"Look UP in the sky, it's . . ."
—**Mike Brumfield**

The Discovery

Mike Brumfield

a.k.a. Michael

"Just imagine."
—**Michael**

The Discovery
By Mike Brumfield

Copyright © 2007 by Mike Brumfield

ISBN 978-0-9740390-8-4
Library of Congress Catalog Card Number (Applied For)

Retail $17.95 plus $2.50 shipping.
Expect delivery in two to three weeks.
To order call 931/657-5815 or 931/261-6697.

First Edition, July 2007

Introduction

Warning: You are about to read my incredible story of discovery. Because of it, I am now careful of what I wish for. So beware, you are forewarned. It all started, as fate seemed to be taking control, by a phone call from a friend in Nashville, TN. Eerily enough, he was pursuing a country music career. You will find out why, later as you read. My search began in 1989. Now, in hindsight, I know why I thought it was destiny. But the evidence didn't always agree. Read on!

I spent my whole life being afraid of evil spirits, a "BELIEF" my parents taught me. They also taught me to believe in good spirits too. Ironic, huh? Which was which? Boy, was that a catch 22. Were they "UP" in heaven or "DOWN" on earth? My parents' religion "taught" that heaven is a spirit world. I found, though, that the whole world has always looked up and still does. I also found religion universally saying Heaven is "UP" too! Why, then, for god's sake, do we continue to say they are spirits? Spirits wouldn't live up in the sky . . . only real flesh and blood space travelers like us. We now live "UP" in the sky too. Why doesn't everyone "SEE" this? "UP" became the most powerful evidence I would follow in solving our mystery. I learned that the evidence doesn't lie . . . man does. I started looking for ancient statues and artworks. I make art. I wanted to know what god and the angels look like. What I found tortured my buddy and almost everyone around me. In our search, you will discover that my "BELIEFS" were replaced by evidence/knowledge. My buddy's beliefs pretty much remained the same. He, like the majority of the world, believed in spirits without producing one, and wouldn't even consider a physical scientific source to cause it. I want to sincerely thank Erick Von Daniken for his "ancient astronaut" theory and hope he considers mine. It is an "infinite astronaut" heavenly one.

P.S. Enjoy my story.

My objective: Find Heaven and the angels

The key: (no brainer) Follow evidence from beginning to end. Please close your eyes for a moment after reading this and just imagine yourself making a scientific discovery, "UP" in the sky, of such a historical magnitude that it radically changes everything your were taught about our past. This very thing happened to me. In 2005 I saw a flying saucer. It changed everything, all right! I was blown away. It was a "discovery" that I would have found hard to believe if not for seeing it with my own eyes. But I did! And in the few minutes that I "witnessed" it, I became overwhelmed with emotion. It exhibited capabilities that are hardly even comprehensible today, if not for my knowledge of space age advancements, that we ourselves have made in the last one hundred years. These achievements have literally taken us from being virtual prisoners in space, living "Down" on earth at the mercy of mother nature—not to mention our constant warring—to where we are today . . . also living "UP" in space. WOW! Right at that very moment, I suddenly had an epiphany. Could "our" future In conquering space have already happened? Religion says so. This flying saucer matched the universal story of religion. It is a story of smarter people who made us to worship/work for them and live "Up" in the sky! Could we be them, imprisoned in our evil human bodies through memory cell transplantation? If we are, then our history in gold and truly improbable existence makes perfect sense now. We use gold for spacecraft. The universal symbol for these heavenly beings is a gold halo. Maybe a flying saucer is made with gold! If so these must be them. This is the only logical reason for them not to live with us. They must be "real" flesh and blood people "like" us, who have already conquered space, which is "UP." Well, I laughed to myself, we haven't conquered it yet, but "we" know heaven is up to our vicious species as well. I began to wonder if they looked "like" us. Then I instantly remembered all the evidence that I discovered in the past. It clearly showed they didn't. In fact, the ancient religious art of Easter Island reveals that they are gruesomely ugly and equal in looks. This became crucial in solving our mystery, which really has only one question to answer: "WHY DON'T THEY LIVE WITH US?" It is called Fermi's paradox. But most importantly, it definitely proved that heaven is "UP" as well; like the book covers show. Finally I understood how they could create a new species like us, when we haven't conquered space yet, and are close to doing the same. We now clone! Wow, I thought to myself, would people see that this matching evidence proves they aren't spirit or dimensional? When we land on a planet with primitive people, they will say we came from "UP." It's now easy to see how primitive man's contact with space travelers started the universal spirit magic story of religion. We could recreate the same story with them today. Holograms would become spirits, cybernetics to mental telepathy, stem cells to resurrection, and last but not least, spacecraft would be fiery chariots. WOW! This is religion's past. My mind was racing wildly, I scientifically saw our future. Suddenly I had another epiphany. Could we be repeating what has already happened on other earths, throughout the universe? Could we be a creation that is a direct result of our scientific addiction to power, through outward beauty? I am addicted to beauty! Is history just repeating itself? I do have déjà vu like everyone else. NO! It can't be! My mind, again, was exploding with questions. Could our species be innately evil and unstoppable because of this scientific human creation possibility? I tried hard not to accept the Easter Island evidence. But those huge bald headed humanoid statues look just alike. It became even more painfully obvious when I looked around and couldn't find a single species that didn't look just alike. This settled it for me, they are nature's creation. Obviously we are their Frankenstein!

"No!," I screamed aloud as I grabbed my face in utter horror. I couldn't stop the ugly vision unfolding in my mind. It was playing out the horrible futuristic dream that I had back in 1989. Suddenly, I was struck by a terrible reality. Will my family or anyone else religious believe me? Would they believe this scientific evidence, or the saucers, when I show them one? My dream had answered that question. It had shown me before, and it was happening again right now. I started to shake when I saw my death, just like the first time! It never got any easier. Instantly, I went back to that moment I saw the saucer hovering above me in 2005. I started yelling for it to please come down. It didn't. That's when I knew for sure that we could be the bad guys or maybe . . . something worse! Could we be them in a different body, like the guardian angel story implies? Is this Hell? I do see hell everywhere. Could we be addicted to the powerful effects of scientifically creating outward beauty?

"Oh my god," I cried aloud. "Please come down."

It didn't move. I knew why, too. I am addicted! I loved feeling beautiful. Was I really ready to go to "HEAVEN"? What if it's boring and everyone looks the same or even worse, they're equally ugly? I ran to get my cell phone only to see the saucer bolt across the sky. I stood there in disbelief. How could this be? I began to shake uncontrollably. "Oh, my god! This evidence will torture the world. We are beauty lovers! We must be these ugly gods in love with our beautiful human bodies, completely intoxicated with this "NEW FOUND" power!" My death flashed before my eyes again. "No, no!" I screamed hysterically, trying to stop the dream, but I couldn't. I clutched my face with both hands and shut my eyes, desperately trying to stop it. The dream played on, I saw the future! Could I have really solved our mystery? Would anyone believe me?

Mike Brumfield

The Past
My search begins.

My first book, June 2001

P.S. I'm sorry I missed so much of your life, Portia Michaels! I dedicate this book to you, and all you kids that I love so much! Warren Alger, we all are so lucky to have such a kind loving person as you in our lives. The same goes for all of my nieces and nephews!

Who the hell is God? And why the hell isn't "HE" here?

(Little did I know the "HELL" I was about to go through in asking these questions! Read on!)

Read: "The Two Witnesses and the Religion Cover-up"

This book is titled after a Bible prophecy in Revelation Chapter 11. It is a fiction based on real events.

Follow along on this journey of two men who are forced to re-examine their religions. They found they were traditionally brainwashed! One of them, Michael, confronts his preachers because of their life-or-death doctrine on blood refusal. Could he make such a life-or-death decision for his own son? He couldn't, not without researching all religions; his wife wouldn't let him anyway.

Discover for yourself the shocking, horrifying evidence that begins to torture him and everyone else around. Could he and Jake be the two witnesses prophesied in Revelation? What could they have to say that would torture their families, friends, and most of all their religions? Even to the point of abandonment and finally physical wrath?

Ultimately Michael sues his religion and wins but not before being attacked and thrown out of his own church. Then Jake drops a bomb on him. He thinks he was abducted by the Mothman! How does this fit in with Michael's alien/angel theory? Could Michael also have been abducted? Is it possible that both were abducted to become the Two Witnesses? Maybe it explains why Michael discovers the Jewish star looking like an atom. Could Michael's theory of the Jewish star/atom be correct? Could the Mayans be right about the return of the gods in 2012? Are these gods the aliens? And if so, then how do they tie in with the Shroud of Turin and the answer to the mystery of life?

Is it a coincidence that Michael was a history major studying to be a lawyer when destiny and his uncle intervened, and he became an artist? And now, it is happening, his songs and this book. He even has his Michael Recycle container. Could May 2012 be the date of a possible nuclear war and the Bible's Armageddon? Will Michael have enough time to help save the world from nuclear destruction, let alone pollution? Can he fulfill the prophecy of chapter 11 and 12 in Revelations to save us from "those who destroy the earth"?

Does Michael's battle begin with the date 1/2/2001? Will it climax with this book being in bookstores all over the world in order to prepare us for the aliens' return? Could those aliens be our religious gods, and the second resurrection of these two witnesses, the final act of proof? Is this the point of time-travel as prophesied in Chapter 10 that time will be no more?

Could this be the moment of contact led by Michael himself for the aliens? If so, WWYD?

FACTS:

Mankind is the biggest mystery of all

Atom looks like Jewish Star

Yin & Yang looks like sperm and egg *(missing link proof)*

AMA symbol looks like DNA

The Ankh depicts the 10th planet's orbit

Halo looks like flying saucer "UP" in air

The Past

Bang, bang, bang! I jerk violently as my eyes suddenly fly open. What happened? Where am I? Have I been shot? I look down to see. No, I haven't been shot. There is no blood. What is this? I am meditating! Man, this is so weird. Is this a nightmare? Is this a dream? I have never meditated before. A newspaper, *The New York Times*, is in my lap. I am in New York City, in a motel room? I pick up the paper to get some facts about what is going on I can't tell if this is a dream or what. I hold up the paper, and suddenly much to my surprise, there before me are three figures. Clearly, there are two aliens, one on either side of a tall thin naked man standing at the foot of the bed. The aliens from Roswell, New Mexico. The aliens? I freeze. I panic. I am speechless. I can't say anything. I just look. They look at me and I look at them. Even through all my fear, I feel at peace. Then, just as suddenly as they have appeared, they are gone. I drop the paper. I am just blown away. What is going on?

I frantically look around. I can't believe my surroundings: a motel room in New York City. I pick the paper up to get some facts. I look first at the date and see those horrifying numbers: January 2, 2001. This couldn't be real. 2001? This is 1989. The last time I could remember I had been in Ohio. I live in Ohio. What am I doing in New York? It's 1989! This means I'm twelve years into the future. As I start reading the headlines, I can't believe my eyes. *Showdown! The Two Witnesses And Christianity*. As I begin to read I am startled to be reading about myself. Apparently I am one of the Two Witnesses. Who is the other Witness? As I read on I can't believe it. It is my best friend Jake from Nashville. Is he still in Nashville? I try so hard, but I can't remember anything. I read on. My Uncle Brice has become famous for his carvings? The story reads like a Hollywood movie script. I have invented a recycling trash can; I have sued the Jehovah's Witnesses and won a lawsuit against them; Jake and I have a hit song; and biggest of all there it is : The Two Witnesses. The Two Witnesses of the best-selling book! Jake and I are the Two Witnesses, who are to battle it out with Christianity! What! What is going on?

Without warning the alarm clock radio goes off and starts playing a song. Not just any song! They were playing our hit song, "One of Us." This is all too unreal and unbelievable. I sit back and close my eyes, trying desperately to absorb all this, to remember something; but I can't remember anything. Just as soon as I close my eyes, the phone rings. Naturally, it must have been the phone, that bang, bang, bang; I must have been dreaming, and the phone rang. It felt like an eternity, but it could have only been moments at best. The phone rings again. I finally pick it up. I expect the caller to be Jake. I just know this has to be one of Jake's bad jokes, but it isn't. It is the lady from the front desk, and she has these words to say: "Hello, Michael. It's your wake-up call."

It is my wake-up call, all right. I need to wake up! I hang up the phone. I know this has to be a dream. I am in the middle of a nightmare. This cannot be real. This is 1989! I am in Ohio. Jake is in Nashville. I don't play any music. My uncle isn't famous. None of this is possible. I cannot remember anything. And most of all, this Two Witnesses thing! What are the Two Witnesses? I search frantically for a Bible. I am in a motel room after all; there has to be a Bible around here. As I get the Bible out of the night stand, I turn and look at the paper again to see where the scripture is. It is a Revelations Prophecy, Chapter 11, The Two Witnesses. I turned to it and as I read I can't believe my eyes. The two witnesses are killed! Killed, for torturing the world with their prophecy! What could I have to say to the world that would torture it? I didn't know anything. I was so confused. I was shaking with fear. I read on. Wow, a second resurrection! "Thank god," I screamed in utter relief. But how could we be the two witnesses? Me and Jake! Jake? I immediately grab the phone to call Jake. I need to make some sense of what is going on. But just as I start dialing, there is an urgent pounding on the door. "Michael!" They are hollering. "Michael, you're going to be late! Let's go! Come on! The limo is waiting! Let us in!"

Let them in? Who are they? What is going on? I can't let them in. I am panic-stricken. Fear is gripping me so tight that I can't move, and yet I have to move. Again I try dialing Jake, and they pound more frantically as I dial. Time is running out. I glance at the paper one more time, wanting desperately for this to be a joke. It looks real. The date didn't lie; the headlines didn't change. Then I see it under the paper: my book! Could it be? It is! *The Two Witnesses*. Obviously, Jake and I are the Two Witnesses! And yet, I am alone. I was suddenly more afraid than ever. This has to be a dream. I have to talk with Jake.

Just as I finished dialing, I hear the mob outside calling, "Michael, Michael! You're going to be late!" Then I hear it. They are going to open the door. I hold the receiver to my ear and listen as the connection goes through. I hear the key go into the door and it is starting to happen. As the door opens, Jake's phone is suddenly answered. By my wife! At least I think it is my wife. And it is. But not my wife from Ohio. It is my wife from Nashville. I have married a woman from Nashville? I am petrified. I can't make heads or tails of it. As they come across the room, I try desperately to talk to the woman. The woman is crying, she pleads, "Mike, why didn't you call? Why didn't you call last night?" I cannot get her to understand I don't know who she is; I need to talk with Jake. I have to make sense out of this. "Please, please, let me talk with Jake!" They are closing in on me with movie cameras and lights, and the room is filling with people. I am losing control of the situation. With phone in one hand and the book in the other, I am being dragged out. They are tearing at me as I cling desperately to everything. They manage to get the book away from me and much to my disbelief toss it into a trash can, not just any trash can, but a Michael Recycle Center. My trash can! I can't believe it. This is all happening way too fast. I scream into the phone: "Jake! Jake!" Suddenly I look up in horror to find a preacher running at me with a pistol in his hand. The phone rings: bang, bang, bang!

I jerk violently as my eyes suddenly fly open. "Jake! Jake! Help, man! I'm shot!"

"Mike, Mike!" A woman's sharp voice broke in. She was shaking me trying to wake me.

I looked and saw my wife. "Yes!" That meant it had to be 1989! "Is it really you, Nancy"?

"Yes, it's me! Wake up, Mike! You're dreaming."

"No, I'm shot! I'm telling you, I just got shot! Where's Jake?" I was still convinced that I had been shot and was feverishly looking for my wound.

I didn't find any. I look up and it is my wife. "Thank god," I said as I grabbed and hugged her tight. I am back in Ohio! "Tell me it's 1989! Please tell me!" I pleaded with tears streaming down my face. I can see my wife's expression is one of total surprise. She tries desperately to get me to snap out of it.

"Well, Mike, of course it is. What's wrong with you? Were you having a nightmare? Are you all right?"

"Yes, but I just dreamed I got shot! And Jake, I need to talk with Jake!"

"How did you know—Mike, you're kidding me, right?" All of a sudden, my wife's expression turned from one of surprise to fear. "He's on the phone? How did you know that?"

"What? Don't tell me. He's on the phone? Let me talk to Jake! I've got to talk to Jake!" I am frantic. I can see she is worried, too. "Please tell me it's 1989!" I quickly get out of bed and walk down the hallway to the phone.

"Mike! You've just had a dream! You're scaring me! Stop this!" She follows me down the hall.

As I grab the phone I ask "Jake! Is it you? You're still in Nashville, aren't you?"

"What? Are you crazy, Mike?"

"Jake, please just tell me you are, man. Don't mess with me!"

"Mike, are you freaking out or something?"

"No, I'm not but I just had an unbelievable dream. I can't believe it I dreamed I could play guitar and it was 2001 and I got shot! We were the Two Witnesses of a Revelations prophecy in the Bible, can you believe it?"

"Mike, slow down. This is crazy, man. The Two Witnesses? You playing guitar? Come on, man, just smack yourself. You'll be all right." Man, I just can't believe it. I stand there in total disbelief.

Nancy just goes on past and gives me that look. "Yeah, it's your friend again. You scared me, Mike! You better quit it. I'll tell your friends, too!"

I knew she wasn't too happy about this. But what she didn't know was that I didn't know Jake was calling. And now that I am talking with Jake, she won't give me a chance to explain. I want to explain. Jake wants me to come down to Nashville. He has been dogging me to get down there. My business is kind of slow, so I figure I might as well go. I look at Nancy, and I know she won't like it so I tell Jake under my breath that I will come. I hang up the phone and face the blues. We argue for quite a while, but that evening after dinner, I head out.

"When are you coming back, Mike?"

"I don't know. I'll call you after I talk to Jake." Little did I know, that after I talked to Jake, things would never be the same.

As I drove towards Nashville, I couldn't help but be amused at the turn my life had taken. It was funny. For years, I've had to struggle between the two people who had become my life: my wife, and my best friend, Jake. And now this dream, what a coincidence, or was it destiny? If it was true then she had every right to be afraid of this trip to Jake's. I thought about the dream and how real it had felt. It was mind boggling to dream into the future, let alone this, Jake and I being the Two Witnesses. I hadn't even heard of the two witnesses before. And I've been a Christian all of my life. But I would discover plenty that Christianity hadn't taught me. I suddenly realized the dream was becoming a reality.

Jake had a satellite showroom on the west side of Nashville. He was relentlessly pursuing a music career. I had just come for a weekend to clear my head. I was in a bad marriage, had a failing art career, and unfinished educational goals. I needed the change. I had called him a week or two earlier and suggested doing a chain saw art exhibition. But I never thought I would. Really, I just needed to get away, but I did need the money. He had thought it was a great idea and told me to come on down. Little did we know that our destiny was about to unfold, or would it be fate. The fate of the world. The Two Witnesses!

One of my first customers was Dave, the son-in-law of Hank Stone, the famous country music star. He was also a customer of Jake's. He was interested in trading a guitar for two statues. I was financially strapped and had explained I couldn't. He left, but called Jake and reminded him of how good a deal he would be getting. Jake became obsessed with the idea of having Hank's guitar and begged me to make the trade. I told him I couldn't do it because I desperately needed the money, but maybe next round. The next day, Dave came right back. He wanted a wooden Indian bad, and ol' Jake had assured him that it was in the bag. I was in no better finances than the last time. However, a different situation began to emerge: I met Angel, Dave's stepdaughter. The following day Dave brought his stepdaughter Angel again and his son Shane. Angel was a beautiful girl, and I immediately fell for her. I felt the same from her as well. Dave told me that he was interested in getting a likeness of his children, but he wanted to make the trade with the guitar first. I explained that I couldn't due to finances. He kept badgering, but I managed to hold my ground. They left with Dave sticking his head back in and saying, "You liked my daughter, didn't you?"

"Yeah," I replied quickly. He laughed and said "We'll be seeing you."

The next morning, I was painting a six-foot cigar store Indian as Dave and Angel pulled up. They got out just as I was finishing. So, I decided to start sawing on a coyote. I had it blocked out already. I made the right choice. Dave would want the coyote, too. Jake headed right for them. It wasn't long before Jake made me shut the saw off and pulled me toward the office. Dave had made him an offer he couldn't refuse. Jake said he wanted that Indian for Angel and the coyote for himself. He was willing to make the trade for both today. "That was a steal!" Jake said. He wanted a thousand dollars for the guitar.

I don't know what made me give way, but I did. I told Jake he owed me when he hit it big. Little did I know then, how big we would both hit it. I just couldn't turn him down as much he idolized Hank. I made the trade and the rest is history. Angel and I fell in love, and we moved in together within the next two months. We left our spouses, families, and everything else to be together. The next three years flew.

I kept in constant contact with Jake and began writing songs, researching religion, and making my Michael Recycle Center. The dream definitely affected me. It affected me so much, that I threw myself into his dream and revived my own dream of writing a song. I had been a song maker for as long as I could remember; I just had no musical influence in my family. Just as I was starting to get into the song-writing with Jake, he threw a bomb on me. He and his first wife were getting back together. I couldn't believe it at first, but it wasn't long before he was asking me to be his Best Man. This was unbelievable to me and everyone. Misty and Jake had been divorced seven years and had never talked about getting back together. Other than their son Moses, they didn't talk much; and when they did, there was never talk about getting back together. Jake had made a lot of headway in the last few years, giving up alcohol and admitting he had a problem with it. He had even given up eating meat and was trying to maintain his physique, something Misty was also interested in. I think he needed Misty at this point between satellites and writing heavily, almost in a frenzy. That became the summer of "Wild One," one of Jake's greatest songs and a perfect description for this period of our lives.

Jake and Misty married in June, and it was mayhem from the beginning, but they did it! I'll never forget that day. Jake was late; Misty was a nervous wreck, and Moses was an overly-excited, big fifteen year-old. Despite all that, the wedding went off without a hitch. It ended with Moses picking me up like a wrestler and tossing me all around in a display of complete and utter joy. He then kissed me as he slammed me to the ground. I'm sure it was like a dream come true for him. But their dream soon became harsh reality. They went through the financial trauma of getting back together and weathered the storm pretty well. Misty and my wife even began to sell Mary Kay. Jake and I worked overtime in the satellite business and carving. We spent a lot of time together and found out immediately that we had something else in common, something so big it would change our lives forever. It was something spiritual.

I laugh now at the irony of it all, the Two Witnesses. Angel was always getting perturbed at the very person who was responsible for getting us together. And yet without Jake we wouldn't have met. I laughed! Our friendship had broken up my first marriage and was almost breaking up this one as well. Jake was such a big part of my life, we were like family. Angel and I had a son whom we even named after Jake. The three years I had been living in Nashville had flown by, filled with a whole lot of satellite jobs, quite a few songs and yep, my recycle container. I even started writing a book about my uncle and his wooden Indian carving career; but nothing—art, music, or books—could compare with what was about to happen. We were about to embark on a spiritual quest for the truth. It was the fall of 1992.

I drove into Jake's driveway. I noticed his truck was gone. That meant too many possibilities to even guess. I knocked on the door and

Misty answered.

"Hey, Misty, where's Ol' Percy?"

She looked puzzled. "Who's that?"

"Oh, I'm sorry. That's just a nickname Jake's brother gave him."

"Oh," she said, indifferently. "He went to the bank."

"Well, is he pretty much ready to go?"

"Yeah, come on in and have a seat."

"Where's Moses?" I asked, as if I didn't know. I headed straight on back toward Jake's old bedroom. That's where the computer and the phone were, two teenage essentials. It was a Saturday morning, and I knew he would be doing either of those or watching wrestling on TV, drawing, or sleeping. It was too early for him to be out. His door was open so I walked on in. He was watching wrestling. We hugged, and he asked about my son James Dean, whom everyone called Jimmy. I called him James Dean, his name sake. Moses liked that. I told him, "I just took him back from his summer stay." He felt sorry for me and said he was so glad he didn't have to do that anymore. I felt real close to him, and I appreciated his kindness to us. We became family. Moses hugged me and remarked how he always felt like I was his uncle. I certainly loved him. I went back into the front room with Misty. We had known each other a while and had been around each other all summer. But this was the first time I had been over this early and caught her up. It was definitely the first time we had a chance to get to know each other personally, one on one. This next hour would produce amazing coincidences in our lives.

I made a comment about her beautiful oak rocker. I knew this would be a good conversation lead, as we both loved wood, and it was a comfortable rocker. She immediately smiled and started telling me about its history. I was listening, but I couldn't help but notice the metamorphosis that had taken place at Jake's. It used to be so unorganized, but not anymore.

I commented on the place, and she thanked me, saying it was a mess. She asked me if I wanted to see her new oak bedroom outfit. She truly loved oak furniture and was obviously a collector. I said yes and followed her into the bedroom. I couldn't help but to notice the Bible and what looked like a dictionary laying on the bed. I asked her about it, but she was already telling me the history behind the bedroom ensemble. I reached down and picked up the "dictionary-looking" book and read the title: *Strong's Exhaustive Concordance of the Bible.*

After Misty described every piece, she said, "Oh, that. That's a concordance."

I said, "It's a concor-what?"

"It's a concordance of the Bible."

I was puzzled and I asked her if it was anything like a bibliography.

She laughed and said, "no, but ironically, it is similar. Well, no, it isn't. It's like a dictionary, a language dictionary."

I explained that in my four years of college I couldn't ever recall using a concordance, but I had done a term paper with a bibliography listing resources. She said that a concordance is a book that has every word of the Bible in it, its origin and what it means. You look up the word being translated alphabetically, then using the reference number, go to the language it was written in. "Okay," I told her, but I think she could sense my nervous hesitation to try it because she waited. I could tell she wanted to make sure that I could do it. I did it with her help.

We went back into the front room, and I continued to look at the concordance as she talked. She asked me if I was religious, and I replied that I had been raised as a Jehovah's Witness, but I didn't stick with it.

She nodded and replied that she didn't either, but had been raised as a Baptist. I laughed and said, "Well, at least you and Jake had the same religion in common; it's tough when you don't, like Angel and me."

"Yeah, I bet," she replied. "But there are more than one Baptist and we belonged to different ones." I laughed. Typical Christianity.

"Are you and Jake studying together?" I asked her.

"No, Jake just bought the concordance to research the name of Jesus."

"Why?"

"He says it has been changed."

"Oh," I remarked, bewildered. I didn't really understand what she meant by that. She started telling me about Jake's research and how she was trying to help him. She never really clarified anything, only that they differed in opinion. That was obvious. I was confused.

I explained that the worst thing about religion is that there are too many to choose from. "It doesn't make sense, logically speaking. How could we get so screwed up in such a short time? Come on, two-thousand years isn't long enough to lose the 'truth' is it? Especially if it will save your life," I ended with a preacher's zest. I recently had a Bible study and the preacher refused to accept scientific evidence of the Neanderthal man and dinosaurs, as contrary evidence against the biblical time frame of six-thousand years. I even suggested that Cain's wife was further proof of a pre-Adam existence. The last thing I mentioned was the absurdity of all the different races coming from one couple, not to mention that incest doesn't work. The preacher had scolded me in his own way and reminded me of "blind faith."

"There are some things you shouldn't question," he had passionately impressed on me.

I had told him, "It's kind of hard to have blind faith and be intelligent at the same time that's an obvious contradiction." Misty just laughed. I just found out another thing we had in common, dissatisfaction with our religion.

I was feeling comfortable with Misty as she began to disclose her biggest problem with Christianity. Not surprisingly, it was "choice," just like mine in choosing Christianity over Buddhism. Who's to say which is better? Hell, it was actually easier to rule out Christianity over the others because it was the most divided. They couldn't even agree with themselves. It was a big problem now, especially since we Jehovah's Witnesses had to die for our religion. "The Jehovah's Witnesses advise you to reject blood transfusion even in the event of death."

"Can you believe that?" Misty gasped.

"Yeah, how would you like to be me? It's unfair as all get out. I have to make a choice with a religion that can't agree and I never really understood it anyway. Even worse, there are hundreds to choose from within itself! Now that's what you call unfair."

Jake came through the door just as I was saying "unfair."

"Unfair? What, Christianity?" He said.

I laughed. "Man, I can't believe it! We were just talking about Christianity."

"I knew it," he said with a smirk.

"Bullshit!"

"Well," he said, "I'll prove it. You were telling her your biggest problem was choice."

Misty immediately jumped in, anxious to support Jake's telepathic abilities. "He does hear the phone a lot before it rings." Then she turned to him all excited and said, "Remember when you guessed the next song on the radio, yesterday."

"Yeah, that's kindergarten stuff, man," he bragged.

"Come on, Jake," I quickly interrupted. "We've got to go."

"Okay, hold on. You might learn something, kid. Let's see here," he said, while he sat positioning himself yoga-style on the couch. He closed his eyes. "Misty was also saying, how choice bothered her most!"

She and I looked at each other wide-eyed I turned to Jake and said, "You've been listening to us from the washroom window."

"No way, man. Gogo would have gone nuts."

"Well then, Smartass, what else did we say?"

"You were saying that Christianity can't even get along with itself."

I jumped up and started accusing him of hearing our conversation, while Misty just sat there in awe.

"I'm telling you, man, I've been practicing," Jake bragged. "I'm trying to be born again as Yeshua describes it in the Gospels."

"I don't mean to sound so ignorant, but my teachers always told me the only dumb question was the one that you didn't ask, so I'll ask this one. I know the Gospels are books of the Bible, but I just can't place what ones. So which ones are they?"

"They are at the beginning of the New Testament," he remarked quietly but sternly. "You know, they're the ones written in red, recording Yeshua's teachings. Our savior!"

"Oh, I guess that's why they say the 'gospel truth', then, huh?"

"You learned something else, young Weedhopper, my student." He extended his hand toward me, challenging me to take a pick out of his hand. He knew I was practicing guitar and wanted more than anything to play, but I just couldn't get it. I didn't get the pick either. Then he continued smugly, "They just so happen to be the accounts of Yeshua's life. I mean, you were also just talking about how the Jehovah's Witnesses make you die for their religion. Don't you think that itself is enough to make you know his teachings inside and out?"

"Yeah, it is, man. And I'm doing that! I feel so ignorant of the Bible and vow to read that damn thing before my thirtieth birthday."

"Gosh, Mike, can't you have a little respect? I mean, it is the Word of God, you know."

"Man, they're just words."

"How old was Christ when he died, Jake?"

"Well, don't worry; you've got a few more years; Yeshua was thirty-three when they killed him. Listen here, Mike, you're at first grade and you really should limit your speaking and do a lot more listening."

"Shut up, Jake," I said, as I wrestled him. "You know it all, don't you."

"I know nothing, man; I'm a beginner. Okay! Okay, man, let go!" He reeled in pain, as I finally let go of his ribs. "I'll tell you, though," he started saying as he straightened up and walked toward his room. "The thing that pisses me off the most about Christianity is how easy they say it is to be saved and born again, when Yeshua clearly said it was the narrow path and a hard thing. They wouldn't know 'born again' if it bit them in the ass!"

"Yeah, the Jehovah's Witnesses believe the same thing," I said, with equal resentment.

"Really," Jake said surprised, although I knew he wasn't. "Well, that's good; how do they become born again?"

"They don't!" I laughed.

Jake asked what they believed. I told him they believe in following the Ten Commandments and separating oneself from the worldly traditions, accept Jesus as the Lord your Savior, confess sins, and then get baptized. "Oh, and of course go to church."

"Well, at least they do one thing right in giving up Christmas."

"Yeah, we never had a Christmas nor saluted a flag." Misty remarked how hard that must have been. I immediately recalled many memories of being ridiculed and ostracized as a kid. "Yeah, it really was," I said in agony.

Jake came out of the bedroom with his Dishout Satellite hat on, and I knew he was ready for business. "You know, Mike, Yeshua says that you must be born again to enter the kingdom of Heaven. So, being born again is a must. I don't understand how they can't all see that they have the same outward religion, right down to their slogans, instructions, and ceremonies. But at least yours doesn't celebrate Christmas."

"Wow, man. We give up the worldly things but don't acknowledge being born again."

"We?" He mocked.

"You know what I mean."

"Well, speak for yourself. I'm not a Christian."

"You were raised as a Christian."

"Yes, but I was never baptized."

"Me, neither."

"You know, there is another thing I like about your religion, and that is they don't pay their preachers. Our little ol' church in the hollow never did either."

"Why not? They're Baptists, aren't they?"

"Yes, but they're not part of the mainstream Baptists."

"Our church was part of the mainstream Baptists," Misty said. "They made pretty good money, too."

Jake immediately criticized any preacher for taking a wage. He ranted and raved that it was the opposite of what Yeshua taught. He started to sit down, and I knew that would lead to a long religious discussion. I didn't want to be all day long, so I grabbed his arm and started pulling him toward the door. "Just one minute, man, and I'll show you what

I'm talking about," he said as he grabbed the remote. "Christianity is making a mockery of Yeshua's teachings." He switched the channel to a preacher selling miracles with a three-step program. All you had to do was believe, give, and get baptized and you could expect a miracle. It was sickening. "The bastards," he growled. "I bet that Yeshua didn't even start Christianity."

Misty jumped in and said that she had heard the Catholic church, which was based in Rome, was the anti-Christ.

"Yeah, I've heard that also," I said without thinking. I was determined to get in on this conversation and get Jake going.

"Well," Jake jumped in, "that's all a bunch of bullshit anyway. It's that kind of sensationalism that they use to sell Christianity. Everybody wants to know when the end of time is! Yeshua said the time was at hand!" Jake bristled at the apocalyptic talk. "And if it ain't written in red, I don't believe it."

We finally got up, when the preacher began to sell a cassette series called "The Signs of the Last Days." It was just like the Jehovah's Witnesses. Jake immediately blasted Christianity saying that Yeshua said there would be only one sign, "the Sign of Jonas," he said boldly. They sell prosperity with 'Jesus,' a fake name. It's sickening."

"I know what you mean," I agreed, but I really didn't. We needed to go and I figured I would learn more about the name change soon anyway. I started pushing Jake out the door.

Jake broke in and said that all the denominations were just glorified Catholics. Rome started Christianity and it had become a world religion within three-hundred years. "Rome ruled the world and the word Catholic means common in it's original language of Latin. Therefore we have B.C.. It means before common era, not before Christ!" I did not know this! "What they did was make everyone Christians, not common," he scowled. "That's what John was writing about in revelations."

"Okay, okay. We need to work." That was all news to me.

"I'm trying to teach you. But I forgot, you already know everything."

"Shut up, man. I'm learning stuff I never knew; I'm a little intimidated. Okay! After all, I'm an ignorant Christian, remember?"

"Well, Christian, there are basically two types of Christian religion: the first is Catholic; the rest fall into the Protestant category. The word 'Protestant' has as its root *protest*, which they did with the likes of Luther and the Lutheran movement around 1500 A.D.. And then, the Bible was translated to the King James Version in English." He wisecracked, "A bunch of people never even understood the Bible unless they knew Latin. That's all that was allowed, for thirteen-hundred years."

"That's crap! It is possible, isn't it, to eliminate the argument of interpretation by going back to the original text?"

"You were looking at it," Jake said somberly.

"What?"

"The *Strong's Concordance*."

"Really?"

"Yeah."

"Jake, I want you to show me about the name change that Misty told me about."

"Are you sure about that?" He asked eerily. "I'm telling you, man, they changed his name." He started rambling. "It lost its meaning, its purpose. Michael is one word in Hebrew as it is in English. They changed Yeshua, man! Bring that concordance and let's go. I've been wanting to show you 'mystery,' and then you can look up the name. If you're really ready for it, then we'll do the mystery." He looked at me with the most intense stare. It was a little spooky. And what was mystery? It was a mystery to me.

Just as we were leaving, Moses stepped into the living room and hollered "Taco Bell! Wow, thanks Dad! I was just coming to ask you to get me something from Taco Bell."

"I knew that, son."

"Come on, man; you're so full of crap," I said grabbing his arm.

"I'm telling you, man, I'm becoming telepathic the more I do the mystery."

"Well, mystery yourself toward the truck."

He started to go back in, but I pushed him on out the door. I knew better than to let him go back in. "Grab that *Strong's* and the Bible. We'll look up some stuff. I'm telling you, man," he said, as he turned toward me. "If you're serious about reading the Bible, you have to buy yourself a *Strong's Concordance*. The original meanings of the words have to be looked up in their original text to get the accurate meaning, and there should only be one word. So get the *Concordance*."

I got the *Concordance* and the Bible and started back out the door. "Well, I feel like a Jehovah's Witness again, going door to door."

"I tell you, Mike, if they just tried to be born again, I'd think they could be living right."

"Well, you can just forget that. If it's got anything to do with delving into the spirit world, they label that as being demonic."

"Yeah, our church did, too," Misty remarked.

"They all do," Jake piped in. "I think that's what they killed Yeshua for. He was obviously doing something radical to be killed. The Jews didn't like that. I'll tell you what I think, man."

"Well, tell me while you drive," I said as I helped him into the truck.

"Hold on, man, you didn't even notice the Shroud, did you?"

"Notice what?" I then suddenly remembered seeing it. He had displayed a picture of the Shroud of Turin, the alleged burial cloth of Jesus, on the living room wall above the couch. It was accompanied by two gold doves. It was a nice wall arrangement. I knew very little about the Shroud. "Do you really believe the Shroud is authentic?"

"Hell yes, man, if Christianity doesn't acknowledge it, it's got to be. Besides, it has a history dating back to A.D.1300. Yeshua said he was going to leave only one sign, and it was his picture. That's unreal, huh: think about it. I'm going to get some books on it tomorrow and check it out."

Somehow, I just knew that he would. Jake pursued knowledge. "Well, you check that out, and I'll get back to the Bible and get it read and learn to use the *Concordance*." We got in the truck and drove on in a hurry. Jake was late. I asked him about the name change. He started educating me again.

I couldn't wait to ask him about the Shroud. It really had an impact on me. It looked like a ghost, a spirit. That was so heavy. And I didn't know anything about it. I couldn't believe there was actually physical evidence to prove Jesus Christ's existence. I certainly didn't know it was left as his only sign. Jake was as eager to talk as I was to listen. I again asked about the Shroud.

"He predicted it, " he said emphatically. "It is written in every book of the Gospels. It's a detailed account that all four writers agreed upon."

"Wow!" I was so amazed. I had read a little bit of the Gospels, but had decided to start again from the beginning of the Bible.

Jake seemed to be reading my mind. "You were bound and determined to read the Bible starting at Genesis, huh? You need to read what

Yeshua wrote. I mean, he is the Savior. That means he's the only one who can 'save' us." He smiled at me.

"Man, you're a sarcastic jerk, aren't you?" I jabbed his ribs. He hated that.

"No, I'm not, man. But you were thinking that, weren't you? Huh, weren't you?" He chimed in taunting me.

"Yeah, I guess so. You'd think that you'd want to start at the beginning of the Bible, huh?"

"Nope, not if it isn't written in red," he said confidently.

"I'd really just like to get right to the root of the problem, man. That's why I went to the Old Testament."

"Well, see what you're missing out on. You better start checking out what Yeshua wrote. You're a Christian, not a Jew."

"Yeah, I'm going to check it out immediately."

"Well, I'd think so," he said sternly.

"I can't wait to get home to read it. How far did you get with the Bible anyway?" I asked Jake.

"Up to the second book of the Gospel, but I had skipped a lot of the genealogy writing in the Old Testament; it's really too much to take in."

"Don't you think you ought to read it all?" I barked sarcastically. "Yeshua was a Jew."

He smiled weakly. I was giving him back some of his own medicine. "I'll read it," he said.

"Yeah, me, too." We would. We would read everything.

He reached toward his glove box, opened it, and pulled out a rolled up paper, tied with something. "What's that, a diploma for the Dishout Satellite school training program?"

"Yeah, yeah, funny man. No, it's the picture of Yeshua. The Sign of

Jonas." It was tied with a neat little silk black ribbon and appeared to be waxed over purposely, like a finish. I took it, and unrolled it, staring spellbound. Jake broke the silence, with the fact that he wouldn't give it to just anyone. "Thanks, man," I replied weakly. "I feel honored." We both just sat there, as he drove on in silence.

"Just taking in the moment?" He asked.

"Yeah."

"I don't think anyone can look at the Shroud for the first time and not be taken back by it. Especially if you know that it was his only sign."

"Yeah, the Sign of Jonas."

"I was in church for 40 years and never heard of it. Even if you're a non-believer of Yeshua, you can't deny the amazing prediction and proof of his fame. He took a picture of himself and predicted it." Jake said.

"Yeah," I replied, "a picture." Jake drove as I stared at the face with complete astonishment. This was so heavy. I just couldn't believe something like this could be taken so lightly. I asked where the Sign of Jonas scripture was in the Bible.

"Flip it over," he said. "I put the scripture on the back. Or just look it up in the concordance for yourself. That's the beauty of the concordance. All you have to do is remember one word of the scripture and go to the main concordance. It will list every scripture that uses the word 'sign.'"

"Wow, that's great, man, but I'll do it when we get finished with this job because we're almost there."

"Yeah, just like you were going to read the Gospels, right?"

"Shut up, man," I said as I jabbed him in the ribs. "Besides, I want to check out the name, too. I'm still not clear on it."

"Ow!" He yelled, as he tried to get away from my jabbing.

I was still holding the picture of Yeshua. Yeshua, I thought to myself. That sounds so much like, "Yes you are." Jake remarked, "Yes it does," as he put on the brakes and turned into the drive of his customer's house. That was eerie.

"Well, Don Juan we're here," I said quickly to change the subject. I flipped over the Shroud as we came to stop.

Jake sneered, "You ain't gonna use the Concordance, are you. No, you always have to take the short cut."

"Jake, it's called time management. I'll learn later when I've got time. I've wasted almost half of my biblically allotted threescore and ten now, as it is." I flipped over the picture to see Matthew 16:4 just as we were pulling to a stop.

"Go ahead, Christian. Take the easy path."

"Shut up, man. Some people have a life and a wife, if you know what I mean. Oh, I forgot. You're new at that again, just learning again, aren't you?" I mocked, patting him on the shoulder.

"Well," he replied with a long deep baritone drawl, "you can't fool me, Christian, but that's all right." He reached up and acted like he was going to pat my shoulder. I jerked away, and he went for my ribs. He poked me as I lunged out the door.

"You know, it's really ironic," I said, getting away. "I was just thinking about the name. I'm going to check and find out, if it is in fact changed."

"It is," he said gruffly, interrupting me.

"Well, if it's true, Christianity bases its whole religion on a false name. Whereas the Jews, who deny him, at least know his name, but they don't think he has come yet."

"Yeah, that's really screwed up, isn't it?"

"Yeah," I said, as we got out and met his customer.

We began working, and Jake started telling me about the name again. How the name came from Yehoshua, but it had been changed. It was split into two names, from Yehoshua to Yeshua and Yoshua. It happened when Israel became divided into two tribes, the tribes of Judah and Israel. The name means the same as Emmanuel in the scripture of Isaiah, in the Old Testament: He will save.

"Are you saying that the name was predicted in the Old Testament and even had a specific purpose?"

"Yes, man, I'm telling you," Jake ranted. "I don't know how they can't see it. Are they reading the same Bible that I am?" he wisecracked.

"You know, I did see that the Old Testament constantly referred to the importance of the name. And even Christianity makes it the most sacred name of all."

"Yeah, man, it's bizarre that nobody else has brought this up. It's the Anti-Christ," Jake said eerily. "No, if it's anything, it's a cover-up man. A cover-up of information," I said defiantly. I don't know what made me blurt that out, but then I remembered the dream. I was afraid to bring it up. But I knew Jake would've remembered. I just knew it.

"Wow, man," I added, kind of stunned. "If this proof is in the Bible—." I started thinking and the wheels were turning.

"It is in the Bible," Jake snapped.

"Well if it is, I'm sure going to feel like a piece of shit."

"Why?"

"Because I've argued with Angel over the blood issue. I marked 'Blood Refused' on my driver's license."

"Don't tell me that, man. You told her you would die before accepting blood? Are you crazy?" He looked at me, and then mumbled, "You did, didn't you? Mike."

"I know, man. I'm ashamed. I'm going to apologize to Angel immediately when we get home."

"You better. How could you make a life or death choice based on information given to us by Christianity? Any idiot can see that they can't even agree with each other. Jake didn't cut me any slack. I didn't deserve any."

I couldn't help but think of Jimmy and Little Jake. How could I have lived with myself, if I had made that decision and caused their deaths. I was determined to research the teachings of Yeshua, more than ever. Jake looked over and he seemed to know what I was thinking. "You've been awfully quiet. Don't tell me."

"What?" I asked.

"Don't tell me. Let me guess." He closed his eyes. "No, no. You didn't tell Angel that you would let one of your kids die. Mike, how could you do that?" He said, as he opened his eyes.

I was in shock. This was too much. "I only talked about it and never enforced it." I said, so ashamed.

"I just knew," he said in complete disbelief.

"I'm telling you, man, I'd like to sue the Jehovah's Witnesses. They've brainwashed me and my family."

"And a whole lot more," Jake added.

I was angry and couldn't believe it. I not only had to research the name, but the Shroud also; and it seemed that the Jehovah's Witnesses, who preach accuracy and understanding, weren't practicing it at all. I always felt if one person could show me something they did wrong, I would quit following them. Today was a bombshell. I would prove it quickly.

We wrapped up the job and headed back to the truck. I immediately grabbed the *Strong's Concordance* as I jumped in and started looking up *Jesus*. It directed me to the Greek text, where it read *Yesous*. Wow, I thought to myself, that sounds an awful lot like Zeus. Makes sense. That was the god of the Greeks and Rome. They just gave Yeshua the name Yesous, which sounded similar, and kept their god's name alive. "Wow!" I said suddenly. Jake said "I know." Then I looked back at the Hebrew text and I read *Yehoshua*, just as Misty had said. There were two numbers there, so I started looking for them, as Jake got in and started the truck.

"Well, did you find *Yeshua*?"

"No, man, it took me right to *Yehoshua* like Misty said. There are two more reference numbers there." I started to look again, when I turned the page directly to *Emmanuel*. "Check this out, Jake: *Emmanuel*. I just opened it, man, and there it was."

"Check it," he said. "I bet it says *He will save*."

I couldn't wait to look it up and anxiously fumbled for the reference number. "Here it is," I said. "What? This doesn't say *He will save*."

Jake looked over quickly and said, "You're in the Greek text; it's Hebrew."

"Oh," I said embarrassed. "Well, it's easy to get mixed up. I can understand Misty not finding something now."

"I don't have any problem," Jake said.

"Well, give me a break. I'm a beginner." I finally found it and sure enough, there it was: *He will save*.

"Now go back to *Yehoshua*."

I returned to *Yehoshua* and looked up the number for Yeshua, not Yoshua, and turned to it. There it was! *Yeshua, He will save*. "Wow, you're right."

"I told you man; they changed his name."

"I don't agree with interpretation," I hollered. "Not if we can do this!" I held up the concordance and shook it.

"Yeah, me neither," said Jake. "That's what I like about the *Strong's*. It eliminates interpretation, taking you back to the original meaning. You can't read the Bible without it and get the correct definition of words. I always wanted to do this, go back to the original Scriptures."

"Me, too," I said excitedly. "Getting back to Yeshua, man, what's the deal? I researched it right to Yeshua. Yeah, but Dr. Strongs doesn't point out that it stops at the Greek. He refers to the Hebrew and there isn't a Hebrew named Jesus. "What," I yelled. "There has to be or this guy is fraudulent."

"Well, the problem is this," he said ominously. He immediately pointed to the other page and there it was: Jeshua!

"What? That means it was Yeshua without changing the Y to J." I remarked excitedly.

"That's right!" He just grinned.

"You know what, man, I think you're right about Jesus not starting Christianity. This name isn't in the New Testament."

"You do, huh," he replied, smiling as if he had accomplished a great thing.

"Wow! We are rewriting history! I can't wait to start reading the New Testament. You read it, too, Jake, and let's research Christianity."

"Well first of all Michael, I've already been reading the New Testament, and secondly, we might have to read outside of the Bible. Like the Book of Enoch."

"Who?"

"Enoch, one of the two prophets mentioned in the New Testament taken by God. He was quoted in Jude, prophesying about the angels, the one-third."

I didn't know any of this. "Why didn't Christianity include his writings?

"Christianity has controlled the writings, too."

"No, man, don't tell me they did the same as the Jews."

"They did worse," he said. "They stopped all writings, declaring 'an end to the writing of the Bible.'"

"Wow!" I couldn't believe it. I had always wondered why there weren't prophets writing today. "How could they do that, when Jesus said there would be prophets to the end of time?"

"Yeah," Jake said. "You tell me. You read that in Matthew, didn't you?"

"Yeah, I think it was Matthew 23."

"It is," Jake said, "That's the reason I wrote that in my song."

"No way," I said.

"No, really, man, I did."

I just looked at him suspiciously. He smirked, "I'm telling you, man, you need to start doing mystery like me and maybe you can do some of these things. Remember how I guessed what you and Misty were talking about."

"Yeah, right. It was just luck; but you know, I've got to admit that I was astonished at the phone ringing when you said it would."

"Yeah, man, and what about Moses and Taco Bell?"

"Well, I have to admit, it is unreal. Are you just pulling my leg? Come on."

"You figure it out," he said with another one of those eerie look-right-through-me stares. He said he was looking at my aura.

We were about to Jake's. We sure had been doing some deep talking. I asked him how long he had been meditating, since I hadn't seen him doing it. He told me that he had started meditating ten years ago, with a guy in his band. Just after his first and only out-of-body experience. He had met him while living in Austin, trying to get a record deal, back in the early seventies. I asked him if Misty had meditated with him. I knew he and Misty had been together then. He started to answer me, but said he'd tell me later. We were pulling into the drive. He did say that she had tried it and something weird happened. "She's been scared ever since!" He looked right through me again. He really had me spooked.

We went into the house where Misty was reading a book about the mysteries of life. Jake immediately loved on her, ever so gently, as she balanced the cigarette, coffee, and Jake at the same time. I headed toward Moses' room to see him again before I left. He was still munching on the sack from Taco Bell. "Wow, dude, you haven't finished eating yet. That's been three hours ago!" Before I finished my sentence, I could see why he hadn't finished eating. There were taco and burrito wrappers everywhere. I laughed and said, "Moses, it isn't any wonder you haven't finished eating. How many of these things did your Dad get you?"

"Oh," he said struggling, while still trying to swallow the last half of a bean burrito. "About twelve."

"What!" I said. I couldn't believe it. "You mean to tell me you've eaten twelve burritos!"

"Yeah, man. Shoot, I've eaten twenty before, in Ohio with mom."

"Really, Dude, that's unreal."

"Yeah it is, isn't it?" He laughed. I knew Jake was fooling me about his prediction of Taco Bell this morning. Moses had probably been eating them since he's been here. I laughed at myself. Then just stared off.

He asked me what I was thinking about. "Oh, I guess I was staring off into space."

"Well, let's see," he said. "I started talking about school, and you just stood there. You were kind of grinning. It was weird."

I started laughing. "Well," I said still chuckling, "your Dad said he had known through meditation that you wanted Taco Bell."

He laughed and said, "That's nothing. I always want Taco Bell."

"Yeah, I can tell. Well, anyway, that's why I was kind of grinning, I guess. I busted ol' Jake," I said a little louder and more enthusiastically as Jake suddenly into the room.

"What do you mean you busted me, man?"

"The Taco Bell thing, man. You know what I mean."

"What did Moses say?" He started to ask Moses if he had told me, but before he even got three words out he looked over and saw the floor and bed covered with empty wrappers.

"Ah, Lord," he said to Moses. "I guess you blew it for me."

"What, Dad?"

"I told Mike I guessed your wanting—" Moses interrupted and said, "Taco Bell."

"Yeah, Taco Bell. Yeah, and did you remember to save some for me or your mother?"

"Well, uh, there's three left."

"Ah, Lord," Jake said, "I guess that would give us one each. He turned to me, looking like a sad puppy.

"No," I said, kind of smirking, "you and Misty can split it." I couldn't help but laugh.

He reached down and hugged Moses and said in a pitiful tone. "Don't worry, Son, we know you're just a growing boy," and kissed him real big.

I laughed and said "Give me a hug, Moses; I've got to go."

"Okay," he said, hugging me.

"I hope you like school."

"Yeah, I do."

We walked into the living room, and Misty asked what we were laughing about. I told her that I had busted Jake and his guru act of predicting Moses' wanting Taco Bell.

"Oh yeah?" She remarked, inhaling long and hard on her Marlboro.

"Yeah, Moses said he's been eating Taco Bell like crazy ever since he got here!"

"Oh yeah," she said, kind of dumbfounded. "I should have known that, I guess. I'm not much of a cook anyway; that's probably why, huh?" She looked toward Jake.

I could tell he got a little nervous. "No," he said, "honey, you're a great cook."

She snapped back at him. "You're just saying that. You know I don't cook very much." They fussed a little, and I watched blankly, while I started thinking about my own situation. Angel and I were also arguing a little bit, over the religion thing. Suddenly Jake directed a statement toward me. "Misty did bring home the book on the Shroud." He must have been trying to appease her. "Where is it ?" I asked quickly. "I want to check it out."

Misty chimed in. "Yes, I did bring the book home and here it is, Mike." She reached the book toward me. "I've just been looking at it."

"Yeah," Jake said, hugging Misty affectionately. "My baby is helping me search for the truth, like us, Mike."

"Wow, that's great, Misty." I complimented her. "Believe me, it's hard to find a Christian who researches anything outside of his denomination."

"Yeah, I know," she replied sadly.

"I don't know about you guys," I said, getting up, "but I'm going to read Jude and see what it says about the angels. To me, if they were created before mankind, then the answer should lie there."

Jake broke in anxiously and said, "Man, don't you know?"

"Know what?"

"We are the angels," he said. "I know I told you this, or how else would you have known about the story in Jude?"

"Duh, don't you remember, Jake, we were just talking about Christianity. The Jews' canonization of the Bible left out Enoch in the O.T.. But the N.T. quotes the writings of Enoch in Jude. You just told me earlier."

"Oh yeah," he replied. "You know, you're right, and I'm gonna get Enoch's book, too. It might reveal something about the angels." *(This became my focus.)*

"Well, you do that, Jake, but what do you mean we're the one-third of the angels?"

"Read Jude and it will tell you the angels left their first estate for a strange flesh. Us! And now we must be born again of the spirit. That's what an angel is, a Spirit! Think of it like this, man. I figured since Christianity doesn't teach about the fall of the angels, then we must be them." *(Little did I know how my spirit "thinking" would change.)*

"Wow, that makes a lot of sense."

"Yeah, I know," he said. "And I still haven't heard anything about it, either."

"Me neither," Misty broke in.

"That's why I think Yeshua was telling us to be born again of the spirit," he said, looking at both Misty and me intently. "It's the mystery. Our spirit is trapped by our bodies, just like the Earth's gravity. And only with our mind or mystery can we release ourselves, by attaining the resurrection."

"You mean to tell me that you really think all you have to do is meditate, and you can go to Heaven?"

"Well that's all relative. But, yes, and it's mystery, not meditating. To meditate means to think."

"Huh," I said, not knowing that either.

"You see, it's not about thinking, man. It's something that they must not have been doing."

"Who?" I asked.

"The Jews. Yeshua was Jewish."

Wow, he was really making sense, but it was a lot to absorb. I felt so ignorant. I vowed again to start educating myself.

"I always thought the Bible said we will be judged according to our works. That's all I know, and that's fair."

"What are your works?"

"How you live your life, I guess."

"Man, don't you think it's easy to follow the Ten Commandments? I mean, I don't do any of those, and I don't even go to church. So, it's easy."

"Well, don't you think meditation is easy?"

"Mystery, you mean? Shit, no, man; ask Misty."

She looked hard at him. Then she carefully replied, "well, I don't know about hard or easy. But I had something weird happen when I tried it." I got all excited and listened as she recanted her first meditation experience. She said that someone or something was moving and it frightened her. She said that she had always felt Jake was playing a joke on her, so she quit doing it.

"Now Precious, you know I swore I wasn't moving or playing tricks on you."

"Well, I'm not doing it again to find out, at least not with you."

"Now baby, maybe you had a spirit experience. We ought to pursue it. We do want to be born again of the spirit, don't we? It probably is weird. How did Yeshua describe it? Like the wind. Wow," he said suddenly, "Remember, Misty, how I told you I called myself the Wind as a kid, and when we got married I was going to call myself the Wind as a solo act?"

"Oh, you were not," she said.

"I was too!"

"You were just going to name your first album 'The Wind.'"

"Yeah, that's right, but I did tell you that I called myself the Wind as a kid and I often referred to myself as the Wind."

"Yeah, he did do that." Jake was relishing her acknowledgment.

"Well, that will come in handy next time you run out of gas or forget something." I laughed and got up to go. I knew Angel would be waiting.

"Don't you worry," he said. "I'll be practicing mystery and just might surprise you. You ought to do it with me."

"Right," I replied mockingly. "I ain't messing in any spirit world."

"Boy oh boy, Christian, how are you ever going to be born again of the spirit, then?"

Misty chimed in and said, "Me neither, Mike. I keep telling him he could get possessed."

"Ooh," Jake said, "you mean I could see a demon. Ooh, I'm scared. Christianity! They're the Anti-Christ. They're anti-spirit. They create demons and scare the shit out of you just to get your money, the bastards! And they make being born again as easy as crying and 1, 2, 3. They wouldn't know a spirit if it bit them in the ass, let alone a demon. Besides, you show me where the word demon is in the Bible and I'll kiss your ass."

"Revelations," she said boldly.

"I figured you would pick Revelations, the only book of the New Testament totally devoted to predicting the end. I don't believe in apocalyptic writing and signs when Yeshua said there would only be one sign," he growled pointing to the Shroud.

"That reminds me man," I said. "I don't want to forget mine. Do you care if I borrow the *Strongs* too?" I asked as I reached down to get it.

That got Jake's attention. "You've got the Shroud book, and you still need to look up the scriptures predicting the Shroud. I even wrote it on there for you."

"Yeah, I guess you're right, but I want to get me a copy of that concordance." I knew he wouldn't let go of his.

"Well, I'm going to get a copy of Enoch so I'll pick you one up."

"Okay, dude. I'll leave it for now. But please get me one quick."

As I started walking out I stopped and remarked that I couldn't get over the Jehovah's Witnesses acknowledging the importance of Jehovah's name, but not seeing that Yeshua is changed. Little did I know that I would soon discover the name change of Yahweh to Jehovah. The name of their church was false, too!

Jake laughed and said, "Yeah, can you believe those Jehovah's Witnesses? I don't understand the name Jehovah being more significant than 'I Am'. 'I Am' was the name given, as a memorial to mankind for all generations. Besides that, the name Jehovah, or Yahweh as it should be translated, doesn't do anything for me. But the 'I Am' and Yeshua have meaning. They answer for me, that we are the angels, the one-third in Enoch."

"Wow, that's heavy Jake! And English has become the world's language. It was just accepted by sixteen countries maintaining the Skylab." We we're both stunned!

I left Jake's with a determination to find the truth more than ever.

How could things be so messed up? As I drove home, I couldn't stop looking at the Sign of Jonas. It looked like a spirit. It blew me away. I had gone to a Christian church all my life and had never heard about the Sign of Jonas. Even worse was the name. How could any Christian not be offended by the name change, especially the Jehovah's Witnesses? However, the most troubling thing on my mind was my blind loyalty to a religion that practiced a life-threatening doctrine, in spite of the obvious problems with their story. I found myself angry at my parents and myself, when I thought of all the things I missed out on, like Christmas, birthdays, and God knows what else. I let their traditions become my own and inflicted the same persecutions on my family. Well, now was the time to eat crow and apologize to my wife.

I pulled in at the house, dreading the hassle that I knew was coming. Our two-hour job had turned into an all day excursion, but this time Angel couldn't blame it on the satellite business. Now she would start blaming our research, something that would consume my time even when Jake wasn't around. Without knowing it, I had spent more time than I thought, talking with Jake and Misty about religion. I grabbed up the Sign of Jonas and headed in to face the music. Just as I expected, she was sitting in the front room with her Mom and the boys.

"I know," I said, as I walked through the door, "but I've got a good excuse this time. "Check this out," I said. "What is it?" Mary asked anxiously. I could tell that Angel was mad, and Mary was good about helping me out. She initiated conversation quickly.

"It's a picture of Jesus' burial cloth, the Shroud of Turin," I said, holding up the picture of the Shroud. She wasn't thrilled. "Have you guys ever seen this before?"

"What?" She asked.

"Yeah, it's a picture of Jesus' resurrection. I brought home this book about it. It's known as the Shroud of Turin because it was discovered in Turin, Italy."

"Yeah, I've seen that on television, "Unsolved Mysteries," I think. What about it?"

"Well, did you know that it was predicted in all the Gospels of the Bible?"

"No," Mary remarked, as shocked as I had been when Jake had told me.

"Yeah, Jake wrote down one of the scripture references on the back." I reached for the Bible in the bookcase and realized Angel still hadn't said a word. I looked up the scripture while Mary was looking at the Shroud and the book. "Check this out," I said as I quoted Jesus' statement from Matthew 16:4: "Woe unto you, you wicked and adulterous generation who seeketh a sign, but only one sign will be given and that is the Sign of Jonas."

"What do they mean, the Sign of Jonas?"

"It is a comparison of Jesus being resurrected on the third day to Jonas being delivered by God from the whale's belly in three days."

"Huh," Mary said. "I've never heard of the sign of Jonas as long as I've been going to church."

"Don't feel bad; neither have I." I figured I better get Angel in on this conversation, so I asked her. After all, she went to a religious school all her life. I turned and asked her.

"No, I haven't," she snapped, and then looked away again at the television.

"Check out what else I found, Mary. Did you know that the real name of Jesus is Yeshua and it's translated Jeshua, not Jesus? It's in the O.T. not the N.T. But it shouldn't have been changed. It should still be Yeshua."

"No, I didn't," she replied with excitement. "What did you say again?"

"Yeshua. Jake has been researching the names in the Bible and found that Jesus is a false translation."

"What made him find that?"

I told her how we both had been getting more religious-conscious lately and had been reading the Bible. I had started with the Old Testament, and he had begun with the Gospels. "Well, apparently Jake started watching religious shows. He heard this guy say Jesus' Hebrew name, Yeshua. He said he knew it from an old girlfriend first, but this guy made an impact with the name. This guy was using a Strong's Concordance. Jake got one and discovered more than this guy. He discovered the truth about the name change."

Mary knew the preacher immediately from watching a lot of religious television herself. "Well anyway, it had struck Jake as odd that this guy didn't bother to correct it, yet he made the truth so important. He doesn't correct the most important name in the Bible, and it's been changed to Jesus, that is, Zeus. It's Greek not Hebrew. Jake is researching names and has found them to be almost identical to their original Hebrew form, except for 'Jezus,' as he calls it. You do know Yeshua is Hebrew, Jewish?" I could tell that Mary became a little uneasy at my mocking the changed name. So I decided to lay my last discovery on her and see her reaction. "Did you ever hear of the Book of Enoch?"

"No," she replied.

"Well, don't feel bad again, girl, neither have I, but it's mentioned in the Book of Jude. It's a scripture about the third of the angels that were cast out of Heaven, only they weren't cast out, they left their first estate for strange flesh."

Mary suddenly proclaimed loudly. "I always wanted to read about the angels who were cast out of Heaven."

"Me too," I said, excitedly. "It should give us some better answers about different races and prehistoric man. And maybe all the other things that just don't agree with Christianity's crazy Adam and Eve story. The idea that mankind's only been here six-thousand years and came from one couple is illogical."

"Yeah," Mary said. "I was always bothered by that."

"Well, Jake and I have decided to read all the books of the Bible and not just what we are allowed to read by Christianity and Judaism. Besides, Christianity shouldn't have trusted the canon of the Jews. Obviously Jesus, I mean Yeshua, was killed by them."

"You're right," she said anxiously. "Come on, let's read Jude."

I turned to Jude, and it was only one full page long. Good. Mary didn't like to read. There it was, plain as the nose on your face.

"Can you believe it?" We both shouted at the same time.

"It doesn't take a rocket scientist to figure this out. Something's wrong, and it has to be in the Christianity story.

And the Jews didn't canonize Enoch, either," I said emphatically.

"Huh, why not?"

"Well, to me and Jake it's pretty obvious that they wanted to keep their outward religion alive. Enoch was a meditator who lived in caves. You can't sell that. I'm going to read every book of the Bible and see if I can find out what's going on. Jake doesn't think that Yeshua started Christianity, and I'm becoming more and more convinced he's right."

"He might be right," said Mary. "Look at all the different sects to choose from in Christianity."

"Yeah, you'd think if there is only one God there would only be one religion."

"Yeah, you'd think so."

"Jake asked me something tonight that really got me to thinking."

"What?" Mary asked.

"How do you think we go to Heaven?"

"We're judged on Judgement Day," she replied quickly.

"What about you, Angel?" She gave me the same answer, sounding even more annoyed than ever.

"Well, you're not going to believe this, but Misty and I said the same thing."

"Well, that's what the Bible says, doesn't it?"

"That's what I thought, but Jake said Yeshua called us dead and said we were already judged: 'Let the dead bury the dead,'" I said. "He quoted Yeshua as saying, 'You must be born again of the spirit to enter the kingdom of Heaven.'"

Mary looked puzzled. "Tell me about it."

"Well, we have to be saved, by being born again. That's what Jake says. The very word 'saved' would indicate past tense, that we're from Heaven, and that we came here in spirit. And the thing that saves us is the mystery. He was teaching the mystery, worshiping in spirit. And it's not easy like Christians believe. They all say the same thing, crying and feeling real emotional is being born again of the spirit. And of course, they would recite the Christian creed."

I knew Mary didn't know what I meant by mystery, like me at first, and I could tell she was annoyed at my remark about Christians being saved. "Don't tell me you've been saved?" I asked apprehensively.

"That's right," she said defiantly.

"I'm sorry then. I didn't mean to ridicule your religion or you. Can I ask what it was like though? Did the preacher put his hand on you and tell you you're saved?"

"No," she replied, sharply. "I was in the kitchen."

"Well, what happened? Did God talk to you?"

"No," she said immediately. "I just became very emotional and started crying. It was as if all my worries and troubles were gone."

"Well, Mary, I hate to say this, but the only difference is the setting."

She didn't care for that. "Well, you'll know it when it happens to you," she said, getting up to go to bed.

"I didn't mean to offend you. It's just that Yeshua said it was a hard thing."

"It was hard and emotional! I was living right and that's hard. Don't you think it ain't!"

I could tell she was aggravated. So this was a chance to make peace with her and Angel. I hugged her and said, "I'm sorry. I don't have the right to tell you you're not saved, but hold on, because I want you to hear this."

I turned to Angel and apologized, for ever having made a decision to refuse a blood transfusion. "I wouldn't have made that decision for Little Jake, Angel."

"You're damn right, you wouldn't," said Mary. "I wouldn't have let you."

"Me either Mom," Angel added boldly.

"Thank you," I laughed, hugging her again.

"Daddy hated those 'damn Jehovah's Witnesses,' as he called them."

"Really," I said, in surprise. "Boy, he sure wouldn't have let Angel and me see each other then, huh?"

"Shit no," she said quickly.

"Yeah, he would have because I would have converted his ass," Angel corrected her as she got up and came toward us.

I grabbed and hugged her and apologized again. We all hugged as we headed for the bed. "Don't worry you guys; it won't ever happen again. Jake and I are going to find the truth no matter what. Even if it means giving up religion, the world, whatever."

"Oh no," Angel groaned, "that's all I need now, for you to be searching with Jake. This means I'll never see you again."

"Aw honey, don't be like that," I said, following her as she went toward the bedroom.

"Don't give me that," she said. "You've been gone six hours, and it's two a.m."

"Now honey," I said, trying to console her.

All of a sudden the phone rang. "Oh no, I bet it's Jake," she said angrily. I grabbed the phone. "Hey man, are you ready for this?" It was Jake.

"Ready for what?"

"Well, first of all, thanks."

"For what?"

"For glorifying your religion."

"It's not my religion anymore, man."

"Well, anyway, it brought an amazing thing to my attention."

"What?"

"You know how the Jehovah's Witnesses glorify a name that doesn't mean squat?"

"Yeah," I said, getting anxious as Angel had already gotten in the bed.

"Well check this out, man: 'I am, Yeshua' the angels." I suddenly remembered our connection earlier today.

"Wow," I said as the significance of both names immediately overwhelmed me again.

"I know, man. I still can't believe it."

I was stunned as well.

"Are you there? Mike, are you there? Did you hear me?"

"Yes," I replied weakly, still absorbing all this and not wanting to annoy Angel.

"It's pretty heavy, huh?"

"Yeah, it is, man. I can't believe it."

"I'm telling you, man," he said with an excitement in his voice. "Somehow I knew this. I knew something was wrong the minute I heard that preacher using Yeshua's name. It's as if I had already known that it was changed, and now, it's lost its meaning. I think something major happened to the truth, and it lies within the Judeo-Christian story."

"Are you really ready Mike?" He asked, almost as if to warn me.

"Yes, I said quietly, but I gotta go."

I woke up the next morning and immediately called Jake. This became a daily routine. "Can you believe this, man?" I asked quickly. "Listen to one of the changes the Jehovah's Witnesses made in their Bible." I read the scripture change.

"Let me hear that again, just to make sure it has changed the meaning," he said. "It's a pretty common thing for the different sects of Christianity to make their own Bible. They say it's easi—."

I broke in and said, "Easier, right?"

"Yeah," he said, "that's right. What, you don't agree with easier interpretations either, huh?"

"Not hardly. It's a load of crap."

We discussed the scripture, the change of mystery to secret. "Yeah, pretty unbelievable, isn't it, and just think, you were going to follow them and even possibly, uh, lose your life. Remember?"

"Yeah, yeah, don't rub it in."

"Well, did we do something when we got home?"

"Yeah, yeah, I did; and I was glad to. Angel wasn't in the best of moods. So it helped to humiliate myself." I knew he was talking about apologizing for my decision with the blood.

"Did you explain how ignorant and selfish you were to force this life-threatening doctrine of blood rejections. Not to mention, birthday celebrations, anniversaries, Christmas, and . . . ."

"I know, I know, give me a break. Did you know Hank detested the Jehovah's Witnesses?" I asked quickly, changing the subject.

"No," he said numbly. "Don't tell me; you offended Angel's mom and now you find out that Hank wouldn't have let Angel go out with you." I agreed weakly. "Man, are you ever lucky Hank was already gone or you probably wouldn't have married Angel. What fate, huh?"

"Okay, okay, don't rub it in. I was brainwashed, all right?"

"Yeah really, just like the rest of the world," he remarked disgustedly. "Christians, that is. That's most of the world. I'm watching this preacher right now, and all that you've got to do are three things."

"No," I said, moaning. "Don't tell me!"

"Yeah, man, they have got this thing down. It's as easy as: believe, give money, and expect a miracle. Isn't that a bunch of crap. The bastards! There are babies, man. I mean sick, starving babies dying every day, and they sell this crap. How sick can these people be?"

"Really," I said. "Their story is so cruel. It's just like their chosen people story. Hell, I can see where racism started, with God, of course!"

"Yeah," he laughed. "You're right."

I laughed too. It was a funny revelation. I don't know where it came from. It's just simple deduction!

"Mike, do you remember the scriptures about the Sons of God breeding with the daughters of men? Well, aren't they angels?"

"Yeah, so what?"

"Well, that's obviously where we got other races."

"Well, that, but aren't we all supposed to be God's children?"

"Who said I didn't see your logic? As a matter of fact, I saw that before you did."

"Right, right."

"It doesn't matter, man. It's bigger than that; listen to this."

"What," I replied anxiously. I could tell by the tone of his voice it was something big.

"You know I looked up 'born again' and just as I thought, nothing. The definition didn't reveal what it was that we should be doing. But then I thought, this was like a mystery, finding the truth. Well, I read on and saw what I was looking for: The mystery. I've been saying it all this time. Yeshua was teaching the mystery to the apostles. Who would know that its definition describes the way, the Sign of Jonas?"

"What do you mean?"

"What do you mean, what do I mean? Let's just see what the mystery says."

I couldn't believe it. We were looking up a word that epitomized what had happened to the truth: it had been hidden; it became a secret. I remembered how the Old Testament had said the truth had been hidden.

Just as I was thinking of the irony in all this, Jake broke in. "Are you ready for this?"

"Yeah, lay it on me," I said anxiously.

"The word is in the Greek, reference number 3466, *musterion*. It is a derivative of *muo, to shut the mouth, still the body and learn secret truths through the idea of silence imposed by initiation into religious rites.*"

I sat there, holding the phone, stunned, when Jake began talking again. "Don't you see it, man?"

"Yes," I rebounded quickly. "But they still say 'secret' in the definition and that's just what the Jehovah's Witnesses have in their Bible."

"Well, get your King James' Version and see. It says 'mystery.' And it's no secret either. The mystery is what has been hidden and forbidden. It's literally been lost. It's in John 3. Have you read that yet?"

"I'm going to read the Gospels, but no, I haven't yet. I told you Angel wasn't too happy about yesterday."

"What other excuse are you going to give me?"

"Look, man," I said, starting to tell him again I was going to, but he broke in immediately and began to explain about the mystery again.

"I told you yesterday," he stammered. "I think Yeshua was trying to tell us to meditate to be born again, right?"

"Yeah."

"Well, don't you think that the definition of 'mystery' sounds like Eastern meditation?"

"Well, I hadn't thought about Yeshua's statement to Nicodemus, but it couldn't be prayer or Nicodemus would have known it."

"Right," he said, jubilantly. "I'm telling you, man, it's eastern meditation, and dig this, it also describes the Sign of Jonas."

"What? What do you mean?"

"Look at your Shroud, man. It's a picture of a dead man."

I picked up the picture and sure enough it did. And he did say, it was the only sign he was going to give us. "Wow," I said amazed. "This is heavy."

"Isn't it though? I'm going to start looking for anywhere it might be talked about in the Gospels." Jake then broke in with something new. "I read in the Shroud book where the author theorized that the apostles were Gnostics. And they might have been meditating to the Shroud."

"Really?" I said completely lost.

"Yeah, but the funny thing is, now the book is missing and I can't read about that."

"No, it isn't. I've got that book!"

"Why do you think I said that! Take care of it man. I'd like to check this out."

"I will man, I've got so much to read."

"Well, prepare yourself. You might have to read a whole lot more to find the truth, especially if it's mystery. Christianity forbid anything to do with meditation, and I bet we might even have to look into Buddhism. After all, Yeshua is Eastern, not Western."

"Well, I know Christianity condemns meditation, but do you think the Jews did, too?"

"Obviously, or Nicodemus would have known how to be born again. Besides, Yeshua said we must go into our closets and pray and give up the world. What else do you need?"

"Jake, do you think it's possible the Bible is altered?"

"Mike slap yourself and then say 3 times, King James, King James, King James."

"Believe me, man, it's been altered, changed, and made just right for Rome to continue the traditions of Jews, Church, and tithes."

"Yeah, you're right. Man, this really is amazing. This is a huge cover-up! Christians aren't really doing anything different from the Jews, are they?"

"No man, that's what I've been telling you. Hurry, turn it on Galaxy 3. The preacher who says Yeshua is on. He's talking about the sixth and eighth day creation. I've been reading Genesis again, and this guy is teaching about the eighth day, when there was no man to till the ground, but on the sixth day man was created. Another joke, huh?"

"Really," I replied, as I hurried and turned on the TV. Jake was talking while I found the program.

"You're right," I said, breaking in on Jake.

"See?" He said. "And another thing he does is point out the scripture in Genesis 6:2 that says God repented the day that he 'had' to make flesh. He thinks that the angels were making flesh themselves on the sixth day, and it went sour between there and the eighth day."

"Wow!" I said. "That's heavy." (*Scientific creation evidence would be heavier.*)

This seemed to make a lot of sense, and the scriptures sure did back up his theory. That sure would explain where other races came from.

"Yeah," Jake said, "I'm going to study with this guy. I like the way he teaches."

"Boy, do we have some studying to do." He started to go on and explain something else when I glanced over and saw Angel coming my way.

"I've got to go," I said firmly into the phone.

"Hold it, man. I need you to help me Friday."

I looked up to see Angel, shaking her head. "You can't get enough of each other, can you?"

I told Jake I'd call him tomorrow and hung up.

"Baby," I said, "I'm coming. Would you cool out, please."

"Well," she said angrily. "Last night I had to make you put the Bible down or the phone away and come to bed. Now I have to see you with it again, and even worse, you're on the phone with Jake about the same thing." I followed her back to bed, trying to hug on her all the way.

"Hon, we are on to something big here. We have discovered proof of a Christianity cover-up, or at least it looks that way to us."

The next morning, Mary came into the kitchen and asked me

about last night. "What's all the talk last night about a cover-up?" I just finished making coffee. So I got us some and sat with her at the table.

"Well, you know I told you about Enoch last night."

"Yeah," Mary replied.

"Well, Jake called after that and I told him how the Jehovah's Witnesses also had changed the original scripture."

"How?"

"Well they changed mystery to secret." He looked up 'mystery' and guess what?"

"What?"

"It describes 'meditation' and the Shroud. It's a physical act, not a secret."

"Really?" She said, raising her eyebrows.

"Can you believe that?" I asked jubilantly.

"No," Mary said.

"Yeah, and did you know also that God repented the day he had to make flesh?" *(I would soon challenge "my god" thinking.)*

"What? Had to make?" I had reacted the same way.

"Yeah. The preacher that Jake talked about is on TV right now."

"I haven't watched him much, but I will now," she said. "Come on, we'll check him out."

I followed her into the living room and started telling her how amazing it would be if Jake and I found the truth. "I mean, a provable truth that makes sense and agrees with science. And you know the mystery is in every culture."

"Yeah," she said. "It would be nice. Shoot, I can't stand to read," she laughed.

"Well, you better wish us luck, because from what Jake and I have discovered, you definitely have to do a lot of reading. We're going to start checking out Buddhism, and I'm reading the Shroud book now. Well, at least I will try to tonight."

Angel came in and sat down beside me. "Where do I fit in between the songs, the book, satellites, and now this? I mean, for God's sake, why do you have to save the world? Let them find it out for themselves." I thought I'd tell her that it was a tough job, but someone has to do it. I knew better!

"Hon, I'm doing it for all of us. Don't you remember last night? I would have sacrificed my life for something I didn't even understand, let alone prove. I can't make that mistake again, and especially not for my children. Besides Baby, we're going to have Christmas now, birthdays and everything."

"Why?"

"I told you last night that I was giving the Jehovah's Witnesses up, and now I *know* I am. I keep finding more reasons. They take the word *mystery* and make it a secret. And now, the act of mystery is unknown to us. It is a secret."

"I know," she said. "I heard you telling Mom, but what does that mean?"

"It means that not only do they condemn the way to do this thing, 'being born again,' but they hide it as well."

Mary started shaking her head. "Yep, you're right. And you know, Christianity is anti-spirit."

"Hell, yes, I do! Go to a Jehovah's Witnesses church. They forbid spiritism. Christianity has always forbidden spiritism. And it doesn't take a rocket scientist to figure out that we are a Christian country. We have God everywhere in our government, even though we're supposed to have separation of state and religion. That's another joke! Hell, if I was an atheist, I'd be pissed off. I am pissed off!"

Mary was nodding her head with every word. My mother-in-law had recently lost her husband who was more atheist than religious, and I was worried that I might have struck an emotional chord in her.

"I'm sorry," I said to her.

"What?"

"I know Dave was an atheist, and there I go again, insulting someone. I don't want to offend you."

"Yeah," she said, "but you didn't."

"Man, wouldn't it be great if I found a religious truth that science accepted, for Dave?"

"Yeah," she said, looking off. Dave would have liked that. I knew that she was thinking about him.

"You know, at times he was religious; but I don't think in his heart he was," she reflected warmly. "He just couldn't buy it. He was too logical to be religious."

"Yeah, who knows." I added quickly to comfort her. "It's just a learned thing anyway. We become what our parents are." I thought I'd change the subject. "Jake mocks the way all old people say the world's getting worse."

"Well, crime is getting worse," she said boldly, stopping me. Uh oh, I guess I said the wrong thing.

"Mary," I said unbelievingly, "surely you know that it isn't? The numbers are getting better, and it's obvious, we don't live in the days of the wild west anymore."

"Well," she added. "You've even said that while you were watching the news."

"Yeah, you're right, but that is what I call a Christianity slip, or learned brainwashing. I'll prove it to you. Remember not too long ago, I told you about Andy Rooney proving this very point?"

"I think so."

"Well, he proved it by doing a comparison of magazines from the sixties to the nineties. What do you think the result was?"

She started shaking her head and smiling.

"You know, don't you?"

"Yeah," she said. "The world is getting better, but don't you think that the crime rate overall is getting worse?"

"No, it just seem's that way. The population is getting bigger, and we are seeing it through television. Which, I'm sure you remember, was just invented not long ago. It's easy to fill up an hour newscast with horror."

"Yeah," she said. "It's funny how you can believe and say such ridiculous things."

"Not really, Mary. The world as we know it talks that way. So it's not so hard to believe; it's just the way it is. We're brainwashed. The ironic thing is that the crime rate is better than worse, statistically, and we know things are getting better."

"We sure aren't there yet, though," she said.

"You ought to know better than anyone," I laughed. "You're a white woman dating a Black man, something you definitely wouldn't have done a hundred years ago. Even twenty, here."

Mary laughed! "That's for sure. Hell, not even now. I was just told by another guy at the lounge to leave the blacks alone."

"You've got to be kidding me."

"I wish I was."

"Wow, doesn't that suck. This world is so racist and hypocritical. I swear this chosen story of the Jews is the reason this crap exists."

Mary just shook her head and said, "I wouldn't doubt it. It makes sense." She laughed again.

We sat and watched the preacher teach. I couldn't help but to notice the American flag behind him as he spoke. It turns out that he was an ex-Marine. He talked like a drill sergeant. From what we watched, the guy explained his theory behind the sixth and eighth day creation, and it made a lot of sense. He acknowledged the repenting of having made flesh, but I just couldn't handle his abrasiveness and remarks about pride. Worst of all was his healing and praying for people through letters.

"Come on," I said quickly. "Can you believe this? I can't believe people go for this stuff."

"What?" Mary asked. "You don't believe in healing and prayer?"

"Not like this, I don't. It's unfair. Hell's bells, don't you think it would be unfair for God to answer any one of those with all the dying, starving, poor, diseased children in this world?"

"Well, yes, but I still think God gives miracles." She just grinned real big and said, "I see what you're saying and it doesn't make sense, but I know he does and I know I'm saved."

Granny was listening in on the conversation, and she quickly agreed with Mary. I hadn't even noticed her being here. She must've been in bed when I got in. She was Mary's mom and the Hank's wife of fifty years. She was definitely a Christian. I turned to her and asked, "When you were born again, did you feel it?"

"Yes I did," she said with that right hand up in the air to swear to it.

"I believe you felt emotional," I said to her softly, "just like Mary and every other Christian who believes in saving, but Granny, it's just too easy." I tried to explain without offending her.

"But it was easy," she said defiantly. "You mean you don't believe God can save you or heal you either?"

"Well, if God has to be fair and we know that 'He' does. He, I said aloud again! Doesn't that offend you as a woman?" I didn't let her answer before going on. "It wouldn't be fair for God to heal and save us Christians, who are born kings, and let the poor, starved, sick children die in India, Africa, and God knows where else, now would it? What about those who don't hear about Jesus? Is it fair that they only get one chance and if they don't hear about him, they're out of luck?"

"I don't mean to be cruel or insulting, ladies, but I just can't believe you don't see the unfairness in your thinking. Don't you want your God to be fair and maybe even a woman?" I could see Angel coming. Granny had turned away from me. She said that I could believe what I want, and she'd believe what she wanted. I finally gave in. Granny was reciting the last thing her mother had done on her death bed. She said she rose up and took one last breath and said, "Jesus" and then passed on. I couldn't leave her thinking that I believed her mother hadn't gone to Heaven. Because I honestly didn't. So I went to her and said, "Granny, I'm sure your momma saw Yeshua and went to Heaven. All I'm saying is that Christianity defies logic, preaching a God who saves one child and lets thousands more die of starvation."

"Well, I know I'm saved just like my mother."

"I believe you, Granny."

"Why are you calling Jesus 'Yabbash' or whatever you said?"

"I am doing that because I just found out what his name really is. You see, it's been changed and why it's important has been lost. My buddy Jake is researching names and Yeshua was changed radically. And when it was changed it lost its meaning. We want to prove the importance of the name. I'll ask you or Mary. What is so important about the name 'Jesus'?"

Granny immediately said that it is the name of our Saviour and it's the only name you could be saved by.

"Well, the only problem I have with that is, it doesn't answer anything for me, as an atheist."

She got a little flustered and started saying that the Bible says we would only be saved in his name.

"Yes, but what does 'Jesus' mean to us as a word? Nothing," I added quickly, "but listen to this, Granny. 'I am, Yeshua', angels, spirit.'" She just looked at me, and then Mary said I better explain because she wouldn't get that. "Well, Mary already knows because I told her last night. It is important because it completes a prediction! I am, Yeshua, angels. My buddy thinks that we are the one-third, cast out, trapped in these bodies."

"Well, I know about God saying his name was the 'I am,' but I don't know Yabbasha . . . just Jesus."

"Yeshua," I said helpfully and politely.

"I only know Jesus because I'm American," she said proudly.

"I know you are Granny, but Jesus doesn't make any sense to me, and Yeshua does. I think I'm beginning to see why the name was so important. Especially, if we are the one-third of the angels cast out of Heaven like Jake thinks we are."

"I don't know anything about that," she said. "I came from Adam and Eve, didn't you?"

"I don't know, really. But Granny, have you ever heard of the Shroud of Turin?" I wanted to avoid that subject. Don't worry if you haven't; none of us have either." I went and got the picture and book to show Granny. Angel came into the bedroom and grabbed my arm. "Mike, remember Papa?" I looked at her with great humility and realized I was doing to Granny what I had done to her Papa. I had tried to prove the J.W.'s to him. What a joke! I was ashamed. I had just apologized for taking up for a religion that I hadn't proven to be true. Worse, I would've died for my ignorance. And now I was upsetting Granny. I knew how I had pressed Papa with the J.W.'s material, and he died shortly after. I just wanted to share my discoveries. This became a valuable lesson to me. I would try my best never to do it again.

I told Angel not to worry and went on into the kitchen. "Check this out, Granny. This is a picture of the burial cloth of Christ, and when he resurrected it was left as a sign to us."

"Huh," she said, picking it up. "What do you know about that!"

"Yeah, remarkable, ain't it! He took a picture of himself 2,000 years ago. We've only had photography 150 years. Now that's a miracle." I said jubilantly. "Jake thinks it was predicted as the Sign of Jonas in all four Gospels."

"The sign of what?"

"The Sign of Jonas, or the Jonah and the Whale story."

"Oh yeah," she replied. "I know that story. God delivered Jonah out of the belly of the whale after three days."

"Yes, and Yeshua was resurrected in three days. Have you ever heard of this though, or the Sign of Jonas?"

"No," she said. "I can't say that I have." She kept walking away. "I hadn't either."

I followed and told her the guy on television believed that people were here before Adam and Eve and he preached a sixth and eighth day creation. She just laughed. "Nope. The Bible says we all came from Adam and Eve."

"Well, what about the different races or Cain's wife? It doesn't make sense."

"Well, it's the way I believe and my Mom and Daddy and theirs before them. So, I'm sure they weren't all wrong."

"No, I'm sure they weren't, Granny, but I think there's more to it. If I find out anything, I'll tell you, okay?"

She started into the living room where Mary was watching TV

"All right," she said lovingly.

I didn't want to offend her like I had Papa. Granny was going on eighty. Besides, I don't want to hurt anyone. I just want to know the truth about us. I wanted to end my visit with Granny on a good note. "I did want to tell you though, Hank would be happy to know that I've given up the Jehovah's Witnesses' religion."

"Good!" She screamed with excitement. "Hank couldn't stand those people for not taking blood."

"I know!" I almost started crying, as I saw Mary smiling with Angel. "Yeah, and we're going to have Christmas, Granny." I hugged her. "Good," she blurted out, "Little Jake needs that." Everybody needs that, I thought to myself. Learning to give is good. "Well, I'm going to get to work, Granny."

"Okay, honey," she said and hugged me goodbye.

I started out after hugging Angel and told Granny: "You need to move on in here, and let's have a regular family and all the holidays, not just Christmas." She just grinned! I went on to work without telling Granny about the mystery and Jake not believing Yeshua started Christianity. But I knew that would have been too much for her to take, and insulting as well.

I thought all day long about my mistake with Angel's grandfather. I had been such a know-it-all with him. And the irony is that I didn't know anything. Jake had said many times to me: "Mike, I know nothing, and I'm ten years older than you. How could you know so much?" I really didn't realize it! What a hypocrite I had been. I hadn't researched anything. I didn't know anything!

I couldn't believe *mystery* was a physical act, to be born again. I only knew that it was a secret as the Jehovah's Witnesses had translated it. Jake saying that it represented the Sign of Jonas, and it's describing the Shroud was even harder to absorb. It blew me away.

If it in fact is true, then none of Christianity recognizes the only sign he gave us as the way to be born again, something Jake thinks was lost. And, from all I could remember in the Old Testament, it seems to be. The most ironic thing about the Shroud is that the Catholic Church owns it, but doesn't authenticate it. Jake didn't know if they quote the "Sign of Jonas;" but if it is the way to be born again by mystery as he thought, then he definitely knew they would condemn it as Eastern mysticism.

"Although, the Pope does preach meditation; it is no different than prayer," I remembered Jake remarking disgustedly, as Misty brought it to his attention. He always ended up scowling how Christians couldn't stop their mouths long enough for their minds to do anything, and even if it did, they'd swear it was demonic.

I had rolled in my seat laughing with him. "I know my religion—there I go again with the Christianity slip—I know the Jehovah's Witnesses would," I said. "They forbid spiritism."

The day had been a long and hard one for me as I had worked on yet another cigar store Indian. Granny had gone back to Spartansville, and Mary was out on a date. I couldn't wait to read the Shroud book and start on the Gospels, but I knew that I had better pay some attention to Angel, since I had just been in hot water the night before.

After spending some quality time with my Baby, I started reading Matthew 16:4 "The Sign of Jonas" as I turned in for the evening. I read up through chapter 22 and started on Matthew 23, the chapter in Jake's song. As I read, I realized that Yeshua was condemning the Jewish preachers' behavior and it was identical to Christianity's.

Then suddenly, boom, more proof of a Christian religion practicing the opposite of Yeshua's teaching, Matthew 23:9: "Do not call anyone on Earth your Father." I couldn't believe it! How did Catholicism get away with this! This clearly is obvious proof that Yeshua didn't start Christianity! Catholics call preachers "Father." I remembered how Jake explained to me that the Catholic religion was the only Christian denomination for several hundred years. And the church didn't exist until 300 A.D.

One thing I knew for sure was Yeshua hadn't started Catholicism as the proof is in the Gospel itself: Catholicism was fraudulent from the beginning with the first Pope. Pope is Latin for Father. Which means Christianity is fraudulent!

I remember Jake saying to Misty that we're all just glorified Catholics with over-rated opinions, too proud to give an inch. I chuckled to myself because we each had belonged to a different Christian sect that believed they were the sole truth. It was so amazing to discover proof of the very thing Jake was saying. Yeshua hadn't started Christianity and the proof was in Matthew 23. I picked up the phone and immediately called Jake. Angel was attending to our two-year-old who couldn't get his days and nights straight. "Hey, Jake, you aren't going to believe this," I said immediately after he said hello. "I've got proof that 'Jesus,' Yeshua didn't start Catholicism." I read the scripture.

"You're right, dude! But what Bible do you have?"

"The King James," I replied.

"You can't," he said. "I have it and that isn't what it says. You must have a concordance version of it."

I looked again and found it to be so. I felt so dumb. "You're right, dude, I do."

"I told you," he said.

"Man, that's a bunch of crap. The first version is what we should be reading."

"Really," Jake said. "Like we can't understand English." We both just laughed. Jake read the scripture and immediately said, "Yep, it sure does, but of course you know I knew that. In fact, didn't I tell you that?"

"No, you didn't, or I would have told you when you said you didn't think that Yeshua started Christianity. He couldn't have according to the Gospel Truth of this scripture."

"Well, there are other sects who don't call themselves 'Father.'"

"Yes, but don't you remember the history lesson you gave about Catholicism being the first and only Christian religion?"

"Of course I do."

"Well, if Catholicism was Christianity, then Yeshua didn't start Christianity."

"I knew that," he bragged, but he knew he was caught.

"Right," I replied mockingly. "That's why you were speculating that Yeshua might not have started Christianity, just the other day. Pretty heavy, huh, and right in your song, *Matthew 23*. Is this a heavy, or what?"

"Really," he replied, "and what about the mystery."

"Yeah man, it sure seems to describe the Shroud. You know I think you could be right. It looks like Christianity is the same as Judaism in structure. It's sure obvious, the Christians do the opposite of Yeshua's teachings. It's a sad day for Yeshua; his new followers aren't true followers. And his people deny him. How sad!"

"Yeah, I think they used his resurrection to convert Jews to the Roman religion. That's why they gave him the name Yesous. It's Zeus to us."

"Heck, yes," I said. "And now they're the wealthiest organization in existence; they own most of New York City, Rome, Mexico, South America and Europe, who knows where else."

Jake started to tell me about some preacher, but I broke in, "I want to finish reading Chapter 23, dude. I just wanted to call and tell you what I discovered."

"What *we* discovered," he said, correcting me.

"Yeah, you're right; I wouldn't have known it if you hadn't given me the little history 'refresher' course. You know I knew it though, the history, I mean."

"Right, right."

"Well, look, I've got to go. Angel's coming, and I don't want to make her mad. Not if you want me to help you Friday. I haven't even told her yet."

"Right, dude; we don't want to make her mad."

"So, I'll let you go."

"Okay, man. See you later."

I got off the phone, just in time. Angel was getting ready for bed. "Don't worry," I reassured her. "I'm just going to read a little more, and I promise, I'll put it away." I really was anxious to share my discovery with her, but I figured I would wait and tell her and Mary together. Besides, I was anxious to read on and wanted to go to bed on a good note. And not discussing it was a good thing. A real good thing!

As I began reading again, I was stunned by the following chapters. They specifically spoke against any hierarchy in teaching. Knowing that he was talking to Jewish religious leaders, it's obvious the traditions and structure of Christianity are basically no different from Judaism! He was right. All churches had elders or some hierarchy.

I thought of how we always went out to eat after church, like the rest of the crowd, and usually at a better place to eat. Everybody dressed as good as they could and it goes without saying that everybody tried to get there early to get a good seat, just like in Matthew 23. We all wanted to eat with the preacher. I couldn't believe what I was reading and wondered how I could've missed this the first time I read it. I probably hadn't understood. I had been taught that there are some things in the Bible not meant to be understood, so it wouldn't have bothered me anyway. I became angry with my teachers, myself, and my parents. I had become their tradition, but not for long.

I continued to read, fighting back feelings that tore at my very soul. Then I read a scripture that really shocked me. There it was! The scripture read, "Woe unto you Scribes and Pharisees, hypocrites! For you shut up the Kingdom of Heaven against men; for you neither go in yourselves, nor do you allow those who are entering to go in." This described meditation to a tee, going inside ourselves. Knowing history, that we were burning witches only a few hundred years ago, it's as plain as the nose on your face. They were forbidding it then as they are now. I couldn't believe it!

I was anxious to read the Gospel of John, Chapter 3. Jake said it was the only place that talked about being born again. I finished reading Matthew 23 and turned to it. I read more proof of Jake's allegations, while I turned the pages. He said that Yeshua considered us dead. He quoted, "Let the dead bury the dead." Well, there it was. He saw the resurrection as something before death, because we are already judged. This is where death is. And there it was, as well.

I found John and started reading again. I laughed when I read the scripture describing the spirit, like the wind. I remembered how Jake got all excited about that. I read on where Yeshua remarks to Nicodemus, "You're a master of the Jews and you do not know this?" Obviously, it wasn't praying, since the Jews, like Christians, pray openly.

I read on and was awestruck at the next verse: "No man has gone to Heaven that didn't come from Heaven, even the Son of Man who is in Heaven." This confirmed Jake's theory that we came from Heaven. Jake felt we did something to get here, and now we have to do it to get back. The mystery. "Be true to thine own self," I mumbled a quote from Joel. Then we wouldn't be scared to do mystery.

I started to put the Bible away as Angel was coming to bed. I laid the Bible down and finished the hot chocolate that she brought me. I hadn't even noticed it. She was the best a guy could ask for! As I picked up the Bible, I noticed that I had lost my place. Oh well, I thought, it's for the better anyway. I started to close the Bible and noticed a scripture in red: Yeshua was telling his apostles that the Kingdom of Heaven does not come with observation, unlike Christianity teaches, but Heaven is within you. I chuckled to myself as I remembered a buddy of mine. He was a Seventh-Day Adventist. They said that everyone on Earth would see Jesus coming at the same time. This seemed impossible, on a round planet. *("UP" and space travel would soon change my thinking.)*

I put the Bible away and mused at Jake's disgust toward apocalyptic writings. He called people ignorant who didn't know the world had already been ruled by Rome. I hadn't known. Finally, as Angel was getting in the bed, I couldn't help but to ask her where Heaven was. I wanted to prove we were all "brainwashed" by Christianity. Sure enough she said, "Up there, I guess!" *(I can't believe I laughed at this now.)*

"Yeah, that's what we're taught, but I just read where Yeshua said Heaven is within us." She kind of looked puzzled. "Do you see how that would explain the mystery, like Jake says?" She wasn't impressed. I just reached and turned out the light, and we did what we did best, made love. Besides, there wasn't enough time to explain that direction was relative. *(I would soon "see" it wasn't to children and NASA, scientifically speaking. "UP" is space from anywhere on a planet.)*

The next few days I shared my discoveries with Mary. I especially liked to ask her where Heaven was. I got the usual response even though she, too, thought it was silly for anyone to believe Heaven was up and Hell was down. She thought the Christian Hell concept was unfair, the same as me. We went over the scripture in John 3 again, verse 11: "No man has gone to Heaven that didn't come from Heaven." She was amazed.

She said, "It says exactly what Jake is saying, that we were in Heaven first."

"Yeah! I can't believe the Jehovah's Witnesses condemn spiritism. They change the very word 'mystery' to secret. And mystery is the function, not a secret."

"Well, they aren't any different from my religion," she said in agreement. "They don't preach the mystery, and they definitely condemn spirituality. Shit, mystery is a secret."

"Man, you ought to read Matthew 23, Mary. It describes Christianity and Judaism to a tee. Heck, organized religion for that matter. The more I read Yeshua's teachings, the more I understand what Jake says. We're going to find the truth, even if it means we become Buddhists. At least they do mystery." Mary just laughed.

I read every night, until the following Friday when I was to help Jake on the satellite job. I waited until that morning to tell Angel and managed to get away without too much hassle. I really found it hard to balance a relationship with Jake and everything else I had going on. After all, I did have to make a living.

I reached Jake's and found him running out of the house, late as usual. It was getting toward Christmas, and he was trying to make all the money he could. I told him I had finished reading Matthew 23 and then John, but I really loved Luke 17:24, where Yeshua said Heaven is within us. He nodded his head in agreement and raised his eyebrows in surprise. Almost as if he knew what I was going to say next.

"Yeah man, you were right about mystery," I said stunned. "Yeshua condemns the Jews for obviously not doing it. He says that not only do they not go in themselves, but they suffer those that do. Just like Christianity, huh?"

"Yeah," he said. "Judaism apparently wasn't doing the mystery."

"Yeah, and Christianity has continued it's traditions. You know, Jake, we have found definitive proof that Yeshua wasn't responsible for Christianity. They practice the opposite of his teachings; and the thing that they need to do most they condemn."

"Yeah," Jake laughed. "They don't just condemn it; they'll kill you for it."

"Yeah, really. It's tradition, man. We're all brainwashed."

"We're not only brainwashed," I said, "but they're hiding the truth like it's a mystery. What am I saying? It is a mystery. It's a cover-up man! An information cover-up by Christianity. The Jehovah's Witnesses did, anyway. I can prove that." *(This eerily became my first book title.)*

"Well let's just keep that to ourselves," he said calmly. "These people are staunch Christians and we don't need to offend them." I laughed at the paradox. Would Yeshua have been offended?

As we headed back home from another Dishout Satellite endeavor, I was telling Jake that we really are a Christian country, not a democracy. He just laughed and said, "So what? What can you do about it?"

"We can tell people."

"Do you think they don't know?" He asked sarcastically. "Most are even proud of it."

"Well, I'm not!" I told him defiantly. "The Christians have nothing but a murderous history. They took this country from the Indians. What's there to be proud of? Pride and religion contradict each other. Where are people's minds?"

"It's not just here," he replied. "It's that way with most of the world."

I told him I was going to read up on Buddhism in the encyclopedia. "At least the Buddhist know pride is evil."

"Well, at least they do the mystery," he added.

"*Life* magazine did an article on Yeshua and said his teachings were comparatively similar to Buddhism."

"Well," I said. "From what I've read so far in Matthew 23, they're right. Yeshua says that we have to make the inner like the outer. Heaven is within us!"

"Yeah, get this," he remarked again. "They even said that Yeshua was an Eastern mystic, but his teachings are called Western."

"Boy, ain't that the truth. It's a trip, dude. They make a mockery of his teachings. 'Let no man be called father,'" I quoted in disgust.

"Really," said Jake. "I read 'teacher,' too, man; and our schools pledge allegiance to God and call themselves teacher. Isn't that bizarre? How can people not see the hypocrisy?"

Jake started talking about the article again. He said all the countries in the world have their picture of Yeshua on the cover and guess what? "They are all men from that country. Typical Christians, huh?"

"Man, what about women?"

"Really," he laughed.

"It's bizarre that Christianity doesn't recognize the Sign of Jonas and preaches signs of the last days. The J.W.'s are the worst."

"They all do," he added again, calmly.

"It's a joke, huh?" I snarled.

"It sure looks that way," he said.

There was silence as we drove on, but only for a second. Then Jake broke in, "He took a picture of himself 2,000 years ago, man. That's unbelievable."

"Well, I think it was too. But dude, more importantly, it is a picture of the thing they weren't doing then and aren't doing now: meditation."

"The mystery, you mean."

"Well, whatever; you know what I mean."

"Yes, but remember the Pope has daily meditations for us to say," he quickly admonished.

"I know, I know, but that's not the 'mystery,'" I said.

"Well, I wanted to tell you what they said in the article, but I can't get over Jesus. It's the name of Zeus. I mean we are going to be saved in his name, aren't we!"

I started to say something, and he cut me off.

"Man," he went on, "let me talk. Anyway this article was saying that the scientific community thinks Yeshua is just a story that four men got together and wrote about. What bullshit! Huh! If that's the case, then their story made one Hell of an impact on the world. I mean, time starts with him."

"Yeah, and that's the gospel truth," I said with a smirk.

"Yeah," he laughed.

"You know," I said, "I can't believe someone isn't trying to prove he does exist and did leave the Shroud. If the world only knew what we did."

Jake broke in, "I think you're right. It's a cover-up, man. That's all I can gather. Look at these churches. They epitomize wealth. That's the opposite of Yeshua."

"Yeah, we have all kinds of street people problems and all these churches have their doors locked."

"Yes, and I'm sure they would even run them off."

Just as we were rounding fifty-first Street, there was a huge, monolithic church on the corner. We saw a street person begging for food, so Jake pulled over. He said, "I bet they drive right past them, too." The old guy came up to the window, and we both contributed to his cause. "Look at that church," Jake said as we pulled away. "It's a mansion." We counted several more before we went another two blocks to his house.

As we pulled in his drive we saw Luke getting out of his car. He was Jake's nephew and one of my best friends. Jake was still giving churches Hell for not being open to the poor.

"What are you raving about?" Luke asked, as we walked up.

"Christianity!" Jake railed.

"Why?" Luke asked.

"Yeshua," Jake said coldly. Then Jake told him how Christianity changed his name. "It has been changed to Jesus, but it used to be Yeshua in Hebrew."

"What?" He asked, puzzled.

Jake looked at me and said, "See, all these Christians and I can't find anyone who knows about his name."

"What do you mean, man? Did you forget about me?" I reminded him.

"You didn't know until I told you, and you still call him Jesus."

"Give me a break, man. I've been brainwashed. It's a Christianity slip." I punched Jake in the shoulder playfully. He laughed, and then started rubbing his shoulder and moaning.

"Oh, sissy, you should've been an actor," I told him, grabbing his ear. Luke didn't understand Jake's offense at the name and asked about it again. Jake told him the name had been changed, and maybe even more were changed, as well. Luke was a little leery, so Jake began proving his point by reciting the biblical names. I was stunned. I hadn't heard him do this before. "Abel was one name, from Hebrew to Greek to English. Adam was also, and so on. But Yeshua has two: Jeshua and Jesus, and we know why Jeshua isn't Yeshua. King James."

"Bingo," Jake suddenly said as he finished, "there it is." Luke mumbled that he didn't understand how they had changed it.

We went in and Jake immediately grabbed the *Concordance.* Luke asked Jake if he still had Mamaw's Bible. Jake replied that in fact he had Mamaw's Bible. She had given it to him when he went to see her in the hospital. They both got a little sad. They were worried about Mamaw as we all were, and Luke and I both grabbed Jake's shoulder. "Yeah, bud, we know how you feel. She's going to be all right."

"Well, at least she's home again."

"She's going to be all right," Luke said assuredly.

"Who?" Moses asked.

"Mamaw," Luke said.

Jake gave me the Bible and said, "we're all getting older, and I, uh—." He kind of choked a second and said, "I think that's why Mom gave me this Bible. She knew it would be our last good moment together." I just about cried, and I could tell Luke was shaken. He hugged Jake, and I did too. We were all hugging, when all of sudden, it felt like Bigfoot was shaking us. I looked up and saw Moses. He was all teary-eyed and grinning like a Cheshire cat.

"Well, what do you know, guys. At least Mamaw gave us our first family hug." What a Kodak moment. Suddenly things were brighter. Love what a great thing!

I took the Bible and started looking up Matthew 23 as Misty walked in the room. Jake forgot his point. He immediately went to her side and started loving on her. While he was busy giving her all his money, I continued to look in the Bible.

"Look here, Luke," I said loudly, wanting to get back to our point about Christianity, "and you're not going to believe this." I started to read Matthew 23 and immediately began, "Jesus, I mean Yeshua—"

He quickly interrupted, "Don't worry; I'm English!" That was all it took.

Jake started in on Luke about the translation, but didn't get far, because Misty said it didn't bother her so much either. I immediately broke in. I didn't want Jake and Misty to start arguing.

"Let me finish reading," I sternly said. "Regardless of whether you agree on the name, let's see if you agree that Christianity and Judaism appear to be what Yeshua is preaching against."

"Is that what you were talking about in the driveway?" Asked Misty.

"No," Jake snapped. "It's how Christians don't care about the name." He started ranting. I started reading and told Luke that Yeshua was talking to Jewish preachers, and that their behavior is just like Christianity's."

"No, they aren't! That's stupid; they don't believe in Jesus Christ."

"Well, no joke! But they have churches just like Christians. And worship basically the same is what I mean. Listen to this," I said, so I could hurry things up. I figured Angel would be anxious for me to get back. I found something concrete, simple. "Here's your proof that Christianity is bogus: 'Let no man be called Father.'"

"We don't call ours that. We call them preachers or pastors. We're Baptists, not Pentecostal." I should've known.

Jake broke in immediately. "It's all Catholic, Luke. That's what Mike's trying to tell you."

"Whatever! I know what I am."

"Yeah," Jake said. "A glorified Catholic."

Luke bristled.

"Luke," I said quickly to stop the arguing. "What would you say if I told you Catholicism was the only Christian religion for hundreds of years?"

"How do you know?"

"He didn't," Jake said. "I told him."

"Well, he did refresh my memory. But, I did learn a little from school," I reminded him. "Well, anyway. Luke, if Christianity started their religion, doing something Yeshua said not to do, don't you think they might be bogus?"

"What," he asked, "Let no man be called Father?"

"Yeah," I replied, "for a start."

"I guess, but like I said, we aren't Catholics."

"Well, I just said that Christianity was Catholicism for hundreds of years. There weren't any others." He didn't seem to understand. "Yeshua couldn't have started Christianity, Luke, it's obvious."

"Christianity comes from Christ so he had to have started it!"

"Well, Luke buddy, that's because you think it's his name."

"Well, it's what I was taught, when I was a kid." We all laughed. Jake said he thought the same thing when he was a kid.

"Luke listen to me. We're still not telling the truth today about the Indians in America and what happened in the name of Christianity."

"Yeah," Jake said. "Those bastards slaughtered women, children, and men, in a way that was more cruel than what we could ever imagine. They were driven into hollows and trapped with bows and arrows against the guns of the Christians. They were slaughtered worse than animals!"

"Luke, believe me, man. We are still being lied to and controlled, by this Christian country. Aren't we?" I said, looking at Jake. He nodded his head in agreement.

"Well," Luke broke in, "I guess you're saying all my family, even my Mom, is wrong, then."

"If they follow a fake name, they are." Jake added mercilessly.

"No, they aren't," he barked right back. "That's just your opinion."

"I know, Luke. You don't care about the name change either, do you?"

"All I know is that I believe Jesus Christ is my Savior, and I'm proud to be a Christian."

"Oh no!" Jake moaned. I immediately knew what he was going to say, that pride was the opposite of what Yeshua taught. "Sure enough, he started. "Don't you know that Yeshua preached against pride?"

Luke got flustered for a minute. Then he rebounded back. "Don't tell me Jesus wouldn't want us to be proud to be a Christian, and want us to follow him."

"Yes," Jake laughed and said, "I'm sure of it."

"Yeshua talked against pride, Luke," I talked slowly and quietly, trying not to get him anymore riled than he was. "Everyone knows that it's one of the seven evils." Or did they? I would find out otherwise, from then on.

Jake changed the subject and asked him if he was born again of the spirit.

"Well, I've been saved, so I guess so."

Jake asked him how he got saved.

"I did the same thing my mom did and her brother George did and right on down the line." He got this serious look. "I confessed my sins on my knees and asked the Lord and Savior Jesus Christ to come into my heart. Then I cried."

Jake piped up, "If that's being saved, then Michael Jackson has done more for God than Jimmy Christ ever could."

Luke moved away from us as if we were going to be struck by lightning.

Jake laughed and started doing his Michael Jackson imitation. "Where's that Jimmy Christ; I'll whip his ass!"

I just rolled laughing, but Luke was getting pretty upset. I immediately broke in and took charge of the conversation. "Luke, I want to finish reading Matthew 23, man. I'm telling you: it nails Christianity, or the Church for that matter, to a cross."

I went on and read where we shouldn't be called teachers and asked if he saw the hypocrisy of that. He didn't. I explained. "Luke, the United States is really a Christian government, started by Christian men, and God is woven throughout its entire structure, especially in schools." I started to recite all kinds of hypocrisy.

"Heck, we have God, in our schools, our courts, and worse yet on our money, even though it's the root of all evil." There was a pause of silence as they all just seemed to be listening to me rant and rave.

Jake looked up and said, "Man, something just hit me."

"What?" I asked anxiously.

"History's lies have become today's truth. A lie, plus time, equals tradition."

"Yeah, you're right, people will follow their traditions, just like their parents did and their parents before them."

"It's the easy path," Jake said.

I turned my attention back to Luke, and continued to read Matthew 23. The next few scriptures held the very thing I wanted to read about. They showed Judaism forbidding meditation and not practicing it themselves. When I finished, I asked him if he had noticed the Shroud picture on the wall above him. He turned and looked, but didn't know what it was.

"Don't worry," Jake said. "Most Christians don't, either."

Luke told him to shut up.

"Don't worry, Luke. I didn't know what it was either. Jake found a scripture in the Gospel predicting it. We explained that the Shroud was his burial cloth. He was wrapped in it. The Jews wrap the body before placing it in the tomb, just like the Egyptians."

Jake started explaining the metaphor between Jonah and the resurrection. "He called it the 'Sign of Jonas' and said it was the only sign he would give us." He finished by saying that Yeshua took a picture of himself 2,000 years ago.

"Well, that's not all he did," I chimed in. "He took a picture of himself doing what we must do to go to Heaven: meditate."

"I didn't say that," Jake said, louder this time, breaking in. "How'd you get that?"

"Remember the mystery?"

"Yes I do."

"Maybe you do, but Luke doesn't."

"What?" Luke asked.

"The word *mystery*, Luke. It's not secret. It's actually meditation as we know it."

"No, it isn't, that's the same as praying," barked Jake. "If it was meditation at all, it would be Transcendental Meditation

Huh," he said. "The mystery is abbreviated the same as T.M.."

"What's mystery, man?" Luke asked again.

"Well, let's educate ourselves, Luke." We looked it up in the *Strong's*

Concordance.

"Remember a little while ago, I asked you how you thought you go to Heaven and you gave the typical Christian response: by living the Ten Commandments and being saved. Well, I did that for a reason, to show you that Christianity is basically following the traditions of Judaism, except for being born again."

We found mystery and read it. "Can you believe it?" I asked. It wasn't a secret like he thought, and me either for that matter. Luke was surprised.

Jake interrupted. "They hide it! Mystery describes the Shroud and it was predicted in the Gospels as the Sign of Jonas. The only sign he would give us, and Christianity doesn't acknowledge it! Hell, they even preach signs, signs, and more signs of the last days. Christianity is bogus, man!"

Luke bristled. I immediately tried to tone Jake down.

"It is safe to say they started misrepresenting Yeshua's teachings, right off the bat. They being Rome. And maybe they were covering up something; something that wouldn't let them continue their lucrative business of religion, if it was taught. And it was obviously the same business the Jews have had since the beginning of history. Yeshua was teaching mystery, Luke, not religion. The definition of mystery not only describes the Shroud, but it also describes the scripture in Matthew 23. Looking back at history it's easy to see that it was mystery, and Christianity has always condemned it. Just as it says in this verse: 'Woe unto you Scribes and Pharisees, hypocrites! For ye shut up the kingdom of Heaven against men: for you neither go in yourselves, and ye suffer them that do go in.'"

Luke just looked lost, as if he didn't understand. I asked him my favorite question, as I had asked Mary and Granny. "Where do you think

Heaven is? I discovered this from reading the Gospel," I said, looking toward Jake to give him credit. *(This question consumed me.)*

"Up, I guess," he said sheepishly.

"See, it's crazy, isn't it? We're brainwashed with *up*. Yeshua says it's inside us and that leads me to my explanation about the Shroud," I said as I looked back at it. We both looked at it. "It was the physical evidence that is so remarkable, it has made him Jesus Christ, Superstar, right? He is the most famous person on Earth, Luke." *(I soon will "see" "UP.")*

"Yeah," he agreed.

"Well, except for Elvis," Jake said bluntly.

"Really," Luke said smiling. I agreed laughingly, as no one in Tennessee was going to argue with that.

I reached over and grabbed the *Strong's Concordance* and held it up. "This is it, Luke, the easy way to prove it to yourself," I remarked. "The beauty of the *Concordance* is, just the remembrance of a single word will find the scripture you want." I showed him how to use it as I looked up *pride*, but he didn't like to be taught anything. I laughed to myself. It's a pride thing.

I found more than what I bargained for as I saw a scripture that exemplified Jake's angel theory and condemned pride. He wanted to know what Jake's theory was. Jake explained it.

" 'Pride cometh before the fall.' Look at all the scriptures that say pride is a bad thing, Luke," I said as soon as Jake finished. "It's even listed as one of the seven evils. Huh, the creation story is based on seven too. Coincidence?"

"It's so obvious," Jake remarked disgustedly.

I watched Luke looking at the *Concordance*. He suddenly asked, "How do you know all these scriptures say pride is a bad thing?"

I looked over at Jake, and he just about rolled over. I knew he was about to bust, so I jumped in. "Luke, look man, trust me. Any one of these will say that pride is bad. It's one of the seven evils, dude." I knew he was not getting the point, so I had to get things moving. I knew Angel would be waiting on me. "Please tell him, Jake." Jake told Luke his theory again on the fall of the angels. "The Book of Jude has the only reference that I know of," Jake said.

"Enoch prophesied about them," I added.

"Yeah," Jake followed. "His Book was not allowed in the Bible, by the Jews."

"Huh?" Luke remarked surprised.

I jumped in quickly and steered the conversation back to pride. I wanted Luke to see that pride is the bad thing here. He wouldn't accept that all of the scriptures condemned pride. So I found another, then another, and he got even more madder. I figured it was useless. So I went back to Jake's theory. "Luke, has Christianity ever explained the fall of the angels to you?"

"No," he said calmly.

"Well, me neither, and what they do say doesn't make sense. It's cruel. God, who can do anything, let Satan do evil in Heaven, and then made man just to let Satan torture him, too. Wow, what a fair God! Thanks, but no thanks."

"Yeah," Jake said. "It's crazy."

Luke agreed, and even said it didn't make sense. It surprised me! He asked about the name change again and why it was so important. We got lucky that he even wanted to talk again.

I quickly explained, as Jake was looking up something in the Bible. I asked him to find Jesus in the *Concordance* and he would see that it wasn't Hebrew. "It stops at the Greek."

Jake suddenly remarked, "Yes, even *Strong's* is wrong!"

I went on. "It's important because its correct translation is Jeshua, not Jesus. It's in the O.T. but not the N.T. But it should be Yeshua. King James changed the Y's to J's, even though we have Y's. Yeshua conforms the I Am, to tell us we are one-third of the angels, the angels who have fallen, at least according to Jake's theory. This has all happened before."

I didn't think Jake was listening, but he perked up and said. "Yeah, and they changed it to Jimmy, or what is it, Luke, Jerry Christ?"

Luke jumped up and said, "You're going to Hell if you say that crap."

"Luke, this is Hell, remember!" I said bluntly.

"I'm already here, outer darkness," Jake said, looking around. "This is where there is wailing and gnashing of teeth." He gnashed his teeth. "Aren't we surrounded by space which is dark? And you Christians sure do moan and cry a lot, especially when you're being persecuted with the truth." He started with the peace sign and Pulp Fiction dance. It was a hoot. The peace sign made me think of the Two Witnesses prophecy. We were sure torturing Luke.

I busted out laughing, uncontrollably. That was it for Luke; he was leaving. I got control of myself. "Don't you want to finish finding out if the name was changed? Think about it, man. I Am, Yeshua, spirit, angels, same thing." *(The ancient evidence would soon change my "spirit" mind.)*

Luke said he was English and that was just language.

Jake started, but I interrupted. "Come on, man, we are just trying to find the truth here. You have to admit, Jake's theory makes sense. At least we get more than one chance. After all, we have to be born again of the spirit. Isn't an angel a spirit? Wouldn't a spirit reincarnate? And in fact it does. We know that. We see it in animals: birds and fish. And Luke, we have proven some fraudulent acts by Christianity."

"That's your opinion."

"Well, yes, you're right; to you it's my opinion, but the fact is that Yeshua said 'Let no man be called Father' and Christianity started out that way, doing the opposite."

"And with a changed name," Jake chimed in. "That's the most important thing. Because it's the only name you can be saved by."

Luke turned again and started to leave in a huff.

I quickly said, "Come on Luke. Let's find Jeshua then."

Luke said that didn't really bother him.

Jake laughed and said, "We know, Christian."

Luke turned like he understood it, but I still don't think he liked it, especially with Jake being sarcastic and badgering the Hell out of him.

He said, "Man, I don't remember being an angel; and why can't we do miracles if we are?"

"Because it's hard," Jake said flatly. "You don't remember when you were born either, but you were."

I jumped in and told him that the Sign of Jonas is the only real physical proof that we are angels, and in my opinion, it represents exactly the way to return. Little did I know about the other physical evidence I would soon find.

"Which is here," Jake said, pointing at his forehead.

"Yes," I agreed quickly. "It's the mystery, man. Look at it," I said, picking up a picture of the Shroud. It even had a dove flying out of his forehead. Jake had a pile of ten or so copies of the Shroud on the coffee table. He had been making them up for the last two weeks.

I asked Jake if Luke could have one, but Luke quickly replied, "I don't want one."

"Well, at least listen to this definition of mystery, which remember we think is the key word revealing the way. It is what Yeshua was teaching the apostles and he guaranteed them Heaven. It is a secret, and you remember Yeshua said we must go into our closets and pray in secret." I turned over the *Shroud* and showed him the definition on the back. At that moment, the TV preacher that Jake liked started praying and healing over national television.

"See," I said, pointing at the TV. "Look at Christianity; it does the opposite of Yeshua. Yeshua told them to pray in secret. There's your proof, Luke, but anyway I want you to listen to this, man, because it is the mystery." I tried to hand him the Shroud picture, but he wouldn't take it. I then turned it around and finished the definition of mystery while showing it to him. "A secret, imposed by closing the mouth, and initiating oneself into a religious rite."

He showed no expression, and I quickly asked him what Yeshua was doing. "He's dead," Luke answered.

"Yeah," Jake agreed. "That's what the mystery is. We have to seek death in order to have life. The ultimate sacrifice is ourselves, our minds. Waiting and learning about life." He pointed at his forehead. "Man that blew me away! I always wanted to know why the Hindus had the ruby in their forehead. The same reason the Judeo-Christians have their mark on the forehead."

"Well," I said stunned, "I think he's resurrecting, the religious rite, and he is showing us the way to do it, the mystery."

"Well," said Luke suddenly, "that's your opinion."

"No, Luke, it's a fact. Let's do this again." I started to get the *Strong's* again to show him, but before I could even reach for it, he was getting up.

Jake said, "We didn't figure you would care about facts, since you don't even care about the name. We know you like Jimmy Christ instead," he said with a whole lot of sarcasm. That's all Luke could take!

He started for the door, telling us we were going to Hell for blaspheming the name of the Lord. Jake was right behind him trying to exorcize that Christian demon out of him.

Misty hadn't had a chance to say much, except for the time when we were looking up the name, so she had started looking at a book. Being tired of Luke's unwillingness to accept any proof shown to him and Jake's crazy exorcizing of him, I turned to Misty.

"What are you reading?" I asked anxiously. She loved to discuss books.

She looked at me and laughed. "*The Mystery of the Ages.*"

I couldn't believe it. It was the very thing we were talking about: Mystery. I asked if I could look at it, and she agreed, handing me the book.

Not surprisingly, it was written by an author who was the founder of the Church of God. When I read through the introduction, I thought how eloquently he addressed the issue of who we are and the reason to believe in God, saying that the footsteps of civilization came from religion.

This was enough for me. I was going to see what this guy's answer to the mystery was. I asked Misty if I could take it home, and she said it was okay. I told her I was sure going to have plenty to read, with the Shroud book and the Gospels, not to mention Enoch and the Bible. I looked over and saw another book that caught my eye. Misty noticed as well. I picked it up, and she said, "That's interesting, but I haven't read it." It was a book about spontaneous human combustion.

"Wow, this is what Yeshua did when he resurrected." I said profoundly and without thinking. "I've never read about this before."

"This obviously really happens, huh? Look at these pictures. This is unbelievable."

It blew me away. "Could I take this home, too?"

"Yeah," she laughed, "but let me get one of those books away from you. I'm reading one that I haven't been able to put down."

I laughed and said, "I know what you mean." We not only shared a love of reading, but also liked the same stuff, mysteries of life. There sure was enough of them. I gave her *The Mystery of the Ages* back. And I didn't mind giving it back. It was written by a Christian preacher!

Jake came back in after walking Luke to the car, and I asked him if he did any good. He replied, "shoot no, man."

"Luke wouldn't know God if it bit him in the ass," I chimed in. "I'm telling you, man, Christians all appear to be anti-spirit.

"Well I don't know about the rest but I knew the J.W. were." I just laughed. "I've got to be heading home, too. I know Angel is ranting and raving. I tell you, man, time flies when you talk religion."

"Yeah, really," said Jake. "But this is for Yeshua."

"Well, my wife wouldn't go for that. I've got to make money and pay bills."

"Yeah, I know what you mean, man." Misty agreed even before Jake looked her way.

I started getting up. As I started toward the door Jake asked what books I was reading and if I thought I had enough.

"Yeah, "I said, "but I still want you to get Enoch and uh...uh..."

"The *Concordance*?" He asked, holding it up from where he had just looked up mystery.

"Yeah," I said.

"You know, dude, I can get you a concordance anytime, but it's forty bucks."

"Wow! You mean they don't have a twenty dollar one?"

"No, the price is not negotiable."

"Man, finding the truth is not only hard, but expensive."

"Oh, too much to spend for someone who died for you, huh?"

"Well, let's hold off right now. Like you said, I do have the Gospels to read and the rest of the New Testament."

"Besides all these," Jake said, reaching and grabbing one of my books. "Oh no, don't tell me you think that Yeshua spontaneously combusted?"

"He did! What else do you call it?"

"He resurrected, man."

"So that's the religious term. I like the scientific term. It's easier to understand, and it's at least somewhat scientifically accepted."

"Well," he said, shaking his head in either amazement or disgust. I don't know which. "It might've involved an intense heat, but your crazy if you think you'll ever get any Christian to believe that."

I broke in. "Well that's not saying much. They believe pride is a good thing and they follow 'Jesus.'"

"Yeah, really," he agreed, just laughing away. He started mocking the name Jesus, and I couldn't help laughing. "Jerry Christ, man. Let's really Americanize him." He taunted. "Heck, he's already got two names now, anyway."

I laughed at that irony. We all have at least two names.

Moses came in and hugged me. I told him I was leaving and asked them if they were going up north for Thanksgiving. Jake said he really couldn't afford it. I knew what he meant. I had just taken my son back to Ohio and I couldn't really afford it either. It was expensive enough just keeping a relationship long distance, not to mention the back-to-school expenses. And now Thanksgiving, and then Christmas, and spring break. Did I ever know what Jake was saying! Angel did too, I laughed to myself. She had lived in riches until our relationship, and now we were struggling just to keep up.

"Believe me," I said, as I reached up and hugged them all. "I know how tough it is, you guys, but hang in there. We're going to get a song cut, aren't we Jake?"

"You know it," he said full of optimism and giving me a thumbs up.

"If that doesn't do it, my book about my uncle will," I said. Beaming like a an award winning author! I was always overly confident.

"You've been writing a book?" Misty asked anxiously.

"Yeah, for a couple of years now. It's about my uncle, his trading post Kawliga and how I ultimately ended up a woodcarver myself. It was like my destiny. I'm like the son he never had. I've always loved art, and now I'm in Nashville because of it, and guess what."

"What?" She asked anxiously.

"I'm starting to write songs."

"Really," she said with great surprise in her voice.

"Yeah, I can't wait to cut one. That reminds me, Jake. I just can't seem to master the guitar, man, but I want you to chart my songs."

"I'm waiting on you, man," he said. "Get on back over here."

"I will, dude," I replied admiringly. I started walking out and stopped and said, "Isn't this all too coincidental, man?"

"What?" He asked.

I looked at him and Misty and then looked away with such a great feeling. "Destiny!" I blurted out. "Us!"

I hugged them all again. I got into the car and headed back. I knew I was going to hear it from Angel for taking so long. I thought hard on the word *mystery.* I couldn't believe the very word that represents a whole spectrum of unsolved phenomena could possibly be an act or thing we do to live forever. That it alone could solve all mysteries is mind boggling. Mystery is life. I remembered a philosophy class I took in college, about the schools of mystery. I thought they were schools of thought. I laughed, because they're actually schools of no thought. I remembered they were just for the elite and not for the common population. A secret organization for the elite. It was pretty easy to understand, why mystery became unknown or lost.

I was really angry that the Jehovah's Witnesses had changed mystery. They preached a total dedication to accuracy of translation. I studied for years from a book called *The Truth Book*. What a joke, knowing this and the Jesus lie. Jake sure opened my eyes to being born again of the spirit: something the Jehovah's Witnesses never really preached and, even worse, criticized the other Christian sects about, being born again. They really did preach it though, as just believing, and then going to church and living right. Just like all the Christian churches. They mocked Yeshua's teachings. But now, I knew why the name was important and the connection to both. It answers a question that the Jehovah's Witnesses also never preached about, the fall of the angels. I am Yeshua, spirit, these fallen angels. I wondered what they looked like.

I was fast becoming wise to an overwhelmingly different story of the Bible. Needless to say, the Sign of Jonas and mystery blew me away. I felt a strong need to share my findings. It was easy to see how people could be brainwashed by preachers and not prove the meaning of the words. Even now, it was hard to stop saying Jesus and Jehovah. I was really brainwashed. Damn this cover-up! I was determined to research every scripture, just like Jake.

As I pulled up to the house, Angel came onto the front porch and laid the phone down. She turned and whirled back into the house, but not before staring daggers right through me. I knew I had blown it, taking so long at Jake's, but I was really in trouble now. It had to be Jake on the phone.

"Hey man," I said, as I picked up the phone.

"How did you know it was me?"

"Are you kidding me? Mystery, what do you think, man?" Angel just looked daggers at me. She turned and stormed away. I wasn't even out of the car yet. I had just pulled up.

"Bad timing I guess, huh?"

"Yeah, you could say that."

"Well, I had to call you, man."

"What is it?" I asked him anxiously.

"You're not going to believe this, man. I found another scripture that appears to be talking about the Shroud."

"No, you've got to be kidding."

"No, I'm not, man. I couldn't believe it either, but see if you think it does. It's in I Corinthians 13:12: 'For now we see in a mirror, dimly, but then face to face. Now I know in part, but then I shall know just as I am known.' Just as I am known, huh?"

I didn't really see how it nailed the description of the Shroud, except for the Shroud appearing as a dim, ghostly face.

As I hesitated, he responded quickly. "Wait until I show you, looking at it through a glass. You've got one; check it out. You're not going to believe it, man."

"Really," I said, sparked by the possibility. "Well, look, man, I'll check it out later." I knew Angel would be wanting me to cut this short, even though she wouldn't say it for anything, until I got off the phone.

"Mike, you've got to read the Gospels first."

"Yeah, really," I said. He had sure dogged me about this the last few months.

"You need to concentrate on reading—"

"I know, what's in red. I'm learning. I'm going to get right on the rest of the Gospels. You know, I finally understand what it means that we're born into sin."

"Don't tell me," he said patronizing.

"We did something wrong already. Not Adam and Eve. I don't buy their original sin story. We created man and have become man. We are the angels who left their first estate for a strange flesh. Yeshua said we're trapped here in this body. This no good body. It stinks, it's sexual, it kills. How could it be good?" *(Again, what do angels look like?)*

"Yeah," Jake agreed quickly.

"Well, I'm going to go and check out the Jehovah's Witnesses concordance and see what it says about being born again. If they changed the mystery, then it's hard to tell what else they did."

"Yeah, really," Jake agreed.

"Man, you're right about the name," I said emphatically. "Ol' Luke didn't care about it, did he?"

"Shoot, no," he said disgustedly. "No one has so far, in my family."

"Really," I agreed. "I can't get over the name. If you don't care about the name, then what else matters? That bothers me worse than anything. And they don't even acknowledge the I Am," I said angrily.

Jake snapped, "No, those Christians love Jimmy Christ— "

I stopped him, as I knew how Jake could get about the name. Still I knew his point and it was increasingly bothering me.

"I agree, man," I said, "but I've got to go. Hey man, look up all you can about angels, and let's see if Yeshua or anyone else calls us angels."

He said he would. I told him that I would too.

"I figured I'd finish reading the New Testament since I've already read the Gospels," he said mockingly.

"I'm reading them, smart-aleck," I rebounded back. I hesitated for a minute. "Well, anyway, thanks for helping me to understand the mystery."

"Yeah, we ought to do it sometime," he said fatherly like. "To know it, you must do it. If you know what I mean."

"First things first," I said. "I've never done it and frankly, I'll admit I'm a little scared."

"Ah, Lord," he exclaimed. "I bet you won't do it. You've been brainwashed by those Christians," he said taunting me. "You think a demon is going to get you, don't you?"

"Shut up, man. I'll try it sometime."

"Oh, I know. Just not soon. Only when an angel comes and tells you to do it, you Christian you. And the angel better have wings and be white. Well, I don't know if that would work. That could still be Satan. Ooooooooh," he continued taunting me.

"Later," I said and hung up the phone.

I could see Angel pacing back and forth inside the house. I went in and sure enough she was mad as a hornet. "It's bad enough you work with him, but do I have to put up with him calling you as soon as you get home?"

"I'm sorry, Angel. It's just that Jake and I are onto some heavy stuff."

Her mother just grinned as I hugged Angel. She knew Angel would calm down soon.

I told Mary about the conversation with Luke. He didn't seem to care about the name or any other evidence that might suggest his family's religion is wrong. I accentuated family and said it finally came down to tradition. His family wouldn't follow something that was wrong, and he knew Mamaw was going to Heaven. They've all been saved already. Mary just laughed, but I knew she considered herself to be a saved

Christian also. I saw that this conversation was a little annoying to her, and not wanting two women against me, I went into the bedroom.

I smoothed it over during the evening and didn't mention the Bible at all. I even watched television with the family. Shane, Angel's little brother, had rented a movie. He was an athletic disciple who devoted all his time to sports, school, and women, although not in that order. He was into having fun. Thank God! My life would become boring.

After the movie, I remembered the scripture that I had quoted to Luke earlier today: "No man will go to Heaven that didn't come from Heaven, even the Son of Man who is in Heaven." So I took the Bible off the cabinet as I walked out of the living room, and went back toward the bedroom.

"Oh no," I heard Angel groan.

"Don't worry, I'm just looking up one thing."

"Right, Mike. See ya!"

"Baby," I sweet-talked, as I turned and hugged her.

"Get away from me, you jerk. Go on. You'll find something and call Jake, I just know it."

"No, I won't," I said softly, trying to hug her but she just pushed me away.

"Go on," she said brooding like.

I went on, knowing that I didn't need to aggravate her. I went into the bedroom and turned on the light. As I sat down, I began to turn the *Concordance* to the entry on "Heaven." Suddenly the phone rang. I cringed as I saw Angel scowl when she answered it.

She responded like a scorned secretary, "One moment, please," then whirled and headed straight for me.

"Don't tell me it's Jake," I remarked weakly.

"Who else?" She growled.

"Hey man, bad timing again, huh?"

"I guess you could say that again."

"Well, you told me to call you if I found 'angel' being referred to us."

"You found something?"

"I sure did." I broke in as he started to tell me about the TV preacher and condemning Paul. "Jake, what is the quote?"

"What quote?" He said.

"The angel quote! And get off Paul."

"Get out your Bible," he snapped back, "and look it up yourself."

"Hey, my wife is a little more than pissed off right now."

"Oh, oh, right. I forgot."

"No kidding."

"Well, I can't stand them glorifying Paul."

"Jake, the scriptures!" I yelled.

"'Know ye not that we shall be judging angels?'" There was silence for a moment as I thought about it.

He immediately followed up. "Did you get it?"

"Yeah, I got it. You can't get much plainer than that."

"Really," he said in complete agreement.

"I tell you, man. I think it was all covered up a long time ago, from the beginning possibly, and as you say: A lie that becomes tradition is accepted truth."

"Well, at least the truth that they sell anyway, their truth," Jake snarled.

"Yeah, I can't buy their truths either, dude, especially when they do the opposite of what Yeshua taught: 'Let no man be called father,'" I quoted again, angrily. "And that's the way it all started. It's a cover-up that is as old as Christianity itself. We're all brainwashed just like our brainwashed parents before us."

"Yeah, I know," Jake agreed, "and that allegiance to family is tough to break. Tradition was something Yeshua preached against. It's in "Matthew 23", my song. Christianity sells it. The Church is their tradition."

"Shoot, man, tradition and pride is a must now among family, country and Christianity. What the Hell is going on here, Jake? How can they get away with this?"

"It's easy," he replied bluntly. "It's the easy path. It's Paul's way."

"Come on, Jake, let's not get started on Paul. Don't you think you're judging?"

"Well, I'm telling you, Paul started Christianity, and there are more of his writings in the Bible than Yeshua's. I'm simply stating facts, provable facts."

I hadn't thought about it. But certainly the latter was true.

"Well, at least now I know what I'm reading. Remember, I've got the *Concordance*," I said reminding him. I knew his memory. He didn't have any.

"You mean you've got mine."

"Yeah, I'm going to get me one."

"Yeah, you'll have to if you want to find out the true meanings of words."

"I know it's like trying to read the newspaper without a dictionary. There are so many synonyms for everything. Man and all his ego. He has to speak bigger and be better than everyone else. Language eloquence is the ultimate weapon now. Why can't we be satisfied with plain old simple words?"

"Yeah," Jake laughed, "It *behooves* me as to why, and oh, what about homonyms, too?"

"Don't you just hate that—*behooves*?" I said mockingly. And he laughed even harder.

I laughed too and then suddenly found myself unsure of what I was laughing about. I weakly asked, "What the hell is behoove?"

"Well," he said, "You do know the meaning, don't you?"

"I think so, but maybe not with the right word." We played our word game.

I knew I better get off the phone, as we had been going on for awhile. "Time seems to fly when you're doing this kind of stuff. I better get off here, man. Angel is not getting any happier."

"Well, one thing before you go. I know you've been saying there isn't a Hell. You do know that there is a Hell, don't you?"

"Well, it just depends on what you mean. I don't believe in a fiery abyss type Hell for everlasting punishment. No, I don't. To me, I think that would certainly make God unfair. And he can't be unfair, can he, Abraham?" *("UP" would soon revise this.)*

"It's the body." Jake remarked flatly and cutting it short, I was surprised!

"Check it out," I said. "Remember I've got the *Concordance*. I believe it's the body, too! I'll try to get in to see you before I head to Ohio, but if not, try to get my books."

"Okay, I will look up Hell. I never have done that, but I know it is here since we do die. Death is here!" He reaffirmed adamantly.

"Yeah and we have wailing and gnashing of teeth. And you know, we are mostly water anyway. The Bible calls Hell the 'lake of fire.' We are ninety-eight degrees. That's hot. How much plainer can you get? Besides, aren't we on the Earth, which is surrounded by an infinite darkness called space? Heaven, the Universe." *(Earth is mostly water too.)*

"Yeah it's unreal, isn't it?" He said in agreement. "You know, I think we are essentially trapped in the body. And when we die within this magnetic atmosphere, we wait on another body until we become born again. We are trapped by gravity." *(Theories to change. Read on.)*

"Sounds logical to me," I responded quickly. "The Earth and body are just alike in the universe. I think they call that science, macrobiotics. It explains ghosts and the light at the end of the tunnel. It's a woman's vagina. It's a win/win situation. Well, unless you're a pig! Even though your body dies, you never die. You just go into processing. Reincarnation."

"Yeah, you reap what you sow," Jake said. "Until the end, the last day, D-day, the second death. "

"Jake, I thought you didn't like that apocalyptic stuff."

"Well, I don't, but I am doing the mystery. My last day is every day. I die daily. Are you?" I would eventually discover Paul saying that exact thing.

"I told you, dude," I said weakly. "I will do it, but not now." I quickly changed the subject. "I wonder why Christianity rejects reincarnation. It's only fair, and it seems that they are the only religion to deny it."

"Yeah, I think so."

"Wow, dude, think about this. The others all believe in it and they have the mystery."

Jake seemed to know what I was thinking and he jumped in. "Maybe Christianity is the Anti-Christ. Christianity turned around is anity christi, anti-christ."

"Yeah," I replied, shaking my head. I laughed at his analogy. He was a trip. "And the Muslims. They're all the same. They worship outwardly. They don't have the mystery either. The cover-up is in the Judeo-Christian story."

"Yeah, really," he agreed.

"Well, I'm going to get off here before Angel kills me. Besides, I wanted to look up Heaven in the Jehovah's Witnesses concordance and see if they changed it."

"Yeah Misty is in the other room. I'm getting ready to do the mystery."

"Okay, dude, do one for me."

"Hold on," he said quickly before I could hang up. "I want to get the Shroud book back from you to see if the Shroud could have been in the hands of the apostles, who I think were Gnostics. I think they could have been doing the mystery to it. That scripture I read about today sure sounded like it."

"Yeah, I'll get it to you, even if I have to drop it off on the way to Ohio."

"Okay, don't forget."

"I won't. See you later," I said quickly, hanging up the phone.

I turned to get the books off the bed as Angel was headed straight for it. It must've been two o'clock in the morning, so I figured I would check her mood out. "What time is it, baby?"

"Two o'clock," she growled.

"Is Little Jake asleep?"

"I'm getting in the bed, ain't I?"

I knew then, that looking anything up right now was impossible. I headed toward the living room where the bookcase was. I decided to put the book away, but right before I reached the bookcase, I broke and looked up the word Heaven. It wouldn't take a second, but the results would affect me for the rest of my life. I couldn't believe my eyes. The Jehovah's Witnesses had separated the quote from Yeshua in John 3:13, to say that no one had ascended to Heaven. I read it and became so pissed off. I finally realized how easy it was for them to do this. They made Enoch and Elijah a liar. I was ashamed of my ignorance. I swore to myself then, that I would never again accept any religion's interpretation. What a joke! *(Enoch and Elijah were "taken." Abduction?)*

I went to bed and just hugged on my baby. I knew better to talk or even think about anything else. Although I didn't say anything to Angel, my mind was doing plenty of talking. I couldn't wait to show my newly discovered facts to my family and Jake, heck, to everyone for that matter. I wanted to shout it from the rooftops.

The next morning I called Jake while Angel was grocery shopping. He was watching the TV preacher again, teaching the sixth day or pre-Adam creation. I told him about my findings and he couldn't believe it.

He said, "Well, that's wrong because Elijah was taken up to Heaven in the Old Testament, and Enoch, too." *(Heaven is Space, "UP"!)*

"Man, that's what I said immediately."

He asked me to bring it in so he could check it out.

I told him it seems like Christianity and Judaism try to cover up Enoch's teachings. "They say that we are angels who shouldn't be here, and that we existed before. They're anti-man, and that's why they were kept out. Christianity, like Judaism, has made Earth and man better than Heaven and the angels. We are responsible for being here, not God, and we shouldn't be here. *(Again, my "god mind" soon changes.)*

"We should be sitting like Enoch!" Jake broke in and took over. "But just watch the preachers reciting 'For God so loved the world he gave his only begotten Son; that whosoever believes on him . . . shall have everlasting life,' John 3:16. It's the easy path," Jake said angrily.

Jake interjected, "I don't think John wrote that."

"Of course he didn't," I agreed. "That's obvious. You know, it says in Matthew, that 'he didn't come to condemn the world, but to save that which is lost.' Doesn't that say that we came here first? I mean, a lifeguard doesn't go in the water unless someone is there drowning."

"We must've made man again and again." Jake said again, quickly taking lead of the conversation. "Enoch says so in Jude, 'A dog returning to vomit.' I mean it's hard to deny that flesh has been here for more than six thousand years."

"Yeah," I agreed, "even our history shows that everywhere civilization spread, people were there. I mean what more proof do you need? Man was here and he changed from prehistoric to modern. From being ugly to becoming pretty, huh, evolution! Beauty must be the downfall of the universe. Desire for beauty, the disease of the gods. Hell, it's the disease of man. It is mankind, 666." *(Addiction to beauty, aha! A clue!)*

"Yeah, the sons of God must've bred with the daughters of men because they were pretty. Wouldn't they have to be flesh?" Jake asked?

"Yeah! But what did the gods look like? That's the sixty-four thousand dollar question." *(And the ultimate evidence to "Believe.")*

I continued. "If they were flesh like us, they have to be ugly. That's obvious! Maybe they downloaded their memory into man as they made him. And then Heavens angels trapped him in it, because it shouldn't have happened anyway. Man, the universal evil! Maybe the future has already happened," I said weakly. Even though I had majored in history, I didn't have anything over Jake. I was totally speculating, theorizing. He was a walking, talking encyclopedia, and he didn't like my theorizing. *(We now clone. How long to actual creation?)*

"You do know about Lemuria and Mu, don't you?" No, I didn't. "Well, here's a theory for you." He explained the theory to me, and I was amazed. It was just another mystery about something lost, something that came from one became two and now is a mystery. Huh, that sounds just like the story of man.

I asked him if he believed my theory. He said it was possible, just like another theory, the lost City of Atlantis. "It's a theory that has influenced the entire world, the Atlantic Ocean."

I had heard about Atlantis and read about it during my high school years of reading mythology. I told him I loved that kind of stuff.

"Yeah, me too," he said.

"Man, I just can't get over the scientific evidence that we have today that definitely refutes the Judeo-Christian time frame of six thousand years. And yet they won't even look at it."

"Well, that is, if you believe in scientific testing. That's what the Christians will say," Jake replied.

"I do, don't you?"

He paused for a minute and then he said, "They've been proven to be accurate." *(His "spirit/religion" addiction made him skeptical of science. He would remain a spirit believer due to his O.B.E.)*

"How can we deny the bones of the dinosaurs, and the fact they aren't mentioned even in the earliest writings of the Bible? I mean, come on, it doesn't take a rocket scientist to figure it out. We have bones of the prehistoric man, too."

"Do you think that the sixth day creation was when we were created?" Jake asked. *(This showed his allegiance to "God." I wanted to know who the hell "God" is and what "God" is. "God" wasn't a given to me.)*

"I just don't believe we were created, period. I think that we were angels, *soon to be aliens (same thing)*, evolving from nothing. We conquered death. But, we created man and weren't supposed to. So, like Jude says in verse six, we gave life to death, again and again, through man. I mean it makes sense. We made flesh. But what do the angels look like, that's the question. Obviously, flesh is bad because it dies and we can be trapped in it."

"Yeah," he said. "And God repented when he 'had' to make flesh."

"Man," I said quickly, to control the conversation. "Isn't it possible that the angels were making bodies and weren't very good at it. But they kept trying until they made the perfect beautiful body. Then somehow, man took over. The angels must've left, but are still here just invisible to us. I think this explains the scripture in Genesis Chapter Two. I never did understand the eating of the tree."

"Wait until you see what tree means." Jake said spooky like. We found that tree meant to shut the eyes and makes ones self firm. The fruit of the tree meant to break through. It was eerie!

"Well, you won't have to worry, according to my last Jehovah's Witness preacher. He said there are things in the Bible we aren't supposed to understand."

He laughed and said, "Yeah, I know, man. Our preacher says the same thing. Don't they understand how ridiculous that is? What kind of a god would do this?"

"I guess! The same kind who gives miracles to them, but lets millions of kids starve every day," I said in disgust. "But how can we get them to wake up?"

"Well," he said, "I use the scripture where Abraham makes God admit that he has to be fair."

"Yeah, I know, then what? I've done that to Mary, Granny and Luke, and it didn't budge them. They know God performs miracles; they're saved already, and don't ask them how they know, they just do."

"Yeah," he laughed. "What can you do? You do know that it will be easier for Mary than Granny, don't you man? She is eighty years old."

"Yeah she's no different from my mom. It's easier to reach young people. They aren't as brainwashed. Well, what is the scripture that you were talking about earlier?" I asked him. I knew Angel would be getting home soon, and I didn't want to start out another day on the wrong foot.

He started talking about Genesis, Chapter Three: 'And I will put enmity....'

I broke in and asked what enmity was and he quickly replied, "hatred."

He continued, " '—between her seed and thy seed; it shall bruise thy head and thou shalt bruise his heel ...'"

"Wow, I can't believe it! This seems to indicate different races."

"Yeah, it sure looks that way, and the TV preacher preaches the same thing." He told me to turn it on the channel he was on.

I went into the living room and switched on the TV, only to look up and see Angel coming. Luckily Mary was getting up, and she liked to watch preaching. I told Jake Angel was coming and quickly hung up. Mary went into the bathroom so I whispered through the door, "Mary, could you please come into the front room? Angel's coming, and I don't want to start the day out wrong. If she thinks I just got up and turned on preaching, she'll gripe." Mary just laughed and said she would. I told her it was the preacher who taught the pre-Adam creation. She said, "Okay" excitedly. Even though she thought she was saved and believed in miracles, she still had plenty of problems with the Judeo-Christian story. Especially their time frame and the scientific evidence that we have to refute it. And now the name Yeshua.

"I'll make your coffee," I told her as I went into the kitchen.

Angel was coming through the door just about that time, so I took Mary's coffee in and put it by her favorite chair. I went ahead and started getting the groceries out of the car. Angel smiled as I held the door open. We finished getting the groceries and even smiled at each other a few more times. I knew how to turn things around. But even that wouldn't stand the test of time!

As soon as we finished the groceries, I got Little Jake out of the car seat. He was sound asleep. He was such a precious angel. Then I laughed to myself. It was amazing how much evidence we have of being angels. Even our puns and sayings confirm it. I thought about the Gospel truth again and laughed!

I put Little Jake in bed as Angel came in and started taking his coat off. It was late October, but it felt like January. We already had a snow, and we usually didn't see our first snow until December. My family really got a kick out of Angel when we visited in the winter. Dad always said she packed more than he had ever owned in his whole life. My brother Jeff, who lived further north by Lake Erie, also ribbed her constantly. We saw the time when the defroster wouldn't keep the windows clean. So Angel wasn't a Southern Belle without merit. My family loved Angel and she loved them. I was happy. That was all about to change.

I spent the rest of the day with my baby, but couldn't help to see a little of the TV preacher with Mary. Mary was eating it up and even talked to Jake once on the phone, while Angel and I were gone. I called Jake that evening, eager to see if he made any headway. I was really bothered that I couldn't get her to see the unfairness of Christianity.

Jake just laughed after I asked him. "No, man. I was just talking to her about the sixth day creation. She's been watching him for a while, Mike. She said it made sense that angels were copulating with Eve, to make other races. I told her we had just talked about that the night before, and I agreed how it made sense. Even the preacher asked where Cain got his wife. He used the same sons of God scripture I did, and everything."

I couldn't help but get sarcastic. I thought his TV preacher was just like all the rest! "Did he get real sarcastic with his flock? Did he tell them if you start a pond with bass, you ain't gonna have any carp? And then he gets onto them for being dummies!"

"Well," he said defiantly, "I don't know about that, but he does encourage them to prove everything with a concordance. He also highly recommends the *Strong's*, just like I do."

"Well, I still have a problem with his healing and saving thing, not to mention the flag."

"You do know, though, that Yeshua says that we can do that."

"Yes, we do heal ourselves and others, with medicine and hard work! But not your man reading over letters. That's bullshit!"

Jake seemed to think that we could get some help from Yeshua through the mystery, whether it be monetary or what. I thought that was ridiculous. The genie syndrome.

I told him to get off that crap. "You know that can't be possible. It isn't fair, remember?"

"Well, he does say that nothing could harm us, even if we ate poison."

"Well, I don't know honestly, and anything is possible. But I just don't believe in what your preacher says. Besides, he's got a big flag over his shoulder and he's proud of killing for it. Is that the kind of spiritual leader you want? It's not for me," I managed to get off the phone before Angel came along.

I was eager to do a little reading of the Gospels, so I turned in early. Angel had her hands full with Little Jake. He usually didn't turn in until one a.m. or better. That gave me some time to read. I had always loved reading, but even more than that, I hated being ignorant. I went in and grabbed the Bible and climbed into bed. I had read only a few lines in Mark, when I looked up to see the Shroud picture on the wall. Angel hung it up. What a great thing to do for me. I felt so good right then. I got up and went to Little Jake's bedroom.

She was lying on his bed beside him, reading. He loved to be read to. I grabbed her up and hugged her so tight. She turned and asked, "What's this all about?"

"The Shroud," I said, smiling from ear to ear. "You made my day, baby."

She said, "You make my life, baby."

"And Little Jake, too!" She lovingly reached down and kissed him. "And Jimmy," I said, showing Little Jake his big brother's picture. "Yep," he said grinning. I went back to the bedroom and thought to myself, "Angel and I are so lucky." I climbed into bed and looked up at the Shroud. It always hurt me to look at it. The suffering pictured on the face must have been a brutal one. I couldn't imagine dying like that. The thought of it shook me to my very bones. What an impact the Shroud had on me. The mystery was overwhelming enough, but the definition of the mystery describing the Shroud was mind-blowing. The Shroud itself is a miracle. It was no coincidence. It was pre-destined, predicted in the Gospels, and fulfilled! We have the Shroud. Suddenly, the pain and anger left me. I was filled with joy. Listen to myself, I thought, bubbling about miracles.

I immediately grabbed the King James' Bible. I wanted to check out the scripture that Jake quoted. He felt it described the Shroud. It was in I Corinthians 13:12. I couldn't get over the dualistic meaning to it, "in part." Jake was always talking about the marriage that Yeshua taught between our soul and our consciousness; or as he said, our spirit and the Holy Ghost. He felt Yeshua had been teaching this, as well as the Buddhists and anyone else who understood what praying in secret meant. It meant to stop thinking, being like an infant without thought. The mind is the bridal chamber and we are the bride. The bride/mind would make the marriage, thus being born again. To him, it was attaining the resurrection, or nirvana to the Buddhist. He knew how much I wanted to know about every religion possible.

I remember how he speculated that it was possible for our Holy Ghost to be trapped around us, but not in us. He said he had felt something at times when he did the mystery, as if something was coming into him. I would get a kick out it, but it really kind of scared me. I hadn't done the mystery. He was determined to be born again, so I knew he would be dogging me soon to do it.

I found the scripture and read it. "We now know in part, but then as we are known." This was starting to come to me in a scientific way, like something that has two parts. Could the angels, us, be asexual? And then it hit me: I had never understood a scripture that I had just read in Matthew. I knew it was around 16:4, the prediction of the Shroud, so I turned to that scripture and started reading from there. I scanned the next few chapters to find Matthew 20:4: "Have you not read that he made them in the beginning male and female."

I couldn't believe it. This says that we are two things, male and female. That would explain why Yeshua taught the inner and outer, the bridegroom and the bride, the Holy Spirit and the spirit. In fact, aren't we two things? The two serpents, DNA. Wow! This was heavy. Male and female. This is why the Jews, Christians, and Muslims, are so cruel to their women. They teach this stuff literally and it's cruel to women! Can't they see it's a metaphor of Adam and Eve and creation? In the beginning we were both, but we became female *(flesh)* and then forgot the male side, the holy spirit. The small still voice, the serpent, they're both the mind! It was all like a science formula to me. I started making diagrams. *(Ancient alien evidence soon explained our "other" side.)*

I turned to where I had left off in Mark. I was now reading with complete concentration. I think we knew we were angels or spirits in the beginning. Suddenly it dawned on me. The Bible was the story of the angels and their fall. The fall didn't just happen instantly, but over time like evolution. And now we must be maintained, Hell on Earth. Man is evil. Heaven is the universe, the Earth is the footstool. Wow! I thought about the Lake of Fire. Wouldn't it be great, if Hell was a metaphor for the body like Jake and I theorized, and we never stopped existing, but only reincarnated. Angel came through the door and looked disapprovingly at the Bible in my hands. I immediately deposited it back in the appropriate spot. I was an organization fanatic.

We made love that night. Mad, passionate love! I honestly and openly loved her. This was Heaven. The Bible says God is love, and I believe that. That's what I would want. I was so much in love with my wife, my kids, family friends, animals, birds, and fish. Even spiders and snakes. I laughed at the pun, and then I started singing the country song. "I Don't Like Spiders and Snakes." But now I do.

The next few weeks went fast. I was putting together a load of Indians for my buyers back home. It worked out great for me financially. "I'm just a poor ol' woodcarver." I laughed. That's what Uncle Brice always said, so it meant a lot to me.

I stopped by Jake's and gave him the Shroud book. Christmas was coming up and I knew times would be getting tougher for Jake. It was a bad time for the satellite business.

He talked me into taking the concordance up north. He wanted me to try and prove to my family the changing of Yeshua's name to Jesus. I told him I would. "I want to give everyone a copy of the Shroud, if they'll take it." They wouldn't. Jake gave me a couple anyway. "I tell you what blows me away more than anything is that it describes the mystery."

"Mike, it's a picture of a dead man!"

"No, it's a picture of the mystery and us, spirits." He started to dispute me, but I immediately said, "Yeah, well, I don't have time to argue with you about opinions. Hell's bells! You just said, it does describe it."

"Well, that's all bullshit anyway, speculation, interpretation. We don't know that, Mike. All we know is Yeshua predicted the Sign of Jonas as the only sign he would give us, and he's left a picture to prove it."

"Yeah, he spontaneously combusted!" I said boldly.

"You're crazy!" Jake blurted back.

"Man, are you blind? The Shroud depicts the way to be born again. You do remember the definition of the mystery, don't you? Boy, I said, holding up the concordance, I can't wait to show them the definition of mystery."

"Well, don't be surprised if they don't buy it," he said. "Haven't you read yet where Yeshua said, 'A prophet is not known in his own country?' Well, that's just about to become your situation. Don't think they will give up their traditions. It's just not going to happen. Shoot man, I can't find anyone who will take a picture of it in my family." He would be right. I wouldn't either.

"The Shroud is the answer, and I'll prove it to my family and the rest of the world," I screamed into the air as I went out the door. "Maybe nobody has ever had this knowledge until now. Knowledge is increasing, you know. We can't stop that. It's now a global world. If you attack the truth, TV will make a fool of you. Besides, we have proof of a cover-up right in the King James' Bible, their own literature! Man can't cover it up. Mystery ain't no big mystery, anymore! They might've made it a secret, and it still may be today. But not for long." I turned to Jake and said, "Man, it is so plain to see how this cover-up could exist.

We're the leader of the world and look at how many lies we live under. We honor murderers in a land which isn't ours. I'm ashamed to be a white American."

"Really," Jake said.

"Hypocrites! I'm telling you, man. I want more than anything to wake up the world. It's living a lie. We're asleep in the Christos." I later read that in the Tibetan Book of the Dead. It's true. Christianity killed the Indians, blacks, and anybody who stood in the way of their greed. Christ Columbus is the best example. Hell, think of how many monuments would have to be changed if history was rewritten."

"Well, that's all good in theory, brother, but doing it will be something else," Jake remarked bluntly.

"That's what I've got you for, dude. Keep that name list going. I want to see what others they change. That's evidence, too, man," I said excitedly. "I'm going to head on out of here. Naturally I'm in a hurry. Besides, Angel will be waiting on me."

As I turned to leave, Jake started to speak. "You know, Mike, you ought to give me some money for your concordance. You really do need one."

"I know, I know," I went ahead and forked out forty bucks.

"Uh-uh," Jake said. "Aren't you forgetting something?"

"Come on, man," I said.

"You know I said fifty," he said. "Remember Enoch?"

"Man, can you catch the slack for me, dude?" I was almost begging. "You know I am going up north. Besides, I haven't told Angel yet."

He just laughed. "Yeah sure, man. Anything for a brother. I mean, after all, you're my first disciple."

I laughed too! "Humble yourself, Oh Exalted One."

"Oh yeah. Yeah, sure, dude." He grabbed me and hugged me. "You make sure and buckle up Little Jake." He loved that name. "I'll report you if you don't."

I waved and said I would. I got into the car and drove off. I knew he loved him like his own son.

I immediately started thinking about all our discoveries. I just couldn't believe the evidence I had amassed at this point. I was determined to scrutinize every religion there was, as well as Yeshua's teachings. If the truth involves meditation or the mystery, it would be next to impossible to get my family to do it. The Jehovah's Witnesses scare the Hell out of you with their Hollywood depiction of demons. And the word demon isn't even in the Bible! What a joke.

I had so much anger toward them, but then I became ashamed for being angry. After all, aren't they brainwashed, too, and wasn't I also brainwashed? Jake thought Christians were being coerced by the Devil, but I knew they were just brainwashed! Besides a devil isn't fair. And we knew God has to be fair, right Jake? I burst out laughing at myself.

We're our own devils as well as gods. Can't we see that? We are above every living thing on the face of this Earth. We're literally gods here, aren't we? Jake had blasted people for hunting and killing and he quickly condemned my hunting. I had learned something from Jake's episodes. I couldn't kill again. "If there is a god I wouldn't want him to be a killing god," Jake would say. It made me shake with regret for the animals, birds, and fish I had killed. I vowed to remember the Golden Rule: "Do unto others, as you would have done unto you!" Practice what you preach, I thought to myself, as I remembered Luke. You can't be more fair than that. I didn't want to reap what I had sowed. What goes around, comes around. I wasn't taking chances anymore. The Indians believe that every living thing is a spirit. Every culture did but the Judeo-Christian cultures! I got all my books together for the trip up north. I was taking the King James' Bible, the concordance, and the book about spontaneous human combustion, as well as the copies of the Shroud. The only book I hadn't taken was the *Mystery of the Ages*. I read that sucker immediately upon returning to Jake's and finding out the definition of the mystery.

It turned out to be eloquently written all right, but it never revealed the true definition of mystery. As a matter of fact, it kept mystery a secret. That was enough for me. Besides, being born again to him was the typical Christian formula, very easy. I told him and Misty how the preacher talked to God throughout the entire book. Jake hated that.

We made our way north and settled in at my parents' home. It was a central point for my large family. I had five brothers and one sister. I was uncertain about their reaction to my newfound literature, so I left it in the car. I did take the King James' Bible and a copy of the Shroud with me. I wanted to compare the changes and slowly present this new information to them.

I really wanted to read the scriptures of Jude, explaining who we are. But I was primarily going to work on the Shroud and the importance of the name. I was saving my theory for my brothers who could handle it. My dad was definitely too hot-headed to talk religion, or anything controversial for that matter.

I spent a good evening with them, before I started talking about the Shroud and our findings. The news had come on, and everybody was either getting ready for bed or had already gone. My boys had played themselves out and had been asleep for awhile.

I turned to Mom and Dad and began to explain my predicament with Angel and the blood transfusions. The Jehovah's Witnesses recommend a life-threatening doctrine of refusal. I went on to ask them about it. My mother did most of the explaining. I really didn't understand how anybody could make a life or death decision, in the face of such flimsy evidence and without giving other religions a look, at least a look. Not to mention looking at the medical science of it. She understood!

Before I let them say anything, I asked them if they believed the scientific findings that refutes the religious time frame of six thousand years.

"Well," my mom said, kind of unsure of herself. "I really can't understand how it could be, if you believe in the Bible."

My dad jumped in. "It's not possible."

"So, you're saying that you don't believe in the skeletal remains of dinosaurs and prehistoric man?"

Mom looked puzzled and Dad was starting to look combustible. "No, I didn't say that," he said angrily already. "I just don't believe in their dating methods. How do you know they're accurate?"

"Believe me, Dad, the world wouldn't allow a scientific thing to be false, unlike religion. I shouldn't have said that. I'm sorry. Anyway," I continued, "how can anyone deny that the Bible makes no reference to dinosaurs or prehistoric man? This has to mean that they existed before our creation and the Bible is the tail end to an incomplete story."

"If you believe that, then you can't believe the Bible," my dad said bluntly.

"That's not true," I said quickly. "That's just what Christianity and Judaism want you to believe, so they can continue their wealthy business of church. They covered up the truth. I've got some questions that might shed some light on my theory. Well, mine and Jake's. Jake is the one who got me started in the right direction, a logical direction. You see, I think God has to be fair. He does in Genesis. God has to be fair. Abraham makes him. Besides, what kind of a person would want it any other way? Who wants a testing, torturing God? That's cruel."

"Get on with your 'theory', lad," my Dad said angrily, "and quit criticizing church. I happen to go to church." Once a year, I thought to myself, on the memorial of the resurrection.

"I'm sorry," I said, "but my findings indicate a cover-up of information by churches. And this religious information could agree with the scientific findings that we have today, if we quit reading it literally."

"How?"

"Well, the Bible indicates the Sons of God came and mated with the daughters of men in Genesis 6:2, and this is after Cain takes a wife in another land called Nod, Genesis 4:17. The first question is where did Cain get his wife, then? And even in the lineage of Adam, not Eve, mind you, there is nothing but males born. Don't you find this odd? We think its possible that Man was created more than once by many gods. Which we think is a synonym or another word for angel or sons of God. Even in Genesis, Adam and Eve had become as 'one of us', to know good and evil, spirit/flesh. One of the gods! Or better said, one of the angels."

Mom struggled to change the subject. They strongly believed in one God, or were monotheistic. I would soon learn that monotheism is polytheism. I found them to be the same, like evolution and creation. Suddenly, Mom said that they were inbreeding. When I questioned that by today's standards, she quickly said that we were perfect then and could do it. But since then, we've grown away from perfection. That's why we can't inbreed now. "We can't be perfect." I hated that. I really didn't understand that logically speaking, I told her. I later found Yeshua to say exactly the opposite. Besides, we have distinct races and that is not possible with only one couple. She gave me the tower of Babel story, which again made no sense. "Isn't dying cruel enough, let alone being scattered, made different and confused? That's really cruel. Mom and Dad, think about that in scientific terms. They were in Hell trying to get back to Heaven. That's the reason for their punishment. The sons of God came and mated with the daughters of men, begetting giants. The ultimate man!"

I asked them if they thought the angels could become flesh, since that was what the Sons of God represented to me. They both said that was what Satan and his angels had done, until God stopped them and cast them to the Earth.

"Like in space, in outer darkness," I said to them in agreement and trying to get my point across about this being Hell. Earth is a prison for man. "And isn't it possible that was why God, the good angels had to make flesh, to save the angels who were already making flesh?"

"There was no flesh man here," Mom said, "until God made Adam and Eve. Then Satan made his mistake."

"But don't you see that there could have been, as angels themselves became flesh. They were with Man. It would answer the question of where Cain got his wife and where different races came from. You know the Bible even says we were made on the sixth day; maybe that was the angels, the perfect evolution. Maybe these 'days' represent time frames that are longer, like a thousand years. Then, there was no man to till the ground and Man was made on the eighth day by the gods. He was made to till the ground, a worker."

They got their Bible out then and started to prove it to themselves. My Mom said that she thinks that it wasn't the eighth day, but just what happened on the sixth day in story form.

"Well, that's possible except that he repented the day he had to make flesh. Did you know that?" I asked her. That doesn't sound like he thought man was good.

"No," she said. "Where is that?"

"Right in Genesis 6:6," I said. "See, the creation on the sixth day couldn't have been flesh, or man anyway, as the sixth-day creation was good. Before I start to confuse you, I need to explain our theory. Jake thinks that we are the one-third of the angels cast out in outer darkness. Jude refers to us as these angels who left their first estate for a strange flesh. That would seem to confirm Yeshua saying he came to save that which was lost. The one-third of the angels."

"Who?" They asked.

"Yeshua," I said slowly.

"What about the one-third of the angels?" She said quickly.

"Oh, don't worry; we'll get to that, but first, I want to tell you the real name of Jesus. That was it! What I just said! It is Yeshua and it has been changed. If it hadn't, it would have answered life's mystery for us. Who we are. I am Yeshua, spirit of the angels. They were spirit." *(I change.)*

" In the beginning of Adam and Eve's creation they were with God; but when they ate from the tree, God could no longer see them.' Genesis 3:9," I said. "Then they saw their flesh bodies. The angels who left their first estate for a strange flesh. Think about it," I said bluntly. "And what are the two trees? Heaven and Earth. Invisible and visible. This story isn't literal; it's spiritual science." *(Scientific human creation)*

"So you don't think there was an Adam and Eve?" My dad asked quickly.

"I didn't say that. As a matter of fact, my buddy does. I don't know one way or the other. I just know that this theory makes sense scientifically. It explains why they repented of having made flesh. It was intrinsically evil. He had to save that which is lost or here already, man/angels, the one-third trapped."

"Do you believe we have a choice?" Mom asked suddenly.

"Yes, but even that contradicts the Bible. Mom, is it fair? The Devil's stuff, I mean. Can't God just do away with the Devil? Why does he have to play these cruel-ass games? After all, life is hard enough for that. That isn't logical."

"Well, that's for the Lord to know, and we just got to have faith."

"See, I just don't believe that God can be so unfair. You obviously believe we only get one chance, too."

"Yes," they both quickly agreed. *(Destiny makes "God" cruel.)*

"Mom, isn't that cruel, too? We only get seventy years if we're lucky, and if we don't get it, we go to Hell. Come on! That's cruel, besides the fact that we don't have any control over what we are."

"No," she said. "There is no Hell. We just die, or we get everlasting life."

"Boy, and that's fair to you? Mom, Dad come on, you can't think that's fair, not with a god who can have it anyway he wants it. I mean, don't we all want a perfect world? I do!"

"Well, I just don't know. There are some things we just shouldn't question."

"No, instead we go to our death tortured by unanswered questions and the prospect of never seeing our loved ones again. Why let us experience such joy, only to possibly take it away? Do you call that fair?"

"Well, I guess it's all in how you look at it," she said softly.

"Well, you're right about that, Mom. At least you don't believe in a burning Hell. It's no good. But I wish you could see that this body, like the Earth, is a burning Hell."

"No, I can't," she said, and then she read a scripture that frankly didn't answer anything about Hell being nothing, like they taught.

"Well, you know, Mom, Jake and I have narrowed Hell down to the flesh body. I mean, it is a pretty accurate description, a burning lake of fire, and bodies are mostly water. And isn't it funny that the Bible starts with Heaven and Earth, not Hell?" I asked excitedly. "Do you have your Concordance?"

Dad asked "What?"

"Concordance," I said. Mom knew it was the *Insight to the Scriptures* book and told Dad so. "It helps you to find any scripture you want by remembering one of the words."

She handed me the concordance and I couldn't find the scripture using the word Hell. So I went and got mine. Besides, I wanted to show them what their concordance or "insight to the Scripture" had done to the born again scripture. I found not one scripture, but three right in a row to explain where Hell was. It was in Mark 9:43-47. The scripture showed that Hell was where you have two hands, two eyes, and two feet. It also describes Hell, where there is wailing and gnashing of teeth. "That's here, isn't it? We have teeth, and Lord knows the Jews and Christians wail like Hell, especially when they pray. The Jews even have a Wailing Wall." I asked them if they believed in being born again.

"Yes," Mom said, then she quoted: "We must be born again of the water and the spirit to enter the kingdom of Heaven."

"We think the body is Hell. Do you know that we are mostly seventy per cent water and we are spirits, which is symbolized by fire. A lake of fire," I said, coaxing-like. "Do you get it? I discovered the Earth was also seventy percent water. The same thing applies to us."

Huh," Mom replied in surprise. "I never thought of it that way."

Enough of that, I thought. I asked her then how you become born again.

She said, "You must first confess your sins, ask the Lord and Savior to come into your heart and then study the scriptures and become baptized." She cited the word water in the scriptures to the baptism. She made a pretty good statement, but I heard it from every Christian that I asked. They preached it as a literal baptism. Funny they couldn't see it as a metaphor of an out of body experience. Even Yeshua noted their baptism as false, not true baptisms. The baptism was representative of an out-of-body experience. I didn't want to make her upset by telling her I didn't think she was born again.

I changed the subject and I tried to explain that we're dead now; that's why we must be born again.

"Yeshua says we're judged already and even refers to us as dead?" She didn't know what to say.

I told them I had discovered that Yeshua considered us as dead. "Yeshua came here to save us by showing us how to be born again, to have life." I brought out a copy of the Shroud. I showed it to them and asked them if they knew anything about it. Of course, they didn't.

"Well, it's predicted as the only sign he would give us, the Sign of Jonas. And he got on to them for seeking signs of the end." They both had puzzled looks. The J.W.'s even have a book with the signs of the end, Revelations. "It's a parable or comparison of Jonah and the Whale to the resurrection. The Sign of Jonas," I said holding it up. "It's a picture of his resurrection after three days in the tomb," I explained. They were confused but finally understood. Then I said, "We are spirit! I think it scarred them." *(How ironic. Their god is a spirit!)*

I continued. "Do you know that none of Christianity acknowledges this as authentic? The irony is that the Catholics own it, and it resides in their mansion, the Vatican. But they don't authenticate it. Even though it is predicted in the Gospels, as the only sign he would give us. And since his message is being born again of the spirit, wouldn't it be a sign of "how"? Yeshua got angry at them for wanting and preaching signs. Don't the Jehovah's Witnesses preach the end of time?" I asked accusingly.

This riled Dad so much, I figured I'd better show them something else. I showed them plain proof of the Jehovah's Witnesses doing wrong. I asked them, "Do you think there are demons?"

"Yes," they both replied emphatically.

I showed them that the *Strong's Concordance* didn't have the word in it. We compared Bibles and theirs was full of the word "demon." I then said that the Jehovah's Witnesses changed the meaning of the word "mystery" too, which is what the Shroud describes to a tee. I showed them the definition and how it exactly described the Shroud. I pointed out that mystery was a religious rite. "Couldn't this be the very thing we need to do to be born again?" They were kind of shell-shocked. I showed them how the Jehovah's Witnesses had made it a secret and therefore had hidden the "way." Then, before Dad could get any angrier, I said, "This brings me to the name and the most important evidence that the Jehovah's Witnesses are hiding the truth. They hide it by changing scriptures, even the name."

"First, I would like to know why the name is important to you?"

They said because it was the only name by which you could be saved by. "Well," I replied, "besides being illogical, the fact is, that a lot of people won't even hear the name.

They were kind of puzzled. "If all you have to do is believe on the name, then wouldn't everybody get saved?" I asked unbelievingly.

"No," they said.

"Why not?"

"Well, not everyone is going to believe in him."

"Believe me, everyone would try if they were dying; don't think they wouldn't, Mom and Dad. That doesn't answer anything logically speaking, I'm sorry. Let me explain why I believe it's important. I don't mean to be rude. Remember," I said, "Jake and I think we came here as angels, the third that was cast out. We think that the name reflects that, as well as the reason the Bible was written. The whole story of the Bible is about trying to convince us that we are spirits, not just humans. And if we become born again, do the mystery, resurrect or eat from the tree of life, like it says in Genesis, before we die, then we would get life again. 'Oh Death, where is your victory?' The name was given to us in two parts. In a voice, the 'I am' which is a statement. It is answered by Yeshua, a confirmation." They looked even more puzzled.

I asked them, "Do you think of yourself as a spirit?"

"Well, I have a spirit, I guess," Mom said weakly.

"I call that a Christianity slip," I said, laughing.

"The spirit has no beginning or ending. The body does. Which are you?"

"I can't remember anything but this," she said, pointing to herself. "So do you really consider yourself a spirit?"

"You know, that doesn't mean anything, as far as not remembering," I said. "You can't remember when you were two years old either, can you, or when you were born?"

"No," she said again.

I toned down a bit. I didn't want to offend her or Dad. "Well, just because you can't remember being an angel doesn't necessarily mean you weren't one. You just proved that possibility exists. Doesn't the name have a logical meaning with this theory? I don't mean to be sarcastic or anything, but I've always thought the Jehovah's Witnesses taught the pursuit of truth. But the real truth is, that they change words and even make scriptures mean the opposite of what they are, like mystery being made a secret. Doesn't that matter to you? And Lord knows, if that doesn't the name change should!"

"It does matter," Dad snapped. "It matters a lot and you better pray you get back to the Kingdom Hall and get back on the right track."

"Doesn't Yeshua tell us to pray in secret, in our closet? Look Dad, I don't need church. I don't want you to get mad. I don't think you need church either. It hasn't done much to help your temper. No offense, I love you! Besides, I want to show you a scripture that proves my point better. Right after Yeshua explains that we must be born again 'to return to Heaven,' he proves that we are spirits or angels. He says in John 3:13, 'No one will go to Heaven that didn't come from Heaven, even the Son of Man who is in Heaven.' We were angels first."

"Now let's look at your concordance and see the proof of the Jehovah's Witnesses' wrongdoing, as I wouldn't accuse them if I didn't have the proof." I looked up the word 'Heaven' in their concordance and there it was. I showed them where they had cut the scripture in two, which also gave it an opposite meaning: "No man will go to Heaven."

Mom was shocked and speechless, whereas Dad immediately defended the right of interpretation. "Maybe it doesn't mean that," he said loudly.

"Well, I don't see how you could see it any other way. Besides, it's right here in bold print, and we know that it's not true."

They both asked why, looking at me harshly.

"Doesn't the Bible say that Enoch and Elijah were taken?"

"Who?" Dad asked.

"Enoch and Elijah. Even worse, Mom and Dad, why did the Christian movement accept the canon of the Jews, when we have proof that their canon was invalid? Enoch was quoted by Yeshua's little brother, Jude in the New Testament. Why not in the Old? This should have raised flags of doubt right away, and all the books should have been revealed to us. Oh, and I forgot. Jude quoted Enoch saying, 'the angels which left our first estate for a strange flesh,' and he said, 'though you once knew this!' You see, Mom, you, me, us, we can't remember because we are retarded by the flesh. It bruises our head and heel, like it says in Genesis. I know it's hard to swallow. But we have pictures. This is Yeshua's only sign, his picture of the way," I said, holding up the Shroud. "It's spirit. And we aren't even told about it, except for *Unsolved Mysteries*. It's still unsolved!"

Dad was quick to question the material I was using. I explained that it was not literature put out by any religious organization. I told him he could prove it to himself by going to the library. "I'm willing to be whatever the truth is, Dad," I said, as loving as I could get. "Even if it's atheism, as long as it's fair and provable. I'm not out to prejudice any one religion," I said frankly. "Can you say the same?"

"Well, that's your damn opinion of what you read," he said, raising his voice even louder. "We need to ask our elders, Mike," Mom said quietly, trying to counter Dad's short remark.

"Well, like I said, I'm willing to become whatever the truth is, Dad. And I sure have doubts about the Jehovah's Witnesses' accuracy and intentions. So much so, that I damn sure wouldn't ever make a life or death decision again over it, especially for my kids. And let me reiterate. Frankly, I'm ashamed of it. I'll check 'em all out first; that's logical."

Dad got fired up then and said, "Don't come in here insinuating that we've done the wrong thing by you, lad."

"I'm not, Dad! Hell, I was brainwashed, too. That's what I'm trying to tell you, It's a religion cover-up." That was the wrong thing to say. He blew up.

"Don't call me brainwashed!" He said, getting right in my face.

"Okay, I'm not going to argue about it. Besides, I'd rather you prove it to yourself, but you'll never do it by just looking at your own mate-

The Five Faces of Man

Proof of competition evident in the different colors and different facial structures. The angels "saw" us for our beauty. Could they all look the same as nature creates life? The heads of Easter Island suggests this possibility. Their lust for power/unique beauty does too!

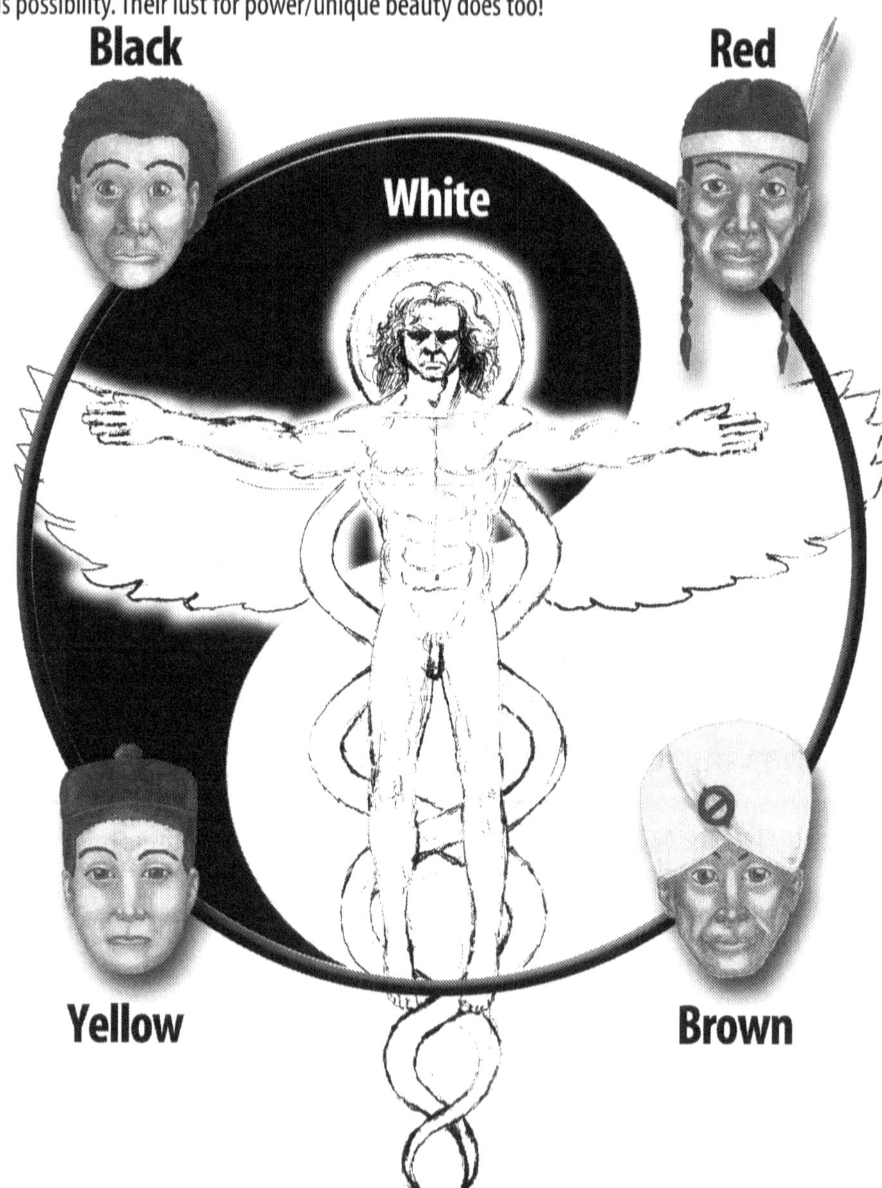

Two sperm and an egg, represents angels mixing with Man. DNA symbol looks like AMA symbol. We create with DNA . . . could they? The evidence suggests so.

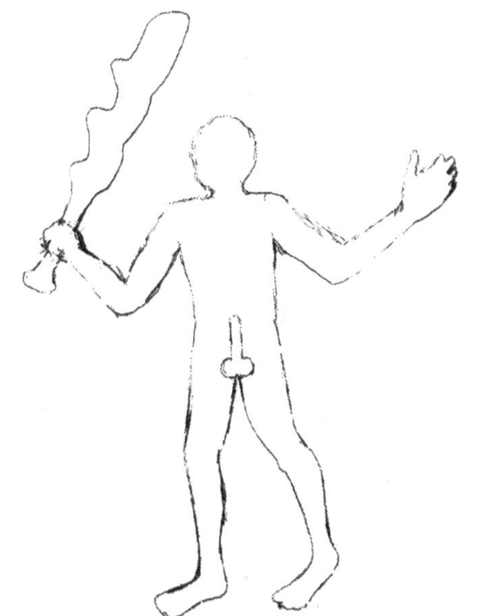

Wiltshire, England
Cerne's Giant

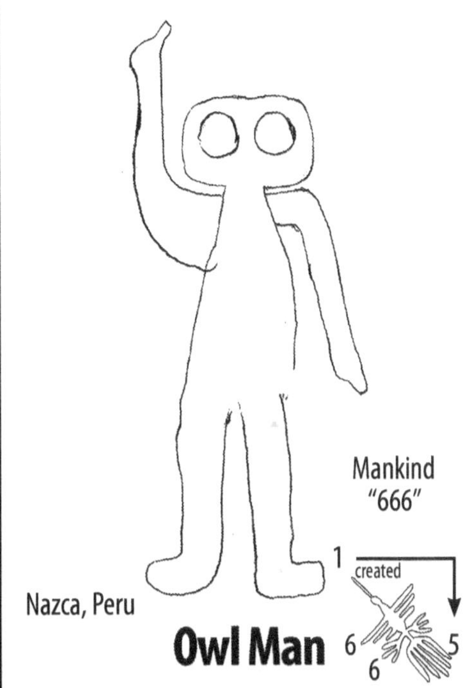

Nazca, Peru
Owl Man

Oraibi, Arizona
A Hopi Prophecy

rial. I'm telling you. I just proved that. The argument that we needed the scripture made easier to read doesn't hold water with me. After all, we are English, aren't we?"

"Well," he said, "I think your intentions are good, but your head is in the wrong place. You better follow your heart and get back to the Kingdom Hall."

"Dad," I said, shaking my head, "the heart is just a muscle."

"Yeah, and you're a smart-ass."

"No, I'm just being logical, and to me, it and Christianity just don't go together. But, of course, they don't see the importance of the name, either, or care that it was changed to Zeus. All you need to do is check the names and you'll see that it was changed. Adam, from Hebrew to English, has one name to each. They changed the name Yeshua to the Greek god Zeus so it would be easy to sell. He has two English names now instead of one and we use the incorrect one: the one in the New Testament, Zeus. How appropriate," I said, "because it is new and it is Greek. The correct name is in the O.T. in Ezra. How ironic, huh? Tell me Dad, how is Christianity any different from Judaism? They both are huge, wealthy organizations that base their lifestyle on the Ten Commandments and going to church, the very thing Yeshua delivered us from. And why are we delivered from the law. Maybe its because mystery is the only thing that saves us."

"I will check on this," Mom said as she got up from the table. Dad was starting toward the bedroom. I knew he had heard enough.

"One thing before you go to bed. Do you think the Anti-Christ is here now or is he coming?"

They both turned and agreed among themselves, about the 1914 theory of the Jehovah's Witnesses. They said he came then, even though Yeshua said he ruled already. John also said he ruled two thousand years ago. "It appears God and the Devil have one thing in common. They're both singular and plural." Dad started to get upset again, but Mom got him turned around and headed him toward the bedroom.

"I'm just quoting the Bible," I said, "but I love you anyway."

"We love you, too," Mom said as she hurried Dad on into the bedroom.

I just laughed to myself. Dad really loved the Jehovah's Witnesses. I was really shocked at how much he loved them. He no longer loved provable truths as much as he loved tradition. As long as I could remember he had studied with them, so I guess it was difficult to accept change. I needed to lighten up. I know I sure couldn't say anything about the blood issue. I had done the same for myself. Boy, he had really gotten riled. I'm sure he felt the same guilt I did, especially the way I had put it, with so much contempt. I realized that I had never really examined the Jehovah's Witnesses' history. Maybe my Dad could make a change. I did! His church had such life-threatening decisions. They always said it was a life or death decision to come back. The only real life or death issue was leaving.

I got up the next morning to the sounds of a full house. I knocked out a good breakfast and then sat around with the family. As evening wore on, I had a chance to talk with Mom again, off to the side. "Ol' Dad must've freaked out when I said we are dead now."

"Yes he did," she laughed.

"You let me know if Dad ever touches you again, Mom, will you please?"

"Don't you worry," she said meekly. "He knows better than to touch me."

"Right, Mom," I replied, knowing better. My Dad had a blind temper, and I knew he did it anyway. "If things aren't so good right now,

I'll lay off the religion." All my life he had shoved the Jehovah's Witnesses down my throat: the short hair, no Christmas, and the crap in school with the flag. Now I'm the persecutor. I thought about the Two Witnesses again. I had other memories flood in and then suddenly I remembered the dream. "I'm telling you, Mom, I've got some resentment that sometimes gets the best of me. And it turns into a rage if I let it. Dad taught me that."

"Don't let it, please Mike," she demanded more than she begged.

"Don't worry, I won't," I responded emphatically. "Mom, please buy yourself a King James' Bible. I'm telling you, yours has been changed in such a way that it has become the opposite in meaning of what Yeshua was teaching. Its anti-spirit, pro-flesh and pro Earth. And think about it, Mom. Christianity and Judaism just aren't fair. If God is great enough to create us, then why isn't he also great enough to make this a perfect world at the snap of a finger, Mom? It makes sense that we are angels. Reincarnation, Karma, it all makes sense. We never stop existing, we must learn who we are. To learn the mystery, if we are lucky. So read everything, Mom. You know I told you about Enoch, right? Well, he was a whole lot older than Moses, the seventh from Adam. Seventh, Mom. You have seven kids, I'm the sixth; man was made on the sixth day of the seventh day creation parable. So I'm going to check out his writings first thing. Besides Mom," I said, reaching and hugging her. "We know now that we were two, once first, right? Or at least that it's possible!"

"Yes," she said, so child like.

"Mom, does it really make any sense that we ate from a tree and then were cursed to death for it? That's pretty bizarre, isn't it? Isn't it just possible that they could have other meanings, like mystery has, that we aren't seeing?"

"I'm going to check that out," she said lovingly, hugging me.

She was a cool mom. And sometimes my dad was a great dad, too. "You know," I looked at her and said, with tears in my eyes, "the ol' bastard does have a good side that makes me overlook everything else. I can't help but to give in. I love him."

"I know," she said and hugged me real tight. We heard Dad coming down the hall. We continued to visit that evening and didn't talk again about my search for the truth. I knew Dad had about all he could take. I had to be getting back to Tennessee. It was prime time for my art season. I was renting a building in Nashville and didn't need to be gone long. Rent wasn't cheap. This was one of my short weekends with my son. I hated the short ones. I was getting into a routine now; I visited three times through the school year and then had him during summer, so this was always hard.

We were going to head out that evening, but we didn't tell Dad that. He didn't like to see us drive at night. I used the Christmas season excuse. I would just tell him that I needed to take advantage of every order I could get before season ends. He could relate to that, being a truck driver for thirty years. There was many a night he had to roll at a moment's notice, headed for anywhere the best rate was sending him. It also was busiest around Christmas.

When he approached, I asked him to use the King James' Bible that Mom was going to get and then look up the name, Jesus. He said he would, but then he said that the Jehovah's Witnesses had translated directly from the scrolls instead of the King James' Bible. He turned to Mom and asked her to confirm it.

"I think so," she said.

"Well, they do believe the King James' is a valid translation also, don't they?"

Dad didn't know what to say, but Mom said they did.

"I thought so," I said. "As a matter of fact, I think all of Christianity does accept it. Except maybe the Mormons or the Amish or something. I think they have a different Bible, and I'm going to check that out too, along with Buddhism, Hinduism, the Indians, all of them. I want you to do the same. You see Dad, I just want the truth, no matter what it is. And there is certainly a wide variety with a short time to find it, so we better start reading fast."

"I'm going to get me a copy of the Book of Enoch as soon as I get home. If Jude quoted him and he was Yeshua's little brother, then Yeshua must've agreed. Jude was a follower of Yeshua. I'm going to find out why the Jews didn't agree with his teachings and why Christianity didn't let us see them."

"You do that, Son, and in the meantime, don't stop looking at your own, the Jehovah's Witnesses."

"Okay, Dad, don't worry about that; they aren't mine anymore, no offense. If they changed the word Yeshua, then believe me, I will be examining their religion with a fine-tooth comb."

"You do that," he said, smiling, like he really wanted me to. What he wanted was for me to go to the Kingdom Hall.

"You keep that Shroud and look up the scripture Matthew 16:4. It's called the Sign of Jonas, and he said it's the only sign he would give us. Think about it. It must've been important," I said. "And remember, I think it's the way to live forever, to be born again. No, no, it's the way to get out of Hell and back to Heaven, Dad. We live forever anyway, even if we don't get it. But who wants Hell, death. We're just reincarnated into mortal bodies again and again. Maybe not always human, actually we know better. Anyway, I am your son, ain't I? You saw me put myself through college for four years, didn't you?"

"Yes," he answered. "What happened to you."

"Thanks, Dad." I said. "I happen to like who I am and what I do, even though I'm not materially rich. I'm sorry, I shouldn't have said that!"

"No, you ain't you poor bastard. You're making your family pay for it."

"Frank," Mom said, quickly.

"I didn't mean anything by it, dammit. I just don't like to see him struggle," he added apologetically.

I had turned away and started toward the door. I stopped and hugged him and said, "Don't worry, Dad. We're getting it together."

He hugged me back and got a little teary-eyed. He grabbed Angel immediately and then I grabbed Mom. Naturally she started sobbing. I had some loving parents, and I never ever lost sight of that; and they loved my wife as much as she did them. I was a blessed man. There I go again with a Christianity slip.

"Do you have enough money?" Dad asked immediately.

"Yes, Dad," I said. "Do you think I would make this trip without money? I am thirty-two."

"Thirty-three," Angel and Mom both chimed in.

Wow, I thought to myself, that was the same age Yeshua was when he died.

"Don't remind me," I said dramatically.

"Oh shut up, sissy," my Dad said, punching me in the arm. "Wait til you're sixty and then let's hear you."

"Shoot," I said. "With the cost of living in Nashville, I hope I make it. This old body can't hold the pace. I'm going back to school and become a psychiatrist."

Dad just reached up and massaged my shoulder and chuckled

warmly. "Well, hang in there, lad. Maybe we'll get something going."

"We will, Dad, I promise you that," I said as I turned and hugged him. That was a good time to make a quick departure. "I still have to get James Dean home, so I better go."

"Who?" Dad asked.

"Jimmy!" I said, laughing. I had a pet name for everyone.

As I pulled out of the drive, I asked Angel if she thought Dad would keep the Shroud.

She laughed and said, "There's no way. Your dad is a Jehovah's Witness, and he'll die a Jehovah's Witness."

"Yeah, you're right. He'll probably use it to start a fire." Angel just laughed and I couldn't help but to laugh with her. I think we saw the smoke as we pulled out. "Mom and Dad are so afraid of the spirit world," I said in disgust. "The irony is that we're spirit. We're supposed to be born again of the spirit. That's the worst thing about the Jehovah's Witnesses. They have two choices, living forever on Earth as flesh, or Heaven as a spirit, but they all chose Earth. They don't want to be a spirit, even in Heaven. Just like Mom said when I asked her: 'This is all I've ever known.' I proved to her it wasn't. She was two once and didn't remember that, so she could have been an angel. Why can't she believe that? Everything is possible with God, right? I can't understand them. Do they believe in God or not? Don't they want to be with him, or not?" *(This would ultimately depend on what we looked like.)*

"How do you know God is a man?" Angel asked jokingly.

I laughed. "It's a Christianity slip. I'm telling you, we're all brainwashed! And all we have to do is just prove it at the local library. I gave Mom and Dad plenty of reason for doubt, and I love how Jude says 'though you once knew this.' He says just what I'm saying. We're angels trapped in Hell, the flesh world, and we are retarded by the flesh. Heck, even science says we only achieve ten percent of our brain function."

I looked back at Jimmy and I said, "I hope you have gotten a powerful lesson out of this. Knowledge is power. It is the key that will open doors and cure ignorance. Do you know what ignorance is, son?"

"Being stupid," he replied with a giggle.

"No, buddy, it isn't stupid. That's what a person is if he doesn't ask the meaning of a word when he hears it and doesn't understand. Didn't you ever hear the old saying in school that the only stupid question is one that isn't asked?"

"Yeah," he said, smiling real big.

"Well, that's right. Stupid has nothing to do with learning. That's just ignorance. Someone who is slow in learning is physically challenged. Someone who doesn't ask questions and learn is ignorant and that is stupid. What's the golden rule?" I asked quickly.

"Treat people like you want to be treated," he said confidently.

He surprised me, because I always thought he wasn't listening. I knew he could learn anything. He was extremely intelligent. "Well, there you go. You wouldn't want anybody calling you stupid. People aren't stupid, Jimmy. That's something we do, not learning as much as we can." That's relative, I thought to myself. Man, life is complex!

I reached back and rubbed his little blond head. I drove on and couldn't stop thinking about him. He was having problems in school because of his outgoing personality. The teachers were always getting on to him and his cousin Rickey. As we pulled into his drive, I pleaded with him to knuckle down in school. "Christmas is coming up," I said. "And you know your mom won't let you come down next summer if you fail. You'll have to take summer school."

"I know," he said. "I will, Dad; I promise."

We hugged, and I got out some money for his allowance. After hugging his little brother and sister and talking with his mom and stepdad, we drove south. Angel was always glad to be headed home.

I didn't know if I was making any headway with Dad and Mom, but I knew one thing for sure. When my son grew up and had to make these choices, he would have a step up on the average kid. I was determined to study. I was going to study every view concerning our history and the world we live in, especially the scientific evidence. No matter what it cost me. I did wonder how I could afford it, though, as I remembered the concordance. And now, I was going to be buying the Book of Enoch and the other Bible. I laughed at the irony of the 'Other Bible'. As I drove that night, I couldn't help but to wonder about life. It sure was a mystery.

We made it home late that night. The next morning I got up and called Jake. I was eager to tell him about my discussions with Mom and Dad. We cut our conversation short as he wanted me to come in and help him out with some satellite work, naturally. But, I was looking forward to discussing the Shroud book with him. He had been reading it while I was in Ohio.

I couldn't help it. I grabbed the concordance and looked up *commandment*. As I was doing so, Mary walked in and asked what I was doing. I told her, "Mom and Dad, like all Christianity, think you go to Heaven by being judged according to the Ten Commandments on the Last Day." She just nodded, and I knew she also felt the same way.

Sure enough, she said, "Well, that's what it says in Revelations, doesn't it?"

"I guess. I haven't read that far yet, but Yeshua delivered us from the commandments, didn't he?"

"Yeah, I've never understood that," she said dumbfoundedly.

"Yeah, me either, until now at least. I'm reading the Bible with a new understanding, knowing that we were angels that left their first estate for a strange flesh, and now it makes sense. The mystery is the hardest thing for us to do."

"Yeah, I've been reading a little bit and even watching the TV preacher while you were gone. It does make sense, and he agrees with the existence of a pre-Adam man. You think it's the angels," Mary asked excitedly.

"Yes I do," I said just as excited.

I finally found *commandment* as Mary continued to talk about the preacher's theory of the Sons of God. It was somewhat the same theory Jake was using to show that flesh was here before Adam and Eve. I nodded in agreement at the indisputable evidence of a pre-Adam existence. "Hell, it's kinda hard not to buy it with dinosaurs and prehistoric man," I told her. "Besides, the preacher is absolutely right about the scripture of the Sons of God. They were either eating from the tree or making bodies, too, and obviously before Adam and Eve. They were flesh bodies. Yeshua had to save that which is lost, the Sons of God. The angels had left their first estate for a strange flesh. Isn't that bizarre. They must not have looked like man exactly. They must've been uglier."

Mary just nodded her head in agreement. "It does make sense," she said wide-eyed.

"There's something about the concept of our being two things that caught my eye with a scripture I read the other night. I can't stand to read something I don't understand. It was a statement by Yeshua, that we were made male and female in the beginning. I'm not quite sure about it, but I think that the whole Bible is a parable of our fall from male to female, from invisible to visible, angel to man. Jake says the marriage is being born again by praying in secret, making our conscious mind/ female unite with our real self, the Holy Spirit, which is male, through transcendental meditation or stopping the mind. I remember that the Bible is always referring to Eve or the female as our downfall for listening to her, the consciousness. Now we have this scripture from Yeshua whose primary teaching was being born again of the spirit, giving up the world. He called himself the Bridegroom. It looks as if the Bible is redundantly telling us who we are: spirit angels who became flesh or, better said, man. The whore of Revelations and the Eve of Genesis."

Mary was glued to my every word. "I found *commandment*," I told her. I needed to hurry. Angel was bound to be getting up anytime. I couldn't believe my eyes. "The Ten Commandments weren't even given for quite some time. The first mention of any is in Exodus. Think of how many people weren't judged by the Ten Commandments," I said, showing her.

Mary was as shocked as I was at our newfound information. She was anxious to talk more, but I had to get ready. I laid down the concordance and went into the kitchen with her. She was a coffee drinker, just like I was.

"I'm anxious to read this book on spontaneous human combustion," I told her. "You ought to check it out," I said, giving it to her. "Jake's been reading the one on the Shroud. I think there could be a connection between it, being born again, the Sign of Jonas, Enoch and Elijah's being taken, and mystery. Yeshua disappeared, leaving his picture burned in the Shroud. The Old Testament is where we sacrificed ourselves and children to God, by literally burning ourselves."

Mary was overwhelmed and blurted out excitedly. "You mean to tell me, that you think in the beginning we were supposed to meditate and spontaneously combust, in order to go back to Heaven?"

"Well, what do you think? Doesn't it sound logical?" I asked. "I mean, you do believe in greater things, don't you, if you believe in God?

How can you think that it's ridiculous if you believe the Bible? Didn't some people disappear?"

"Well, Elijah was taken," she said, shaking her head in agreement.

"Yeah, Enoch walked with God. Not that it's any different, but the word taken seems to imply against the will. But think about it, Mary. The Old Testament is full of parables like 'lift up the serpent,' 'make straight the crooked path.' These are all examples of being born again. And in the scripture John 3, he tells us plainly that we are spirits, from Heaven. He gives us an example, as proof of who we are and what we must do: Lift up the serpent, this body. Deprivation, fasting, celibacy, praying in secret. All the monk-like behavior in every culture is further proof of it." *(I would soon see it as mind control exercise.)*

"Wow," she said, completely dumbstruck. "This makes so much sense."

"I know," I agreed excitedly, just as dumbstruck as she was. "Sometimes I wonder if I would have gotten it. I doubt I would have if it wasn't for Jake, Mary! And it's so agreeable with the Book of Jude. I love how he says 'though you once knew this' because that's what it's all about. The flesh retards us, and I don't think we really believe we're spirits and not these bodies." We looked at each other. I told her about my dream. She said she had looked up the Two Witnesses in Revelations. I told her then, we could be them. She listened as if she was in a trance. Then she got scared.

Suddenly she started talking. "You know, Dave said that we only use ten percent of our minds," she said with admiration.

"Yeah, he's right. But we can use more."

"I know," she said. "Dave was so scientific, believe me, I know." She was nervous!

"Was he religious?" I asked softly.

"No, but he wanted desperately to believe in God or something greater."

"Don't we all ," I said quickly. "I don't know how he couldn't if he was truly an educated scientific person."

"Oh, he was that," she replied quickly.

"Heck," I said boldly, "the structure of our world is all too perfect mathematically not to have something greater. Something greater than us anyway. Man can't get along with himself long enough to create anything, let alone the universe. We're the biggest threat to it, as it is. I'm going to see if Einstein himself was religious."

"I don't know," she said, "but I do agree with you that it is all too perfect to have just evolved."

"Well, I do believe in the evolution of life-forms. I do believe in change, adaptability, and improvisation. That's the only thing that stays the same. The Earth is constantly changing and has plenty of evidence of evolution. I just don't know about Man. Well, yes I do; we are improving. But why do we have a missing link between Neanderthal Man and Modern Man or Cro-Magnon Man? It has to be that the angels sped up the process. If we accept that, there is no missing link." I later discovered our unique disadvantage of having an overly large head!

Shane walked in and must've heard us. "Science has proven evolution of the universe," he confirmed. "The sun itself is a star that is constantly expanding and shrinking, imploding and exploding, recycling itself."

"Really," I said. "Being born, aging, and then dying. Then it does it again. Huh!"

"Yeah." Then he started to go into the living room, to show me what he was talking about in his science book. I was eager to see this.

"Does this mean that the sun will expand or contract to the point that Earth is uninhabitable?"

"Obviously, it does," he said. "If an asteroid or meteor doesn't take us out first. Or maybe a comet."

"Yeah, I guess we've already had proof of that with the Ice Age and the flood. Man, how much more proof of that do we need?"

He showed me the article in the book, and I was completely awe-struck. After we talked, I remarked that I thought science would prove God someday or at least what God is. Shane turned and said that it has to happen. "God made man; man made science; science will prove God."

"Wow, dude, what a profound truth. It has to be. If God is the truth and science has as its foundation provable truths, it has to happen. We just haven't evolved to that point of truth yet. We haven't evolved to that level of knowledge yet," I said.

"Wow, son," Mary chimed in. "I didn't know you had it in you."

"Yeah. Obviously, I take after Dad," he said laughing.

"Yeah," she said. "You're full of crap."

"I'm scientific, not religious."

She replied quickly, "No, Son; you take after me. I knew your dad; he wanted to believe in God, but didn't. You don't have a bad bone in your body, but your dad had more than his share."

I chimed in. "Would he chase down people if they made a wrong move driving?" I laughed, knowing my dad did.

"Hell, yes he did!" She and Shane said at the same time.

"Yeah, my dad had a bad temper. His childhood is what I think made him that way. And as far as religion goes, he was too logical to buy it." Shane said, real sad-like. He missed his dad!

"Well, it is hard to buy. The whole story is full of unfair contradic-tions. And the worst is this 'I'm saved' crap that they sell. They get you with the one-two-three easy sales technique. You think you're saved so you start paying them from then on. What an irony, huh? You don't pay 'til you get saved. But then you pay for the rest of your life. Even though you're saved. What a joke!"

Mary just smirked and looked away. I saw her disgust.

"What?" I asked quickly. "Don't tell me you can be logical one minute and not the next, just because you want to believe something is so. Mary, how can anybody believe in God giving miracles to some and not to others? How can you believe in this at all, when you see children starving and dying every day? Misery is everywhere, wailing and gnashing of teeth."

"I'm not going to argue about it," she said in an aggravated tone.

"But you still believe in healing, miracles, and that you're saved, don't you?" I said unbelievably. "Mary, it's a miracle Yeshua's name has now been recognized by us. That's a miracle, and it looks like a biggie. God didn't do that. Jake did! And I can't find anybody else who cares about his name being changed. God doesn't have anything to do with this world; that's obvious by the dying children in it, but I think children get another chance and another and another through reincarnation. And I don't base that on speculation. We have plenty of proof in animals, birds, and fish. That way, God or life isn't so cruel. I think we're on this ride, until we finally realize that we shouldn't be here. I'm finding that the world seems to be dominated by cultures that believe we came from Heaven, where we are immortal. The Aborigines believe this world is a dream, and in our dreams lie the real world. Spirit."

"Yeah, I saw a documentary the other day about them, and you're right, they do."

"Isn't it funny that the world is dominated by cultures that believe in a spirit world, including the Judeo-Christian story, but the only ones who don't do the mystery or worship in spirit are the Judeo-Christian people?"

"Huh?"

"I'm telling you, the twenty-third chapter of Matthew describes Judaism and Christianity to a tee. It and history say it all. Even now they forbid spirituality." That's why Yeshua taught this mystery.

"What do you call praying?" She asked quickly. "Isn't that worshiping in spirit?"

"How could it be, when we know the Jews pray. Yeshua made it clear it was something they weren't doing, in the Gospel of John, Chapter three. Nicodemus was a Jew who prayed diligently, so it couldn't be prayer. It was something the Jews should have known."

Angel was getting up, and I knew I had one last minute to talk about religion. "I've got the concordance of Jake's and I'm taking it back today, so let's look up the Lord's Prayer and see what it says."

"I know what it says," she said.

"What is it?" I asked. "I remember reading it in Matthew, but I just read over it without absorbing it." She recited the prayer as I looked up the word "pray."

I found the scriptures and went and got the Bible. I started to turn to Matthew, but instead, found I had turned directly to the prayer in Luke. "Wow," I said.

"What?"

I turned right to it in Luke. Can you believe that?" As I started reading it, we were both surprised at an amazing piece of evidence. The scripture further proved that praying wasn't what you do to become born again. Yeshua wasn't praying, but doing the mystery. The apostles saw the Lord doing something, they thought was praying. They asked him to teach them how to pray. He obviously wasn't praying, as he told them the only prayer to say. "If he was saying something, wouldn't they have heard it?" I asked Mary. "Besides the apostles were twelve Jews who knew how to pray. And it only takes a few seconds to say the Lord's Prayer."

"I would think so," she replied.

"I can't believe this either, Mary. This scripture is a commandment to pray only this prayer, but I don't even know it. Hell, the Jehovah's Witnesses pray whatever they want. And look at this prayer. It's short and specific, not long. And Mary, Yeshua asks why they pray when God knows what we need anyway. Remember, the cares of this world, he calls the 'evil one.'"

"Huh! I never thought of that. It's pretty heavy, ain't it?" She said.

"No, it's actually pretty light because it is so full of holes. In Matthew 6:5 it says not to pray in church and in public. It's obvious that Christians do the opposite of Yeshua's teachings like the Jews. They pray everything but the Lord's Prayer and they preach the Ten Commandments. And they do it in church and everywhere. Yes, it is heavy! Is it heavy enough to convince you that prayer isn't how you become born again?" She hesitated for a moment. "Huh?" I asked.

"Well, he obviously wasn't praying," she said.

"So, do you still think you're saved?" She just started walking away. "I don't mean to sound sarcastic, but you seem to be a logical person; and you did indicate that being saved was something you prayed for, right?"

"Yes," she said, in a much harsher tone than I wanted to hear. So I went ahead and got up. I started to the bedroom. I didn't want to end on a bad note.

"I just want you to see that you aren't born again by praying, and I think we both proved that today. It's not that easy."

"Right," she said, just waving me off as she headed in to watch television.

As I started past the kitchen table I noticed a check lying next to a religious envelope. I stopped and looked at the check. Mary was tithing to the TV preacher's ministry. I turned to ask her about it when I saw him on the television. He was on the biggest street corner of all. And he was praying over letters for financial help and everything else under the sun. Even though God knows what we need and blessed are the poor, woe to the rich. Hypocrite. He criticized other preachers. He was the pot calling the kettle black.

"I hope you aren't tithing to this guy, Mary. He's praying something besides what the Lord told us to pray. He doesn't care about the truth, Mary, only what benefits him, and without your tithes he wouldn't be in business. Hell, don't be naive; give your money to the poor directly. Do you think he pays tithes? Hell, no! He uses your money to increase the size of his organization. It means more money and a bigger salary." She was clearly getting upset, so I told her I loved her and didn't want to see her become brainwashed like they clearly are. "Give your money to the poor, Mary. It's not hard to find them. Some of them hang around churches even. Trying to get help! Oh," I said as I started away, "but don't think you'll ever find one of the vagabonds in a church with nothing but his rags on. They'll throw him out! He's the one the Christians will pass by with their windows rolled up and their doors locked, saying 'get a job,'" I said sarcastically.

I started to leave I guessed that Mary had probably never given a beggar money more than once. Angel dogged me about my giving all the time and Mary always took her side. It was only because we were struggling ourselves. I apologized to her before I left, saying, "I don't mean to stereotype all Christians that way, but why give to the church when Yeshua said to give alms to the poor. The church is sure not poor?"

"Well, they do help the poor with food drives," she remarked. "At least I think they do."

"Yeah, ten percent of what they take in. Who's getting more? Anyway, I know some are giving, but if they don't further Yeshua's message, then what good are they? Religiously-speaking, I mean? Please give your money to the poor. You can't buy your way into Heaven."

"I know that," she snapped, resenting my remark.

I knew I had gone too far, so I ended it there. I didn't waste any time getting ready. I was just about finished when Angel and Little Jake came out of the bathroom. "I've got to run and help Jake for a couple hours."

"Oh no," she replied grimly.

"I promise I'll hurry."

"Right, Mike," she replied with a scowl. "That's what you always say."

"Well, this time it will be different." I knew she wasn't buying it. So, I went ahead and slid past her and went to the bedroom to get a few things. I quickly wrapped it up and sailed through the kitchen, giving her and Little Jake a kiss on the way out. Angel and Mary were whipping up a first class breakfast. I think it was just to rub it in for leaving early.

When I arrived at Jake's I couldn't wait to tell him about the Lord's Prayer and all the scriptures that contradicted each other. He had already convinced me with Nicodemus that praying isn't what you do to be born again. I was eager to show him my newfound discoveries.

Jake answered the door, and I immediately saw the button. It was a huge, like you get at a political fund-raiser. He was wearing it, right on the front forehead of his cap. It read Yeshua.

"What do you think?" He said, tilting his head down.

"Man, that is cool. Where'd you get it?"

"Moses," he said. Moses grabbed him and picked him up like a wrestler, ready to body slam him. "Son, son," Jake pleaded.

"Oh, oh, sorry, Dad." Then he came over and did the same thing to me. He loved his dominating height. He had grown six inches over the last year or so. Misty told him not to hurt me. She was right!

"Don't worry, I love kids, big or small," I said, looking up at Moses. He just grinned real big and then used my head for a prop to lean on.

"Let's go," I said, wriggling out from beneath his thirty pound arm. "Bring your concordance," I said grinning at Jake.

"Oh yeah," he said and started into the bedroom. "Thanks," Jake said as he came out and started toward the door in almost a jog. I couldn't believe he reacted so fast. With the mystery and music, he must've really needed to work. He must've needed to make some money. But didn't we all? However, he didn't catch it. I had his concordance.

I hollered and said, "I've got your concordance, Jake."

He hollered back and said, "I know." I waited for him to say something, wondering what he was doing and then he came back in. "And I got yours."

I couldn't believe it. I finally got it. This concordance was the first and most essential tool in my library of tools in this search, even though we would find it to be flawed. The Jesus lie. It was free of religious influence and billed as the most exhaustive concordance of the Bible ever. It was plain to see that the concordance of the Jehovah's Witnesses was incorrect, if not outright fraudulent. I think both. No, it was both! Read it and weep, I thought to myself.

"All right, man, I can't believe this. I'm making progress now."

"What did Angel say about you buying it?" They both asked, almost at the same time.

"Well, she wasn't thrilled, so I'm going to have to hide the Book of Enoch."

"Yeah, I know what you're saying," Jake said. "I haven't told you, Honey," he said looking toward Misty, "but I want to get a book about the Dead Sea Scrolls. First, I've got to make this good paycheck," he said with a big ol' grin. Before Misty could respond, I gave him a little shove. He definitely needed money!

"Of course you do, we both do. Come on, let's go. What's it about?" I asked quickly. "Oh, and get me the Shroud book while you're at it. Hurry, man. We've got to go."

"Well, I can't believe it," he said, shockingly. "The author theorizes that the Shroud was in the hands of the Gnostics from the beginning."

"The who?" I asked. Bewildered. I had never heard of that religion. I would find almost no one who had.

"He repeated. The Gnostics. I'll tell you about them later. She even traces this thing down to the fifth century. It's a pretty viable theory."

"Well, get it," I said. "But we've got to go if I want to save my marriage. Then we'll worry about saving ourselves."

"And buying more books!" Misty added snidely.

While he was getting the Shroud book I began telling Misty my theory about the Lord's Prayer. She was surprised to find that it was the only prayer we were supposed to pray, according to Yeshua. Jake walked back in, just as I was showing her the scripture. He asked me what I was looking at, and I told him.

"Did you know that the Lord's Prayer was the only prayer we are supposed to say?"

"Yeah," he said. "You told me already."

"Well, why doesn't Christianity?"

"I guess it's because they're too busy praying for other things," he said laughing.

"Well, forget that and get going on the name list. That's more important." I said tapping his new badge while I pushed on him to leave. He couldn't keep from watching the television. "Come on, man. We aren't going to start watching this stuff."

"Okay, okay," he said.

As we were leaving, I hugged Moses and told him what a great present he had gotten his Dad.

"Now he can really torture Christians," Moses remarked. I just laughed. I wondered if he had read about the Two Witnesses. How else would he know that?

"You are going to stop back in, aren't you?" Misty asked.

"Not if I want to save my marriage," I told her laughing.

"Oh, I forgot to ask, did your family care about the name change?" Jake interrupted.

"No, or at least they didn't seem to. They still called him Jesus."

"No, don't tell me," Jake said, as if in agony. "They liked 'Jesus' better, didn't they?"

"Yea—" I started to say, but Jake broke in.

"Don't tell me; they speak English, right?"

"Right."

"Man, can't they see it?" He complained. "Adam is Adam, Moses is Moses, but Yeshua is Jesus and Jeshua, come on! Did you tell them about the 'I am' and how it is answered or fulfilled by Yeshua?"

"Yeah," I said. "But they don't think we're spirit or the one-third of the angels. I told them about Enoch, too. They didn't care about that either."

"Boy, I'm telling you, these Christians. You can't find a one who cares about his name."

"Well, at least you've got something to remind them," I said, pointing to the button.

"Yeah," he said, reaching and hugging Moses. "My offspring sure surprised me, and I couldn't have asked for a better gift." He kissed Moses on the cheek.

"Aahhh!" Moses squalled. "Dad!"

"Come on, man. Let's head out," I said. "I'll finish telling you about the Lord's Prayer."

"Well, you better get the Bible. I know how you remember scripture. That's why I watch this stuff on TV, man. They might be ignorant, but they do teach scripture."

As soon as he looked at the TV, he saw the preacher again. I knew we had to go then. I pushed him out the door. "Oh no," I said loudly. "We aren't going to watch that proud war veteran pray again." I went ahead and started telling him about the Lord's Prayer. As soon as we got into the truck, he made me get the Bible out and read him the exact scripture in Luke. As soon as I finished, I asked him if he got the same meaning out of it that I did. He gave me that impressed look, but then said that I would never get Christianity to buy that.

"I don't care. I don't have a church business. Anyway, what does that matter? I can prove that Yeshua said to pray only this prayer. And look, what do they do: the opposite." I said it with an embittered growl. I didn't like my anger. I knew I wanted to love everyone. "This is no different from the scripture about praying in Matthew. He tells them not to pray on street corners and church and they do the opposite of that, too. Hell, they've even mastered prime time TV, the largest street corner of all."

As we drove, I changed the conversation. "You know I can't believe Christianity doesn't believe in reincarnation."

"Really," Jake replied. "I wonder what their answer is for the scripture about Elijah being reincarnated as John the Baptist?"

"Wow, I've never read that," I said excitedly. "Where is it?"

"You've got the concordance. Look it up."

"What should I look up, John or Elijah?"

"Look up Elijah," he said. "I know it says Elijah."

I found the scripture and grabbed up the Bible. As I looked it up, Jake reminded me that if I had read the Gospels first I would have known about it. I read the scripture aloud. We both looked at each other and shook our heads. It was so clear that we are reincarnated.

Jake started to talk about the TV preachers' teachings as I read on. I went back to the chapter and right off found something that blew me away. *"And verily I say unto you, that there be some of them that stand here, which shall not taste of death, till they have seen the kingdom of God come with power."*

I couldn't believe it. This was more proof! Yeshua told his apostles, who are all dead, that we reincarnate or resurrect before we die. I busted out and said, "Check this out, Jake. This scripture gives us irrefutable proof of reincarnation and the resurrection being before death, an individual event."

"Where?" He asked skeptically.

"In Mark, at the beginning of the chapter about Elijah."

I read the scripture to him and nothing happened. He was playing it safe. "Well," I said. "Did you get it? I don't know how you couldn't," I added mockingly.

"Well, who says I didn't get it?" He said indignantly. "We just might differ in opinions here."

"There's no room for opinions here. This is what it says." Then I repeated the key quote; there would be some of you standing, which shall not taste of death, till you see the Lord coming in all his power.

"The end hasn't happened yet, has it?"

"No," he said, "not that I know of."

"Well, then wouldn't these guys be reincarnating? He said that we all will see it."

"Well, you see, my lad, you have in fact jumped the gun. Although, you do have a good point. I do think the scripture confirms my theory, of attaining the resurrection before we die. When we do, we overcome the second death. We're dead now."

I sat there for a second as I didn't want to stick my big foot in my mouth. I was good at that, and Jake relished the opportunity to embarrass me. "I see your point, man. That's exactly what that scripture says. Wow, dude, I can't believe this. This also proves that it doesn't happen at once. We all have a last day, our own death. Wait a minute, I just said that."

"Yeah," he said, giving me another Mr. Impressed look. Then he said, "This certainly implies it is an individual thing and not a worldwide apocalyptic event. You said science proves this Earth was born and it will get old and die. It has its last day and that would be ours too!"

"Exactly," I hollered.

"Well, you'll never get Christianity to buy that. Not with Revelations."

"I don't care about Christianity," I said angrily. "Just the facts." I looked up the word 'death' in the concordance to try and find more scriptures. "Wow," I said in astonishment. "I can't believe this. It's amazing how you comprehend the Bible, when you have the knowledge that we were spirits first."

"Yeah, I know. See, man," he said condescendingly. "You should have started reading the Gospels first. It's important to study the teachings of Yeshua and what's written in red."

"I know already, okay dude? I just figured, since we made the mistake in the beginning I would start with the beginning. Oh, that reminds me, here's your concordance. I had yours out at the house to look up 'commandments.' I wanted to read about Yeshua delivering us from them and how he explained that to the preachers."

"Why?" Jake asked.

"Well, you know how I used to think that we are judged according to the Ten Commandments?"

"Yes, then I told you Yeshua said we're judged already."

"But why don't the Jehovah's Witnesses acknowledge that? And that you have to be born again, of the spirit."

"Well, they just call that believing, getting baptized, and living right. I guess, like all the others!"

He started to rail against the "living right" thing. Then he began saying it's easy to see that the Ten Commandments were just given to us for law and order. That we were uncivilized. And since we reincarnate, it was more important to establish order so we could increase in population and knowledge. "To Hell with knowledge. Just survive." I added with contempt.

"The commandments must've overshadowed the fact that we shouldn't be here in the first place," he said defiantly. "You're right," I agreed. "I found out the commandments weren't even introduced until Exodus. And they couldn't sell mystery. It isn't good entertainment. It's a hard solitary thing."

"So?" He said.

"Dude," I said in disbelief. "There were thousands of people, if not millions, by that time. The only Commandment was the Tree of Life. Weren't they judged too, though, according to the Judeo-Christian story?"

"Huh," he said, surprised-looking. "The Tree of Life was the only commandment."

"You know, I think that the angels were creating man up to this point slowly. Yeshua becomes man because he has to save the third that can't save themselves. Whether it's because they're killing themselves off or they lack the knowledge of how, I don't know. But it's obvious, the scripture of the Tree of Life is what we must do."

"Do you believe there was an Adam and Eve?" Jake asked.

"No, I'm not sure I do. Even you said it was a parable."

"Yeah Mike, but it is a true story, according to the Jews, a well-documented and proven Jewish history."

"Well then, why don't we have any books written by Adam?"

"Mike, do you think they came into this world with paper factories?"

"Well, Adam was perfect, wasn't he? And he lived long enough too!"

"Mike, even Moses, who was far from Adam, only wrote five books. At least I think he did. Scribes usually did the writing though. Most of the books were passed down through tales and folklore and written hundreds and even thousands of years later by a follower," Jake added firmly.

"I know that, pea-brain!" I barked back. "Anyway," I said excitedly. "Let's look up the Tree of Life and see what it means. That's what I've been wanting to do ever since I thought about this. I was just saying that to Mary. It doesn't make sense that they actually preach this literally and remember, this was our first commandment for a long time."

"Really," Jake said. "Just look up "tree," though. That is what we ate from."

I looked up 'tree' and was totally blown away. "You're not going to believe this," I said. "Jake, it has two meanings, just like 'mystery'. And guess what they are."

"Well, one is tree, like an apple tree, and the other is dimensions or worlds, right?"

"Well, check this out." Man, I was shaking with shock and excitement. "It says to make oneself firm and close the eyes."

"Wow," Jake said, completely awestruck. "Yeshua said that our eyes had been closed. We closed our eyes when we opened our eyes to this world. We must've just closed our eyes in the beginning. Now if we could just close our eyes to this world we could become conscious to that world."

"Yeah, man, can you get over that?" I said, just as overwhelmed. I agreed with him, but had totally been blown away by a different perception of this definition. Although it was along the same line as Jake's. I saw it as two definitions that describe the Sign of Jonas to a tee, which I think was the way to be born again. Now, it and the mystery together became the Shroud! I told him my point of view.

"How do you figure?" Jake asked skeptically.

"If you look at the Shroud, it is a perfect picture of these definitions," I said. "Both, not one, as if they fulfill each other just like the name." I said in complete amazement.

"Well, I don't know about that," he said, challenging my judgement.

"What do you mean, you don't know about that?" I snapped back.

"What is he doing?"

"He's dead," Jake replied.

"Yeshua's dead, huh?"

"Well no, but you know what I mean, he is there on the Shroud." Jake then started saying that we need to mimic death to be born again.

"Jake," I said, shaking my head. "Don't you see the whole point in the Sign of Jonas?"

"Yeah, he took a picture of himself."

"Well, maybe to you. But I see it as a picture of the way to be born again, as well as a picture to prove what the whole Bible was written for. To prove that we are spirit angels and can resurrect ourselves by doing mystery or eating the Tree of Life. You know, spontaneously combust."

"Oh no," he groaned. "You can't just speculate those things."

"I can too," I said brashly. "I can prove it."

"How?"

"He resurrected, didn't he? We got his picture to prove it. That's what made the imprint, and that's the religious rite. It was his message and it can't be changed. Even you say that we must resurrect before we die."

"Yeah, but we don't disappear."

"Enoch and Elijah did, didn't they?"

"Well . . . ."

"Well, nothing. Isn't that what Yeshua and this whole story is all about, resurrection? Invisible life. We've got the mystery of spontaneous human combustion. Those definitions could not singularly describe the only sign that he gave us, but they do together. Just like the name," I said. "And I think that the whole message of the Bible is to tell us we're male and female, two things, invisible and visible. The Bible is written in two parts. And even in Genesis where we ate from the tree,

God calls himself 'us' in saying, 'Look, he's become as one of us to know good and evil'. And God is just a voice then. We're two things, one of us, angel and man."

"Well, I think that the Sign of Jonas was just a picture to prove his existence. However, I can see where the mystery and the Tree of Life represent basically the same thing, and it's obviously transcendental meditation. Huh, funny," he said. "They call Eastern Mysticism, T.M. Yeshua was teaching T.M., the mystery."

"You know, not to change the subject, but I'm going to keep checking out the commandment thing. Yeshua only quotes five, not ten. I think the angels might've created man five times." Little did I know, I would discover the exact number of races; it was five.

"Man," he said, as if disgusted by my theorizing, "it's obvious that they were just implemented to keep mankind from killing themselves off." He started with some Satan crap, like Christianity. "Well, I really don't believe in a Satan, but I don't believe in miracles either, at least not the Hollywood kind anyway. You better quit watching that TV Christianity crap."

"Mike, you know the Bible refers to the leader of the third. If there is a good spirit there has to be a bad spirit."

"Yeah, mankind. And we left our first estate for a strange flesh here, remember?"

"Yes, but I think there is a devil or at least a leader of the one-third, and he is more powerful than the others. He's too smart to trap himself in flesh, and yet he can't return to Heaven. Why do you think the church still reads this story literally? They must be possessed. Why else wouldn't they see this?"

"Probably the same reason you do. You're possessed," I said laughing. "You're just like Christianity. They all say the devil works through religion. Besides, your devil theory sounds just like your god theory. The oldest and most powerful. Come on!"

"Man, you're sick, aren't you?" He said, in his own defense.

"That's the cruel Christian story, Jake. It isn't fair to give us life and let this devil run around screwing with us. God is capable of anything, right? I mean, it's bad enough that we have to experience death, sickness, and all the other miseries of life, without having a devil thrown into the mix. Besides, Yeshua told the apostles not to call him good. Was he evil? Only one is good, those in Heaven."

We arrived at our job site and quickly knocked it out. Jake had made real good money on this job and had things going his way.

When we returned back to the house, Misty met us at the mailbox where she surprised Jake with a check. Jake remarked how all this good fortune must be a result of the mystery. He quoted the scripture where we would be rewarded openly.

I just laughed and said, "Come out of there, demon. One minute you believe in miracles, the next you don't. And a minute ago, Satan, too. You better help him, Misty. He's falling back into the grips of Christianity."

"What?" She said, not really getting it.

Misty looked puzzled. I told her Jake's theory. "Jake thinks that if you do the mystery all things will be added, right Jake?"

Jake broke in. "Nothing, Misty," he said, going toward her and getting the check.

"Watch out! He's got a demon inside of him," I said to Misty. I laughed and headed toward the car. I had to get home if I wanted to save marriage. I stopped and got the Shroud book. I said, "Please make sure you read Enoch," then I hurried on to the car.

"All right, Satan," he said. "Give me my money."

Boy, this learning was not only time-consuming, it was expensive. "You need help," I told him as I jumped in my car and started pulling out of the driveway. I threw the money at him.

He was really talking two stories. I was totally convinced that there was no Devil. And it was Jake who helped me. Yet, he did think there was a leader of the angels. It was so obvious to me that the quote by Yeshua. "In the beginning he made them male and female" was not only us, but was also an explanation of our fall from spiritual to flesh. Maybe we downloaded our memories into these bodies. I don't know! But we now can clone man and the president has made that illegal. Man is evil here just like in Heaven!

It was all so ironic. It explains why the traditions of the Jews and Christians are the way they are. They preach a literal story from the Bible with exact lifestyles; and all of it named after words in the Bible. It was so obvious that most of our knowledge comes from the Bible, if not all of it, all six thousand years of it. That explains the reason their God is a man. Man has ruled for that long, up to the present day. His-story, I just chuckled to myself. Christianity taught the marriage scriptures literally, but I thought to myself intuitively that we are two things, one flesh, male and female. What God has joined together, let no man put asunder. I laughed again. The angels sure must've been ugly.

I pulled into our drive as the dogs came running toward me. They made their way over the creek on our swinging bridge. It was too far into the winter to get their feet wet. Boy aren't we lucky to be human. I found Angel in a fairly good mood, so I didn't bring up the discovery of the tree's definition, but I sure was anxious to tell Mary about it.

As the evening wore on, I managed to catch Mary alone. Angel had taken Little Jake and our neighbors to the movie rental store. I told Mary about the definition of the tree and then wrote all four definitions down. I got the Shroud off the wall for her to see. She was as blown away as I was. I told her about Jake not being able to see this either, and she just laughed.

"He just thinks it's a picture to prove his existence."

"How could he not see this?"

"You've got me. These definitions describe the Shroud, his message exactly," I remarked with complete confidence.

"They really do," she agreed.

"I don't know about Jake, though," I said quickly to Mary. "He believes there really is a Satan, the leader of the one-third. And when we got home he had a rebate check in his mailbox. The car dealer had accidently sent it to him, instead of putting it on the car. He implied that spiritual intervention had caused this to happen, along with all the good business he was getting lately. I quickly nipped both ideas in the bud, though. That's the Christian mentality. God breaks the law to help a rich man."

Mary just smiled and didn't say anything. I knew she didn't like to hear this. "My God has to be fair, Mary," I said bluntly. "Fair is a choice between two things, right and wrong, and if we have to make the right choice, shouldn't God? Wow, isn't that just coincidental, the story of us, who we are? We're also two things, male and female, good or bad, spirit and flesh. The very concept of fairness requires two things to make a choice possible. You can't have one without the other. I think that is karma, isn't it? You reap what you sow? Isn't that a Buddhist belief? Hell, that's Yeshua's quote." I was rambling again. My mind was racing. I thought about the Yin and Yang and how they resembled sperm in an egg. And black and white. "Wow! It is a picture of the angels, creation of man. Their DNA and prehistoric man's DNA, in a cell or an egg."

"I think it is," she said in agreement. She got my attention. Mary was only a high school graduate, but she had a wide arsenal of knowledge. She watched a lot of TV, and her husband had debated her at every turn. She maintains he was pretty damn smart, especially scientifically-speaking. I asked her about her dad, Hank, and she said he believed in God, but didn't do anything about it.

"He was Agnostic, huh?" I said it without thinking.

"What's that?" She asked.

"That means they believe, but don't do anything about it," I said. We both broke into laughter at the same time.

"That was simple enough, wasn't it," she said.

She suddenly asked. "Do you think I'm Agnostic?"

"Aren't we all? I know I am! I'm not doing the mystery yet. If we aren't meditating as much as we can, wouldn't we be? Or going to church in your case. I mean, that's what Christians do, right?"

"What?"

I didn't want to offend her so I changed the subject.

"Where is Heaven?" I asked her. She immediately remembered that I had asked her the very same question not too long ago. "Well?" I prompted, noticing her smirk.

"You said the other day, it's within."

"No, I didn't say it. The apostle Luke said it, remember? Then, are we all Agnostic or what?"

She just shrugged. "Yes, okay." She said, looking somewhat shocked.

"Think about this, Mary. Isn't it mind-blowing that the Bible was written in two parts? As if it was to be evidence itself of God, it is something invisible that we can't prove, tangibly-speaking. Like the voice, I am."

"What's tangible?"

"I like that about you; you ask questions. It makes it easier for me to ask you things, when I don't know what a word is. And we know life's a word game."

"Really," she laughed.

"Why don't they have only one definition for every word or just one word? Life's a synonym game," I said with great frustration. "It would not only simplify things, but people wouldn't have superiority over one another in conversation, which is intimidating. That's why we do, I guess."

"Damn right it can," she said. "I certainly agree with you. What the Hell is 'tangible' anyway? Here comes Angel," I said nervously. "It's the opposite of intangible," I said, getting up. "It's an accounting term, but you can apply it to anything. It's something measurable immediately: cash versus accounts/receivable, food versus sunshine, visible vs. invisible."

"I got you," she said.

I got up and went into the bedroom as Angel came in. I put on my slippers and hurried to help get in the groceries. After putting away the groceries, Angel and Little Jake headed straight for the tub. They loved to soak together in a tub full of bubbles. I smiled to myself. I was so happy. I wish I could've frozen time.

As I went into the bedroom to read, I noticed Mary getting ready to go out. I had to tell her one more thing before I went to bed. I thought I saw her cringe as I approached her. I didn't want to annoy her, but I did want to ask her what her interpretation of the Prodigal Son parable was. I really wanted to tell her that Jake said it is obviously a parable of the fallen angels. They are both set up in thirds. "What do you get out of the Prodigal Son parable, Mary?"

"The one where one of the three sons goes and parties his inheritance away? You trying to be funny?" She asked me suspiciously.

"No, I'm trying to make a point to help you see the possibility of our theory. That maybe, we're the third of the angels which left their estate for a strange flesh and not this creation story. The third factor is sure a coincidence. What is your understanding of the parable?"

"Well, that God will forgive you if you ask."

"Wow, I said that's what Christianity's view is, and it doesn't really describe the parable at all. Just come back to church. No wonder it's their view. They own the church! It contradicts Yeshua's teaching that it is a hard thing to do and few will be chosen. But if we were taught that we are the angels which left their first estate, the one-third, then we could see this is a parable of us. It makes perfect sense, just like the Adam and Eve parable representing who we are, two things, and our fall." Her expression changed to that of disbelief. I knew how she felt. I was just as amazed to see the connection. "I'm telling you that reading the Bible with this knowledge makes sense and seems easily proven by the parables within the Bible."

Then I said boldly, "Believe me, the best example of the marriage, or being born again, is Yeshua's statement that I quoted earlier. We were made male and female in the beginning, angel/man. Angels could do anything. So they immediately made man. The big question is, what do the angels look like? I guess we must have to be born again of the spirit to know." *(Finding ancient evidence changed my thinking . . . evidence.)*

She nodded her head in agreement and then asked me to help put a necklace on. I stepped over and fastened the necklace and whispered. "Don't worry about going out and partying. Forget those Ten Commandments. We're delivered from them, remember? Just love everyone. And eventually do mystery. I've got to. We all do. We shouldn't be here. We are just too retarded by flesh to believe it, or we're too scared to prove it. If you're a Christian, you're scared. Scared, because Satan will get you if you worship in spirit."

"Why, Satan isn't tangible," she said mockingly. She just laughed.

We hugged and I whispered in her ear. "You're scared, like me, huh? I'm scared to do the mystery."

"No, I'm not," she said quickly, but I could tell that she was bothered.

"You're scared too, aren't you?"

"I don't know," she said. "I guess I am a little." She hesitated then suddenly asked me, "Do you really think I am Agnostic?"

"We're all Agnostic," I replied.

"But I do believe that God gives to those who ask. I guess I really want to believe that I am saved. I don't want to die." She said with tears in her eyes.

"Mary," I said apologetically, reaching and hugging her. "None of us do. That's what I'm telling you. First of all, we are dead now. Our body dies, but we, the spirit, keep going, reincarnating. Hell and death are here. It is a place where there's wailing and gnashing of teeth. Us!" Then I chopped my teeth. "No other culture believes death is the end. That's a Christianity thing. If we don't get it we are cast into the Lake of Fire, right? What's the Lake of Fire?"

"The body," she said smiling.

"Doesn't that make sense?" I asked. "Doesn't that make God fair? Have you ever asked yourself why God can't just show himself?" I asked.

"Or herself?" She said mockingly. Yeah really. Why can't people take the logical choice to answer that.

"Well," I laughed, "everybody is entitled to a Christianity slip. After all, we do live in a Christian country. And we're brainwashed, believe me, especially me."

She quickly agreed, laughing. As she turned to leave I said, "Remember, don't worry about those Ten Commandments."

Mary just smiled. "Well, if we don't die, what the Hell!" I laughed. As she left, I wondered if she ever really thought about that. The Hell life experiences on Earth.

Angel was getting out of the bath with Little Jake. So, I figured I had better head to the living room. I wanted to end on a good note, and so far, Angel wasn't complaining.

We played all evening with Little Jake. Mary and Shane were gone. They both had dates. We were in for a rare treat: being alone.

I was right in the middle of my busy Christmas season, and I didn't have much free time left. I would be headed back to the log yard to carve soon. The log yard was located on the main street of a little town in Tennessee. It was a small town of about ten thousand people and was what we called home now. Fortunately, the yard was only a half-mile from the courthouse square and only a few miles from the house. Ironically, I had gotten lucky and landed a big order from a boot company. I didn't have to leave the shade tree in my front yard all winter to get orders. But knowing that the orders would eventually end, I figured I had better take advantage of the moment and continue to carve at the log yard. Christmas, thank goodness! It was tough being a starving artist. But this year we weren't starving. I would've thought the Acme order was divine intervention, but that kind of stuff I left to Jake.

I read the Bible a little bit, when I got into bed. Then the phone rang. Angel answered and grumbled, "Oh no," as she brought the phone to me.

I just laughed weakly. "Baby, I'll get right off, I promise." It was Jake.

"What are you laughing about?"

"Well, don't you know?"

"Yeah, yeah," he said, knowing all too well. It was also starting to annoy Misty. I knew that.

"Well, when you called I just finished reading the Bible and was going to bed."

"Oh," he said. "That's bad, huh."

"Yeah, that's bad."

"Yeah, Misty's been complaining about me, too."

"Hell, I can understand that," I said quickly. "You watch that crap on TV."

"Hey, if you watched it," he snapped back, "maybe you could learn something."

"What?" I asked. "Pride?"

"I guess you're right, and they love the name Jesus more than anything," he said, disgustedly. "He does at least say Yeshua, though."

"Are you still torturing people about the name?"

"What do you mean, torture? It's the truth," he said demandingly.

"I know, I know. But you know what I mean. You do get people pissed off about it."

"I can't help that," he said. "It's the only name you can be saved by. It's not my fault."

"Really," I agreed, laughing. "I'm glad you called. I was just talking with Mary about the Prodigal Son parable. She was blown away."

"Did you tell her I told you?" He replied quickly!

"Yes, oh Wise One. I did!"

"Come out now, Satan. She got the connection, huh?" He asked.

"I said she was blown away, didn't I?"

"I don't see how anybody couldn't be," he said. "The one-third thing is just too coincidental."

"I also told her about the definition of the tree and how I think it has a connection to the definition of the mystery. They both perfectly describe the Shroud. I told her that I think is a picture of the way to be born again, meditation, the Sign of Jonas."

"Mystery," he added, coldly.

I didn't respond.

"Well—"

"Oh, don't worry, I told her mystery."

"I—" he started.

I broke in again. "I know you think that he just took a picture of himself; I told her that as well. Oh yeah, anyway dude, I followed up with the next scripture, male and female, one flesh, and how it was another parable of 'In the beginning there was the Heavens and the Earth,' One thing."

"Would you give me a chance to talk?"

"Yeah, go ahead."

"I think we need to stick to the facts, don't you Mike? Don't you think there has been enough theorizing? I mean, we do have hundreds of theories to choose from already. What makes yours any different?"

"Because mine makes sense. Mine is based on physical evidence. It proves spontaneous human combustion."

"Oh no, you didn't tell Mary you thought Yeshua spontaneously combusted, did you?"

"Well, didn't he?"

"Mike."

"Well, did he or didn't he?" I asked again.

"Well, that's your opinion."

"What?" I asked. "Now you don't believe in the Shroud?"

"I didn't say that," he said quickly.

"Well, what made that imprint then?"

"Well, I guess you could be right about that," he said meekly.

"Hell yes, I'm right. It's proven, isn't it? And to doubt the authenticity of the Shroud is ludicrous. If it was a fake it was a failure. It wasn't sold to anyone as we know. Wouldn't the motive to fake it, have been money?" *(I wasn't "aware" of how wrong I could be.)*

"That makes sense," he said nodding his head in agreement.

"Well, it didn't, except for the church and they don't validate it. And you can't deny that it is a picture of the way to be born again. After all, the resurrection is what made it. And we have to be born again to achieve the resurrection, don't we?"

"Well yes, but you don't think we'll disappear, do you? Come on."

"Enoch and Elijah did, didn't they?" I asked coldly.

"Well, yes."

"God's invisible, right? Yeshua said, 'God was a spirit.'"

"God's not invisible, Mike."

"It isn't, huh? Show me then," I said, thinking back to the other day when he put me in this similar situation.

"You got me." He finally spoke after several seconds.

"You see, Jake, I think that Yeshua was trying to tell us that we are all gods, but we just don't know what God is. It's spirit, us, trapped by this body mass. Mass creates gravity. Heaven and Earth."

"Are you saying that you're God?" He asked mockingly. "Because I'm not saying that I'm God."

"Look it up! He says plainly, 'You are Gods'!" I continued with intensity.

"Yeshua said we all are. I'm saying God is invisible within each of us. A spirit body that is male. And when we make this marriage and become born again, we can resurrect ourselves."

"An O.B.E." Jake just grunted in contempt. I would soon read this very statement in Revelations, "Come up out of her my people."

"So are you saying we can't make ourselves disappear, Jake?"

"I don't know, Mike," he said flatly. "I know nothing."

"Oh believe me, I know you don't. Even though Enoch and Elijah disappeared! And Yeshua said the only sign he would give us was the Sign of Jonas. Then he disappeared, and left us a picture that looks like a spirit. But don't worry, Jake, I know you think that's ridiculous."

"Well, are you through now?"

"Yes, you can talk now, but don't speculate a thing! Just the facts, remember," I said sternly, giving him a good dose of his own medicine.

"Mike, all that we know right now is the mystery and the name. Remember, we know nothing, or at least, I don't. So we need to always be in a learning mode instead of a teaching one. We both know there is but one teacher."

I just shut my mouth. How easy it was to sound self-righteous when talking religion. "I know," I said, "but it all makes sense to me. We do have the mystery of spontaneous human combustion. Those pictures in the book don't look fake to me. And their feet are the only thing left. It's as if, this is another piece of evidence to help convince us who we are, spirits. Something that doesn't need feet, spirits."

Jake laughed out loud, but with a hint of doubt in his voice.

"What," I jumped and asked. "Are you telling me that you don't see those feet in every photograph? The authors already acknowledge this phenomenon, but don't know why it occurs. At least, not until now," I added.

Jake just laughed. "Mike, do you think that you have done what most astute minds of the world haven't done?"

"Well, I am pretty convinced by the evidence."

"Evidence!" Jake piped up sarcastically. "If you think Christianity will ever buy this, you've got another thing coming. I haven't been able to get one to even care about his name. And it's easily provable. It just blows me away," he remarked appallingly. "If you ordered a tombstone for your mom or dad and they changed the name, would you take it? Hell no! But they don't care about Yeshua's name, the only name they can be saved by. I mean, he is our savior. Isn't he?"

"Yeah, I know what you mean. I can't wait to see if Mom or Dad check to see if the name's been changed. I gave them enough information to doubt the reliability of the Jehovah's Witnesses translation. And I gave them our theory."

"Whose theory?"

"Okay, your theory, but I combined our findings and the definitions of mystery, the tree, and the name together on the Shroud. They'll get the picture with my scriptures describing Christianity and Judaism and their outward traditions of church to a tee in 'Matthew 23'." I knew he would get a kick out of the rhyme, using his song.

"Well, we'll see. Tradition usually wins."

"Tradition?"

"Yeah, that's what Yeshua's parable of the burning house is about. There will be some that just don't desire to come out, to search elsewhere."

"Wow," I said suddenly. "Can you believe that? The parable is about us, in our house, this body, the Lake of Fire." Then I couldn't help but to think about spontaneous human combustion. "Why couldn't people see the connection? Look at the parables in the Bible. There is a sacrifice story of burning flesh. It was all too coincidental. And we are one-hundred degrees."

"Huh," he remarked musingly.

"I tell you, Jake," I went on before he could mock my theory. "I honestly think that all the words in the Bible are preached literally. Can you believe that people really believe this cruel crap? This makes so much sense! We are already cast out and the Lake of Fire is the body. This body is just like an Earth. We are reincarnated! That's fair. We reap what we sow. Memory is the system of justice. One that doesn't judge us but we judge ourselves. If we don't get it, we just keep trying. We never stop existing. But some lives are worse than dying. That's the cold hard reality of life."

"You can't read the Bible without the concordance," he said. "That's obvious with what the Jehovah's Witnesses did to the mystery."

"I know," I replied angrily. "I just hope others can see it, too."

"They would if they did the mystery. When are you going to do the mystery, Mike?" He asked bluntly.

"I'm going to," I told him, "but for awhile I'll be working hard to finish up Christmas season. We need all the money we can get."

"I know what you mean," he replied dreadfully. He was a working class stiff like I was. We both needed all we could get and then some. He started to dog me again, anyway.

"I better sign off, dude. I just don't want to end a good day with Angel, on a bad note. Besides, you know how she feels."

"Right," he said. "I need to pay a little more attention to my own wife."

Then I heard Misty in the background: "That's right, you do!"

"I'll see you," I said quickly and hung up.

I had hung up just in the nick of time, but Angel caught me putting the books away. I had the concordance out with the Bible. "Don't worry," I said as she came through the door. "I was just putting them away."

"Oh, don't worry," she replied back. "I'm getting used to them. You've only been reading the Bible for a year now, every night."

"I know, and I really didn't understand a thing until now, or at least until just recently." I felt that it might be a good time to share some stuff with her. She really didn't seem too mad at the moment. "The concordance proves that the Bible is being taught wrong. You can't read the Bible without it, and make head or tails of it. Tree doesn't mean tree, and mystery doesn't mean secret; they both mean transcendental meditation."

"What?" She asked completely dumbstruck, innocent of their meanings.

I asked her if she minded if I showed her in the concordance. That way she would be able to check it for herself. She said she didn't mind. I got so excited. As I got the concordance, I explained. "Both definitions nail the Shroud's description. It was so unbelievable." Then I told her that Jake didn't quite see it that way. He saw it as a picture of Yeshua, as physical proof of God. I thought it was how you do the mystery. Mimic death.

"And he's right. It is his picture. Although, I think I see something even more startling. The tree's definition has; close the eyes and make oneself firm. Then the mystery has the other two, shut the mouth and initiate oneself into a religious rite."

"What do you think?" I asked as I finished. I had given her the concordance and had written down the four definitions: Make firm, shut eyes, shut mouth, initiate oneself into a religious rite. "Doesn't the Shroud fit the description exactly of these definitions? And we know that Yeshua's message was being born again of the spirit."

"Wow," she said. "They really do."

"Isn't that overwhelming?" I said, totally convinced. "Check this out." I got the book about spontaneous human combustion and showed her the photographs. "Notice anything common about all the victims?"

"They're gone," she said, "except for some ashes."

"What about the feet, they're not completely gone," I added.

She agreed that they were there, but didn't know what I was getting at.

"We don't need them; we're angels." She looked amazed. "I know," I told her. "It's unbelievable." Then I pointed to the Shroud and said, "That's the most amazing thing of all. We finally have proof that it could have happened. And in my opinion, it did happen. It supports the story of Enoch, Elijah, and the resurrection. It gives it credibility, in my book. Especially with the evidence of spontaneous human combustion, not to mention the Bible itself. Which is the testimony of things unseen, spirit. Besides, if the Shroud is a fake, it was a complete failure for the perpetrator. The entire religious community, even the ones who possess it, deny its authenticity." I stopped suddenly.

I remembered how I had asked Jake if the book had any history of the Shroud being sold. I hadn't completely read the book yet. I kind of drifted into a trance, remembering that occasion.

"You haven't read the book yet, have you?" He had chimed with great pleasure.

"Well, I—"

"Don't tell me. I know, you just read some of it."

"That's right, but I plan on reading it all. I need to finish all the Gospels first."

"Just concentrate on John," he said sternly like a father. He relished that moment.

Angel caught me wandering off about Jake, and I quickly came around. I just finished my point and started putting the books away. She asked me several times what I was thinking, but I didn't hear her. Anyway I knew the answer would make way for trouble, so I didn't say.

I couldn't stop thinking about all the new information I had discovered. Could it be possible that we really resurrect ourselves through the mystery? Were we supposed to sacrifice ourselves through mystery? It seemed so obvious that we started out that way, with the flesh sacrifice and all. But religion gave way to an easier, much more saleable way. Religion! Religion is entertainment.

Angel had turned on the TV and at the same time, Little Jake hollered. As soon as she went out of the room, I started reading the spontaneous human combustion book. I had remembered seeing a chapter called The Kundalini Fire and also The Fire Within. How could I have missed this connection? Then I realized how. I had been reading the *Mystery of the Ages*, the Shroud book, the Bible, *Life* magazine, the Jehovah's Witnesses Bible and concordance, and a little of the Dead Sea Scrolls. So I guess it was easy to see how, after all.

I had read both chapters and was stunned. They confirmed my theory! One chapter even cited an experiment, in which the subject burned her hand imprint into the table at the concise point she nodded off. This was called twilight sleep. My buddy Jake had mentioned that to me. The subject was meditating.

I discovered an amazing fact. The Hindus meditate to activate this force within us to give us transcendent power. Their whole belief system was based on this, spirit. We should learn who we are, spirit. They live this life, for the next life, and so on. Reincarnation. But, the ultimate goal is nirvana, resurrection.

This was a lot like Jake's description of Buddhism, in the *Life* magazine, and ironically, a lot like Yeshua's. He makes it clear that this world is evil. He even says he is not of this world. Wow, I thought. If people would just examine all the cultures, they could see an overwhelming common theme. This is Hell. The spirit world is the superior world, Heaven. Universe is a better word. The spirit manifests itself as electrical energy, life. Even fire, like with Moses and the Burning Bush. The Egyptians, Indians, Mayans, and God knows who else, see the sun as god. And in fact, I remember reading the same thing in the Bible last year. I read not once but several times where God is a consuming fire. The most obvious place is in our own temperature. A fire within, I thought as I started to put the book up. Angel was headed this way. She finally got Little Jake in bed, and it was getting late, somewhere around two o'clock. I didn't want to cause a stir, so I kept this new information to myself. But I couldn't help thinking about Jake's response. I knew that he hadn't read all of this yet, and I could get him back. It was almost a challenge to see who was going to be first in discovering more evidence.

It was obvious that Christianity was not started by Yeshua. It was started by the world's ruling power at the time, Rome. All roads lead to Rome. Might makes right even to this day, I laughed to myself. The U.S. government being labeled a democracy is a prime example of might makes right. We are a democracy founded by white Christian men. First, this country wasn't found; it was taken. The very word democracy means "people rule," but only the men did, not women. They couldn't vote! Blacks were owned and Indians had a bounty on them. The Christian religion and the Bible was woven into our Constitution and throughout our entire governmental structure. Schools had the Pledge of Allegiance and the courthouses had their oaths sworn on the Bible. This cover-up was deeply intrenched.

We have the best example of might makes right, with the Columbus holiday. Yeshua addresses these Christians with a scripture from Matthew 23: "How can you say you had no part in the blood of prophets, when you honor your fathers who did kill such prophets; therefore you yourselves are partakers of the blood of the prophets." He said it best. How can any American honor the memory of Christopher Columbus, the leader of the holocaust on the American Indians, and all in the name of Christ? Can't they see it! There's enough monuments and other things named after him. That's what I was going to do from now on. I decided it. I was going to explain the history of Christianity. It's very easy to prove the cruel, inhumane, criminal history. I was determined to scrutinize it, with every fiber of my intellect. I had been persecuted by it. We all have in one way or another. I even let myself become brainwashed, to the point of sacrificing my life. For what? A scam. What had I been thinking? How could I have done this? More than that, I had even thought about this for my children, without examining all religions. How could billions of people do this? Easy I thought. I had done it. We all fell prey to it, the Religion Cover-up. Tradition!

I just lay there and fumed at myself, and then it dawned on me: I was just brainwashed like everyone else. It was the very thing Yeshua preached against, tradition. It was Matthew 23. Tradition had ruled because of our state in evolution, primitive. We are still a might-makes-right world, but not for long. I was determined to study every culture and science. I was convinced of the truth of Yeshua. Our oldest recorded history lies in the Hebrew story. And we do measure time after him. I finally crashed and went to bed trying to do the mystery. I remembered Jake's instruction, after he insinuated that I was scared. He said, if I couldn't do it the grown-up way, the way a real man does it who isn't scared of ghosts, then I could do it at night. Just mimic death. Don't think when you lie down to go to bed. Say the Lord's Prayer, I laughed to myself, the only one we're supposed to pray. Then just do it, Nike. He said to use Yeshua's name as a mantra to stop my inner voice (*conscious thought*), but to eventually let that go and don't think. So I did. I was finally trying it.

I remember hearing a tone in my head like the Emergency Broadcast Signal but more gentle and steady. That was a mystery to me, itself. I honed in on it, to stop thinking. It was hard to do, after finding out all I had found out. But I could do it, if I listened. I did do it, and I couldn't wait to tell Jake about it. I had to admit that I was somewhat afraid of spiritual things, but now I was also excited. I was actually anxious to make a connection. Now I knew why we counted sheep and the rosary beads.

The next day came and went just like the next three months, cold, hard, and fast-paced. Jake and I were staying on the phone with each other several times a day looking up words in our concordance. Both of us were overwhelmed by the spirit meanings. It was plain to see Christians preferred a physical meaning to everything. It perverted the truth.

I had told Jake my theory again about the feet in the spontaneous human combustion book, and he just laughed. He also laughed about my theory of our disappearing when we resurrect, but I told him Elijah and Enoch did it. Jake laughed a lot. That was good because I was getting more depressed.

We had looked up a lot of words in the last several months, and I was passing on everything to Mary and Angel as I discovered it. I was sure getting some resentment toward our findings, from everyone that I shared them with. However, Mary was glad to know living according to the Ten Commandments didn't have any bearing on going to

Heaven, at least for drunkenness, fornication, you know, the enjoyable ones. She was a little bit confused though, as was I.

Jake and I purchased *The Other Bible. The Other Bible*! What a joke! Huh? Nobody knew about it and could care less. Except Mary and she didn't read! I did! I was blown away. We began to research constantly.

Jake had gotten so excited about the closing of the eyes, being the definition of tree. He had often commented on Yeshua saying that our eyes have been closed. He quoted "lest we be converted and become as humble as a little child, we would in no wise enter the kingdom of Heaven". A little child doesn't think. We even discovered their brain wave length was Delta, death. I looked closely to find the scripture and discovered it just before the Sign of Jonas in Matthew 16:4. It was amazing how it now made sense. I continued reading, unable to put the Bible down. I discovered the five commandments were proof that the seven-day creation in the beginning of Genesis is a parable of the fall and is ongoing today, evolution. The sixth day is where man had been made, by nature from nothing! The race of the immaculate conception. The sixth day, huh. Why the sixth? We have a sixth sense. This was all so weird. It took him six days to make man and three days to resurrect. Why? I'm the sixth child born in my family. How bizarre. The immaculate conception sounded like alien abduction. *(They aren't here either.)*

We looked up "converted" and it meant reversal. Jake was blown away, because he had always liked a song called "Pride of Man." He said the guy was a heavy writer, almost as heavy as John Lennon. He quoted "Turn around go back down." He felt that babies came into this world in perfect mystery, but we steal it away by demanding their attention. His theories were founded in humility, knowing nothing, he always reminded me. Only children know humility. It's a dog-eat-dog world. We have to work hard to know it. Adults! Adulterers! Think about it, I told

Jake. Children don't know racism either. It seems so obvious Heaven is more a frame of mind, logic. Without knowledge of the world, ignorance is bliss, as they say. It was obvious that Yeshua was here to tell us and show us the mystery. The Ten Commandments are common sense, we all know that.

I had read on and found Yeshua referring to a Samaritan woman as a dog. It also implicated the true reference to bread and what it really means. This helped support my theory about the five commandments and words. The Jews had perverted the words, which had spiritual meanings and applied them to physical things in the world. The Jews consider only their race man. This was a perfect example. Yeshua's reference to bread was spiritual, not physical. I remember Jake laughing at my theory, but he was at least agreeing with some of my findings.

The scripture is in Matthew 15:26: "It is not meet to take the children's bread and cast it to the dogs." I thought this was so cruel literally, but then I realized that this proved to me, that the Jewish race was the only true man to them; all the rest were Gentiles, and she was a Samaritan. I discovered the definition of Gentile and found Samaria!

He had said that I would never prove this stuff to a Christian. I told him that I didn't care. I just wanted to prove it to myself, for my kids.

"It was obvious that bread was spiritual truths, not food. The woman had come to him, asking that he cast a devil out of her daughter." After I had pleaded my case, Jake was surprised. I told him that it made sense. "The words of the prophets and seers had been given physical meanings. I don't think that kill means kill. I couldn't accept killing as approved by God or done by God. Why make something out of love, only to kill it? Come on."

He had just laughed. I remembered how we reacted, when we looked up *kill* and found a scripture. Kill them "with the two-edged sword of my mouth." We both immediately looked at each other and said, "The tongue! Being talked to!" The story was taught literally or physically. I knew that Yeshua saw things spiritually. Even Peter's vision of the scroll only contained the first five days of creation, not man. He was told to kill and eat. The meaning of the dream was to talk to all five races of man.

Jake somewhat agreed with my findings, but he kept hammering about Yeshua's name change. "Yeah," he said, as if he finally saw my point. He remembered how hard it was teaching me about relativity and absolute truth. He admitted, it could possibly apply to him as well.

"Now you're getting it," I said. "Just like I finally did, huh?"

"I know," He said, braggingly. "And it's the perfect example of good and evil. There's nothing in this world good because we shouldn't be here in the first place. That's why Yeshua teaches this world and that world too. They're worlds, not things we do in these worlds." We even rediscovered he called all men evil and chastised the apostles for calling him good. Only the Father in Heaven was good. Who was the Father? That's the question! I started to target that question. My mind was working overtime!

I don't know how much good I did, but we continued to discuss theories with each other. He always reminded me that he knew nothing, and I usually thought I had it down pat. We were a great team. It was fun. It wasn't long before I was going to Ohio again.

We had found some amazing scriptures indicating that we are angels. Jake had found one while reading Paul and called me about it. It was in I Corinthians 6:3: "Know ye not that we shall be judging angels?" I looked up a Revelations scripture, and found: "The measuring of the walls of Heaven, the measurement of a man, that is of an angel." How much plainer can they get? This even showed that Heaven is within us literally; Jerusalem is the body of man, and it says we're angels. Jake and I were trying to figure out how the Bible could've ever been preached otherwise. But then we both knew, tradition. Christianity's bloody, cruel history was today's truth, tradition. I had a lot of evidence to show to Mom and Dad, everyone. However, I was not prepared for what was about to happen.

Christmas had come and gone without a hitch. Jake had made it up to Misty's parents and even exchanged a few gifts. Although, he was only doing it for Misty. Jake made it plain that Christmas had already been a traditional celebration of the Winter Solstice by the Greeks and Romans. It was celebrated long before Yeshua, and Jake really got pissed off about it. "They used Yeshua's fame to continue what Jeremiah preached against in the Old Testament. Jeremiah described it to a tee. Just look up 'tree.'" I did. I couldn't believe it. What a sad irony that was. It was so easy to look up. Yeshua called himself the truth. Don't they care? Their traditions mocked his teachings as well as his name.

But at least the Jehovah's Witness didn't acknowledge it, I thought. There I go again, thinking of myself as a Jehovah's Witness. What a spell, this traditional religious brainwashing was. Jake had said that it was good that the Jehovah's Witnesses didn't acknowledge celebrations of days, times, and events in this world because, that at least agreed with Yeshua. But I told him if they practiced one false thing, it blew it for me. They even preached something life threatening. Besides, they don't do mystery.

"Yeah," he said, "and they do love Jesus."

"Not to mention," I added quickly," what they did in changing the scripture in John 3:13 to say that 'no man would go to Heaven.' Did they just happen to overlook Enoch and Elijah? And they don't love Jesus; they love Jehovah the most. It's a chosen thing."

"Really," Jake replied.

"Besides, man, they absolutely preach a literal, cruel story. I remember asking Mom if she believed in or wanted a God that would order people killed. Of course, she didn't but her religion did. She really didn't know what to say. I could tell, she thought that was cruel, but since her religion preached it, she didn't know what to say. I told her this was a perfect example of how traditions became more important than logic. And that's what truth is, what it has to be. Love and logic are the same.

Before I left, I begged them to be just as skeptical of their own truth, as they were of mine. Mine had no ulterior motive of increasing congregation size or money. Besides, I was examining all literature and encouraged them to do the same.

They never would. I gave them all kinds of reasons not to trust what we have been taught by religion and country. But they won't look; tradition has won! There are so many lies, that we now have a real history, TV network. What a joke. Thank God for shows like it, the Learning Channel, Discovery and all the others that reveal truths. The world glorifies killers every day as heroes. Might does make right, here in the United States. The biggest lie of all!

The trip to Ohio was a long time coming. I was going to spend a good week with my son and do a little carving. We arrived, late as usual. I had taken my *Strong's Concordance* and the King James Bible to prove the changes made by the Jehovah's Witnesses. I also brought the spontaneous human combustion book. I wanted to show them proof of the resurrection. Little did I know the reaction I was going to receive.

The next day started like all the other traditional mornings, with a big pot of tar black coffee. As we were getting into the third cup, I turned to Dad and softly asked him and Mom if they had checked on any of the information that we had last talked about. Dad immediately puffed up! So Mom quickly said, they had taken my questions to the meetings and asked one of the elders.

I figured as much, but I kept that to myself and only replied with a very honest, "Boy, I was kind of hoping that you would have checked out the name at the library or at least the Book of Enoch. But anyway, what did they say about the name, Enoch and the other books of the Bible. Or the mystery?" I continued on, probably too fast and a little too excited. "And most of all, what they did to the scripture of 'no man will go to Heaven that didn't come from Heaven'?" I remembered her writing these particular things down, in our last conversation.

"They interpret that differently, Mike," she said weakly.

"But Enoch and Elijah went to Heaven, Mom," I came back immediately. "Besides that Mom, it is a scripture, with a comma, saying we came from Heaven. The Jehovah's Witnesses have taken it and made it two. Worst of all, it becomes the opposite of the true meaning, that we came from Heaven. Don't you see that they twisted it to glorify the flesh existence and to make it anti-spirit in meaning? Did you even read Jude? He quotes Enoch." I couldn't believe it. They hadn't researched one thing! "You make it such a life or death issue. Why not?" I asked her a little too demandingly.

"Well, uh, uh," she said, trying to find an answer. Dad had gone from the table over to his recliner. He was putting his shoes on, obviously getting out of there. I could tell he was getting upset.

"Have you guys even read Matthew 23 or 16:4 about the Shroud? By the way, I don't even see it. What did you do with it?"

"Ask your Dad," she said with a half-smirk.

"Hell, that's all you had to say," I said with a laugh.

"No, you sonofabitch, you. It ain't what you think. I accidentally burnt it."

"I'm sorry" I said softly, not wanting him to get any angrier. "I figured you might've been a little spooked and all, since it looks like a ghost. I mean you probably still believe in the Devil and demons, don't you?" I went too far.

He go up and looked me squarely in the eyes. He had an anger that I had seen all too often, in my life. "By God, I not only believe in the Devil and Jehovah God, but I know that you are on the wrong track, lad. And if you aren't careful, you just might find yourself falling into the Demon's hands."

I just looked at him and said, "Dad, doesn't the truth matter? I've showed you that demon isn't in the Bible anywhere, at least not in the King James version. And you said yourself that it is an accurate translation, accepted by all of Christianity. This proves that the Jehovah's Witnesses pervert the writings. I'm telling you, this interpretation argument is a bunch of bullshit!"

Dad immediately hollered back, "Who wrote your books?"

I grabbed my concordance and showed him the letters PhD. "Doctor Strong? Not preacher. He is educated, and this is simply an exhaustive translation. What about the other books of the Bible that the Jews didn't canonize, like Enoch. What did the Elders say about that?"

"By God, they weren't accepted as legitimate books; therefore we don't read them."

"By whom, the Jews? They killed Yeshua. Yeshua was condemning the Jews. Enoch is quoted by Yeshua's little brother. That's my point. You know Dad, I'm finding that the Jews and Christians are just alike. It's all religious brainwashing. Jake and I can't even find a Christian who cares about the name change."

Dad blasted back and said "Mike, dammit, we're Americans; we speak English."

"Well, what's so important about the name to you, Dad? I mean after all, your religion makes it a life or death matter, doesn't it?" I shouldn't have done that because he blew.

"By God, I know why it's important, and that's all that matters!" He screamed. "You live your life. I'll live mine."

What a reversal, I thought. He used to always dog me to be more righteous than him and go to church. He used to make the truth so important. "No, you know your answer doesn't make any more sense to you than it did to me, and you're angry because mine does. I want to show you something, please before you leave. I love you Dad." He sat back down. "I found something else that supports our theory of the mystery, to be born again. That's the correct word. Even meditation has been perverted by western thought. They've made it to think. Doing the mystery is to not think, mimic death. It's what the picture of the Shroud looks like. That's the way to be born again. Paul said it plainly, 'I die daily.' It was lost by the Jews, and Yeshua came here to show us the way again. He even said he was the Way. Remember in the beginning of Genesis, in Chapter 3 after we had eaten from the Tree of Knowledge, we became flesh and God couldn't see us? Well, God said we had become 'as one of us,' calling others obviously God, too. That proves polytheism not monotheism, but they're really one and the same. Trinity! But that's another story. I want to prove that mystery is what we are supposed to be doing. God told us unless we take 'again' of the tree of life, we would die. The tree's definition and the mystery give us all the characteristics of the Shroud, the Sign of Jonas, the only sign he would leave us."

I reached and got a copy to illustrate my point. But first I turned to 'tree' in the concordance. I got the definition and read it as they watched. I had written down the four definitions on the Shroud. Each of the words, mystery and tree, had two. I highlighted this fact for them.

"Anyhow," I said, seeing that Dad wasn't going to sit long, "here's proof. Tree means what?" I continued. I held up the Shroud and read the definitions of the words tree and mystery.

"Make firm and close the eyes. Would you say they describe the Shroud?"

They both agreed weakly.

"So," I went on, "here's the biggie. The mystery means to shut the mouth and initiate oneself into a religious rite, to learn secret truths, to be BORN AGAIN," I blurted out excitedly. "This proves Matthew 23 as well. The Jews and Christians are the only cultures that forbids spiritual exercises. Everything they do is outward, especially praying. It says that very thing in Matthew 23."

Dad looked at me. "You mean to tell me that you think we can go to Heaven by doing this?" He folded his arms, leaned back in the chair, and gritted his teeth as hard as he could. I laughed because he was really letting his anger get the best of him. He looked ridiculous. The angry prophet. He was the perfect contradiction. "I must be making some sense. The tragedy is that the Jehovah's Witnesses have won. They've made us both afraid of the spirit world. For your information, I haven't done it yet, but now I will. Your resentment toward it proves my point even more."

"To Hell with your proof," he blurted out. He got up and started toward the door.

"The proof is in your own house, Dad. You don't even have to go to the library. Mom said she had a King James Version Bible. Read John 3:13, Jude, and Matthew 23. Now the ball's in your court. It's easy to prove to yourself that Yeshua is describing Judaism and Christianity to a tee. Hell, it doesn't take a rocket scientist to figure that out. They teach the same things, down to the Ten Commandments and church. Besides, Dad you don't have to go any further than the word Jehovah. It comes from the consonant YHWH. We have Y's and if you put the vowels in from the A, you get Yahweh, not Jehovah. Even the E is right, but in Jehovah you miss on both."

He went on out the door, but not before telling me he would mash my mouth for blaspheming Jehovah's name. I didn't say anything else. I went ahead and wrote down a couple of teachings of Moses that were opposite of Yeshua's: An eye for an eye versus turn the other cheek and the Ten Commandments versus being delivered from the Law.

I showed these to Mom and she was pretty shaken by the obvious differences between Yeshua's teachings and Moses'. "The sad truth is, Mom, that Christianity has followed the Jews to a tee. They even preach the Bible literally, making physical things that have a totally different spiritual meaning. Mom, Yeshua came to save that which was lost. The angels which left their first estate for a strange flesh. It's mankind, obviously. But we keep returning, like the Bible says, 'a dog to his vomit, a pig to mud'. Reincarnation! Isn't that great, Mom?"

She just looked dazed and said, "I guess so."

"Now that's fair mom! Jude quoted Enoch. Mom, that alone ought to make you skeptical of the Jews' canon. It should have made Christianity, too. The cruel history of the Christian movement is hard to swallow anyway. How can anybody take up for an organization that killed millions of people in the name of God. The very person that supposedly preaches peace. That's a joke, Mom. Only a hundred years ago or less, this Christian government killed men, women, and children for being witches."

She was becoming visibly shaken. I lightened the conversation up.

"The end of the Bible is the best proof," I said calmly. "They have symbols for tree, bread, and wine, but they don't for Hell and Lake of Fire. Why? If we give it a physical meaning, it's obvious that it is the physical body. We are 'Lakes of Fire,' wailing and gnashing our teeth. This makes life fair. If we don't become born again and learn who we are, spirits, then we are simply reincarnated. Doesn't that make sense? Don't you want your God to be a fair God?"

"Yes, but we believe that Hell is just symbolic of death, or sleeping."

"Mom, can't you see there is no room for interpretation? This symbolic and literal argument is crap? Besides, is it fair for God to toy with us like that? What about those who aren't preached your interpretation? Is that fair? Believe me, there are many people who have never heard of the Jehovah's Witnesses, and they won't, before they die. That can't be fair. Your story, or Christianity's story for that matter, is cruel and full of contradictions. Yeshua would order no one's death nor kill anyone himself. Shouldn't you as a Christian follow his teachings instead of Moses'? I mean, after all, you are a 'Christian,' aren't you?"

"I suppose," she said softly, "you do have a good point. It does bother me that we have a killing God in the Old Testament."

"Mom, he isn't really. You've been preached a story physically that is spiritual. The prophets received these visions in meditation, sitting and repenting in sackcloth and ashes, spiritually.

"The problem is that you are taught man is good," I continued. "But Yeshua says that this world is evil, that man is evil. He was created on the sixth day. John says the devils' number is six hundred sixty-six. That's what I am saying about mankind. It's all happened before. What is, what was, and what will be! Six-six-six. Time travel, destiny, the same thing. It makes sense that the two trees represent two worlds, Heaven and Earth, just like Yeshua taught. Two worlds that he has already been tried in and overcame. It's pretty ridiculous to think that this is all there is. Yeshua makes it clear that he was here in this world before us."

Mom started to ask why I thought this world didn't have any good in it.

I told her about the scripture, where the apostles ask Yeshua who was good, and he answered "No one is good except for the Father. The Father in Heaven, Mom." I went ahead and got the concordance, and began to look up the word "world." I explained that this one word proves how Yeshua saw the big picture. I showed her how to use the concordance, as I was looking it up. We found it and she couldn't believe her eyes. It was full of quotes by Yeshua, saying that he is not of this world.

She was getting nervous as she heard Dad come back onto the porch. She started to close the book, but I heard Dad leave again. So I followed up on a scripture that I noticed her reading. It was a scripture in Matthew.

"I can't believe it, Mom. Here is a scripture that really proves my point. That we are the angels Jude and Enoch prophesied about, the one third in the Prodigal Son parable. Remember, I said we came here on our own accord, by eating of the tree, which really means sit down and close our eyes, not tree."

"Yeah," she said, glued to my every word.

"Well, the scripture is a quote from Yeshua explaining to the preachers that John didn't come into this world eating and drinking." She looked puzzled so I emphasized the words "didn't come into this world." She immediately understood. "The eating of the tree wasn't a physical eating of fruit. Men gave it a physical meaning that I never understood. Now I do."

I thought of bread, and went to the scripture in Matthew, that even further explained my position. Yeshua makes a statement, that it is not meet to take the children's bread and waste it on dogs. "Mom, he is talking about a Samaritan woman wanting a little spiritual truth. This scripture proves that only the Jews were considered man, and all others were dogs, beasts, creatures, water, darkness, or Gentiles to be nicer. It is a perfect example of what Yeshua considered bread, something spiritual, not physical, something hard to understand. It obviously wasn't taught. In the Lord's Prayer, the only one we're supposed to pray, it asks to forgive us for our trespasses and deliver us from evil. It says exactly what I'm saying. Our trespass is here. And the evil is not returning, being where we shouldn't be, in this body. Man. Six-six-six is his number. Mom, I'm your sixth child." She looked sheepish.

I read on and showed her where Yeshua says "My Father will pluck up every tree that he did not plant." This was more proof, that we were indeed coming into this world on our own. "Mom, he came to save that which is lost."

I went ahead and looked up bread and found it to have two meanings just as I said, a physical one and a spiritual one. The spiritual one was "to lift up." Resurrect, I thought to myself, resurface again. After I read it, I quoted John 3:13, "No man will go to Heaven that didn't come from Heaven, even the Son of Man which is in Heaven. And as Moses lifted up the serpent in the wilderness, so must the Son of Man be lifted up."

"Now do you see what I'm talking about?" I asked her pleadingly. "They preach physical meanings instead of spiritual ones. It's obviously ridiculous to think that Moses went to Heaven by lifting up an actual serpent. What do you think the serpent really is, Mom?"

She didn't know what to say, other than worldly temptation. That was a typical Christian answer to make it a worldly act that they label right or wrong. They always forget being delivered from them.

"But Mom, Yeshua gave a thief the promise of Heaven and stealing is a bad thing. Couldn't it mean flesh, DNA? It even looks like two serpents. It is our America Medical Association symbol. Get it? Medical symbol, to save. It would explain the forty day thing, Yeshua and Moses had in common."

She laughed weakly and said all bewildered, "I suppose."

"Christian doctrines are basically pretty easy, Mom. Yeshua said it is hard, a narrow path. It isn't hard to be a Jehovah's Witness, is it? It isn't physically hard living according to the Ten Commandments is it?" I asked her.

"No," she replied weakly.

"But it is to lift up the flesh, for forty days and nights. Huh Mom? You know that all too well. You do diet. Don't you?" She laughed and agreed completely. "I tell you, Mom, Jake's pool parable is the Prodigal Son story. One-third went astray. There's nothing you can do while you're here, only returning. The mystery is the truth, secret truths, Mom. This is Hell! Heaven is the universe. And we're inside it." I think we're the one-third of the angels who were cast out. It's all about being born again, lifting up the serpent. Remember that God is in the still, small voice. Still as being shut down. I know it sounds radical, Mom. But that's why they killed Yeshua. He was doing the mystery or T.M. And they have the same abbreviation, how appropriate.

"I'm telling you, Mom," I continued exuberantly, "I think I am finally making some sense out of this whole religion mess. And it looks scientific, that's the beauty of it. Religion has been created by man and his own physical interpretation of words. And believe me, they defy the truth, even when proven otherwise. Just because they can! Man, the prince of the air. Until now! The Religion Cover-Up is about to be uncovered! I'm telling you, Mom. The other books of the Bible are available, and there are concordances not made by religious organizations. The truth is out there and it's easy to prove. Christianity isn't the only religion in this world. It's a world full of choices, truths. Hell, what about science? The problem is that we live in a religious world that preaches against science. Worst of all, Mom, they've brainwashed us to love the flesh. They scare us with demons or evil spirits. And Mom, I've shown you proof that the Jehovah's Witnesses created demons, not Yeshua. He said we're all evil, even himself. Does that make him a demon?"

"No," she said. "I'm going to check on that."

"I want you to, Mom, because it's pretty obvious that Dad won't."

Mom got up from the table and looked out the window. "I heard a car pulling up. It's Jeff and Little Jeff," she said as if relieved.

I was anxious to see them since it had been about three months. Mom told me that Little Jeff had gotten a pretty bad whipping, recently. He had been caught by the police drinking, smoking, and partying at a football game. He was only fifteen. It wasn't any different from what we did, except that he had been caught. I was shocked. Big Jeff had never whipped Little Jeff at all, while he was growing up. I always felt it was because Dad whipped him a lot. And I know, like the rest of us, it affected him. He had only been back home in Southern Ohio for the past five years, and it was easy to see Dad's influence on him again. We all would make this same mistake, that I would soon realize. We all can break, especially when kids get older and look us eye to eye. I would soon experience plenty of major traumas with my own son. I would break, too.

Little Jeff came through the door alone and looked like he had grown a foot taller. He was sure taking after his mother's side of the family. They were all tall except for one or two, but that wasn't saying much since there were thirteen kids. It was a good ol' Christian family, pro-creation. He came over and hugged me as I got up. "Oh no," he said as he looked down and saw the Bible and concordance spread out. "Dad told me that you were getting into some cult or something."

"What do you mean, a cult? I just want to find out why there are so many God-awful religions out there. Get it, God-awful?" I laughed.

"Mike," Mom said.

"Okay, Mom, don't panic, but do you realize, Jeff, that we have a recorded history of only six thousand years? Isn't that mind-boggling? And recorded history comes from the Jews, who predict a Messiah, or messenger that will come to save us. A story of time-travel! And guess what? We measure time after him and he has become the most famous person on Earth! That was only two thousand years ago, twenty-five men's lifetimes. Can you believe it?"

"Save us from what?" He asked.

"What do you think that is, Mom?" I asked quickly, to refresh my point with her.

"What?" She said, puzzled-looking.

"Mankind. Where we don't know who we are, six-six-six! I think Yeshua, the Messiah, left us a sign. Only one, Jeff, to answer that question. And we don't even acknowledge it. I left one for Mom and Dad, but Dad burned it accidentally. But I've got another one with me," I said quickly. "Thank God!"

Angel looked at me scoldingly as I asked her where it was. She said that it was in the luggage, but that I needed to quit talking about it. It was getting Dad pretty upset.

"Ah, he can take it. He's a big boy. I got the Shroud and the spontaneous human combustion book." I wanted to show Little Jeff the other proof I had. "Have you ever really thought about why you believe in

Yeshua or God anyway, Jeff?"

"I don't know who Yeshua is," he said, "but I do believe in God."

"I know you do. I do to, and it's because we're brainwashed. It's a Christian country, Little Jeff." He was looking a little confused. "Let me explain, first of all, that his name has been changed. But the thing I've discovered, that blew me away most is the shroud. I now know about the burial cloth he left behind. It's what he gained fame for and it was only nineteen hundred years ago. The resurrection. How could Christians get so screwed up? He disappeared and left a picture. It's what we have come to know as another mystery, spontaneous human combustion. Have you ever heard of that? I hadn't. The Shroud is the physical evidence that really staggered me, Jeff." I handed him a picture of the Shroud and said "It's the only sign Yeshua, who said he was the Messiah predicted by the Jews, gave us of his existence. It's a picture of his resurrection and the way to return to our first estate, Heaven. We're lost here, and this is Hell. Can you believe this? And his story is supported by this physical evidence. This," I said holding up the Shroud. "That's powerful, huh? And he comes from the oldest history we have, the Jewish history."

"What is this?" He asked, looking at the Shroud.

"What's it look like?" I asked.

"It looks like a ghost," he said, with a blank face.

"Exactly," I replied excitedly. "It is a picture of us, who we truly are, spirits. I think it is also the way to return to Heaven, or be born again of the spirit as Yeshua put it. It's called the mystery."

He asked who Yeshua was again and I told him. He then asked why I was calling him Yeshua instead of Jesus. I told him his name had been changed.

"It has no logical explanation as Jesus." Then I asked him why it was important. He gave me the typical Christian response. "That doesn't answer anything, does it?" I asked bluntly. "But listen to this, Jeff. It helps us to know history and the way it was given to us. The name was predicted by prophets. Guru-type guys who meditated. They said that the Word of the Lord, what the Messiah was called, came to them and told them the name of God. And not to mention all the knowledge that we know today. Guess what that name was? And by the way, it was predicted thirty-five hundred years ago."

"I don't know," he replied.

"It was 'I am.' What a crazy name, huh, unless it has some importance. It does! The Bible emphasizes the importance of the Messiahs name, who is to fulfill the prediction. He was sent to show us the way. He comes a couple of thousand years later, and his name is Yeshua. And, by the way, Little Jeff, today English rules. It is even the language of Heaven. We have adopted it as the universal language in our skylab. That is why I think the name is so important. He left us a sign, the Shroud. A picture left in his burial cloth, from the resurrection of his body through intense heat. With it, we have the best proof of his existence being possible and maybe even spontaneous human combustion, another mystery. Now let me finish my reasoning. I believe that the Shroud you hold is authentic. It proves Yeshua's existence and purpose. Remember earlier, when I asked you what it looked like?"

"Yes," he said, nodding his head.

"Well, knowing the story of how it was given, put them together. I am, Yeshua, and yes you are spirits, angels/Gods."

"What?" He said. "You're saying we're gods?"

"Exactly, gods/spirit, same thing. We keep reincarnating back into this world. And if we don't become born again of the spirit, before we die, we'll do it again."

"What?" He asked really confused looking.

"Here's proof of the resurrection or spontaneous human combustion." I then showed him the book and gruesome pictures of ash and feet. I asked him if he saw anything the pictures had in common. He said no. I pointed out the feet and told him my theory. "We don't need feet as angels or spirits, what we truly are. See how it further supports the Shroud, which is proof of our being spirits. Well, what do you think?"

"Wow, it makes sense," he said, agreeing with me.

"Think about this," I told him, as he looked at the Shroud again. "All the other cultures do mystery except for the Jews and Christians. They can't stop praying long enough. See how I get that the Shroud is also a picture of the way to be born again, transcendental meditation? Why do you call it Transcendental? Think about it. Yeshua wanted us to be born again of the spirit. Isn't that what transit means? The spirit leaves the body, like a baby leaves a womb at birth. It's actually called mystery, that's the religion cover-up. When you pray, you're using your mouth and brain, thinking and talking."

"You could pray with your mouth closed," he said. "What's the difference?"

"That's the beauty of the resurrection. Yeshua's body was dead. It's a picture of death. To become born again, you have to practice dying." He was finding this all too much to swallow. "Do you know that we still can't burn a human bone to ashes. It even takes nine hours to completely burn the flesh off the bones, and then we have to crush them to dust. But spontaneous human combustion can reduce the body to ashes within seconds, and it leaves the feet. Now, that's why I believe in Yeshua and the theory that I am now pursuing. Our theory is that we are spirits, the one-third of the angels in the Jewish story." I started to explain further, but the kids were getting fidgety. They were getting anxious to go to the hotel. Angel and I had decided to give Dad and Mom a break. They didn't care about what I was saying. It went against their traditions.

"Little Jeff," I said getting up to go. "Go to college, Son, and unlearn what you've already been taught. Everything's a lie, or at least they were the last time I looked," I said, getting out a dollar bill. "Nope, there it is. It's still a lie." I showed him the words, "In God We Trust." "We're supposed to be a democracy, Jeff, yet God's on our dollar bill. And money is the root of all evil. You call this freedom of religion; we're brainwashed." I said shaking the bill. "It's all lies!"

Just at that moment, Jeff and Dad walked in. "What lies?" Jeff grunted with a little smirk as he came toward me to hug. We had a very affectionate family. I sure gave my loving mother credit for that. Dad wasn't a hugger. "The ones we're brainwashed with, I added quickly.

"Little Jeff was just telling me that you told him I was in a cult, huh, Jeff."

"Well, that's what it sounded like to me. Mom told me about you and Jake meditating to some damn picture."

"We don't meditate to a picture, or at least, I haven't yet. Heck, the Jehovah's Witnesses have done a good job of scaring the shit out of me about meditating. I even thought that maybe, just maybe, I could be possessed by a demon. But I found out that there aren't any. It's just one of many lies Christianity uses as a scare tactic to get us to join their club. Pay their tithes."

Jeff went over and hugged Angel. "What have you let this boy get himself into, this meditating shit?"

"It's not my fault," Angel replied. "Ask his other wife, Jake."

"Jeff, I haven't meditated yet. Well, it's actually called the mystery, but I'm going to start. I'm convinced that Yeshua left his picture to prove it. Oh, by the way, this is a picture of Yeshua's resurrection." I held up the picture of the Shroud. "His behavior seemed cultist to the Jews. In fact, he was killed by them. The church. At least that's what I think. And Christianity/Rome did nothing more than take over. They seized the opportunity to sell Yeshua's fame and start the same wealthy organization of church. They changed his name and sold his fame, man. I think that we're all brainwashed. Lies became truths. We can even prove these lies. Might doesn't make right anymore. Not as far as I'm concerned. I can prove that we aren't a true democracy, but it won't change anything. We know the Indians had the country taken from them. There were eleven million killed. Hell, the Indians aren't even called Indians. Indians isn't an Indian word. I can prove that Yeshua was anti-religion, saying that Heaven was within us, but we would still go to church. The only way to find the truth in today's world, a world that teaches and lives lies, is to seek. Watch real history. Go to college, Little Jeff," I said as I turned away from Jeff. I could see Big Jeff cringe at the word college.

"He doesn't need to go to college," Jeff blurted out. I knew it was a bad topic since I was the only one of six boys who went to college.

"He would if he wanted to be a surgeon," I said boldly.

"Well, you said to learn. He can learn by going to the library."

"Jeff, you know damn well he needs to go to college. We all do. That's how you get knowledge. That will open doors that can't be opened otherwise. Knowledge is the key to success. Knowledge is power."

Jeff walked by and saw the Shroud as I was talking. He picked it up and looked at it with intense scrutiny.

"Do you know what it is?" I asked.

"No, but you just said it was Jesus."

That name really annoyed me. Jake had affected me. "His name is Yeshua. They changed his name. I didn't realize its importance, since Christianity doesn't acknowledge it. It is a clue to the Shroud's message. The Shroud was predicted in the Gospels as the only sign he would leave the Jews, a wicked and adulterous generation, which seeketh a sign."

"What do you mean, it was predicted in the Gospels? What's the Gospels?"

Funny, we went to church all our lives as kids. I told him I hadn't remembered either, and then explained the phrase gospel truth. He knew the phrase.

"Who is Yeshua?" He asked, just like everyone else.

"You see what I'm saying about Christianity and ignorance? They go hand in hand. I'm not saying you're stupid, just ignorant. We all are; we're Christians. Christianity forbids questioning or looking outside of our own religion. The sad truth, Jeff, is that the Jews know his name, but they deny him. Christianity/Rome changed his name to Zeus, sold his fame as the new religion. They used the resurrection, yet deny the Shroud's authenticity. They even own it. Screwed up, huh! And now, even worse, they call themselves Father, the opposite of Yeshua's teachings. Hell, we don't even care about the provable lies. We buy them easy. We just never check it out."

Dad began to get up and come at me, looking like he was about to blow. Angel seized the moment to get us out of there. "Let's go to the motel, guys," she said, jumping up.

"Jeff, can Little Jeff go to the motel with us?"

"Hell, no, he can't," he said, laying the Shroud down. "I'm afraid he might slip away to the 'hood and hang with the niggers drinking and smoking crack."

"Jeff," I snapped. "Watch your mouth, man."

"What?" He snapped back at me.

"You know what," I said. "The word nigger. I don't want my kids to hear it."

"You say it," he snapped back.

"That's a lie," I hollered.

"You're the liar," he said. "We all say it."

"I know you all do, but not me, bud. I might have said it in my lifetime, but not for a long time. You can ask Angel." She shook her head and said she had never heard me say it.

"Well, what's it matter, anyway? You know I'm not a racist, man."

"But you strive to teach your kids honesty, don't you? Then you know it's a racist word."

"That's only because they make it a racist word. Besides, they call themselves that."

"That's them, Jeff. From a black man to a black man. You're a white referring to them as niggers. That's wrong and racist. It doesn't change the truth. The truth is all that matters to me, Jeff. It doesn't matter what we learned from our parents, if it's wrong. I just talked to Mom about your whipping Little Jeff. I can't believe you are whipping your son now. You are the one who convinced me it was wrong, and now that I've read some of Yeshua's teachings, I know it's wrong, man. We can't whip dogs or adults, but we can children. Things are screwed up, huh?"

Dad couldn't restrain himself anymore. "By God, you'll have to prove to me where it is wrong."

"Hell, that's easy." I quoted "turn the other cheek."

"Well, by God, none of you turned out bad."

"No, we all left early, Dad. Let's get ready and go, Babe," I said, turning to Angel. He was visibly shaking and I knew the potential for a violent explosion from him. And me too, verbally anyway. We all had our Dad's temper. The apple doesn't fall far from the tree, another religious pun. But Jeff and I could control ours. We both knew Dad couldn't. I started getting my books together, but couldn't keep from saying to my brother, "I'm telling you, Jeff, if you care about your son, you'll set an example and strive to be loving and know the truth. I am, and believe me, it's hard. We are brainwashed by lies that are preached as truths. I mean, isn't honesty the most important thing, Jeff?"

"Well, what's truth to you could be a lie to somebody else."

"Well, personally, Jeff, I think that's a crock, and the interpretation argument is a bunch of bullshit. We can prove written history. It's very short!"

"Well, until you do, I'd rather you not preach to my son."

That just blew me away. I couldn't believe he said that. "Well, I'd appreciate it if you don't use any more racial slurs around my kid. But I have to give you credit: at least you aren't a hypocrite. You don't go to church. To me there's nothing worse than a person who professes to love the truth and openly does the opposite. Like the name and Christianity." I knew that would piss Dad off, but I was leaving anyway.

"What is it about the name, you sonofabitch?" He hollered. "We're English!"

"Well, do you have two English names like Yeshua does?" I snapped back. "I told you it's been changed, but you don't care. Just like you don't care about the word demon in your Bible. It isn't in the King James Version. I can prove that," I said to Jeff.

"How do you know this shit?" Dad hollered.

I held up the concordance. "This is how I know! I went to the library to read everything, unlike you! How many books have you read, Dad? How many religions have you studied? After all, you are making a life or death decision for your kids. How many Dad?" I got loud again. I had so much resentment.

He was beside himself, but before he could answer, I blurted out. "Don't answer, because I know already. What you have read is the Jehovah's Witnesses material, but I proved them wrong with *demon*. I proved that the name Jesus, Jehovah, Jimmy Cricket Christ has been changed! Adam is one name from Hebrew to English, Moses as well. But the only name we can be saved by is changed. Changed by the most cruel movement in history, Christianity! And you don't care!" I blurted out.

He came at me with his fists drawn and in a rage. "You sonofabitch, don't you ever blaspheme the name of Jehovah in my house again! Get out!"

"Jehovah!" I hollered back. "Don't you care about ol' Jimmy Cricket Christ's name? It's the only name you can be saved by, and all you can say is Jehovah. He supposedly started your religion, didn't he? Doesn't that count for anything? Jehovah is such a joke. Where does it say that name will save you? Can't you see that your precious Jehovah's Witnesses have everything to gain from your membership? I don't want your membership, just your respect. Hell, who am I to ask for that? I'm just your educated son."

He got right in my face. I couldn't believe it! I had witnessed this same event my whole life. "Go ahead and hit me, Dad, in the name of your almighty God Jehovah!"

"You sonofabitch, get out and don't you come back until you respect my home."

Jeff came leaping in between us. I came right back at Dad. "By God, don't you come to mine and disrespect me either, with your racism. You taught us that, just like beating kids."

He went into a rage and started saying that he would always be a Jehovah's Witness and if I didn't like it, I could stay away.

"Yeah, we all know how you love them. Even to the point of abusing your family, not to mention making life or death decisions for them without researching anything else!"

Then Jeff jumped into my face as Dad shoved me. "Frank," Mom screamed.

"Jeff, let me prove it!"

"You believe what you believe and let us believe what we want to believe!" He screamed bloody murder. It shocked me.

"Don't worry, I will, pal," I said, letting the tears fly. I turned to Angel and told her to take the kids to the car. Just as she started to leave, I stopped her. "Kids, I'm sorry this just happened. I didn't want this. I'm sorry."

I turned to my Dad. "I just wanted to show you the facts I found on my search. I shouldn't have pushed them on you. I'm sorry." I went over and hugged him and then hugged Jeff and said I was sorry. "The next time I bring it up, I'll be giving you a copy of my book. I don't want you to be offended, but the title is *Two Witnesses and the Religion Cover-up*." Anyone can prove it unless they love their traditions more."

"I've got to give you credit," Dad said quickly, as if to change the proving-to-yourself conversation.

"I'm sure proud of the way you stand up for what you believe in."

"See how brainwashed we are, Jeff? Dad, Yeshua spoke against pride and defending oneself. I'm ashamed of what just took place in front of these kids, and I don't ever want it to happen again. It's something I have to deal with."

"No, it's something we all have to deal with," Jeff said, as he hugged me. He was crying. "I don't know what kind of religious kick you're on,

Mike, but you're out of control and you might be getting into something you can't handle."

"You're certainly right about that, Jeff. I can't handle the racism, the lies, but most of all, the hypocrisy of our own government. Hell, the Indians owned this country and there were eleven million killed. We glorify killers. The world is screwed up, brainwashed by this cruel lie called Christianity. All roads lead to Rome. I can't hardly stand this world. It's full of hypocrites, racists, and killers, and we glorify them. You're right about one thing, Jeff, I can't handle it. If it wasn't for my kids, I wouldn't handle it, bud."

"I'm sorry to hear that," he said, shaking his head. "I'm telling you, you need help, and I hope you get it."

I got the kids and Angel out the door and headed for the motel. Boy, I sure knew what Yeshua meant when he said, "A prophet receives no honor in his own country."

Angel was blown away by Dad's rage as well as my own. She commented that she knew where I got my temper.

"Yeah, but at least I'm not physical, and that makes a big difference." Then I thought about one time with my son. One bad time. "I'm sorry, Jimmy," I said as I turned toward him and hugged him. "Not only for whipping you, but for acting like that with Dad. It's wrong. It's best to walk away when someone starts getting upset. Can you ever forgive me for the one time that I beat you?"

"One time . . ." he said shyly. "What about the board, remember?"

I did, but tried to downplay the severity of it. I was ashamed. After all, it was a paddling to me. But his impression was different, and that's all that mattered. "I'm sorry twice, son. Please, would you forgive me? It won't happen again." Then I remembered how I spanked him for peeing the bed. I was so ashamed. That day changed my life. I was no longer following the path that my Dad chose, disciplining my children. It was important for me to set an example. How could I not practice what I preach, when I condemned hypocrisy. I was determined to set an example. That's how we change things.

I pulled into my brother's driveway to pick up my nephew. As soon as Randy got in, he asked if I had heard about Little Jeff.

"Oh yeah," Angel said. "He heard all right."

"What?" Randy asked. "What happened?"

She told him all about the incident at Dad's. He wasn't too surprised. He knew the Jackson temper. We started talking about the discipline thing, and I was surprised to find that he approved of whipping. I asked him if he could see the hypocrisy in it. He couldn't. But ol' Randy sure enough asked me to explain. "How do you figure?" He asked. I liked his confidence.

Jimmy snickered! I scolded him and said, "The only stupid question is the one not asked." I continued to ask Randy, and it was like pulling teeth for him to admit that it was hypocritical. "Randy," I said, frustrated, "my Dad beat us all for smoking and now five out of seven smoke. It obviously doesn't work, and now the same thing is happening with the rest of my brothers. I've even heard that you're beginning to smoke. And you've already got a whipping for it yourself, just like your older brother and sister. Can't you see that it doesn't work?"

"Well, that's your opinion," he said defiantly in an effort to protect his dad's good standing.

"Randy, we all make mistakes. I'm not trying to place blame, or make one person better than another. I just want a more loving, understanding family that cares about the truth. Hell, Dad forbid, and we all rebelled. Forbidden fruit is sweetest, right? You smoke, don't you, and they taste awful, or at least did for awhile. But they're cool, entertaining, and fun. I know, I tried; I admit it." I paused. "Besides adults can't physically abuse adults or animals without breaking the law. We should treat children the same. Actually, we value children more than anything. And we should."

We had driven a little while and were just about to the motel, when out of the blue my little nephew boldly stated. "Mike, even if you find that we're supposed to meditate, I never will."

I was flabbergasted. "What?" I responded, shocked by his remark.

"Jimmy and Memaw said that you're in this cult or something and they got you to meditate."

"Randy," I said bluntly. "You know me. Come on, man."

"Well, do you meditate?" He asked me quickly.

"Not yet, but I plan on it, as soon as I get back to Nashville. I just might do it at the motel if you don't cool out. You see, Randy, for your information, all religions have meditation as their oldest form of worship. Moses in the wilderness for forty days and forty nights. Yeshua, Buddha, and Gandhi, too. Hell, Sitting Bull too! But now, and for a long time, I think meditation has been lost in the Judeo-Christian world. And surprisingly enough that is our world. The Jewish story is our oldest history and language, Hebrew. It's where Yeshua came from. We can't help it, if these are true facts. We are just looking at facts. Another surprising fact is that Jews condemned spiritism. So if you don't want to meditate right now, that's cool, but at least think about these facts and give it a second chance. I'm finding that Judaism and Christianity created this Devil thing, which in turn has created a Hollywood truth that's a load of crap. It scares people away from meditation. Hell, Randy, if there's a Devil, then that makes God pretty unfair, doesn't it? I mean, after all, God can do anything, right?"

"You don't believe in a Devil?" He asked, kind of shocked.

"No, Randy, I don't. And you know what else, Randy? I don't believe in a God who gives punishments and rewards to us either. And he sure isn't an ol' man with a long flowing white robe, sitting on a throne of diamonds, sapphires, and rubies and God knows what else. But there is one thing I believe in, Randy, and that is whatever these prophets and seers and the Messiah were doing, they got killed for it. Not only that, but it explains why the 'mystery,' which is what it is called, is all over the world in every religion. Believe me, Randy, I was. . . .well, I started to say scared, but I'm not anymore. I know now there isn't a Devil and demons, right Jimmy?" I asked quickly.

"Right," he said back just as fast.

"So Randy, I'm no longer scared, but looking forward to mystery. I just hope I can keep gathering enough evidence to prove to you that Christianity and Judaism have been killing people a long time for meditation. Maybe the reason is we wouldn't need their churches anymore. Not that I have anything against church, the concept; but I do with this Devil and Hell thing. They scare kids! Their cruel scare tactics prevent us from meditating, because we're scared we will be possessed by demons. It's all hogwash. If there's a devil, where is he? Have you heard him? Seen him? Well, I haven't either, but if you do, let me know. Where you at, ol' Devil? Where are you? I'll join you. Come on, I'm easy!"

"Shut up," Randy yelled, kind of irritated at me, which I'm sure wasn't fear. Randy's too proud for that.

"Where are you, Devil?" I said as spooky as I could, then I lunged at Randy. He almost jumped, out of his skin, and the rest of the kids just shrieked with laughter.

Angel didn't though. She hollered and grabbed the wheel. "Watch out!"

I jerked around and retrieved my composure. I had almost missed the entrance, and Angel just sneered at me. "You'd better come back to Earth," she said, with a smirk.

"Well, I was just trying to help my young nephew, to at least see there is a world of truths out there, and maybe, just maybe, they all seem to have one thing in common: the mystery, or meditation, or rather as Yeshua predicted, the Sign of Jonas," I said as I pulled into the parking lot.

"What?" Randy asked me.

"It's a long story," I said, "but it's called the Shroud of Turin. It's a picture of the mystery and who we are, angels who live forever through reincarnation. It's the burial cloth left by Yeshua's resurrection."

"Don't tell me you believe in reincarnation!"

"Yeah Randy, I do, and if I don't say so myself, it is a whole lot more fair than your story, or Christianity's rather, wouldn't you say so?" I asked him.

"No, I wouldn't," he replied smugly.

"Well, that doesn't surprise me there, Mr. Jackson. You know everything at fourteen. But you would argue that one and one doesn't equal two, wouldn't you?"

"It doesn't. It's three."

"Shut up, Randy," I said and grabbed him.

Angel hollered and I let him go. Jimmy took over. Angel went to get the room and scolded me. She left me instructions to get everything unloaded and quit horsing around.

We settled into the room that evening and even got a drink from the bar. Angel got the kids pizzas and Nintendo, so we were set. I heard Jimmy tell Randy about my incident with Dad. He was saying that the word demon wasn't even in the original writings and that Christianity had made it up. I heard him explain a few more things. I sure was proud. Proud? What? I'm sorry, Jehov–, I mean Yeshua, dammit to Hell! I couldn't help myself. I was so brainwashed. I had said these things all my life. How could Christianity make pride a good thing. I wasn't feeling pride. I was feeling love. Love and hate. A hatred for lies, Christian lies!

Before we turned in, Mom called and checked to see how the kids were.

"Okay," I said. "How's Dad?"

She just laughed softly. "He went to bed after you all left. He worked pretty hard outside today."

"I'm sorry for what happened," I said quickly.

"Don't you worry about it," she said. "He's got to learn to control his temper."

"Me too," I added apologetically.

"Yes, you do," she said, but laughing to not seem critical. She was a great person. I started to talk to her, but she heard Dad get up. "I'll see you tomorrow," she said and quickly hung up the phone.

I laughed to myself. Ol' Jake was right. I was starting to annoy my family, talking about religion. I was even torturing them. Torturing them? I laughed to myself. Could we be the Two Witnesses? I started to wonder, remembering the dream.

The next day Mom came in as she promised, and Dad wasn't with her. We all grabbed dinner and headed for the pool. The kids didn't swim too long. It was early spring and the pool was still cold from lack of use. We endured as much as we could and headed back to the room.

"Even the hot tub's cold," Little Jake said, with his lips shaking furiously. Memaw just laughed and grinned from ear to ear. Mom was getting itchy to go, so I went ahead and told Angel, "Let's get ready to load up." It was a perfect sunny afternoon to leave early and get back south where it was warm. Besides, it was about three o'clock, and we still had to take Jimmy home. The drive took about six hours.

I walked Mom out to the car, while Angel organized our departure. She was always glad to do that. I laughed. Mom asked what I was laughing about, and I told her. She laughed, too. Then she looked serious, "You've got a good woman, Mike. Take care of her. Don't blow this one," she said and hugged me.

"I sure blew the last one, didn't I Mom?"

"Yeah," she said, and we both knew how badly I did. "But now you're happy and that's what I want to see."

"Yeah, Mom, I'm happy."

As we hugged and went out onto the parking lot, I asked her to please look into the scriptures I gave her and most importantly get a concordance. "I proved that Jehovah's Witnesses are hiding and even changing definitions to words. Worst yet, Mom, they glorify the flesh. And that's what we must overcome. Remember, Jake and I think that we're spirits already cast out and we have to get back. The angels who left their first estate for a strange flesh. Mankind, six-six-six."

She smiled at me. "Lighten up on this religious thing, Mike. You're going at it too fast."

"Mom," I said disgustedly. "I'm not going at anything too fast. I'm just going at it! Checking it all, Mom, everything. I've found all kind of things that Christianity does that is the opposite of what Yeshua taught. Besides, they can't explain the importance of his name. This alarms me, Mom, because I thought I was a Christian. And I would think that it should alarm you. Mom, if there's one thing I want you to leave here with, it's the importance of the name and rock-solid proof that it was changed. The name Yeshua is in the Old Testament as Jeshua although it should still be Yeshua.

"Where" she asked, kind of puzzled?

"It's in Ezra, Mom. Ask a Jew. Mom, think about what it means with the 'I am.' The I Am is in the Ten Commandments movie with Charleton Heston. Do you know why?"

She didn't.

"Because it's the only name in the Old Testament so important that it was to be kept as a memorial forever. Not Jehovah."

She looked so confused. I grabbed her and said, "Don't worry, Mom. You guys need to worry more about yourselves than me. You're brainwashed. We all are. I think that Yeshua probably encountered this same problem when he started rebelling against his traditions. Mom read Matthew 23. And remember that I've proven there aren't any demons."

"I don't care about that," she said.

"Yes, you do," I said. "Don't make me get my concordance again."

She laughed and said, "No, no, you proved it."

"Okay," I said, "but seriously, Mom. This world is so full of pain and suffering. It's Hell. We know that God has to be fair. It has to be a mistake. 'God repented the day he had to make flesh,' and he had to do that to 'save that which is lost,' us. We came here and we don't know who we are, where we came from, or how to get back. All these questions can be answered by the Shroud, the only sign Yeshua would give us, spirit. There you go!" I said excitedly as I started to go. "But Mom, the best proof of Christianity practicing a lie is the Sabbath. Just look on the calendar. We all know it's Saturday. The Jews maintain the true Sabbath, but Christianity has changed it. Do you know why?"

"No," she said.

"Neither do I," I said laughing. "But we know they changed it. We have the calendar as proof. Proving it just takes a trip to the library. I would find it to be a Roman holy day or holiday."

I looked at her seriously. "Mom, I know one thing for sure. I'm ashamed I ever thought about sacrificing my children's life, without researching everything. But I did. It was easy. That's what I'm telling you. If we truly believe in Yeshua and I do, and I know you do, then it's up to us to prove it for our kids."

"I know, she said and hugged me. "I've got to go."

"Mom, before you go, I want to tell you what Randy said yesterday, out of the blue."

"What?"

"He said he would never meditate," I said coldly. "Mom, I know what Yeshua meant, when he asked forgiveness for his killers, the Jews and Christians. 'Forgive them, for they know not what they do.' Because they were brainwashed from the beginning by tradition, religious tradition. It becomes us, traditions get carried on. Mom, I love you! But I just want the truth, and I'm discovering that we live in a world of lies. Lies that are easily provable, if we can accept the reality of it. Because the truth just might be hard to swallow. We might have to radically change, like I seem to be changing. I'm doing something dangerous, meditating," I laughed. "It all fits, Mom. Please don't worry about me being brainwashed by Jake and this Yeshua thing. Remember yesterday, Mom, when I said I would commit suicide if it wasn't for my kids, Angel, and my family? I wouldn't! It was a Christianity slip."

She hugged me again and we bawled like babies. "Besides, isn't everyone my family?"

"I guess," she said.

I knew she was anxious to get back to Dad. "I know you want to go, Mom, but please promise me you'll care about the truth more than religion."

"I will," she said and turned to open the car door.

"Remember, read the King James Version Bible. At least they don't have demons," I said, laughing. She laughed, and I was glad. She needed to. I was pretty hard on her. "Oh yeah," I said as she started the car and began to pull out. "Don't forget to read Matthew 23, the whole chapter. You'll see how it describes Christianity to a tee. Christians/Jews, same thing. Church is church. Better yet, read it to Randy, so he can see where Yeshua said the Jews forbid mystery. They don't want you to meditate. It's evil," I sneered and laughed. "You might get possessed by those demons the Jehovah's Witnesses created."

"Oh, get out of here," she said and started pulling away.

"Mom, I'm serious," I said, waving. "I'll send you a copy of Jake's song, *Matthew 23*, to remind you, and I'll even try to sing it someday."

"Good," she hollered. "And I will read Matthew 23, I promise you."

"I hope so, Mom. And I will sing and play Jake's song one day. I really did dream about it."

She blew me a kiss as she burned rubber, to miss the light.

I laughed as she went through a yellow, nope, red light. I sure loved my Mom. I turned and headed to the motel. Then I thought about the dream of the Two Witnesses. Wow! Maybe I would sing and play. Poor Dad. "Forgive them, for they know not what they do," I mumbled to myself. I felt a little better as I stepped onto the elevator. I thought about this trip. "A prophet knows no honor in his own country," I said loudly, looking quickly to see if anyone was around. It was all making so much sense now.

This confusion exists because of religion. The truth was perverted right from the beginning. Now, it can't be hidden. We've finally become a global world. It couldn't be suppressed anymore. Little did I know how wrong I was. But it wouldn't stay that way for long. Not if I could help it. It is actually written in Isaiah, "when the world increaseth with knowledge, the truth will be revealed." This is it. There is a world full of lies. Daniel even said; 'At the time of the end, Michael will come forward with the truth.'

We made it back to Tennessee that evening without a hitch. I was as glad as Angel was. The next day came and went just like the next few weeks, fast and eventful. Jake and I were on the phone morning and night. He just laughed at my being thrown out of the house over Jehovah.

"What did you expect?" He scoffed. "They are Jehovah's Witnesses."

I guess he was right. My family wasn't any different from his, and they weren't any different from any other family defending their tradition. I told him about my slipping and saying Jehovah myself, and he just laughed even harder. But he didn't laugh when I told him about my threatening to commit suicide. I told him I did correct my mistake. It made me so ashamed, that I was more determined than ever to prove the importance of the name. Besides, I didn't want to come back.

"Good luck," he said. "I can't find a Christian one who cares about it." He had even been calling toll-free numbers of any Christian organization he could. One guy actually said that the name Yeshua gave him the willies. I couldn't believe it, but then again I could. I had just experienced it with my own family. I told him I was going to check out the name Jehovah and see how they get it is so important. "You won't find anything if you don't start doing the mystery," he taunted.

"I will," I snapped quickly to end that topic.

"Don't worry, Mike. I know you're scared. Hell, I can't get any of you Christians to try it. You're afraid you'll get possessed! You're just like Misty."

I was determined to overcome my fears about a spirit world, and I admitted I was somewhat afraid. "I'll do it soon."

"Sure," he said, laughing.

I began to pour myself into reading. I was going to prove what name was important and what wasn't. I got the concordance and turned to name. I looked in disgust at how many scriptures glorified the Messiah's name, and yet Christians can't produce a rational explanation of its meaning.

Then suddenly Exodus 3:14 seemed to jump up at me. I hurriedly grabbed up the concordance and looked up the scripture: "my memorial unto all generations." It was the first time I actually read it. I was blown away. I couldn't believe it. I checked to see if Jehovah, or any other name, was given this importance as a memorial forever, and it wasn't. They quote the next verse, Exodus3:15 with Jehovah, and skip Exodus3:14. How could they get away with this? I had missed this when I read the Old Testament last year. Good thing Jake got it. I was sure reading the Bible differently now.

I finally made it to Jake's during the next several weeks. I was working hard, to get ready for my son coming down, and a vacation with my brother. I hadn't been in town much because of work, but finally mustered enough courage to go do the mystery with Jake. I got goose bumps as I pulled in the drive. Misty still wasn't back. I went in the back door and didn't hear a thing. I nearly peed myself when I walked in on Jake doing mystery. He was sitting in the middle of the living room floor Indian-style, with his palms turned upward and resting on his knees. He had the room darkened with black blankets draped over the windows. A fan and air conditioner was circulating an eerie, but sweet-smelling incense. It burned on the floor besides the candles. They were placed in front of the Shroud and cast an eerie light on the face, just in front of it. I became stricken with fear. I literally jumped back into the kitchen, and before I could catch myself, headed right back to the truck and drove out of there as fast as I could. As I started pulling away, I got so angry at what the Jehovah's Witnesses had done to me. "Christianity!" I screamed.

I began to pound the wheel furiously as I became filled with anger.

I turned that truck around on a dime. I was determined to carry this thing through no matter what, even if it killed me. If I didn't, Christianity would win, and I couldn't let them win again. They had already caused me enough pain for a lifetime. I cared about the truth. I had to! I had kids!

"There aren't any demons," I blurted out as I whipped back in the driveway. "And I sure as Hell ain't going to let you win again, Christianity. This world, that world! That's what Yeshua said. The spirit world, the flesh world; good and evil; and this world's evil," I mumbled as I headed in the back door. "Even Yeshua said he was evil. I'm going to do this. I'm ready for you, Satan," I said laughing, knowing it was a Christianity slip. "We're all brainwashed Christians, and my family thinks I'm in a cult." Somehow I was reassuring myself just to talk.

I went into the kitchen, and Jake was starting to get up. He heard me. "Well, I thought you would chicken out."

"No way," I said confidently.

Jake smirked as he noticed my nervousness. "You're not going to back out on me now, are you?"

"Nope, let's do it."

"Let me get a drink," he said as he shuffled to the kitchen sink.

I went on in and looked for a good place to support my back and sat down with my legs crossed. I hadn't gotten my arms relaxed and my eyes shut before Jake came in.

"Hey man, don't you have any respect? Let's pull those shoes off."

I pulled my shoes off and sat back, regaining my position. "Sorry, bud."

"That's all right. Just don't let it happen again."

I just laughed. "Okay, okay." I was going to recite the Lord's Prayer, but right then I started to tell Jake about my leaving earlier. He just laughed and said he knew I was here. "That's why I continued to do the mystery."

"Sure you did, Jake."

"Believe what you want, O Ye of Little Faith," he said as he sank to the floor effortlessly.

Jake, the Actor, I mused to myself. He was attempting to imitate a guru or something. I just laughed. "Damn Christianity," I said suddenly. "They not only succeeded in scaring the shit out of me about spiritism, but I realized that I don't even know the Lord's Prayer. Jake, would you please recite the Lord's Prayer, and I'll join in."

"Hey, I was raised a Christian, too, remember? I might not be able to remember it myself."

"Right, O Great One. You forget? Come on."

"Yes, it's possible. As a matter of fact, I'll just look."

He started to get the light and I stopped him. "Come on, man. You can do that later. Let's do the mystery."

He sat back down, but not without putting in the last word. "Oh, really," he said. "We know how you're so busy and ain't got time for the Lord."

"Oh shut up. I do, too."

"Well, Yeshua did go out of his way for you, didn't he? Like dying on a cross!"

"All right," I said. "I'm sorry." I looked at the Shroud and almost wept. What a cruel and inhumane way to die. "You know, I'll never understand how Christianity adopted such a cruel symbol, the cross. They don't let their kids look at such a horrible graphic display of flesh being tortured and killed on TV. How could they let their kids see this and worse yet, glorify it?"

"Really," Jake said, with disgust in his voice also. "And they don't even now about the Shroud."

"You know, Jake, the Shroud really is a picture of the truth. It's who we are, and how we get back."

"It's a picture of Yeshua's dead body, Mike."

"I know that. That's the way, isn't it? You said we have to die to this world, didn't you?"

"Well yes, but . . . ."

"I know, I know. You think it's just a picture of his resurrection and I agree. But I also think it is the way to be born again of the spirit."

He started to argue the point, but I piped in, "It doesn't matter. I respect your opinion. I even want to thank you for your theory, Jake. But time is precious. Let's do mystery."

"What theory, though Mike? It's mystery, man, not theory; that's the only thing worth trusting."

"And I agree man. It's mystery, so please, let's just do it." I joined in as Jake recited the Lord's Prayer and closed in the name of Yeshua. I couldn't help but to think about the name again, I am, Yeshua. How could people not see the connection between it and Yeshua's message. We must be born again of the spirit. I was going to go home and design the cover of my book: the Shroud with a cross on Yeshua's face bearing the words The Religion Cover-up.

My first mystery went off without a hitch! Nothing happened. No voices, no visions, no nothing. It was just the beginning of what would become a lifelong endeavor. From the very first moment that I closed my eyes and tried to stop my conscious thought, I knew it was hard. It was boring as well. It became harder to sit, but we did. We knocked out an hour. Afterward, I confessed to Jake that I had a hard time stilling my mind. He hugged me and then recited, "Heaven was like a seed you sow in the garden." I knew the parable and helped him to finish it. I now understood it. I was in a hurry as usual.

Before I left that day he said something that really made an impact. "You know, this is probably the first time in nineteen hundred years, that a couple of guys have done the mystery, in his true name."

"Wow!" I said in amazement. It probably was. He often told his apostles not to tell. It's a secret."

I had thought about that hard then, and do every day now. It all seemed so cruel, but it made sense. They would have killed him quicker if he hadn't kept it a secret. As anti-spirit as they are now, you can imagine what they were like then. Lord, they even stoned you to death if you said the name. Jake would always make a joke about how cruel the Jews were. He would kill me with his accent. He hollered for Little Yahweh, and then ducked and hollered again. He taught me that people were killed if they said the name. I didn't know it. He was a trip, and did he ever give me a good education. I was on fire to know it all. But most importantly, I was going to prove that I could do the mystery. I was determined to de-brainwash not only myself, but also everyone around me. I wasn't going to let Christianity win.

Jake continued his name search and made a startling discovery with the word Messiah. It was the only accurate translation. Not Christ. We would soon be adding it to our list of words. It radically hid the truth by being changed. Its root form is Hebrew. When it became Greek, it was given two words, messias and christos. One acknowledged its accurate definition as the expected King of the Jews, Messias, while the other was a Greek concept void of any Hebrew importance. They made Zues Christos their Savior. We now had found four words that ended with more than one English word in their translation, Yeshua, YaHWeh, Yacob, and Messiah. We would discover how they changed history. Especially Yacob. He became "King" James!

We continued to read the Gospels while Jake tortured my family, his family, and everybody else about the name. He really blew them away, asking if they know they're dead already. What was the worst thing that could happen to them? My wife was starting to come unglued with all this. I started doing the mystery every day, besides my reading morning, noon, and night. She really thought I was going off the deep end! I guess I was, to her.

I was blown away, by how Christianity could preach a one-time existence and deny reincarnation. Yeshua said, that "there are many who are first that will be last and last that will be first." Reincarnation! That means we'll all eventually enter. He also told the Apostles, that "some of them would not taste of death before seeing the Son of Man coming in all his glory." This was the second coming according to Christianity, a literal second coming that every eye shall see at once. This is not possible according to these two statements. In fact, they clearly show that the resurrection or second coming is an individual occurrence and it happens before death! Death, where is your victory? This sums it up best. It supports reincarnation. Even Yeshua gave an example of the Jews believing in reincarnation, citing Elijah's return as John the Baptist. I continued to read the Gospels over the next few months. Jake had begun to fall prey to the TV preacher. I heard him slip again and say that Lucifer was an angel, the leader of them in fact. I always asked

Satan to let me work for him. He never showed.

Why does God talk to the serpent as a person? "She was! It was Eve's consciousness." I explained how I felt it refers to our dilemma here and how it gives meaning to the scripture in Genesis 3:15 if we know the tree was mystery: "And I will put enmity between your seed and her seed. He shall bruise your head and you shall bruise his heel." This is a perfect example of our dilemma. The serpent, or conscious thought, keeps us from knowing who we truly are, and our flesh prohibits our sitting ability in order to still the mind. It's the Eve and female curse. Jake was impressed, but yet continued to suspect a real Devil. He began to look up the serpent. It meant whisper. She listened to her consciousness and stopped doing the mystery or eating from the tree of life.

"See," I told him, "It couldn't be literal, man. If it was, it makes God out to be so cruel." I couldn't believe this stuff now. Christianity could be so cruel to teach this story literally. Jake even remarked how it was funny that the Jews made God a meat eater right away, with the Cain and Abel story. And they do. Cain is a farmer. Jake made a joke about the scripture where God gave us dominion over the animals. He said that they meant Demenu. He could have been a stand-up religious comic.

I was determined to prove that life had become a word game. I couldn't believe it. A religion cover-up!

Jake and I started doing the mystery together as much as we could. It gave us a chance to research together and read. I loved reading the Book of Enoch! Angel wasn't so thrilled. I read the ending and was amazed. Enoch had seen a solar system. I thought of my recycle container. Everything was about recycling! I asked Jake if I could borrow it. He wanted to read it first. I got to read bits and pieces of it as I went to do mystery and research, but I didn't mind. We shared to keep the cost down.

I was researching words galore in the *Strong's Concordance*. While I continued to research my theory, he was determined to find out what happened to the mystery. Jake educated me that the Catholics sure had the mystery, and still might, but they obviously don't know what it is.

"It's a secret," I laughed, knowing that it was a perfect example of the religion cover-up. I asked him how that was possible, since they do so many things Yeshua condemns, right down to calling each other Father. He explained that they had monasteries where the monks took a vow of silence, abstained from sex, and fasted. "So," I said, "I bet they pray." He didn't know, but figured as much. There was so much I didn't know, and Jake loved to let me know it.

I saw clearly, as I continued to read the Gospels, that the behavior pattern of Yeshua was very monastic. It must be where they got it. No, Rome had schools of mystery. It's just not easy to sell. There's nothing more torturous than physical torture. Suddenly, I remembered the dream. The Two Witnesses! Jake sure tortured people with his Yeshua button. We continued for the next couple of months researching relentlessly morning, noon, and night, while we worked as much as we could, too. We were taking advantage of the summer season's long hours and good business. Jake and Misty had their first anniversary. I wish that I could say everything was rosy, but that would be lying. Jake was working his brains out, and needless to say, their spiritual pursuits were going nowhere. She and Jake still argued about the name even though we purchased the other Bible and it said it should be Jeshua, if not Yeshua. It got worse.

Well, anyway, Angel and I weren't having any luck with our spiritual pursuits either. That was something else Jake and I had in common. I didn't spend much time up north. I tortured them. So, I waited right until the last minute to take Jimmy back. I hadn't been fun for him, either.

It all seemed like a nightmare. My reality was coming unglued. I lived in a world that was religiously brainwashed. Religion was history and history has been cruel, unbelievably cruel. The more Jake and I studied, the more we uncovered meanings to words and parables, that we didn't have before.

We both worked hard through the summer and into the fall. I went in as much as possible to do the mystery. And if I didn't get to do it with Jake, I did it alone. I finally realized that I was dead now. Death was all around me. Time was flying. I knew what Jake meant by "what's worse than death?" This was a hard thing for Angel to understand and everyone else.

One of Jake's band members moved to Nashville that summer and got a studio going. He and Jake immediately put a band together just like old times. I was about to start recording my own music. The dream was coming true. I remembered Paul; I met him in Portsmouth. We had become good friends. They had a band together back in his early twenties. We anxiously shared our newfound evidence with him, and he was surely amazed. He had been doing a little exploring himself. Jake made sure he got a copy of the Shroud and explained the name coincidence. Paul was really impressed. I told him that it was the way to be born again. Jake might've been a stickler for facts, but I just wanted to clear up the big picture. He made sure he stated the facts. It was a picture only.

Paul agreed that Christianity was anti-spirit. He thought the Devil and demon story was a bunch of bullshit also. He had been doing the mystery and was glad to have us to do it with him. Jake and I were both making it our regular daily routine now. We finally got together and did a Buddhist mystery. It was pretty groovy. I asked the teacher, a Buddhist monk, what their goal was, and he explained Nirvana. Jake thought that I was crazy. It did attract the interest of others. I have to admit, that I told them my Jehovah's Witness background and revealed their anti-spirit attitude in a bad way. I was so angry. I poured my guts out in front of the congregation of worshipers. We never did go back. I think Paul and Jake did once more, but they wouldn't let me.

We saw Paul quite a bit, though. They got a band going and really committed themselves. I started recording some of Jake's songs, until I put my own to music. I became their number one fan and apprentice. Well, me, Angel, and Little Jake. We went to all their gigs. Needless to say, it was all costing us money, so I was working my brains out.

We managed to get a vacation that summer with my brother. I shared all the information I had. It tortured them, too. His wife had recently started going to a Baptist church. I read the scripture in Matthew 6:5. It condemns preachers who pray on street corners and in church. That did it for them. But like everyone else, they didn't become affected one way or the other.

I did explain the best I could to Jimmy. He was my main concern. He was my son, facing the age of understanding, twelve. I told him that we don't ever stop existing. I believed the Bible taught reincarnation. What we get in the next life is based on how we treat others in this one, providing we don't do the mystery and attain the resurrection. It was a little more difficult to explain, although he seemed to understand from the Shroud. I had sure preached it enough. I told him there isn't a Devil or demons and that God is a synonym for spirit, and Satan for flesh. Yeshua even called the Jewish preachers Satans. I explained that Yeshua had washed feet at the Last Supper, to show us that we're equal to him, and if he's God, then we're God. Equal! That was most important of all.

I taught him Yeshua's Golden Rule. Jimmy needed that most of all. He was being mean to people, playing jokes on them. I had been working on the theory that the seventh day of the creation parable was further proof of the way, the mystery. The seventh day was a day of rest. The holy day. I argued with Jake, that when we attain the resurrection we could disappear. After all, Enoch and Elijah did it. He found this pretty bizarre. I explained that the Mount of Transfiguration and Moses' arm incident was good proof that we could. He was the Doubting Thomas. I believed spontaneous human combustion, and the Shroud; it was all too real. I would soon find that every Christian I encountered didn't either. Jake finally would.

I found that Yeshua became disgusted with the Jews thinking that there would be one final last day, an apocalypse. He said, "Time is at hand. These are the Last Days." Jake had finished his Gnostic book, a critique of the Dead Sea Scrolls. He was sure that the Gnostic book was in line with John in the Gospels. He said it was the only book in the Bible that was worth reading. It had the big lie, he grumbled, John 3:16. I chimed in as well. I knew he felt that was added later.

I was continuing to read the Gospels and had just finished Luke. I sure had more than enough evidence to prove that we were indeed spirit and we became flesh, that Heaven was within. The mystery and the tree was the function. I also found an unbelievable connection between Yeshua and Buddha when I looked up Buddhism in the dictionary. I was amazed to find that it was spelled out, plain as day, in black and white. Buddha had reached Nirvana through silent meditation. They both did the forty day thing in the wilderness. The way to achieve stillness of the mind. Annihilation of desire. Just like Yeshua said in his sower parable. He called the devil the cares of this world. Lift up the serpent. I turned to Isaiah and read that very passage, "Only in quiet and rest will you be saved." Yeshua, Buddha, and Isaiah have six letters each!

I also read a passage that further proved that the seven-day creation parable in Genesis was indeed a metaphor for creation of men. The passage read, "Have no fear as I will be with you as you pass through the waters. Seven times I will pass over you." I wondered as I read through this scripture, is it possible that there are seven races of men? I thought I had counted five. I was so excited I wrote them down: White, Black, Indian-red, Asian-yellow, and the Arabic-brown. The tan man from Iran. I laughed at Jake's rapping. We had so much in common. But why five times and why don't we know this? I would soon discover no one else knew. I hadn't found anyone. It seems to all point to the sixth sense, spirit. It's yet even more proof of us being spirit. I was stunned! I suddenly again realized that we were created on the sixth day. I was the sixth born in my family. What a coincidence. The Jewish star had six points. What was happening to me? I remembered Enoch talking about the archangels. He mentioned five. Jake informed me, that Moses' writings were called the Pentateuch because he wrote five books. The pyramid had five sides, and we have five senses. I held up my hand and looked at it. Five races of man. Wow! Why didn't people know this? Little did I know, that by the time I finished this book, we would have a world population of six billion. And a history of six thousand years. Enoch was a seer, with a six sense. He lived a monastic lifestyle in caves, communicating with the angels, staying away from mankind. The most remarkable thing I read was that the angels didn't look him. They were different. I suddenly remembered Shadrack, Meschack and Abendigo. The fourth man was an angel. He had the appearance of the sons of God. They had to have looked different. Radically different. I remembered how amazed I was to find the beginning of John to be just like Genesis. How much plainer can you get? The Jews didn't understand

Genesis. John rewrote it in the gospels. And it is today's science. Quantum physics! In the beginning there was the word! In John 1, there are four references to Yeshua: the voice, the word, seeing him, and the Shroud. "That which we heard from the beginning, that which we hold in our hand, that which we have seen and that which we look upon." This was solid proof of the Shroud's existence. I would soon discover paintings in Europe that proved the shroud. My mind was exploding with information. Brainstorming!

I even finally understood the Trinity. It was the triangle, the pyramids of the Jewish star. It represents time. Time is three things. The past, present, the future! The angels are a little higher than man. They made him and conquered time! I was making charts for everything. Heaven was composed of two-thirds and one-third was cast out. Heaven was literally three-thirds. Three, huh! It took three days for the resurrection. Is this a coincidence or what? The third time is a charm. I found three to be woven throughout all cultures.

The good angels in the universe control the bad, imprisoning them on Earth, stuck in time. Obviously trapped within man. I took a deep breath, and realized suddenly, the whole thing had a mathematical factor so enticing that I couldn't leave it alone. I started making diagrams like Einstein or some lawyer. I even bought a big chalkboard and put it in my bedroom. I drew the Jewish star. Two triangles pointing the opposite way of each other. It represented the Gnostic concept completely. I thought of the Yin and Yang. They believed we were spirits trapped inside man. I read the first book of John and discovered this very thing. "There are three that bear witness in Heaven; the father, the son and the holy spirit; and there are three on Earth; Earth, water and spirit." There it was, Holy Spirit/Spirit. I finished reading the other books of John, while Jake read the Gnostic book. I loved what the word

Gnostic meant, knowledge. I learned another Greek word besides tetra, penta and Messias. Jake said he didn't know how anybody could not see that John was Gnostic. We would soon find out they did. The religious community would call it Essene. We even discovered that the Gnostics gave us the right hand shake. It was their way of maintaining secrecy, within their group. This evidence was in the book of Acts, in the King James version Bible. John extended his right hand to Paul and Barnabas! We knew John was Gnostic. We looked it up on the computer and confirmed the time frame of this religion. It started around 100 B.C. and disappeared by A.D.200. Duh! Rome! This explains John the Baptist and the Dead Sea scrolls. John lived outside of Jerusalem and had no part of organized religion. When Yeshua was killed, the apostles fled for their lives and buried their writings. I just about fell over! I was looking at the chalkboard. There it was, the Jewish star! I took a deep breath and suddenly I had a horrible shocking revelation. The star not only showed us who we are, the angels who went astray. But there was something else! I reached up and drew a ball in the center of the star. It was the nuclear symbol! "Oh my God, no!" I sat down in disbelief and cried. This is our biggest threat today. The extinction of mankind through nuclear proliferation. I knew the Bible was a story of time travel. Einstein gave us nuclear technology, the theory of relativity; and the quote 'Patriotism is an insidious disease. He was a Jew. He felt time travel was possible. I literally shook in fear of this possibility. I couldn't stand the thought of my children seeing my mistakes. I had made some bad ones. And most were sexual. And the history of man was savage beyond belief. No, I cried! Please make it all go away! I sat and sobbed uncontrollably. I suddenly remembered the dream. The dream of the Two Witnesses. Could it be possible? Could we be the two witnesses? I would soon find out. It was obvious, the future has already happened. Mankind had already been made in Heaven/universe, just like he was now able to be made on Earth. And just like it, the leaders of the Earth have declared it illegal. Even we can't escape the horrible truth about man. He is evil. I looked at the nuclear symbol and begged Yeshua to intervene. Please don't let this happen to my children. Please! Please don't let this happen to my children. I cried again even harder. I realized that it already had! I thought about Hiroshima and Nagasaki. No, no, this can't be real. Please Yeshua, I'm begging you! I pointed to my forehead. This is my suicide! I now understood the Hindu ruby and mark on the forehead. This was all a spiritual inner experience, that I was convinced was hard and time-consuming. Time was the only thing on my side. And our families didn't understand because they were brainwashed by their literal interpretation of the Bible. We're brainwashed! The whole world!

I was beginning to feel the impact of my findings. It was clear that Yeshua's teaching was causing the Jews to revolt, to leave the church.

Jake felt that the Jewish custom of worshiping at the temple was right, since Yeshua went there. I couldn't buy this. Really, I think Jake just liked church. It was apparent that he suffered no one outside the Jewish race. He pursued them he said in Matthew, "even as you sat in the same seat as Moses sat in". That explains why he delivered us from Moses' law. I knew he went there because the Jews were supposedly pursuing Heaven. Therefore he wasn't imposing himself upon them. We would try this, eventually. We got the same results. Jake always pointed out that Elaine Pagel said John and Ecclesiastes were the most dangerous books in the Bible. I quickly started reading Ecclesiastes. It began with "all is vanity". It was totally anti-man!

Jake was sure starting to have some problems with Misty. Their conversations about religion were becoming more serious. In fact, they were getting heated. Misty would never do the mystery, and when Angel tried she heard a voice in her head and immediately quit. Jake didn't help with believing that crap about Satan, the devil. I eventually changed his mind, but not before it was too late. Our hopes and dreams were about to be shattered.

Jake had explained the Gnostic religion to me as he read it. I was blown away that they felt we are spirits trapped in flesh bodies. That was Yeshua's whole message. I thought of his simplest question that proved this point. Isn't the body more than meat and raiment, clothing that is? I was blown away. The Pope said that Elaine Pagel's book and the writings themselves weren't anything more than a resurgence of third century Gnosticism which was effectively conquered by the mother church, Rome. It was heresy then and still is now. That pretty much solidifies it. Why do we would buy the ridiculousness of the church killing its founders? Christians killing Christians, come on! Why would anybody believe this? And yet we have. It's the traditional lie.

They were killing these Gnostics. That's how it has to be. Logic dictates. The evidence does too! The books say they're Gnostics, don't they, and the pope confirms it. The Gnostics were conquered by Christians. The Gnostics like Yeshua, probably didn't even defend themselves. They obviously didn't or we wouldn't have found their writings buried in the desert, the find at Nag Hammadi. They obviously ran for their lives. Yeshua and the Apostles weren't the first Christians, but Gnostics like John the Baptist. He baptized Yeshua.and paved the way.

Jake and I were even more fascinated when I read in Ecclesiastes "better is the end of a man, than the beginning." What is man but a worm. Jake started reading it, too. From that day forward he would answer his phone and say, "All is Vanity." We were on a roll.

We were making great progress in our search. The problem was that Misty and Angel were freaked out on spirit things. Jake and Misty were continuing to experience a presence, a ghost in their bedroom. Jake used to do the mystery there. Now, Misty made him do the mystery in the living room. Jake started telling Misty that he was anxious to go to church and asked her to go. She said she would and was even happy about it. It wasn't as scary and a whole lot more entertaining than mystery. However, it would never happen. Only Jake and I tortured the churches.

Jake and Paul were playing heavily, working every gig they could. The weeks had turned into months. Time was flying. They had put quite a bit of time and money into a showcase for some record people. Jake conveniently named the band Big Run. It was the name of the road that he grew up on in Ohio. It was my old school bus route. Coincidence or what? Being their number one fan, I helped watch the door. I even chipped in; every dime counted. We hoped desperately for a big run. It wouldn't happen yet. Jake would see hard times first. And I mean hard times.

Paul recommended a church, one that meditated. Well, at least for five minutes, anyway. Needless to say, Angel and Misty were communicating with each other on a daily basis several times a day. Just as we suspected, they stayed home for our first round. It was too early for Little Jake and Angel didn't really want to go, anyway. Besides, Misty was still in bed. She was a night owl.

"Is she going?" I asked Jake as he got in the car. Angel would've gone. It was a beautiful sunny day in December. One of our last picture perfect days. A cold hard winter was about hit. So was Misty and the Spirit!

"No, she couldn't sleep last night."

"Is she still wigged out on that room?"

"Yeah," he said. "She's scared to death."

"That's sick, isn't it? Christianity," I growled. "They've got us all the way, and we don't know it. The bastards," I railed. "Yeshua isn't their father. They're illegitimate! Their the real bastards! I'm going to sue them one day. You wait and see."

"You can't sue them. They're protected by the government," he remarked quickly.

"No, maybe not! But we can prove them wrong and then maybe, just maybe, it can be corrected. At least it would get some publicity. Christianity sued for fraud in a civil suit. Preponderance of evidence. The majority rules. Yeah! Remember, two-thirds. The future's now, dude. The angels won't contact us until this cruel Christian-Judeo world crumbles and the truth can live. Live without being killed. Man is a killer. Finally live, man, woman, and child in peace." I held up my two fingers. I just grinned; Jake did too. We just knew. We didn't say a word. Logic dictated the peace symbol!

We both argued as usual the next few weeks as we studied my seven-day creation theory. He was blown away at the sight of my chalkboard and the Jewish star. I left the atom in the center and drew the nuclear symbol beneath it. He finally agreed with it.

I was studying Buddhism and I would say, "Yeshua's teachings were just like Buddha's". Jake would always say, "Mike, you can't say that to a Christian, man."

We would always argue and I would tell him that I didn't care. I wasn't doing this for the Christians. I was doing it for my kids, so they wouldn't have to sort through all the lies that we have to. History hasn't been rewritten, and it has to be, because it's provable. We can change. If we aren't too proud to face the truth, I thought. Hell yes, America the proud. Where it's okay to be religious and proud at the same time. It's

America's dirty little secret and the Indians' worst nightmare.

The one thing that Jake and I argued about relentlessly was god. He felt that God did exist as a life-form, not flesh, but greater than any man or thing. The oldest thing in the universe, the universe itself. I told him god is everything and it's Spirit, invisible! He had a hard time with it! Soon we would learn about quantum physics and the study of sub-atomic particles. It proves everything is invisible that is visible. Ultimately, the only thing that exists is just movement of information in electric form. Information. The Word! I guess it came through mystery. I don't know. I now can plug holes, make logical conclusions. I felt that we are spirits, from the moment I saw the Shroud and figured out the name. Yeshua's teachings in John were clearly telling us who we are and what we must do. We "must be born again of the spirit" and it's hard. Even more, what is it? Spirit. *(It matches the atom and we are it!)*

Throughout our disagreements, as to whether we are gods or not, Jake and I really hammered the scriptures. It was clear that Yeshua was showing us that we are all equal and we could do anything that he could do. We just forgot who our Father was: Spirit!

"It's that clear!" I hollered and told Jake, "Don't you see? We're spirits! That's what we've forgotten. That's what the Shroud is, man. You're right about the angels, dude, and this, the Shroud. I thank you for it." I hugged him. "It's a picture of us, all right. But most importantly, it's a picture of the only way to get back. Worship in spirit, the mystery, the tree, or even better yet, the rest. Enter into Yeshua's rest. I don't want to argue anymore!"

"What?" Jake would ask, making his usual sarcastic, dumbfounded look.

I told him it was easy to see that the seven-day creation parable was a fall from Day One. The angels created the five races of mankind.

The sixth always existed. They evolved from nothing! Spirit! The angels obviously conquered death and time travel. They actually created the first five and got trapped in them. And "the way" got lost. Until the sixth day. Then, Yeshua and two-thirds of the good angels became/created true man, the son of man, the Jewish race. The race of the immaculate conception. This was to assure us that there would be adequate proof. Proof to convince us of the way to be saved. The seventh day, the holy day of rest. Yeshua, the tried cornerstone, gave us the same message," enter into my rest."

Jake was pretty amazed. I couldn't get over the connection between the amount of races and the connection to the creation parable. I was determined to study and see if all the other cultures/races had the mystery. I knew the Buddhists did, and the Indians. But what about the others? And we know Aladdin does, I laughed. Well at least his Jeanie anyway. Jake had a lot of Indian in him and acted like he was proud of it. Funny, that all Americans do the same thing and yet we had a bounty on them as little as one hundred years ago. There's a good example of how a truth can be so perverted. What was once evil, is now good. Jake became a wealth of information for me, and he sure liked his teacher role.

We had started seeing less and less of each other as Christmas closed in. I had gone to see the family for Thanksgiving and ended up staying for deer season. I had totally intended to quit hunting, but still clung to eating a little meat. It was the hardest habit I ever tried to break, and it tortured my family. Jake had quit eating meat on the moral issue alone. Although, he did want to live as long as possible. Didn't we all! That became a controversial subject. A torturous subject! He always asked, "What kind of gods are we?" I understood it and from that day on I struggled with it. I really wanted to quit. I was having a hard time because my family didn't understand it. Thanksgiving and rabbit season was tradition. Then came deer hunting. How was I going to resolve this? I didn't know. I failed and killed not only then, but for a couple of years later by eating the meat that was killed. I understood perfectly the oath-taker scripture. I was guilty! I killed a deer in front of my son, that year. I did apologize later, when we were alone. It was an awful moment telling my son I was wrong. I had shown so much enthusiasm in killing that deer. I felt like a killer. That would become the most torturous memory. How could I! A killer! A killer! I was so ashamed and sorry!

"We're just brainwashed, son," I said with tears in my eyes. "All of us, my Dad, me; and his dad before him. You see, my Dad taught me to hunt, and he thought it was okay, just like his Dad did. But when we ask ourselves if it's fair, we don't have to think very long, do we. Especially if we were the deer! Just because some tradition tells you something is okay, son, doesn't make it so. Let fairness and logic be your guide. We can't hide the truth. We could've been that deer." I never hunted again. We came back to Tennessee with my trophy. I felt ashamed, but not too ashamed to have it mounted. I was worthless, as a prophet and Jake rubbed it in. But it didn't stop me from doing the mystery. I eventually gave the deer to one of my brothers. Maybe it would help. It tortured them. We honed in on the vegetarian thing, and it was clear that Yeshua found meat abominable. He called the things they put in their stomach abominable. I later discover the Eastern Vegetarian Festival. The fish thing is Catholic. I didn't know that. Jake quickly explained to me that the Catholic monks eat fish on Friday, the day before the Sabbath. Rome still had an effect on us today, even in our school systems. Fish on Fridays. We are Romans, with a Jewish foundation of course. All roads lead to Rome.

When I was looking up these scriptures, I saw the abomination of desolation scripture. I told Jake about a theory of mine. It was that, "time, times and a half a time, equalled seventy years." It was proof of reincarnation every time we die. Our last day. The abomination of desolation, our death. When we see our dead body, just like the meat we put in our mouths, it is the abomination of desolation. Jake was again impressed. He then filled me in on history. I didn't know, that most scholars interpret this to be the time Zeus was put in the holy temple of the Jews around A.D. 70, when the temple was destroyed.

"Yeshua said our body was the temple," I said with disgust.

He immediately remarked back to the scripture of Yeshua throwing the merchants out of the holy temple. He liked church. I quickly quoted John 3:16. He started to defend the idea of church. I didn't want to argue about the concept of church. It was the content I had a problem with. He knew what I meant. If one thing can be written in, then so can another. He had been trying to get me back to the church that meditated for five minutes. I wasn't going back to a church to worship, especially just for five minutes. Everybody exalts themselves by dressing up. I could do the mystery at home. As a matter of fact, I could do it longer. He always made it clear how little I knew, and started asking me, if I had been to a so-and-so church.

"No, I haven't, but we can start with the name. If they don't know that it's been changed, then forget it." I knew that would do it. He taught me well. I now knew the importance of the name. It and the Shroud kept me going. I tried my best to quit eating meat, going for weeks at a time. I would eventually win and destroy my marriage and my life in the process. I did the mystery relentlessly, morning and night. I even let Jake talk me into going back to that church. It turns out they held a private Zen meditation. Jake was elated; Angel was fit to be tied. It was every Saturday morning at seven-thirty on the other side of town, an hour's drive from my house. We did it for a couple of weeks before everything came to a head and blew. And boy, did it blow.

In the next few weeks before Christmas, our studies revealed even more grim facts about Yeshua and his behavior. I studied the meaning of the eunuch scripture, after discovering that Daniel was a eunuch. I never even knew what a eunuch was! It was standard procedure for priests, preachers, prophets, shamans, medicine men, monks, and whatever else you want to call them. They were eunuchs, spiritual advisors. It was clear that eunuchs were seers for the king. They were neutered and maintained a pious monastic lifestyle. Most were taken from their families as young men, like Daniel. The parable of the eunuchs, by Yeshua, clearly shows that attaining the resurrection took daily practice and required first priority. Thus the reason for "Blessed are the eunuchs". We had plenty of evidence that was anti-creation. Jake and I knew all too well family responsibility. But that didn't alleviate the truth. Nor did the truth alleviate our situations. Whether or not we could make a compromise was about to unfold, or rather, be thrown into high gear.

Jake had been working every minute he could. He had tried to ease off the religion thing. Misty was getting upset by it. She wasn't going to do the mystery, because of her hang-up with evil spirits, and she didn't get the opportunity before she snapped.

Angel was also having a hard time. She was becoming paranoid that I would leave this world through the mystery and spontaneous human combustion. I tried to console her, telling her I wouldn't do that without exposing this Judeo-Christian lie that we live under. Besides if I could do that, it would be a miracle. Because, then I could come back and get rid of death, for all of us. I told her I was going to finish my book and win a lawsuit against Christianity.

"Yeah, and you'll get killed," she screamed. "The Two Witnesses, remember?"

"Angel," I said, shaking my head. "You don't get it; I'm dead now. I've already got a death sentence. We all do!"

"Well it's going to happen a lot sooner than you think if you keep this shit up. Jake's brainwashed you." She started to cry. She started to scream. She just started freaking out.

I quickly tried calming her. "Honey, honey, calm down. Don't you see the good side to this? We never stop existing! If I did leave, wouldn't that be the greatest thing that could ever happen to me, to us?"

"No!" She cried even harder.

How could I ever get her to see this, or anyone for that matter? It was the hardest thing I had to overcome. How do you get them to take the hard path? We have to do the mystery. And my wife had the Christianity curse just like Misty. But I would do the mystery. The mystery and more, much more. I became dangerous.

It finally happened. Misty broke! Jake had been paying more attention to his satellite business, books, music, and mystery than Misty. He had really been absorbed in the other Bible, and TV preacher. He only let me take the Gnostic book for a week between our Saturday sits. I gave it back and stated beyond any doubt, "The Christians killed the Gnostics, the Apostles."

"Yep, looks that way, huh?"

"No wonder this will torture people!" I exclaimed loudly. "The Gnostics think we're spirits trapped in this body. They see it as evil, not good." Misty couldn't handle the spirit thing! She was openly afraid, when we returned from our morning mystery. She heard us discussing this, and practically ran into the bedroom. I looked at Jake and he looked at me. We didn't know what was going on! I jokingly said, "It's your devil curse, Jake. Fragile humans!" We could hear Misty moving around and the television came on. It didn't take a rocket scientist to figure out that it was time to go.

Jake was having financial problems that Saturday, as I left his driveway for work. He had sunk quite a bit in the showcase and hadn't even thought about Christmas. Misty was still upset over not having a good Thanksgiving with her family. Things were not good.

I hadn't been at work anytime, when Angel called. I became faint with terror at the possibilities. Angel never called me at work, because of the inconvenience to the gift shop owner. He had to come outside to get me. I ran to get the phone. "Hello."

"Misty is on the run from Jake!" She screamed hysterically.

"What?" I asked, almost panicking myself.

She was crying and said that Jake became possessed, and tried to kill Misty! When I tried to talk further, she just screamed for me to leave and come home now. Now! Frantically, I hung up the phone and told Jerald I was going to the house. It was an emergency. I asked him if he would please watch my stuff. He agreed and asked me if everything was all right. He noticed my obvious change in personality. I told him it was and left. If he only knew.

I raced home not knowing what kind of ordeal had taken place between Misty and Jake, but knowing damn well that Jake wasn't trying to kill anyone. Misty was just wigging out. As I pulled in the driveway, Angel came outside. Her eyes were swollen from crying, and I could tell she was still pretty shaken up.

"Have you seen Jake?" She cried out. Then she immediately ran toward me screaming. "Did you know Jake was going to kill Misty? Did you? You knew about it, didn't you!" She started to lose it and pounded on my chest. "You guys lost it, Mike, and I think Jake's talked you into leaving with him!" I reached for her in an attempt to quiet her down and she jerked away screaming. "Don't 'Honey' me!" She screamed. "I want to know. Do you have anything to do with this?"

"To do with what, Angel? This is all new to me."

"Well, according to Misty, it ain't new. You're leaving with Jake."

"Hon, I'm not going anywhere. And Jake wouldn't kill Misty; that's crazy. Hell, Misty believes in demons, dammit, get real. Doesn't that tell you anything? Have you seen my head spin around and spit out pea green soup? Am I the one losing it here? Come on!" I found myself getting louder.

"No, but you have changed and Yeshua, Yeshua, Yeshua—!" She screamed and stomped, shaking her head violently. "Yeshua is all you care about, dammit! I've lost you!"

I tried my best to console her, but she just screamed harder. "Jake and Yeshua have won. They've got you!" She wailed as she turned away from me and started running toward the house.

"Get hold of yourself, dammit, or I swear I'll leave right now, Angel," I suddenly screamed out of sheer panic! I didn't know how else to calm her down. I ran and caught her. I hugged her tight as I could and pleaded. "Look at me, Misty has wigged out!" She was trying to pull away screaming and crying. I pulled her around and screamed, "Dammit! Stop this for Little Jake's sake, Angel, I'm telling you the truth. When have I ever lied? Misty has just wigged out." She started to pull away again and I broke. "O.K. dammit, you win. I'll leave!" She suddenly stopped. It worked.

"How come you and Jake have been talking on the phone and then when I come in you quiet down or hang up."

"I do it for the same reason I do with your Mom, Angel. It tortures you. I don't want to torture you anymore."

"I want to help you, Mike, but I can't. Jake has won." She tried to pull away from me.

"Jake hasn't won a damn thing. You're making it a contest. You and Misty will go to church, so you could put on your fancy clothes and eat at the best restaurants, just like it says in Matthew 23! But if it's hard, forget it! Especially if it means giving up this world. Dammit, snap out of it. I'm trying to help us all. I love you!"

"You've changed!" She wailed, uncontrollably. But she wasn't pulling away.

"Haven't I changed for the better, dammit?" My temper was flaring, and she knew that I couldn't take that. I would run then. "I didn't want this to happen. But since it has, I can't help it. I will never again love this world, and I can't pretend to. The bad part is trying to be of good cheer in a world full of people who are cosmic waste. Your problem is that I just don't eat, drink, and be merry anymore. I don't make plans and goals for wealth, and I don't turn my mind off to poverty, starvation, and racism. I don't go with the status quo! I'm not the old Jehovah's Witness Mike. But that's good, isn't it?" I started to cry. "I'm headed in the right direction! I want to recycle. I want to right some wrongs for my son, for our son." It was my turn to lose it.

She hugged me and started calming down. She agreed with me about my changes being good. She promised she would even start helping me recycle that year.

"I know you will, honey. You've put up with a lot. But you know me better than this, and I've proven to you that demons don't exist. Hell, I've proven it to everyone, haven't I?"

"Well," she stammered with great effort and started to hug me and cry again. "I'm just so scared."

"Well, haven't I or not?" I asked softly. "You were there, when I showed Mom and Dad the word demon isn't even in the Bible, weren't you?"

"Yes," she said meekly.

"Angel, dammit, we're just brainwashed. This world is full of lies that have become truth over time, but whose truth, Angel? There isn't a devil and there aren't any demons. If there is, where is he? I'll work for him. And if there's a god, where is the cruel bastard!"

"Stop it, Mike!"

"Baby, please, I'm just trying to show you that they aren't real. The devil wants us more than anything Angel, according to Christianity. So, why doesn't he come get me, huh? He isn't real! I'm going back to work. We're gods! Please get yourself together, before you go back in the house. Be a good god for little Jake, please. I'm begging you!"

She did so reluctantly, but told me not to listen to Jake if he came around.

"Angel," I reassured her, "Jake is fine. It's Misty that needs to get it together." Her, too, I thought to myself. "Now please, I'm begging you to get yourself together. Jake wouldn't kill anyone, and I'm shocked that you would believe this. Don't pay any attention to Misty. And leave the phone off the hook, until I can find out what happened." I pulled away as she went inside. I hoped she would go to the bathroom and straighten her face. Little Jake was so sensitive. I just shook my head in disbelief as I hurried down River Road. I couldn't believe what was happening. The winter of 1993 sure came in like a lion.

"The Two Witnesses," I suddenly said out loud. Then I looked in the mirror at myself. I started to cry. I didn't want to torture anybody. I didn't want to, but I couldn't stop it, either. The findings of our search would do it for themselves. Heaven would soon become irrefutably clear to me. It was universally Space/"UP!" I can't believe it took me so long to see that Elijah and Enoch went "UP" too. "UP" becomes my focus. Why? Because we go "UP" in fiery chariots, too!

I would soon find plenty of ancient evidence of what the angels/gods looked like. The Easter Island statues held the most convincing clue. They all looked the same! This matched their equality story in heaven. The problem is they looked like aliens! No! I was fast becoming an archaeologist. Physical evidence would soon torture all the spirit thinkers around me, including my buddy Jake, *"the other witness."*

My search for heaven was and is very painful. The reason for this was and is that most of my family, friends and readers of my books held fast to their traditional spirit teachings from the Bible. I can't believe how much it has influenced people all over the world, just from hearing it quoted by preachers. I often tell them now and unfortunately told them in the past that this wasn't and isn't scientifically seeking evidence. This is called tradition. All prophets/religion speak against tradition and **MONEY/WEALTH.**

I promise to give to the poor and never attain material wealth. Will they? This is my challenge and **Yeshua's** as well.

(I am not a bible-thumper; just pointing out that simple message of all religion is anti-materialism. This was Atlantis and all other pre-flood stories' perfect culture's "DOWN-fall." Word "UP", people, equality!)

JESUS SAID UNTO HIM, IF THOU WILT BE PERFECT, GO AND SELL THAT THOU HAST, AND GIVE TO THE POOR, AND THOU SHALT HAVE TREASURE IN HEAVEN: AND COME AND FOLLOW ME.

—MATTHEW 19:21

To finish reading the first book of my search, buy a copy of *The Two Witnesses*. Then follow up with the next three books of which covers you will see in the fifth book. Enjoy!

I had to share my past so that you could better understand where I am today, and clearly "see" where I am going tomorrow.

The evidence!
ABC-Phoenix, Arizona rejects
my flying saucer discovery.
May 29, 2007

Fifth book, February, 2007

"People, without religion, we'd be looking "UP" for spacecraft when contact happens. Primitive man said heaven is "UP" and they created us! Science compels us to look for this evidence. Why? Because it matches today's knowledge. We live "UP" and create too. Heaven is Space, UP to us as well."
—*Mike Brumfield*

HEAVEN IS SPACE... UP!

MIKE BRUMFIELD

"MICHAEL"

"If the evidence changes, so must the theory."
—*Grissom, CSI of CBS*

"The evidence hasn't changed! The 'story' did."
—*Michael*

Did Flying Saucers Create Religion?

Could our sudden appearance without the skull evolution from an elongated cranium to the obvious upright bulbous large head be directly related to religion's god? Our short recorded history is!

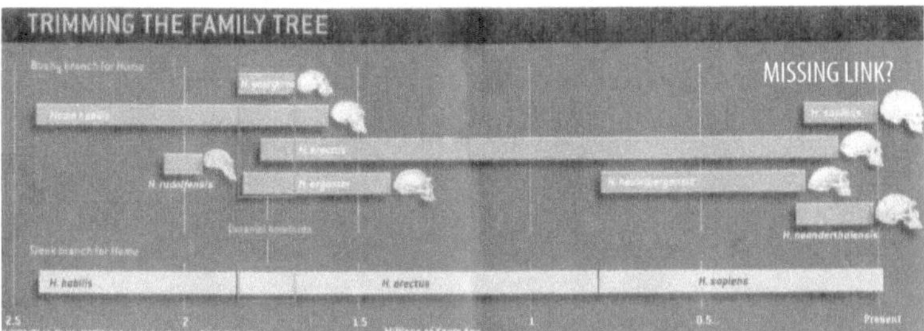

Could the large-headed statues below be primitive man's god/angel, and nature's creation/evolution?
Nature does create life through evolution that looks "equal," like a flock of geese, a herd of zebras, etc.

Dedication

*I dedicate this book to Barbara Walters
and her special, "Where is Heaven?"*

THE FOLLOWING is my scientific answer, based solely on evidence, to Barbara Walters and her famous question/interview that was recently aired in August 2006. The question that she asked of all the world's major religious leaders: "WHERE IS Heaven?" Of course she said we all know it's up from the onset of every interview. But do we really? Well, her esteemed panel didn't. None of them took this seriously, and the majority of them said it was a spirit or dimensional world. They certainly didn't think it was up in the sky and never referred to the sky as space. The funny thing is, that one of them even said it wasn't real. He said it was a metaphor. You know like the good and evil in "US" all. What! Who does this guy think he is? How dare he judge us and say we all have evil in us. That's not for him to say and remains to be "SEEN"! Maybe he needs to confess? But what else can we expect from a RELIGIOUS scholar?

Religion is synonymous with judging/RIGHTEOUSNESS / hypocrisy (well maybe not all)! Well, what can we expect? For a start, some day, is hopefully science. Science would let the evidence be the judge and not him. It would have no feeling with its verdict, either. If scientific evidence can answer this question, will Barbara even see it?

This remains to be "SEEN" as well.

I'm begging her to do a follow-up show with scientists who acknowledge the ancient flying saucer and alien artwork evidence. Maybe the answers will surprise her and agree with the universal ancient "UP" evidence of heaven in the Bible. Barbara laughed after each interview that none of them said "UP," like ALL ancient writings say. And I did, too. The evidence clearly says it is up, and she even mentioned that we all still look up today. I'm sure her laughter wasn't because she saw the irony of this scientific reality—and she tells us so at the end of the show—of Heaven being "UP" and us going "UP," like I now do. I'm sure, because she never mentioned it and at the end of the show even said herself that she still wonders if we will ever find Heaven. Well, I would love to show her as a scientist presenting evidence of why it is up, that we have already found it, like I wrote on my fourth book's cover, *SCIENCE FINDS Heaven!* But will she let science do what religion couldn't or is she religious and "CAN'T SEE THIS SCIENTIFIC MATCHING EVIDENCE"? Will any religious person see the shocking matching evidence of SCIENCE AND RELIGION'S "UP" FACT OF LIFE!? Take away the magic spirit factor, and I think they could. I think some will, like I finally did. I did it by proving it to myself. I've seen no proof of instant creation, magic spirits or anything living that can't be killed! PROOF IS SCIENCE and "Heaven" began irrefutably "UP!" If you don't "BELIEVE" that Heaven is "up," then please give my answer and evidence a chance. Please, Barbara, for our children's sake. Religion has us on the brink of global nuclear war!

My answer is scientific hard provable evidence. It is the reason I titled this book *Heaven is Space . . . UP*—and after all Barbara does agree!

At least in premise. Please laugh here, everybody, and for me, take life easy today. Let religion go. Sing along: "Let it be." Let's all sing! Singing is good for the soul, and I'm a soul man! Oh, how I love to sing. Let's all sing, please? It will bring peace to our valley. I can promise you that. Oh, by the way, don't ever "promise a rose garden." Somebody's life ain't so rosy today even if yours is! And please don't ever forget that. Now, let's all have a coke, Lionel Richie, and teach the whole world to sing in perfect harmony! Please? Let it be, let it be!

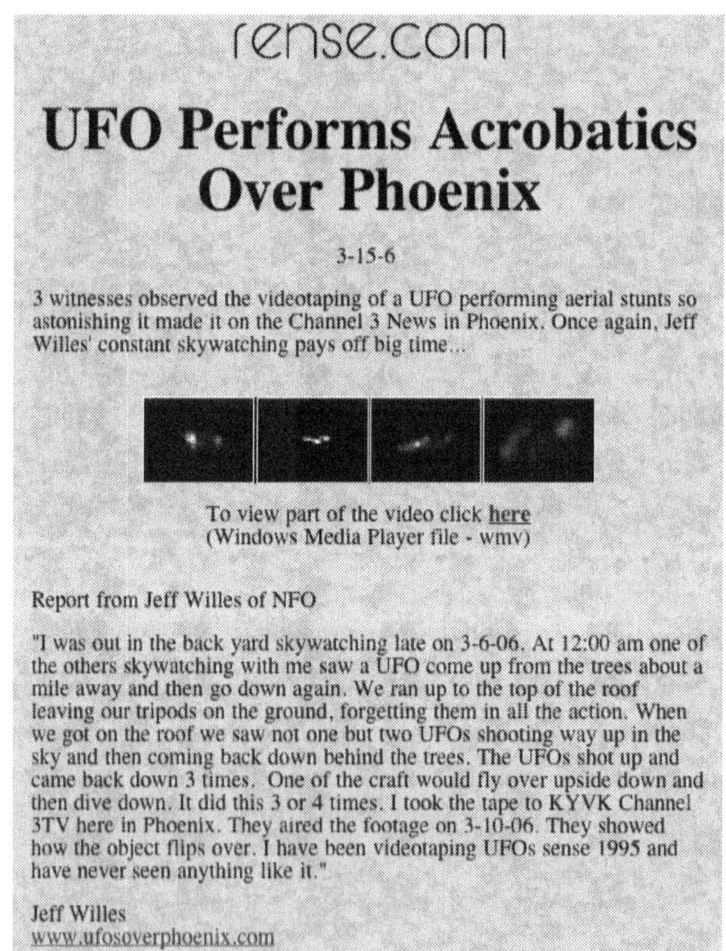

rense.com

UFO Performs Acrobatics Over Phoenix

3-15-6

3 witnesses observed the videotaping of a UFO performing aerial stunts so astonishing it made it on the Channel 3 News in Phoenix. Once again, Jeff Willes' constant skywatching pays off big time...

To view part of the video click here
(Windows Media Player file - wmv)

Report from Jeff Willes of NFO

"I was out in the back yard skywatching late on 3-6-06. At 12:00 am one of the others skywatching with me saw a UFO come up from the trees about a mile away and then go down again. We ran up to the top of the roof leaving our tripods on the ground, forgetting them in all the action. When we got on the roof we saw not one but two UFOs shooting way up in the sky and then coming back down behind the trees. The UFOs shot up and came back down 3 times. One of the craft would fly over upside down and then dive down. It did this 3 or 4 times. I took the tape to KYVK Channel 3TV here in Phoenix. They aired the footage on 3-10-06. They showed how the object flips over. I have been videotaping UFOs sense 1995 and have never seen anything like it."

Jeff Willes
www.ufosoverphoenix.com

Author's family struggle now turned world-wide!

(Please bear with my sometimes rambling passionate brainstorming)

Did Flying Saucers Create Religion?

SPACE IS "UP" AND RELIGION IS A STORY OF PEOPLE WHO LIVE "UP" IN THE SKY! WE LIVE "UP" IN THE SKY!

I was shocked at my lifelong primitive spirit thinking when this scientific matching reality finally dawned on me. Moreover, these two things agree, living in the sky and creating. We're doing both! I truly understand how my life changed from a boy whose religion teaches/believes the universal spirit story, to being a scientist. My parents' religion started with the commandment to "have no other gods before me" yet says he's the only one. And then, to add insult to injury, we sanctified our prayers to "HIM" with an Egyptian God named Amun/"Amen." No way! What a contradiction and joke. I understand why I didn't see this scientific reality as I so well know now. My parents weren't teaching me science. I finally know we must conquer space to save ourselves from each other, let alone natural disasters. But do they? No!

This is as much a scientific fact for us today as it was for the ancients who gave us religion thousands of years ago. But how can this be? How could they know this then and we not know it today? They weren't scientific and certainly were brutally primitive by today's standards. But even more importantly, they were religious followers of "heavenly creators!" WHAT! Who the heck are these people? This can't be a coincidence. We need to go "UP" and find them—they say we came from "UP", and we are going "UP"!

THIS IS INDISPUTABLE MATCHING SCIENTIFIC EVIDENCE in solving our mystery! There must have been contact with life that had conquered space. Could these religious heavenly occupants be real flesh and blood beings who have always existed like space itself? Space Dwellers? If so why the hell would they stay away?

And we surely want to know if they look just like us. I mean, after all, it is a given that no one has been able to take us to their leader or make them show up. This I find applies to both religion, scientist, ufologist or atheists who think life does exist elsewhere in the universe. Huh, think about this. Are all these really coincidences? Are we so naive to think we're the only ones in this INFINITE universe? Maybe we are an unstoppable scientific creation. This certainly supports and explains their absence more than them being spirits. Can't we just imagine the scientific possibility of discovering new evidence to solve these questions? Science does. And what if they don't look like us and are ugly? This goes even further to explain their absence. It supports the lust for power "Fall from Heaven/"UP" story." We all lust for beauty. Could this be Hell? The evidence confirms it. HELL IS HAPPENING RIGHT NOW! BABIES ARE BEING RAPED! WE ARE "BEAUTY ADDICTS!"

Today DNA is solving cases that were once thought unsolvable in our past. Science will likely conquer this and much, much, more—possibly even immortality itself, through nanotechnology, cloning, DNA duplication, and even resurrection itself. Maybe even storing memory or even finding that it is infinite anyway within the atomic universe! "WHEREVER THE SUN SHINES LIFE WILL EXIST." *(See ancient Chinese disk!)* Even if this sounds unreachable to you then at least realize that space is our final frontier! And we have reached it. We live in a space station. People, Space is our final frontier. SPACE, THE FINAL FRONTIER! Captain Kirk made this the most famous universal simple scientific fact that we know today! All children are looking to the stars for our future survival. All religious adults look "UP" to the stars. Coincidence? Not if you consider the flying saucer evidence/future reality. And did he sum it up best by saying "to boldly go where no man has gone before"? Is he absolutely sure that no man has gone there before? Are any of us? I'm not. I have déjà vu, and the teaching of reincarnation exists. Besides, religion teaches prophecy (predicting the future, that we could have done this before). Oh, and don't forget "immortal" spirits too.

But what is a spirit? Could it be a body that can convert its mass to light, or could it be like a hologram? Could it be a form of communication to a primitive species in which it needs to manipulate because of its subservient use and their flesh-and-blood reality? It makes sense, if they're real like us and don't want to be hurt. Could it be something that we just still don't know what the heck it is and that's the reason we have ghost busters/science?

If we don't know then let us investigate further, please? I think that any logical human on Earth would find it hard to believe that we are alone. I think that this commonsense scientific mentality is understandable in looking into an infinite sky full of circles just like our own. In fact, being "alone" is not possible in an "infinite" universe. Please let yourself start thinking infinitely, as both science and religion confirm this possibility. It is the foundation of both. The atom and God are both infinite. And so far, the universe is infinite too, until proven otherwise. This is a "Beautiful" fact of life. In fact, it is logical to assume that life is watching us even if it isn't making contact with us.

It is also logical to conclude that space has already been conquered by people who would be light years ahead of us in technology. If the universe is infinite then it is a given that they are! To give them numbers like light years is a contradiction, an oxymoron. Religion says this very thing. They have no time! If the "FINAL" frontier is in fact conquered then reincarnation makes sense if this is our/their incurable disease/lusting for scientific human creation. This is where they would not be able to cohabitate with their "former" heavenly inhabitants. Carl Sagan let us know like Einstein that matter/energy can't stop existing. We can't create it, so looking for the beginning of our universe is like buying the beginning of creation in every religion: then you find out "Heaven" doesn't have time! We can't create what makes up atoms!

And the bible says we are Adams! People, come on! This mystery is all about "Why the hell would they stay away?" (Fermi's Paradox). And in my quest to find that answer, I was shocked to find that it may have to do with "what the hell they look like"! Let's stop being afraid of this unknown. They aren't hurting us, and if someone says they are then let them scientifically prove it. "If not, then they're the good guys!" There is ancient and modern evidence to prove they don't look just like us! Frankly they're ugly! And the writings prove that they are real flesh-and-blood people who can be hurt, killed, and have sex with us! What? No way!

Most of all, there are plenty of references to these divine encounters that show the person was horrified upon seeing this angel or God! Why am I not afraid of the evidence? I guess because of my experience with this happening to me when I was only six. It's in my second, third and fourth books. But were they gruesomely ugly and what we embellished to now call them monsters today? The evidence must confirm this, and it must be ANCIENT ART for it to be so!

I am not afraid of monsters, nor the dark. I grew "UP." I am afraid of being ugly and dieing. If I get scared in the dark, it is because I can't SEE! I guess I'm like this because the Jehovah's Witnesses, my parent's religion, couldn't answer these questions for me. Worse yet, they scared the hell out of me with demons and devils who are spirits that I can't SEE! Religion terrorized me, taught me nothing and turned me to science. Science gave me a whole new understanding of religion! I wanted answers. As a loving parent, I want to help all children from being tortured by ignorance, religious terrorism, and DEATH.

Science proves that our atoms always exist! Scientific evidence is our future, and we shouldn't be afraid of challenge! And it, like our children, should be nurtured for the sake of their future! Here's to the future. The scientific religious evidence that you are about to read and see has persuaded me to be scientific about religion's heavenly occupants. This evidence that I have discovered and still am learning, in my quest for answers about our origins, has changed me forever. It made me a scientific believer of these mysterious "PEOPLE "UP" IN SPACE" and answered the torturous question: "Why would they stay away?" This in turn answered for me: "why the universe isn't perfect and why they can't stop us from killing each other?"

Finally, it has answered the ultimate question: "What do they look like and where did they 'come from?'" Again "come from" is a contradiction to an infinite universe and energy/matter. The following evidence "should" tell you why our mystery exists. If it doesn't, then maybe it flies in the face of your religious prejudice as it did with some of my family.

Please don't let words hurt you. We teach children "sticks and stones may break my bones but words will never hurt me." Come on. This evidence is also about helping the brutality of humanity as science represents today. It will speak for itself, without any prejudice on my part. I follow the evidence only as any scientist or neutral seeker of answers should! If we all wouldn't die for our children today then we need to re-think even looking for answers. Can religious "BELIEVERS" see the matching scientific evidence between religion and flying saucer evidence? Scientifically, I already know most can't because of the evidence that exists now. They can't give up the "magic"/omnipotent god. Most religious people don't know where Heaven is and believe in spirits, without seeing proof. So seeing flying saucers won't change most of them.

My brother Brian said it best in a recent interview for my new DVD, "Why The Blank Don't They Care?" I was getting his eyewitness testimony of seeing a silver-disk in the sky above a commercial jet while building my billboard *(see back cover of this book)* last August. I asked him if he thought seeing one will help religious people. He said he asked a preacher this, and even the preacher told him that he would still believe in his God! Even worse, "He" has to come back on the clouds "riding a white horse." No, this can't be happening! Please somebody slap me! I've already asked my family the questions you are about to read in my struggle. If their reaction is any indication, then, indeed, their religious one-third *(those cast out of Heaven)* will be cast again onto another "lake of fire"/body/Earth to infinitely be religiously doomed. Coincidentally, to a final test of NOT BELIEVING THE SCIENTIFIC EVIDENCE SO OBVIOUSLY ENTRENCHED IN EVERY SOCIETY ON EARTH as a result of non-cohabitation. All this in spite of looking "UP" and giving God a halo symbol that looks like a flying saucer.

We are ruled by religious leaders who all look "UP" to Heaven, but believe in spirits. This is chiseled in stone. I've asked them, my family

and many people at my book signings or lectures, why? I'm not surprised to find that none answer scientifically or don't remember they
were taught this ignorance and obvious contradiction. Why would
spirits come from "UP?" Let alone be riding white horses! There parents don't know why, either! Only the scientific will see this matching
"UP" evidence. Scientists will let the evidence and lack of it say who
these gods are. What's really scary is that our world leaders are religious.
They believe in Heaven, kill children just like their god, and have NU-
CLEAR WEAPON capabilities to destroy the world! That's the scariest
thing of all. How could this be any scarier than the Biblical Hell? People, this must be Hell!

When I press the issue that "Jesus"/Yeshua himself saw religious
people didn't know where Heaven was and would kill too, they would
get very angry. I have also been attacked and received religious death
threats. But, I still want to ask the world: WHERE IS HEAVEN AND
WHY DON'T YOU KNOW IT'S SPACE? SPACE IS "UP"!

Yes, I would especially love to ask Captain Kirk this very thought-
provoking question. If nothing else, to see how much his wonderfully futuristic-based scientific phenomenal show influenced his scientific awareness of "OUR" religious world around him. Did he and does
he see the matching scientific evidence of flying saucers to heaven's fiery chariots? They are both "UP" in the sky and this is where they came
from. And of course, this is where we are going . . . "UP." We all know
that conquering space is the logical course of events for our species to
survive. Or at least I thought so, until I scientifically examined religion
and its adult followers. Most don't think scientifically. They don't know
this fact and, yes, I'm shocked that they believe God's magic will super-
sede science. Only God will save us! And of course, they all want you
to send God money because he owns all the wealth and is our ultimate

lien-holder. To prove you believe this to them you should give to God. But of course, again, through "Pat" who handles everything.

I just heard Pat Robertson say this on the *700 Club* at 10:00 A.M. this morning. To my horror he was on NBC. No! This is influencing our kids, people! How can this be? He's the "pResident's" friend. He is also the same guy who preaches revenge instead of forgiveness, totally the opposite of whom he represents. Just like the President! I can't stand how both use science when they want and use religion when they don't. How can we let religious people use science when they want and then attack it otherwise? This is the height of hypocrisy. Of course I know how. Religion rules our White House too! You will see why this is so when you view the *J. W. Magazine* using science to prove God exists through intelligent design, but then saying science is not to be trusted either. Crazy, huh? Worse yet, they say something can't come from nothing! What they don't see is that's exactly what their story is. Their "invisible"/spirit God just thinks it into instant existence! Although, when it comes to all children, religion doesn't rule here. They want visible, scientific proof. They know, because of science, that we need to get off this planet and conquer space.

But, what if there was proof that it already is, contrary to Captain Kirk's popular sound-bite's "to boldly go where no man has gone before" made oh-so-famous by *Star Trek*? And if there was, why wouldn't he or any of his cast members have "seen it" by now, especially the logical one, MR. SPOCK? Could they also believe in the magic invisible God who lives in the sky? Would evidence change them? You should already know the answer. It's already written in the religious "EQUATION", two-thirds will and one-third won't. If they did "see it" we'd already know—they're famous. So, just imagine that it's you who discovers flying saucer evidence and sees this similarity between "it" and religion. And how hard it would be to get respect. Well, this is my story. Now, just imagine trying to get an Intelligent Design religious proponent who says "SOMETHING CAN'T COME FROM NOTHING." That is exactly what his God story is—to REALIZE, that's what it does and is. His God is invisible and just speaks things into existence. VOILA: SOMETHING CAME FROM NOTHING! COME ON, RELIGIOUS PEOPLE, GET SOME SCIENCE/COMMONSENSE. If you don't know where the hell God is, what he is, and why the hell he would stay away, then just say I don't know and start researching it scientifically. If you were buying land you would, wouldn't you?

I mean, after all, nobody buys swampland in Florida without going to see it! Isn't your God worth proving? Well, what if we could present scientific evidence to prove this very thing or not and that space is inhabited? Before you think this is impossible, let's look at our history. We all know the old saying: "To learn about our future is to look at our past." That's the only way to see where we are going, to know where we came from. The historical evidence might surprise you. Our history began with religion universally saying that Heaven is "UP" and inhabited. Science agrees with these two basic simple premises. We send space-craft "upward" to the "HEAVENS and monitor them every day in hopes of living there, just like religious people look "UP" to the "HEAVENS" every day in hopes of living there as well. AGAIN MATCHING EVIDENCE! *(Read about J.W. convincing most followers and my mom to stay on earth in paradise; they are afraid of Heaven because they don't know what to expect. They've always known this. Talk about fear of the unknown!)* But, why hasn't Kirk or his co-stars come out and disclosed any awareness of this "coincidental" matching evidence. Recently, we've even spread Scotty's ashes into space. He was famous for beaming people aboard their craft. This would scientifically explain religion's "magic" teleportation through science if it was possible. We have successfully done this with gas atoms and the future looks "bright" for carbon atoms as well!

We are also levitating things, which is another universal religious teaching that is being done scientifically. However obvious this matching scientific evidence, does it change the minds of the Japanese people who lead the way in this technology? Shouldn't they or the Hindus be the most likely to see this "coincidence"? Does it change their president or our own? NO, it hasn't!

So, it's easy to understand how Kirk and his co-stars are still enslaved by primitive man's magical spirit God teachings, if they are. It's painfully "CLEAR" how this scientific blindness exists when it comes to religion. Could this matching scientific "UP" evidence alone prove that space is, in fact, inhabited? I think it is possible only through the scientific examination of religion's "spirit" history. We all know how stories can get exaggerated from the same exercise of story-telling in school. All religions say Heaven is "UP"! How could this be, if the ancients were primitive and these beings are spirits? Spirits wouldn't need direction. And for that matter, neither would today's quantum dimensional theorists—who like religion say that dimensions are a fact— need direction either.

DIMENSIONS AND SPIRITS ARE NOT PROVEN FACTS! If they don't admit to this then forget it. This is not debatable; only one scenario "MATCHES" the ancient evidence. "RELIGION" is a "UNIVERSAL STORY OF PEOPLE LIVING IN THE SKY"!

WE NOW LIVE IN THE SKY on the International Space Station. This matches! If you think this is just a coincidence, that primitive people would have this scientific knowledge, then please look at the pictures on the front and back cover again. These are all ancient religious artworks by primitive man who drew what he saw! We know this because he also drew the animal and plant life too!

The following evidence will disprove the "SYMBOLIC" argument in religion and science, which is just their theory/opinion. It isn't a law. It takes "MATCHING SCIENTIFIC EVIDENCE" to establish laws of science, like the law of gravity! If you throw an apple up it will come back down. These RELIGIOUS artworks are all looking, pointing, and going "UP" into "SPACE." For this reason and one other that you will read about in the last chapter of my story, I titled this last book *Heaven is Space . . . "UP"*. I did it because we say Heaven is "UP" every day; we see "PROOF" of it every day on television around the world; we read it in all the religious text; and we even look "UP", but we don't really believe it's "UP" there "in" space. My religious family struggle will epitomize Heaven's ultimate confusion later, for those of you who don't get it that we're in Heaven/Space/UP now and that Fermi's Paradox is the real question to be answered.

Well, I mean, besides the obvious ultimate reality that we will "FACE" upon their return. Which is: "What will their 'FACE' look like?" Remember, though, I think you will "CLEARLY SEE" why one causes the other to exist, with we humans who love outward beauty! And if you don't know "FERMI'S PARADOX" term then science and education is the only thing that will really "TEACH" you—not religion. It is the same religious question that they can't answer with proof as science does.

Anyway, if this "POWERFUL UP" evidence was the only matching scientific coincidence I had to answer our mysterious loneliness with, then maybe it wouldn't be possible to accept it as a fact. But there are more scientific examples of matching evidence. Plenty more! Like the "GOLD" halo symbol, given to these heavenly people as a result of them not being with us and again coincidently "UP" above their head, resembling a flying saucer. (Cave art on back of aborigine god in flying saucer going "UP" protected by gold halo!) YES, A FLYING SAUCER, and yes, there are plenty of ancient artworks showing more all over the Earth! Besides, I filmed them and found my footage to match these ancient artworks as well as my buddies in phoenix. And it is on Dan Aykroyd's video right now called *Dan Aykroyd Unplugged On UFOs.* (Check out our new video, *Why the Blank Don't They Care.*) Yes, he and many others—including Jimmy Carter, a former president, and also another president, Ronald Reagan—saw one. I don't have to ask how they can't entertain the idea that maybe these craft started religion? Because I already know. They all believe in the primitive, magic spirit God story!

Even more important, though, than all these famous people seeing them, too, the footage and still image MATCHES the so-called HATS of Easter Island. And they are looking "UP!" It is shown on the front cover. Come on, people, this is good scientific proof that religion was started by bald-headed people in flying saucers "UP IN THE SKY." This also matches other cultures' "hats" and baldness, which is well-established in religion, like China's rice hats and Buddhist monks. So is uniformity! IT ALSO MATCHES THE UNIVERSAL TEACHING THAT Heaven IS "UP" and they're all equal!

The Easter Island statues are all bald and look the same, like Buddhist monks and the Olmec gods. They all look "UP" to Heaven. For "GOD'S" sake, the Owl Man on the back cover is pointing "UP" to the sky as well and has a huge bald head and big eyes! The aborigine God below it shows the bald alien in a saucer going "UP"! Come on, people, again! This is hard scientific evidence of what primitive man's God looked like and where he is! If you are religious and this doesn't sway you then nothing will! You will be forever allegiant to your religious faith, which is the absence of evidence and your saying that you don't need it.

Well, I'm not saying you need it either! But don't try and convert a scientist to your magic spirit/invisible God when you have no proof of him, don't know where he is and certainly—it goes without saying—don't know what he looks like, because he's invisible! This will make you look insane. Funny, huh: no "COMMON" sense! Religious killers get off on insanity pleas like Andrea Yates, but we don't see the insanity in the religious God killing his children. Now that's crazy as hell, and religion created both the killer and the insanity defense for it— and we don't see RELIGION as insane! Even worse, we now see why Andrea got off but the mother who killed because the devil told her to do it didn't. She got the death penalty while Andrea's God defense spared her! What a twisted scientific conundrum, huh? How do we cure it? We can't. I recently told Jehovah's Witness to do one thing for me and that is to read, proving to themselves that their God is a murderer. He kills innocent children in Sodom and Gomorrah. They don't "mind," though! If you don't get it by now you won't unless you continue to look at the evidence. THERE IS LOTS MORE!

I like the Olmecs best. The Olmec gods look the most like the Roswell gray alien—JUST LIKE HIM AS A MATTER OF FACT—and the statues from Israel found along the banks of the Jordan River! And, yes again, the worldwide Roswell saucer crash exists. But it is nothing like the Washington, D.C., evidence in 1952 of a living president knowing they exist and not making a worldwide effort to find them! This blows me away. And for this reason I made my latest video, which is a follow-up to the "proof" video internationally nominated in the Film Fest for the study of UFOs. It came in second place at the 2006 convention! See,

I don't mind not winning. Uh oh, Karma just ran over my dogma, and humility is lying all over the floor.

The follow-up video is titled *Why the Blank Don't They Care?"* and has the footage you see on the front cover of my book. I finally filmed them March 6, 7, and 8, 2006, after making the proof video with Jeff Willes in 2005. You can see the proof for yourself. Fourteen flying saucers are clearly visible in the live footage and pictures over the White House, and we couldn't stop them or catch up to them with our fastest military jets!

But enough of this POWERFUL SEEING IS BELIEVING EVIDENCE, because, believe me, seeing a picture, video, or newspaper won't change a skeptic. It seems nothing will change a religious follower but themselves. I guess it takes seeing one for yourself—and this ain't easy. You have to look a lot! I finally saw one for my brothers' recently and asked them if they landed and said they started our religion would they believe that. They both said if the evidence was there they would. Cool. It is! Look at pictures on both covers.

For now, let's get back to the gold thing. I always thought that if I filled in our history with all the evidence, revealing that real flesh-and-blood aliens in flying saucers existed, then that is the way I thought it could work. I am also proving that they wanted our gold and created our religious stories. Much like convicting a criminal with DNA, fingerprints, blood, footprints, eyewitness testimony and every other piece of matching evidence would. But then again, I remembered O.J. We had all that evidence and he was found innocent. How? How did he explain that his blood was found at the crime scene? Oh, I remember, a racist cop. But is it just a coincidence that his finger was cut, too? Oh, how I wish lie detectors were perfect and everywhere. More importantly, I wish there was a God who could make this world perfect and it didn't happen. But there isn't and that's why I challenge the perfect magic/God story. Most importantly, I hope I have the strength and love to forgive him if it did.

If he did it, then it was a result of "SICK LOVE" like the God story. Really, I deeply feel for Nicole's death and O.J.'s life because the "COLD HARD FACT" is that God kills his loved ones, too, when they don't love him back—or for even far less. People, this love/worship-demanding, killing God story influences everyone. It is the same sickness O.J. could have if he had done it—killing someone because they wouldn't love him! For Nicole's sake, the Yates' children, and the perpetrators, too, let's solve this mystery.

I thought my last book about gold's historical connection to God and space exploration would. But it didn't. Anyway, what I discovered about gold is unbelievable! Our history was founded in gold mining. Why? It was clearly used by the ancients for their sacred offering to the "SKY-PEOPLE"/God, and not because it was rare, either. It is abundant. I discovered this scientific fact during the writing of my second book and it also astounded me. I always thought it was rare. What I discovered awakened my scientific mind.

Gold is essential for space exploration. Our astronauts have a gold-covered face visor. The aborigine God on the back cover is protected by the same gold halo over his head—and he looks like an alien! Heck, all the pictures on the cover do! Bald, big eyes, and indicating "UP"! The religious quotation "Heaven's streets are paved in gold" again MATCHES TODAY'S SCIENTIFIC EVIDENCE OF SPACE EXPLORATION ONLY MADE POSSIBLE WITH GOLD! WE PAVE/EXPLORE IT WITH GOLD! Come on, people, this was hard scientific evidence that could solve religion's mystery: WHERE ARE THEY? WHAT DO THEY LOOK LIKE? And WHY DO THEY STAY AWAY? I thought this would make my second book not only a world-wide best seller, but also finally convince my family that "Heaven is in fact UP or space" as we know it is today. But it didn't. Neither did all the other amazing scientific matching evidence either.

But, here's a few more matching examples just to prove my point even more. Not that it will change anything, but I'm an optimist and really do hope for the best always. Primitive man was drawing what he saw even if it was not his knowledge and obviously God's like the flying saucers, atoms, and DNA. It is clear that they all play into primitive man's story of his "SCIENTIFIC CREATION AND THEIR SPACE-FARING FLESH AND BLOOD REALITY." First, the double-helix coil of the A.M.A. symbol. It looks like DNA and does match the double-helix strand we all know so well today as "the invisible scientific creator of life." If he was scientifically created then he could have seen this symbol at some point, given they used it instead of magic/instant creation. The matching evidence indicates this reality as well as universal snake worship and the same squiggly-lined-looking design all over the Earth. The second is the obelisk, which looks like a rocket to me. And in fact, the known Egyptian origin confirms it to be a weapon of the sun God. A weapon that eerily looks like our nuclear missiles today! Third, the atom looks just like the Jewish star and matches it point for point. I put it on every book.

Our universal religious story is one of pre-destination—a creation known to end in our own demise from threatening the destruction of the earth through war! Come on, people. North Korea has nuclear weapons and Iran wants them. We have just now gotten the capabilities through nuclear weapons to destroy the Earth. Iran wants to wipe Israel off the map! Please help me, people. Do any of us really want to see our children put through nuclear hell? Isn't this hell bad enough?

Listen to me pleading as if it can be stopped. If destiny can be stopped, then it has to start with religion itself. Religion agrees! Don't you see the cruelty of Iran's religious president or our own? Do you really still buy the magic spirit God story with all this scientific evidence of our species being a scientific creation like plastic. We both have an instantaneous occurrence on history's scene. I found that most of my family did believe in the same God as the Iranian president and ours still does too.

They just don't get it. Most people even get angry because of their lack of evidence and just tell me that I'm going to hell for questioning God. I tell them it's their God, not mine. They're the ones with faith, who don't need evidence, and worse yet, don't "mind" God-killing children! No. Please don't tell me that this is the way our world truly is. Somebody, please wake me "UP" and tell me that I'm just having a bad dream. Dream, hell. This is a nightmare. Our Earth is literally surrounded in darkness! No, not the outer darkness they call hell! Could it be? No, please?

If it is, then the fact remains that their lack of evidence and looking for it, feeds this monster mentality called religion and its killing God. It creates presidents who kill, too. I can't believe this is real, but it is. Well, I finally accepted the reality that nothing scientific will change a religious person like my mother who has been a Jehovah's Witness for fifty years. She says they don't preach hell, though, just the killing-God thing! I told her that it doesn't make them any better, because they're not. They're all the same! You can't get worse than killing. The sad irony is that she still doesn't know where Heaven is, only that it is a spirit world. And remember she's afraid of spirits. This is crazy! This really frustrated me as the "UP" evidence was so overwhelming, besides religion's lack of magic that they claim God has. And it really kills me when they say God's power isn't magic. I don't know what the hell they think it is then. He does just speak things into existence. That's pretty damn magical to me. Nothing sways their "belief." I even gave them example after example of situations that would cause this same magic spirit story if we were to land on a planet inhabited by primitive mankind. He would say we came from "UP". And if we weren't able to live with his uncontrollable brutality, we would leave. This isn't realistic if we couldn't be hurt like a spirit. If we scientifically altered his intelligence to serve as a slave for us, his story would go as follows. His God came from "UP" in a fiery chariot or cloud, is magical, and they were created to serve him. The reason he's alone, is because he rebelled with his "new-found" intelligence. They also would have a slow evolutionary growth until this moment and then civilization would just have suddenly appeared culminating in a very short history of rapid growth.

Wow, Wow, Wow. SETI, eat your heart out (just kidding, karma)! THIS IS OUR MYSTERIOUS PAST! Even more, their need for gold would also be obvious as they live in spacecraft. Our history started with gold mining everywhere, and it still backs all currency today!

The scary part is that all religions say that we are doomed to destroy ourselves, and they knew it before they gave us the ability to do this and yet did it anyway. But the good news is they also stop this from happening with a world-wide famous "UNIVERSAL" Second Coming ending! And where do they come from? The world's largest religion knows this all too well.

"JESUS WILL BE COMING ON THE CLOUDS FOR EVERY EYE TO SEE!" My mother says this is not only symbolic, but the Jehovah's Witnesses said it already happened in 1914 "INVISIBLY"! Come on! Please tell me that there is one Jehovah's Witness who sees the ridiculousness and danger of this religious fraud. He's invisible with no way to prove it! What! No way! Why aren't they teaching Religion 101? When did the God story start, where is he, she, or it? And most importantly, why the hell would he stay away and torture us with this mystery of mankind's brutality, anyway? WHY, WHY, WHY? If we are afraid to accept the possibility that he, she or it isn't a magic "ALMIGHTY" spirit person then I finally know how this happened and why it will be this way "FOREVER"! Religion breeds a traditional incurable resistance to any scientific evidence that refutes it.

HEAVEN IS "UP" IN SPACE, AND HELL IS DOWN ON EARTH! Space is "OUR" scientific final frontier! This is scientifically logical. Earths make great universal prisons. "Our" is the key word here, and that is speaking as a scientist seeking scientific evidence—evidence that should speak for itself! I've even discovered that the Mayans painted their gods blue because they needed to distinguish them from mortal humans. Blue because they live in the "SKY"! It's obvious how all man makes God his race. Mom's God not only lives in the sky, but is a "man" spirit and she doesn't know why "HE" would be. She doesn't know because she gets my point. Spirits wouldn't need to live in the sky, only us flesh and blood humans and anybody else trying to escape the hell of their ignorant, beast-like population would. Just like the aliens with us! Get it!

And they would be in spacecraft as the scriptures say: "Flesh and blood can't enter the kingdom of Heaven." SPACE WOULD KILL US! But does she really "GET IT" or is she just pacifying me to stop this torture? I was torturing everyone, even my buddy who videos flying saucer and yet believes, just like mom, in spirits. What the heck is wrong here? Could I get him to finally look for proof of his spirit world? He looked for proof of saucers! I couldn't, even at the writing of this book. What can I do to get them to prove or challenge religion's spirit world. It has "BRAINWASHED THE RELIGIOUS PEOPLE OF THE EARTH." (Thanks for the quote, Brian!)

Hell, I wish religion's magic God did exist. If he did though, I would still ask WHY, WHY, WHY? And we all know the questions. But they don't and won't ask why? Why are they afraid or why don't they care about answers backed by evidence? They care about me and getting me to join their church, don't they? Voila! This proves that they are brain-washed by the church! This is what the church wants! People, Space is the final frontier and we can't escape the evidence laid out in the groundwork of our primitive religious forefathers. It still exist to-day. WE LOOK "UP" TO HEAVEN! Evidence and scientific knowl-edge will prevail over ancient religious traditions. Even this is a good scientific piece of matching evidence. The bible says that knowledge will increase all over the earth and finally prevail over religious tra-ditional, superstitious ignorance. Is it a coincidence that this has hap-pened? Don't these Bible-thumpers see this? It is provable by the his-tory of progress and religion's story of "the inevitable global increasing of knowledge." It is increasing and can't be stopped.

Now I know why the word "FINAL" created religion's reincarna-tion tradition. Beast will always remain beast. And like beast, I know what the power struggle is in religion's universal story. I see all of our addiction to outward beauty. This is the power that humans possess, our unique difference in looks. Nature all looks the same, from bees to trees. I know all too well! As a matter of fact, my name is at the fore-front of this struggle and it again confirms energy/reincarnation and the way our universe works. The most famous religion of the Jews is waiting on Michael as is some of Christianity, like my parents' religion. That's the reason I use it as my pen name. I use myself as an example in my story. I haven't found anyone who seriously entertains the possibility that I could be him. Well, except for the ones like Brian who want me to prove it. But the only way I can prove this possibility is to solve our mystery with scientific evidence. I can't make anyone show either. Funny again, huh? I'm trying to solve a religious mystery with scientific evidence. And we know how the Jehovah's Witnesses view scientific evidence. They use what they want to support a magical God of instantaneous creation, but totally reject evolution, which is universally accepted. Yet, there isn't one example today, nor in our past, that they can give of instant creation!

I beg them to do it, or at least admit the Earth evolved. Anyway, the current evidence PROVES we are forever doomed to be separate from these heavenly beings that are equal. The evidence clearly shows them to be so because of their looks. According to all religions this separation is because of a desire for power to be greater than God! If Earth is a mirror-image of Heaven as it says, then I know they created our species to give them this power. Plastic surgery is the ruler here. Could they have created our "NEW" species for the power to be greater than one another through outward beauty and uniqueness? Are they this advanced? It's clear they can transfer memory from one body to another or possibly transfer the memory cells themselves, just like reincarnation implies. It's also clear that they can be invisible. We are on the verge of doing this, too. *(Look at newspaper evidence!)* Again, see the matching scientific evidence! WE LIKE WATCHING OURSELVES!

People, we are beauty addicts. I am, and I see it every time I go to RED LOBSTER to eat. We like to look at each other! This story is so scientifically provable that it is pathetic. It's so simple, we even tell our children to not judge a book by its cover. Why can't we see all these parallels in our scientific world today? We are on the verge of all this and even more. Heck, we are even creating new species of life today that wouldn't exist, just like us, without science. Please ask yourself: Do I want to be outwardly ugly? I don't! Humans are cruel when it comes to this. That's the reason I put the Olmec gods in the evidence. They are equal in looks, just like the heads of Easter Island. They are ugly (abnormal compared to humans). This is the reason I use my name as a fictional possibility of being the biblical Michael. I am addicted to beauty—worse yet, to my own beauty! I am no better than anyone else. Our sexual ego or desire for power tortures us! It tortures me! I want help. Scientific humility is my only answer, not judgment.

Love of others is scientific humility—forgiving others and myself of falling prey to this most "POWERFUL" feeling. I can easily imagine being an ugly alien addicted to humankind's unique beauty. I also can easily imagine life doing this "somewhere else" in the universe. Right here and right now. Anyway, back to my name and the reason I use it. Michael the archangel wars with the devil (who is an angel) and his angels, according to the story, and they are cast out of Heaven and down to Earth. I found this to be the biblical prison that we can't escape called hell as well as the human body. If we are an alien then it would make sense of all religions saying this body isn't who we are. They all say this.

Plus, one person is the creator of any new invention. Was this angel just that, the inventor of human creation? Then, at the end of the story, Michael returns from the "SKY" to war with those of mankind who are destroying the Earth. He then cast them to hell again. AGAIN, INFINITELY REPEATING HISTORY! I propose the evidence to be perfectly clear. This story reflects the possibility of an unstoppable creation of mankind, which they called the devil. This is likely the reason YESHUA/"JESUS" called the Jewish preacher "SATANS," plural. This also could be the reason he called the good guys, "only the father in

Heaven." He even called himself evil because he was a man when the apostles called him good.

The evidence is clear that these beings all look the same; therefore one is many, monotheism is polytheism. They are a perfect example of nature's creation. They are just like zebras in this sense many but all looking the same. We have plenty of evidence of these angels/gods breeding with their creation in the mother-goddess statues. This would explain why they are called "FATHERS." There is evidence of aliens with a penis. The head of all these mother-goddess statues are bald and big, like the alien fathers. The bodies are all fat, exemplifying the story in Genesis saying they were doing this because of their beauty.

This makes painfully clear again that the power struggle is all about the power we have from our unique beauty. Human mothers with alien fathers. And voila, we all look different. We have a missing link in our fossil record that reflects the lack of a skull between primitive man's small one and our "OVERLY LARGE" one. This is again beautiful evidence that we are science's creation. We have this evidence. *(See fossil chart.)* Nothing else in nature does this! When it finally comes down to contact, what they look like will not be acceptable to us narcissist beasts. Yes, I love myself outwardly. Sure, there are some things I would change, but plastic surgery is to expensive. I couldn't do it now, anyway, unless I was grotesquely "UGLY." I still don't know if I could, though, as long as my kids weren't repulsed at it.

I want to share money with the world to help the ones who are. They "need" to feel the power of beauty as they are tortured by this dreaded "UGLINESS." NO! I can't believe I just said that! Like I said at the end of my third book: "EVERYBODY WANTS TO GROW OLD. HELL, WE EVEN WANT TO LIVE FOREVER, BUT LET'S 'FACE IT' NOBODY WANTS TO 'LOOK' OLD! LOOKS GIVE US POWER

The Discovery

OVER ONE ANOTHER!

You know what, folks? When it's all said and done, we aren't going backwards. Children know this cold hard "ugliness" fact all too well and that space is our only hope for survival. They know this as a result of living in a world faced with daily nuclear destruction. Space is the Final Frontier! Unlike them, little did I know the scientific reality of this fact, in humanity's quest for survival, as I was growing "UP". This famous quote by Captain Kirk of *Star Trek* did become a staple for me, though, as a child. However, it only "happened" from an occasional glance on the TV as my dad or mom skipped through the channels in search of traditional Fifties & Sixties westerns or family-theme shows.

I was never really taught science by my religious parents. I now know why. They themselves weren't aware of it either, and this was obviously due to the same obvious non-scientific religiously dominated world and upbringing, just like my own. God is everywhere! This is good old tradition at its best. Religion "preaches" against tradition and yet patriotism makes it null and void as a fact. Besides tradition, it was easy to not be scientific in a pretty primitive state back then. And this is only fifty years ago. Just think of where we will be fifty years from now and how today will look in another fifty. It will be history "REPEATING ITSELF"! Hell, it still is a "pretty" primitive planet by any universal standard today—we haven't conquered space, moved into it and still don't see the significance of the universal religious "sky" God story as possibly being scientific. I mean, after all, nobody is healing dying babies right now. If they were we would all know it!

We need to conquer that sky; space is our final frontier and it is obviously where these religious inhabitants live! But why don't we see this when we even have evidence of a historically long UFO phenomenon and they, too, are in the sky as the acronym so "clearly" spells out UNIDENTIFIED FLYING OBJECT. "Flying" being the key word. "RELIGION'S UNIVERSAL HALO" looks like a "FLYING SAUCER"! Why don't they see that tradition proves the ancient origin of Heaven is "UP" AND POSSIBLY CREATED BY FLYING SAUCERS? THEY DO MATCH!

This is irrefutable. Heck, we even show all gods flying like the saucers do! Really, I know why religious people like myself didn't see this matching evidence and it becomes excruciatingly apparent in the reading of my story. So much so, you may even empathize with me at the end, that even in the face of contact this mystery will still continue as it does today. It is infinite like the religious hell story. The reason for this will be easy to see after you're finished reading.

I *can* promise you this! I'm sorry it took me five books to finish this journey. This is the last chapter of my harrowing saga. With it, the God mystery is finished, for me, anyway. I'm okay with the evidence. My thinking is now dominated by my brother Brian's "PROOF" factor, or science. They are one and the same as the Jehovah's Witnesses so eloquently show and then look ridiculous by retracting science as a method of proof *(again see evidence)*. I'm a big boy; I've grown "UP". I know Santa doesn't exist. I can do the same with religion's god, not science's god. I can't believe it took me so long to see their similarities. I believe the scientific evidence that "shows" me what God is and why the world isn't perfect, and why magic miracles don't exist. It has answered for me the logical questions on the cover of my book: Who, Where, and Why?

Scientifically, I am not afraid of the repercussions from my parents' religion. Ironically, I am also addressing the religion that rules the Earth, which also consists of five books like mine. Judaism, Christianity, and Islam. Coincidence? Like my parents, I too believe the evidence proves the God story to be a scientific fact. I "BELIEVE" the evidence without the magic. There's no proof of it so far. I have too, based on this. Therefore, I don't have religious questions for their God anymore.

Science has given me the technology and desire to find what I was looking for, religious answers. I am a scientific believer in the God evidence without the instantaneous magic factor and evidence that will scientifically rewrite it. I didn't become a scientist overnight, and in fact science never ends. We will agree with the evidence if it warrants rewriting itself. Competition is non-existent where evidence is concerned. The competitive nature hurts all fields. Like religion, I knew very little about science, but I certainly knew nothing about religion. Not to mention the fact that you spend the first twelve years of your life just slowly learning about what life is and who we "humans" are, but I really had no clue of anything. I was a kid.

The answer for this is simple. Life is a painfully slow learning process. My parents didn't know "why," and their parents didn't know either. I quickly understood tradition. The questions on the cover of this book are simple questions. My parents were childishly simple with their humble answer, "I don't know the answer, Mike." I could've dealt with that but yet a commandingly complex admonition always followed: "But there are some things you just *can't* understand because 'God' works in mysterious ways." What the hell was that all about? There's no way this can be true! I was completely unsatisfied religiously as well as scientifically. I just wasn't scientifically taught about religion! And when it came to science, well, school was slow like I said and I obviously wasn't "gifted" or it wouldn't have taken you this long to read about my story.

When I did go looking for religious answers elsewhere some twenty years later, I was repeatedly told this same thing by the rest of them and I am still scientifically examining "all the knowledge in the world." And, man, is it complex! It is what this confusion is all about. My life! The world and its origin. I mean, after all, I came from "it" and I am in "it." So what the hell is "it"? If I came from "it" how dare anyone to tell me that I can't trace "it"? As a matter of fact, I am "it."

I love hunting. It was a sacred family tradition. Except this became a hunt unlike any other. I was endangering my life for "it" and it was my life. I wasn't taking a life; I was giving one back. I was essentially finding "me," and according to my mom and dad, "God" made me. I had to know where Heaven was and ironically, laughed at the idea of it being "UP" just like every other religious person. This is so funny, as you will read about in my first book *The Two Witnesses and the Religion Cover-up*. I didn't know where Heaven was and what God looked like. I wanted to talk to him, her, or who the hell it was that could give me some answers. First of all, a NO-BRAINER question: WHY? Why the hell would anybody stay away from us and cause this torturous disease of humanity, our mystery and religion's birth? Why are we alone and why do we have such a short history and why are we so God-awfully, brutally primitive. Wow, now I finally knew where the "God-awful" saying came from. Funny huh, always learning.

But this wasn't fun, these nagging questions, pain and death of children. Hell, these questions alone were so scientifically frustrating for me. At first I didn't even dare, but I did finally ask religion the merciful question, "How could a loving God not stop a baby girl from being sodomized by her savagely brutal and certainly horrible, evil, sex-crazed, mentally deranged supposed "father"? Forget about that—well, I wish I could, but I can't. I learned to live with it, like everyone else. Those who couldn't commit suicide. Only we humans commit suicide.

Finding ancient alien evidence as the title of my second book says,

The Discovery

Aliens Gold Tenth Planet, I asked the question that was so beautifully illustrated in the movie *Bruce Almighty.* Why can't God do better—we could with magic. Heck, children would make it perfect as was so beautifully illustrated in a poll about this during the movie's ride of fame. Even worse, I put religion to the test of open-mindedness when I asked on the cover of my third book *The Future Alien Contact,* "Could primitive man's God be the universal Roswell alien and not make the world perfect as is the evidence before us?" I know this seemed crazy and dangerous. I wasn't crazy; I wasn't a "sadist"/Satan either. Another funny pun, huh, so I won't mention any more.

But I never cease to be amazed at how religion's creation and molding of our language gives us clues to the mystery of God. Like being awful? This didn't jive with our standards or their own for that matter. You can't be merciful and at the same time kill, except to end pain. Why couldn't my mom or any religious person get this simple scientific fact! We must be "HUMANE," mustn't we? Again it's simple. You've got it! It's simple. Religion isn't "HUMANE" itself. God is a killer who refuses to make and keep the world perfect!

Religion doesn't teach, anywhere in this world, "THE GOD STORY" scientifically. That's why my previous book, *2012 Gold's History Solves Mankind's Mystery,* utilized good hard evidence, scientifically speaking, to address this issue. But my fifth and final book has a title that directly answers "WHERE IS HEAVEN?" Let's just get down to the brass tacks of it. Let's take it apart—religion, that is. The scientific evidence of God being a real ancient astronaut needing gold for space travel was overwhelming. Erich von Daniken became famous for his ancient astronaut theory but never saw the alien-looking God evidence. The evidence of God being "ALMIGHTY" and yet the world being flawed also was overwhelming! The evidence for God detesting wealth but yet living "UP" in Heaven with streets of gold on a golden throne and us kissing his feet was overwhelming. We were mining gold for them from the get-go. This is all so overwhelming unless you open your mind to the possibility that science can explain primitive man's magic spirit miracle story. And ultimately having to accept that religion's omnipotent God doesn't exist! This happened to me! I gave up the traditional RELIGIOUS examination and opted for the "logical" scientific one. Even those two things became synonymous to me. Scientific and logical. They have now graduated from a long "short" process of growth to where they now are today. They have become synonymous in the world of religion, too. Again, read any Jehovah's Witness magazine. They even use notable scientific members to prove that the intelligent design theory of science proves there is a God. They just don't answer why he remains invisible to us—THAT'S THE TRADITIONAL MYSTERY. They don't use science to prove what he looks like either or when he began, just that he's always existed and works through time (HIS MASTER PLAN, WHICH SOUNDS LIKE EVOLUTION) but could instantly make it perfect. Again another contradiction of evidence. It isn't perfect and he has no time, but works through time! Try and scientifically figure that enigma out! Only religion can, and the answer for that is simple. Hopefully, you got it. But if they are using science, it could come back to haunt them if science defies THEIR UNIVERSAL SPIRIT TEACHING or, even worse, God forbid, solve the ultimate riddle. What is God really? What if he's "real" and the answer REFUTES their teachings? Can anything change or cure this persistent disease of religious people not believing the scientific evidence when he comes back? If you're scientific then—you got it—again the answer is no. This mystery exists now. Science rules the universe through "REAL" evidence. Logic is believing it. Religion is a story of non-belief when they return. This mystery is incurable. It's all about "Heaven mirroring Earth." We lust for power also. Here, it's all about wealth and beauty/greatness. Maybe we are them, lusting to be greater "looking" for this power.

We all exist now and are alone. This is indisputable and inescapable evidence. This is the "cold hard truth" of our species so inappropriately labeled humans. We are far from humane, and we are "down" on a planet, literally in a universal prison. Since religions don't know where Heaven is and what God looks like then let's look to the scientific evidence for these answers. This was made very clear in a Barbara Walters special. She interviewed every religious scholar across the board and they all said it was a spirit world, dimension, or frame of mind. They all thought that it certainly was crazy to think "UP" in the sky. This is where the simplest of evidence (Occam's Razor) can come back to haunt them. From the beginning we have looked "UP", it has been written "UP", the ancient art like on the front cover and back of this book indicates that it is "UP." Yet they don't see it and most hate me for this. They hate me because I certainly think their "spirit" story is more crazy. At least mine is supported by our spacecraft "UP" today. This matches.

I know their anger is a direct result of having no evidence for their teaching of a spirit world. Thank God I had the ancient statues of aliens and flying saucers. And, yes, I consider my footage of a saucer a miracle, but only in the sense it is rare, scientifically done, and evidence that maybe they are primitive man's God. Heck, we're lucky they even care about us. Wake "UP", people, please? If you can't entertain this notion then please stop religions from saying they are evil. This isn't "right" without the proof to back it up. *(The Jehovah's Witnesses do this; see evidence.)* And for this reason I set out to answer Fermi's Paradox: why they don't make global and open contact with us. I am doing this with scientific evidence. In science the evidence doesn't lie. Knowledge is power. Religion can't stifle this, and why would they—or any of us— want to. Don't we seekers have the same goal, religious or otherwise? Aren't our intentions both good? Could the God story be too "good" to be true? We must accept it if it is.

I can only say that science is a wonderful life, and I love a fast ride in my little red Corvette listening to Prince singing it on the radio. Science made all this possible. So please, my religious daddy, if you exist don't take my T-bird away. Let science be you; please let it be true. This would explain all the hell and misery existing because it can't be stopped. I can only imagine the future of science and the world it will provide for us and our children. We all know this. Not a one of us would deny our children a heart when they need it if we could grow one! And guess what, everybody—great news. WE WILL SOON! This is the wonder of science. Why would religion or anyone be afraid of it. Please, for GOD'S SAKE, let us solve the God story. Let not one of us do this if he or she isn't willing to die for our children. This is the greatest love of all, to find something you would give your life for. I can think of nothing more worthy and beautiful for this honor than our children. And indeed it is an honor to be a parent. They are the most wonderfully precious and scientifically logical things to celebrate in this universe. They are the future and they will outlive us and carry on our legacy. Let it be to flourish scientifically.

Religion is killing us with the killing God story. Enough is enough! "Stop the insanity." Will religion let logic solve this mystery by scientifically examining the evidence of our past and its brutality? Or will they continue not to see that "ALL GODS ARE KILLERS"? Do we want this to be true? Do we want to be with "him" if it is? Are we really prepared to get what we wish for if we believe in this "KILLING GOD"? If you're religious, like I was raised, then these questions have to be answered because science will do it whether we want "IT" to or not. It is where we came from (increasing scientific knowledge) and it is where we are going. Word . . . UP!

If Heaven is Space, as the evidence suggests, then the evidence will tell us how this God mystery came to be and where they are now. But most importantly, it will tell us why they stay away. All of these answers point to Religion 101's first question—or at least it's a no-brainer that it should be—"What does this God look like?" I am willing to accept the scientific or religious evidence. Shouldn't they? Why should either be afraid? I mean, after all, I do believe the scientific evidence of "God" and it hasn't warped my mind. I have scientific evidence to support it. The evidence does convince me that primitive man started the magic factor of religion because of this contact between him and "GOD." But it still has to be answered: What does "He" look like? The little two-lettered, but oh-so-powerful scientific word "UP" yields the greatest clue. Primitive man's God gave us a scientific fact of life. But primitive man was ignorant of science. This proves what the evidence scientifically confirms. His God was a spaceman! Nobody created the universe. It infinitely re-creates itself over and over again with time, not magic! It exists unseen and bursts onto the scene in an explosion of light to the eye as a gas and then brings forth "touchable" matter. The water of life with all its necessary ingredients becomes aware of itself through evolution. To finally know that it always exists. It is the thing it can't see. It "is" the universe, and didn't come from it. This is infinitely cyclical, just like the ice cube that never stops existing, even though it melts before our eyes and then disappears. And yet we know it still exist as a gas. Why can't we see this about the earth, sun, galaxies and most importantly ourselves!

Carl Sagan said we are the suns/sons of the past and will be them again in the future. What a beautiful reality. They are both beautiful and amazing to look at! I can only conclude and am glad to do so, in lieu of my nephew's freak accident, which resulted in his death that I would give my life to have kept his mother and father from experiencing such pain. Wouldn't any father? I saw their pain and it was unbearable! The reason bad things happen to good people is that there is no magic, and there is no reason for it. It is the same reason asteroids destroy life as they collide with planets in a universe full of wonder. Life happens! *Happens* being the key word. Life is magical, but certainly not my nephew's freak death. This was an accident and for this reason life isn't magical because the religion story makes people wonder why God wouldn't stop this. Danny's death was horribly painful, and it helps me to look at the God story scientifically. Religion's account of the Genesis creation mimics scientific evolution, but the magic factor muddles the scientific picture. Anywhere that it is thought or blinked, has to be challenged, like in the very beginning. How can we create atoms or Heaven? There is no proof of this magic process as we know it and science like religion, says it isn't possible. Heaven nor atoms have a beginning or ending. However, "Something does come from nothing," contrary to the scientific Jehovah's Witness testimony of Science proving God is the Intelligent Designer, but yet attributing it to this invisible God. Something/everything is energy/nothing but movement creating an image. I told my brother Brian about this quote and their lack of scientific knowledge. Ultimately, they have to prove their God! If "he" doesn't exist, then so be it, we wouldn't have religious wars! If it came from God and they can't prove what God is then it came from nothing. If it came from him and they can prove what he is then it still came from nothing—he's invisible! Voila!

This controversy still brews, because the contradiction is clear even in their own text. Well, anyway, if they have proof of their God or he's invisible again this means it came from nothing! If we are able to deal with this fact, then life is still beautiful. Except for one thing, my precious nephew's tragic accidental death, as well as my little sister's, and every other child who is a victim of it! For God's sake, people, their's, and ours—there can't be a logical reason for freak tragedies.

Please let us solve the God mystery and our own? I propose that they are maybe one and the same. Could primitive man's god be a real flesh and blood alien?

Read on!

**The final chapter of *"Heaven Is Space . . . UP"*!
begins on page 286.
Enjoy the explosive ending!**

Mike Brumfield

Are all the ancient religious monuments made of huge stone circular patterns, like Stonehenge, really just flying saucer representations/art?

FINAL CHAPTER: *Heaven Is Space . . . "UP!"*

December 23, 2012, "The final frontier is 'BAK'!" The story continues.
(What goes around comes around? Life is indeed an atom, yeah!)
The mayans believed in infinity
It's all about the money
The Golden Age
RETURNS
NOW,
UP
!

"All right, everybody, it's happening," I said as I looked "UP"! I looked over at the President and he was looking up, too! *Wow,* I thought for a split-second as a big smile came over my face. Everybody must be looking up! Finally, science was making religious people come face to face with this "UP"/space-traveling/flying saucer reality. Without religion we'd be expecting contact from space! Why did it take us so long to realize this? But have we really?

Why does most of the world not think this way? I knew why: religion. But today, science won out! The president was religious and yet he WAS looking up! If only he could be open-minded to his Jesus being an alien, which looks like all the other aliens. One species whose worst nightmare couldn't be stopped: "HUMAN CREATION."

This was Heaven's occupant's lust for power story in religion, "THE FALL." Our unique looks give us power over one another. We're all addicted to beauty of the flesh. I knew it all too well. Hell, just watch television. Beautiful women and fabulous wealth is the ultimate reward here. This is as much an irrefutable fact as heaven's "UP"-ness!

It was D-Day for me as well. Was I cured? Was I really ready for this ultimate reality of mankind? The whole Earth must be looking up!

The saucers began to land. I watched as they descended within seconds. I couldn't believe what was happening. I was just as excited now as the first time I saw one. My mind was racing with all kinds of thoughts. What had happened to me in the past six years was incredible. I finally saw and filmed flying saucers.

But enough of this, I thought to myself as I turned again toward the president. I had to stay focused on what was happening. I was worried about little Jake. I knew little Jake was okay, though. He loved riding on a saucer. I had taken him on one after my arrival back from Jerusalem. And I sure wasn't about to stop him from coming today.

Besides, he wasn't little Jake anymore. Although, I knew he'd always be little Jake to me. My anxiety left me as my smile grew even wider. I knew he was looking down at me now. Nothing would do but for him to come with me this morning. *Little Jake,* I mused. I laughed aloud and maybe even cried tears of joy. He may have grown up. But just like I was always little Mikey to my dad and older brothers, he'll always be little Jake to me. Somehow, I now felt good about all this. I knew deep down that he and Jimmy were all right with it. Hell, it was Angel and the rest of this crazy-ass world that I was worried about. Especially the religious ones.

But then again, I knew they would be stopped if they resisted. Why did I know this? I guess it was just scientific logic that dominated my thinking. I was always amazed at the SETI program thinking it would make contact with extraterrestrials. Everything scientifically and logically pointed to them being more intelligent. It was ridiculous for me to think beings who have already conquered space would respond to our repeated attempts to make contact. There wouldn't be a mystery if this was the case. Believe me, if a more intelligent species could help us, they would! This is only logical intelligently speaking.

The same thing applied to the God story; he loves us and created us because were a "good" thing. If we were either "good" or worthy of being contacted then this mystery wouldn't exist. Their reason for not bothering is clear by our disease of war and lust for power over one another. We are the most destructive thing in the universe. It's unbelievable that people don't think scientifically about this lack of contact from an intelligent, loving extraterrestrial. For god's sake all our wars are over religion. Why wouldn't God or this extraterrestrial just never let this mystery began. Hell's bells, people, they could just stay up in the sky and never let us forget why they don't live with us. There must be a logical reason they don't. Serving a purpose working for them is the only thing that makes sense. How did religion make us a good thing and how does it continue to hide the provable fact that they live in the sky as real flesh and blood beings capable of death, pain, and addiction just like us? When religious people would counter—and they always did—that god did this because he wouldn't want robots, it made me sick. I'd always tell them how it would stop war if he would just make it clear what the hell he is!

What hogwash and lack of logic, not to mention cruelty. It's illogical and down-right sick for any loving parent or adult to let innocent children be tortured and killed to prove our "LOYALTY" to this "mysterious" God. What a sick compromise from people who wouldn't do the same nor would want to be worshipped either because society sees it as a sickness. I can't stand their free-will argument. Hell, the word wasn't even in the Bible. And it still doesn't take away from their God being responsible for all mankind's hell and a chaotic universe. Why don't they see he is a killer of innocent children in the Sodom and Gomorrah story? Why?

If all this isn't bad enough, they have another creation gone awry to add to mankind's temptation, and that is the devil story. Their God is inept and a killer to boot. Besides being a sadist who chooses not to make it perfect! In every book I drove this PROVABLE POINT home! Come on, religious people! Where's your logic, when you demand it from your children? This religious sickness was almost just as bad, though, as scientists who think this lack of contact is due to the vast distances in space. Isn't it logical to think that the infinite universe is already conquered? Concepts like distance and time are irrelevant because they wouldn't live on planets. They would just rest on them. I always quoted Yeshua/"Jesus" for proof of this reality. He said "HEAVEN IS THEIR THRONE AND THE EARTH IS A FOOTSTOOL!" They also don't have time or distance! Isn't it logical that if we have "UNIVERSAL" stories of beings that live in the sky, to look for the answer as to why they stay away? Shouldn't we be realizing that these flying saucers must be them? I knew why religion didn't think this way. My search is about heaven's change in status from "UP" to a spirit world.

But isn't it logical to never let religion make heaven some place other than what the facts clearly state? It is UP/sky! Why doesn't science see this "UP" word as "CLEAR" proof that space is conquered? How can we have scientists who believe in spirits without proof? Isn't it logical that this one common theme is enough to make us all see this religious being/god is real and not a spirit magic guy who has already conquered space time and infinity! I suddenly realized that, in my barrage of scientific wonder and horror, the most powerful man on Earth who believes in this very thing was standing beside me looking "UP." Now, even he was faced with this harsh reality. The seeing-is-believing factor made us all swallow this cold, hard fact. It stood before us, front and center.

The flying saucers were landing now! I looked at the president in total disbelief. This was happening! THE PRESIDENT IS LOOKING UP. We all were! Again, I had a sudden chilling realization that I had not only seen one way before this, but had actually filmed them. What! *No way,* I thought to myself. *This can't be real.* Wow, but it was.

It was all coming back to me now. I did do this. I had done it with a man named Jeff Willies from Phoenix, Arizona, back in 2005. Seven long, hard years ago! Sure, my books got me world-wide attention and hatred. But this event became my final obsession. This piece of evidence became the catalyst for me to find an even bigger piece of evidence. With it we would become *The Jeff and Mike Show, REAL-LIFE FLYING SAUCER HUNTERS!*

Before I go on with CONTACT, let's first get back to how our paths became destined to cross in the first place. And how fate teamed us up to find and film REAL-LIVE FLYING SAUCERS. And find them we did! We're still finding them now! You'd think that after actually doing this six years ago, it wouldn't have taken so long for us to garner world-wide attention. But it did. There were lots of photographs of flying saucers, Jeff's included, and believe me, it along with mine were big. I'll tell you in a second why it was so big, but for those of you who have already read my books, you know!

But, until we proved it by showing them live, we were still ignored. And then we couldn't be ignored. Television time could be bought, and we bought it. Throughout all of this amazing evidence that I had put in my books—and I do mean some truly amazing stuff—none of it worked. Not the evidence of Jesus being a false name or the criminal changing of it, to finding a great saucer picture. And not just any picture. But a picture of a saucer that had none other than one of the most famous entertainers of all time in it. HE WAS ALSO LOOKING UP AT IT!

I had found a photo of Johnny Cash that matched Jeff's flying saucer footage from the infamous Phoenix lights. I used it in my third book. It didn't get the response I wrote about until . . . read on. Well, that picture is real, but the story part was fiction. Like I said, it didn't get me world-wide fame. Hell, it didn't even get the attention of Nashville and I protested in front of their newspaper! One of the editors came out and told me he couldn't review every book. He said there were plenty of pictures besides mine. I told him, "Not with the Man in Black." I quickly added, "Get it, 'man in black'!" He wasn't amused nor impressed and seemed a little angry. I asked him if he believed in God. He said yes. I knew why he was angry!

That's why I finally use my real name on this last book. I knew it was real; this wasn't fiction. But hardly anybody thought that me putting the evidence together would solve our mystery. Thank God for my brother Brian and Terry! They finally would. Seeing is believing to them as well! Well, I'll get to that in a second.

First, let me tell you what happened as a result of finding and using this picture. This is the actual story. This is what really happened with no embellishments. In 2003 when I found "THE PHOTO" Jeff and I became great friends and immediately set up a venture together. This resulted from an attempt of mine to get on a nationally famous radio program that was using Jeff's photo. Like I said, I wasn't famous; that was fiction. But this event was real. My fame wasn't world-wide, anyway. I, well, we would soon get there. I had no clue that he would become the new "other witness."

Anyway, if you read my first books, you'll know what that reference was. My first book is called *The Two Witnesses and the Religion Cover-up.* This will give you a clue. He was religious just like my other buddy from the beginning book. But at least he had found and believed in flying saucers. He still believed in spirits, though, just like my other buddy, and he didn't have any answers for why they wouldn't openly live with us, either. Spirits can't be hurt or killed. Well, he did have the stereotypical ones "like maybe we're not ready yet" or, like I said before, "God wouldn't want robots." These were both illogical if "he" loves us. To make something lovingly perfect through pain is ridiculous. Not to mention the freak accidents and senseless acts of killing and torture! But they both had the world-wide religious answer, too! It included them to be demons, and I sure couldn't stomach that lack of proof or logic.

It was, in fact, harmful to our purpose of wanting to figure this mystery out. It blinded them to scientific logic. It scared the majority of people. It was terrorism! I showed them both that they were no different than the Jehovah's Witnesses. They refused to see this or couldn't! I thought these were one and the same, and then I saw a similarity in science. They don't see the "UP" significance of religions heaven. Maybe they didn't see it, even when presented matching evidence, science didn't. I didn't know how this was possible, except for their stubbornness to change theories. I always liked what the show *CSI:* and Grissom would say: "If the evidence changes so must your theory!" Theirs didn't, just like the rest of religions.

Anyway, I presented this evidence in my last book as well to prove it to them. They saw the matching evidence and refused to change their belief in spirits! I had used proof of this religious reality in my last book. It was universal. It was truly a religion cover-"UP" on a universal scale.

Back to the radio show and possible interview. Here's what happened. They declined an interview with me, but told me my picture looked similar to another famous photo and then used Jeff's to compare. This is how I met Jeff. I finally asked the host if he was religious, too, and he said yes! He was a Christian. Wow, what a struggle. Scientific evidence vs. religious pride.

Anyway, this one rejection started the *Jeff and Mike Show* rolling, whether I knew it or not. I didn't. Believe me, I too, never thought I'd see a flying saucer, either. It became an adventure that would change my life forever. It really was the catalyst for our fame—and for one huge reason. I believed Jeff, and we found and filmed saucers! I first saw one that year before we did. That blew me away. I didn't get a picture of it, though. But when Jeff and I filmed them and got on television a year later, it received world-wide media recognition of flying saucers, then and now! It wasn't just this, though. After all, I had a picture of Johnny Cash and a flying saucer, for God's sake. Why wouldn't it? Right.

Well, seeing is believing, believe me! Anyway, I was using this as proof that aliens in flying saucers started religion. I had compared it to a cave drawing of one in France on the front cover. We even made billboards together. *(I will write about this later. It is what happened in the years succeeding the third and fourth books. All of this was eerily coincidental. It all led up to and precipitated this world-wide contact by flying saucers. Remember, this is 2012. I have déjà vu, and religion knows our ending. It's from the sky! It is now. Coincidence or Destiny?)*

Well, I used his video picture again on the fourth book and had advertised a video using this footage called *PROOF!* But it was Jeff's and not mine. Remember, I had only seen one in the fall of 2005 and I don't think anybody but him truly believed me. He did and, needless to say, I believed him one hundred percent! And now I was going to film them. At least I hoped. No, somehow I just knew it. I saw one. I was so excited. I hadn't filmed them yet. But, I had pre-advertised a new documentary. Little did I know what was about to happen, and I just couldn't pass this off as a coincidence. It would be the smoking gun of all smoking guns! I was going to compare Jeff's footage to the world's largest ancient statue of one on top of the heads of Easter Island and many other ancient pieces of evidence.

It turned into something much more. He had told me in 2005 that I could find them with him. I wrote about his evidence and claim to find and film them in my fourth book. This claim drove me to investigate after participating in the International Film Festival/UFO conference. I went straight to his house afterward. Before I left, though, I have to say that his proposal to find flying saucers was pretty unbelievable to me. Even seeing one wasn't enough because I hadn't seen any more. Besides the fact that I couldn't really afford to keep trying!

But something happened that drove me to give it a chance. While I was there, I had a contact moment which left a mark on my face. It was filmed by a local TV station there in Laughlin, Nevada. Jeff also experienced contact. Needless to say, I went. Nothing was going to stop me now! When I arrived at his house, we immediately set up the gear outside and started to relax for an evening of sky-watching. I told him that it was funny for a guy who believed in spirits to be sky-watching. He didn't comment. You see, I had asked why we were sky-watching back in Nevada, if everybody thought aliens were among us and believed in spirits. I reminded them that Heaven's UPness was irrefutable, like our going up to conquer space.

Nobody cared to comment. They were tired of me. They believed heaven was a spirit world or didn't know where it was. Neither one made any sense. None of them said UP. Why? Why didn't they get it? I knew why! But why didn't they look for spirit proof? The out and out lack of hurting or killing a spirit begged for logic besides this OBVIOUS MATCHING EVIDENCE! Why just an apparition or white noise, anyway? They can't be hurt if they're a spirit, can they?

I couldn't get them to see the lack of logic in this. I couldn't get them to understand that this doesn't reflect evidence of a spirit being, but one that is real and can be hurt or killed! Worst yet, I couldn't get them to see mankind as an evil creation, and this is why they don't help us. We can't be helped, that's what the religious story says! The majority is predestined for doom. And God forbid that I tell them that we could be an alien addicted to the scientific possibility of being in another body that we created in a lab. One that is used for its outward beauty and its powerful effect over other humans. One that we can control or at least influence its thoughts.

This came true in 2006. We finally achieved "scientific" invisibility and made robots that we could control with mental telepathy! Nothing I said or showed them seem to work. Not even their own admission of wanting power and being addicted to outward beauty, MATCHING the religious story!

Anyway, that night I found them! Before I go on, I want to make it clear why I used Jeff's photo from 2003 again on this book cover. It's because I videotaped the same one at his house in 2006. The next day! Yes, I did it. Look at the picture of it compared to his and, yes, Johnny Cash's. I couldn't believe my eyes, and it solidified my futuristic scientific thinking that space was conquered. By all appearances they exhibited all the characteristics of HEAVEN'S occupants. They could cloak their craft and render themselves invisible. Their craft had no sound! They weren't hurting us, nor helping us either. They weren't stopping accidents. Therefore they couldn't predict our every move. However, they did seem to know that we were watching them. Mental telepathy seemed to be obvious as well. I watched them for three days and could hardly bring myself to leave. I think they knew it! But again, they know we're an evil creation. We just don't know it yet.

Why help us to prosper? Maybe this is the way it is. Us wanting to be them isn't forcible, nor possible. We're just a disease running its course. No, we're gold-diggers and they need gold for spacecraft. Our every move can't be predicted, just our/mankind's outcome. The best proof of this is Yeshua/"Jesus" not knowing the guard's ear was going to be cut off by an apostle. I mean, come on. It doesn't take a rocket scientist to figure this out. And what about him asking why his father had forsaken him? This doesn't make sense if he already knew he wouldn't.

I always wrestled with this religious teaching of pre-destination, but worse with my own déjà vu. Déjà vu indicates we've done this before. Religion and scientific probability points to this reality as well. The idea that energy can't be created or destroyed and that all matter is energy, agrees also. But these scientific concepts are "deep," like infinity itself. I thought all of this wasn't as important as contact. We have a history of alien/flying saucer evidence, and I filmed one. To me, contact would eliminate our doubt about everything. It does! Read on!

Our doubt about not existing is really selfish. Why else do we want to know if the atoms of our body will always exist? Knowing we are atoms/energy isn't it ridiculous to ask, "Could they ever be manifested as me again?" If we only had one shot wouldn't it be best to try and conquer death for our children? How could we be so selfish and expose them to the same fear of death that we have? The sad reality of mankind is that the majority of us think we would be brutal without religion's reward-or-punishment doctrine. The evidence indicates otherwise. More deaths occur from religious acts of violence than any other. This is second only to people committing crimes for money, but proportionately quite larger. I hope this information provokes research into such a startling fact. Are we truly better off believing in life after death? Wouldn't that make us even more likely to live viciously, for the moment thinking we will have another chance? Maybe, we would have wealth, beauty, and power next time. The evidence indicates we are brutally and religiously vicious. Does the killing god story create this? Please consider it. He is a killer.

I was recently studying the scientific research of Michio Kaku. He stated that the universe is mostly composed of much more than atoms. In fact the majority is made up of dark matter (fragmented atoms). It is made up of elementary particles. I dug and dug until I realized that the smallest part of matter is termed nihilistic atomism. It is really all that exists. However, it is moving and only a part of the whole which is constantly appearing and disappearing. This is microcosm science and deep, but I understand it from the ancients. Almost everybody knows the quote "I think therefore I am"! This ancient quote is clearly quantum physics. But I haven't found too many people who know what an atom is, let alone, it being what they are made of!

So, it is simpler for me to use the sparkler at night example. It will explain how this "movement" relates to the infinite nature of matter, just changing form. The circle you make in rotating it really doesn't exist, just the sparkler. We are the sparkler/energy that just changes form! So do we, the universe, or anything the atom makes really exist? In effect we don't exist permanently, but just as a temporary image. But we need to remember we are the "moving"/stationery atom. I like the ice cube example to explain how we don't doubt the infinite existence of gas and its ability to turn into water then freeze and ultimately disappear. Yet we know it still exists.

This is the holy grail of mankind to understand that everything is nothing but moving energy. It didn't come from anywhere and isn't going anywhere. It is the godism quote of the ancients and Michio Kaku's theory. I wanted to take the time now, before I go on to share my latest discovery as a result of looking at Michio's umbilical bubble theory of the universe. In a moment, I will return immediately to March 6, 7, and 8, the date that I first FILMED FLYING SAUCERS!

Anyway, back to my overwhelming scientific discovery. I was shocked, after watching an interview of Kaku recently on *HARDtalk*, to find him answering questions about the universe. Like where did it come from and where is it going. He was clear about it being a cyclical dance of expansion/birth and contraction/death. He was also clear that we seemed doomed by it. Wow. I listened on—he was talking my language. I wanted to see if he saw the parallel to Buddhism and nirvana. Their goal is to break the cycle of birth, death, and reincarnation. If the universe has us doomed, religion has us doomed, and science sees the likelihood of our doom, given the ability to destroy ourselves with nuclear weapons, why bother with all of this? He said that it is our nature, and I agree! We are in effect gods of science, and it is in effect what drives him to try and overcome our "mortal" challenge.

He sees this as an exciting time to discover the tantalizing possibility of a loophole and escape the expansion or contraction of these bubble universes (the multiverse, which is really "one" infinite universe made up of an infinite birth of new ones). He sees this opportunity, through what appears to be a white hole umbilical cord blowing out of a black hole. Talk about blowing out, I was blown away! I saw this very solution to achieve the immortality of our species several years back and put it in my fourth book. However, my hypothesis was based on the membrane theory. It says that space is flat, which makes sense if it is spinning matter out from a central point. I felt the ability to stop this cycle, birth and death of a universe or membrane of matter/universe, was only possible through conquering space. We would have to out-distance the gravity field caused by it. My theory is based on space being flat as supported by the cave grid. His is made of bubbles, which I think could also be flat.

Either way, our principle theories are the same! He went on to say that science gives us an edge over the inevitable destruction of every universe, which is just one of infinity. He said we can only do this through space travel! Wow! My point exactly! If I can just show him flying saucers, maybe he will get my matching "UP" point. Religion is a story of people who *live* "UP" in the sky! I say the ancient evidence will give us the answer that we are so desperately looking for. Like the cave art of a grid showing our solar system exactly with a rocket/shuttle and the asteroid belt! It will prove religion was created by space travelers. I wanted to show him that his bubble theory is supported by the ancient religious yin and yang model. It has a black and white hole, the spinning motion of both galaxy or black hole, and looks like a bubble. It also has two sperm in an egg, which maintains life through an umbilical cord. I first used it to confirm the story of angels/ gods mixing with man, as two sperm in one egg would do this. But, now I see it could do both—and indeed does. Whoa, the parallel of religion's message is the same as his goal, to achieve the immortality of our species! Religion is a story where they are omnipotent, omnipresent, and omniscient. They have conquered space and live in it, just like he and I theorize that we could do as well. We would do it by going "UP," and they came from "UP!"

Wow! I hope he sees this MATCHING EVIDENCE. It irrefutably proves space is indeed conquered. The matching of ancient religious symbols to today's scientific ones are amazing and universal. If this doesn't convince him then I will show him a flying saucer. This will do it if he's a "true" scientist, one that follows matching evidence. If it does, then maybe I will get some respect for my scientific theories. First, they have to be watching us! We both agree that life in space has to be infinitely more advanced than we are. We also both agree on the natural progression of this intelligent being and that is to live in space. If I can continue to film and find flying saucers, then it will make us address Fermi's paradox. Answering "why they don't contact us" with logic will force us to accept this ancient religious evidence. They have to be real flesh and blood people who live in space, just like they all say. And they "CAN BE KILLED JUST LIKE US."

Secondly, they can't cure our primitive nature. The final question to be asked is why make a destructive scientific creation and yet we have already answered that with nuclear technologies! It can't be stopped, serves a purpose, and creates the desire for power that it will afford us! WOW! This is our story, people. Finally, a eureka moment that gives me a simple understanding of the universe I live in. It is infinite and space travel is the only way for scientists to separate themselves from the brutality of mankind. Thank You, Michio Kaku!

I went through all this hell the past fourteen years only to confirm what I always felt inside, anyway. It was my CON"SCIENCE"! Wow, we can't "CON SCIENCE." Man, these word coincidences are a trip. What goes around comes around. We can't stop existing. We are atoms/adams! I really hoped to explain the structure of the universe in a much simpler way. The big bang starts with the atom, and in Buddhism we must become one with the self. Adam must learn he is the atom! Wow, I discovered this to be the ultimate scientific knowledge that children and adults lack, myself included until now.

Asking what the universe is became an eye-opening question for me. I asked Angel, and she said it was everything as we know it. I asked her what is everything. She said it was us, the planets, space, etc. I asked her if she thought there was more than one universe. She said, "Of course, I just heard of the multiverse thing that you were talking about the other day."

"Well," I asked, "Where are the other ones?"

She didn't know. I asked if they were next to ours. She didn't know. I asked how there could be multiverses if there was only one universe. She didn't know and looked really confused. Hell, this was understandable—almost everybody is including myself. I wanted to ask her if she is the universe, but know better. I always sang John Lennon's *The Walrus* song, where he sings, "I am the eggman, I am the walrus, koo koo kachoo!" We are the universe. I wanted to explain how giving numbers to anything infinite is an oxymoron. I could see that Michio was saying that the multiverse theory is really infinite. Therefore, the term *multi* is a contradiction. To better clear up this confusion over one universe being composed of infinite multiverses (again, this is an oxymoron: one being multiple vs. infinite) it would be better to call them fields of matter as stated by the membrane theory. The reason I say this is that they are not really separate from the others. The gravitational pull is the only thing that separates them. The black space is infinite and expanding through the creation of baby "universes" born out of the bubbles of matter.

This would agree with both scientific theories. It also confirms the way matter continues to be born out of the union between it and anti-matter. This intercourse leaves one part matter over the one hundred per one hundred parts explosion theory. Therefore, this is what creates and sustains the ongoing and infinite existence of the universe, which is really just matter. We are it. This is so, because if it didn't exist, would any of this really matter?

Therefore, we have now come full circle to repeat an ancient religious philosophy of "mind over matter" that has become today's science. To conquer our understanding of it is secondary to space travel. Funny that it might take actually conquering the atom and making anti-matter to achieve this! We are doing this with the particle accelerator, but at a very slow rate. I was surprised at Michio stating that another universe could exist within his living room. I was always under the impression that two things couldn't occupy the same space, like matter and anti-matter. I will look up this law in the deep theories section of my physics book. I find it hard to understand how another "universe" could fit in such a small space given the expanse of what we "think" ours to be.

Anyway, I think that calling these flat fields of matter floating in an infinite universe a "universe" or dimension itself is a mistake. It gives the person the impression that is world-wide today, dimensions exist. This has led people to speculate that worlds/universes can exist within matter itself. I think this is called the "grandfather paradox" of time travel. The bottom line is that if there were other dimensions we wouldn't have the "UP" evidence of these religious beings and we wouldn't be going "UP." Spirits nor dimensions have yet to be proven and until they are, the evidence should dictate which is correct. We are going "UP" and have ancient stories of people who live "UP." I film the sky/"UP" to see flying saucers!

Now, back to my flying saucer career. It's still hard for me to believe that I not only saw one in 2005 but actually filmed them this year. And what's really hard is having to finish this book, before I can chase saucers again! I know I can find them now! Let's go see what happened. I'll give you a hint: nothing! "Just kidding," my Uncle Brice would say. Well, at least nothing had happened yet, anyway. Read on to find out if it does! I will tell you though, if it did you wouldn't be reading this book and not know about me.

Remember, up until now my story of world-wide fame was fiction, excluding the scientific discoveries. Now, I am telling you the real ending! If you look at the copyright date on this book, it says 2007. It is right now Christmas of 2006. I will be releasing this book in February 2007. It's been almost a year since the Barbara Walters special was on. While I was typing this it was advertised to come on again. I got pretty excited about this. Maybe, I would have another chance at getting her attention with this new book and new video. Here's why. You see, I gave her my fourth book and video proof last year, right after I left Jeff's. Well I gave her *WHY THE BLANK DON'T THEY CARE*, too. But, it was mainly just the footage I told you about already. I will get back to that in a second, though.

But before I do, I know now why it didn't get her attention the first time. Maybe it's fate. I mean, after all, my last book did say "SCIENCE FINDS HEAVEN," but it didn't "prove" it. I think it was the combination of a poor title (*2012 Gold's History Solves Mankind's Mystery*), no still shots, and poor video. Now I will have a new book and a new reality-show quality video with amazing stills! And this book has a title that "CLEARLY" addresses her question: "WHERE IS HEAVEN?" Besides, I'm better prepared. I got several still shots of my video saucer footage, daytime and night, to prove that's what they are. The footage was shaky, but the pictures left no doubt about them being saucers! This new *WHY THE BLANK DON'T THEY CARE* video has a new beginning that also pitches us as "THE JEFF AND MIKE SHOW: REAL-LIFE FLYING SAUCER HUNTERS!" I hope to attract the investigative side of her television nature and capitalize on the reality show phenomenon that's so hot right now. To me this is the ultimate reality.

Entertainment would take a back seat to "NEWS" if we could do this. Heck, the whole world would be immediately drawn to catching one or making contact. They would converge upon Phoenix and other areas of high activity. And wouldn't we want to know why just these spots and not the same everywhere? Are these places like Phoenix and Mexico City in jeopardy? This would take first priority all over the Earth. I am sure of that. I'd tell you why I'm sure, but that's my ending. I know we can find them, and we will! You'll see why it becomes the "SMOKING GUN' as I told you earlier. We did it once; we can do it again!

So follow me as I go back to where I left off that fateful day—the day I actually filmed saucers in Phoenix, Arizona, in 2006 with Jeff Willes. Wow, that still blows me away! Now, let's continue on: here's how it went. I left off at Jeff's house in Phoenix, March 2006. I had one video out called *Proof* with his famous video shot from 2003. I had put it in my fourth book and was already advertising my new book, the one you are reading. Coincidently enough, I had also advertised a new video called *WHY THE BLANK DON'T THEY CARE*. But little did I know I would find them as I headed out west, that fateful cold February morning before all this happened. I wish I could have filmed myself then. As soon as I pulled out, I began talking about how crazy this was. Did I really think that I could just drive out there and find them? I literally laughed out loud at the thought of this coming true. And believe me, I did talk to myself, a lot! It was crazy, or I must be. I couldn't stop thinking about it as I drove, because I hadn't found them again since I saw one over my house in 2005. And I looked hard damn near every day! Since I hadn't been able to find one for over a year, it seemed ridiculous to think that I would. I was losing hope, and I certainly never thought, for one minute, that Jeff and I were destined to do this. But we did!

Hell, I was naive enough the first time to think my buddy Jake and I would find spirits or even Yeshua/"JESUS" himself. Jake just knew he was a spirit! Right. He never proved it! As a matter of fact, the few times we experienced the apparitions or a voice out of thin air, it made me even more certain these angels/gods were real/flesh people, and this was proof of that. This is how real advanced people who will be hurt by us would communicate. Anyway, we never made contact/open communication, and they never answered questions telling us they were spirits! This to me was what we all were looking for, like the Ghostbusters. A spirit is the "HOLY GRAIL." Well, like I told you earlier, he wasn't looking for them scientifically. I became the Ghostbuster. He is a spiritualist!

Man, what a turnaround over the past fourteen years. I went from believing in spirits to ACCEPTING THE EVIDENCE OF ANCIENT ART DEPICTING ALIENS AND FLYING SAUCERS! My theory was now based on "PHYSICAL EVIDENCE"! Surely, advanced technologies of these aliens in flying saucers must've created the magic spirit factor of religion and its universal stories—incredible scientific stories of fiery chariots taking people (which sounds like abduction) "UP" in the sky. It was this ancient evidence that assured my sanity when I did see one. It was "UP" in the sky as well. It was then that I was one hundred percent sure they had seen them, too! Now it all made so much sense to me, especially the hell of life. They were "real" flesh-and-blood people/aliens, not spirits. Now we know what's real and what isn't.

Funny, I remember as a child how Mom would tell me that spirits didn't exist. She would do this to calm me down after I got too scared in church or after one of Dad's sermons at home. The irony is that she really thought they did. They scared her, too. (Check this evidence out; it is both sad and ironic.) They made her scared of the very thing she was supposed to be looking for! If she only knew from the beginning that it was her belief in something she couldn't prove that scared us in the first place. But she never proved it, just like Jake and my new "OTHER WITNESS." The whole world began to hate my challenge to prove a spirit. But they wanted me to prove the saucers. I do! No, we do! First me and Jeff, then the whole world.

Oops, I am telling you a little too much. Remember, it hasn't happened yet. But earlier I had said the world might be better without religion. Well, at least we wouldn't have this fear of monsters and spirits. We wouldn't have religious wars either, huh. That's a given. Wow, what an unbelievable transition, huh!

Well, anyway, back to finding saucers! So, like I said before, after my sighting of 2005, I looked and looked but never saw another one. And in not finding any more, I had already planned to use more of Jeff's footage and ancient matching evidence to support my theory. I was going to prove that flying saucers had created our religions. But what a surprise I got, huh! I filmed flying saucers! Just imagine me doing this with you. Pretty crazy, huh? Well it gets even more eerie. I told you about us making billboards. Well, I mean literally. You'll never guess what happened, or maybe you will.

Anyway, I'll go ahead and finish the story up to the present. It's Christmas of 2006. I left the story leaving Jeff's house after three days of filming over ten flying saucers. I called everybody I knew—family, friends, and some potential newspeople, thinking that would definitely seal the deal on my fame. But it didn't. We got on TV, however, our short three minutes of exposure on a local public access channel failed. We couldn't believe it.

I left Jeff's telling him to get ready and board an airplane to L.A. or New York. That's where they were telling me to go. I did. I left Jeff's and went straight home to prepare for this trip. I now had footage to make a new video. This changed my whole plan for *Why The Blank Don't They Care*! I wanted to show the whole world that the media didn't jump on this! I needed the world to see how "OUR" saucers matched the hats of Easter Island and that this was not only an ancient statue of a flying saucer, but proved religion's heaven was "UP" and caused by flying saucers. So, that's what I started doing the days, weeks, and months upon my return. I found it harder and harder to be normal again. I really became the weirdo now. I did, however, find more saucers over Nashville and tried to show one to my brother Brian, but he didn't see it. I never saw any more over my home; even as I write, I am looking. But I did when I started building my billboard. That didn't happen until early September. In the meantime, Jeff finally got our new video done without the new reality show introduction. He told me that would take awhile. We were doing this on a shoestring budget. Man, it was just killing me to wait. My book sales were down to nothing and even my trip to Roswell didn't do much good. I always do their annual Fourth of July UFO festival. While I was there I advertised on the street: GUIDED FLYING SAUCER TOURS! Nobody bit. I couldn't wait any longer. So, I went to New York with a three-foot poster showing Jeff's saucer over the Easter Island statue's head and my new unfinished video. Naturally I didn't have this book yet, either. But I was hell-bent to show Matt Lauer my new Easter Island evidence and tell Barbara Walters that I did know heaven is "UP." I thought my poster would prove it! It didn't.

When I returned I became very depressed. I called all the TV stations in Nashville and never got one bite. This drove me to do a protest in front of the newspaper, located right downtown on Broadway. I got a lot of support from passers-by, but still no press. All I could think of next was the billboard. My brother Terry lives on a major four-lane highway in Ohio. I knew it wasn't going to get me the attention that I could get if I jumped the gates of the *Today* show. I actually thought about this. After all, I had live footage of flying saucers, for god's sake. Needless to say again, I didn't or you would have known about me! I went home. The protest thing is what spawned the billboard idea. I had a lot of people come by me. This proved to me that patience is a virtue. I wasn't going to jail when I couldn't change things anyway. I wasn't able to just make them show up. Hell, I couldn't even spot any more, after that. How could I with everything I had going on?

I needed to start this book. I knew I would have to have all this in place, anyway. I desperately needed the money to do both—the book and a full-time flying saucer hunting career. It wasn't easy, making the money and finding more flying saucers. But in the back of my mind I knew I could guarantee a sighting in Phoenix the first day. The amount of activity there vs. Nashville is phenomenal. However, I did still see one after Brian left in November. I did it on the way to Nashville while I was making deliveries for business and seeing my editors. They were pretty excited about it. I wanted to put them in here as witnesses to the event. Even better though was finally getting to show one not only to Brian but my sister-in-law Vicki too! Brian helped build the billboard in September. The first day after it went up, I spotted them as he was getting up on the scaffolding to help me stabilize it. It was twenty-six feet high! I couldn't believe it, but as I looked "UP" to guide him, I was blinded by the sun. I quickly moved over and let the billboard block it. That's when I saw them! I saw one big one and a faint smaller one off to the side just above it. I really got excited and started screaming for Brian to look at it. He thought I was bullshitting him, but I yelled, "I'm not, goddamn it, just look." After not being able to find it on the scaffolding, I didn't think he would believe me. But he did, finally. How could he not? I was screaming and telling him I saw another one and . . . and.

Wow, I saw two definitely and what appeared to be some flying by it. A lot of them really high "UP." They were really visible in the white glare that I was looking at in blocking the billboard. He had a hard time finding them, but when he did it was great because he didn't just dismiss it. In fact, he abruptly replied quite surprisingly, "What the hell is that thing?"

"It's a flying saucer," I remarked. (I remember Jeff telling me the same thing back in Phoenix, when I first saw an irrefutable UFO I got on tape.) I hollered again that there was more than one.

He said, "It ain't either, goddamn it."

"Well, what the hell is it then, if it ain't?" I snapped right back.

"I don't know, Michael Duane," he said, less angry this time, "but you've got an awful big imagination." He called me by both first and middle names like mom or dad did when they were angry. I laughed.

"Well, what is it then?" I demanded. "It is round and it ain't no balloon, that's for damn sure. Now is it?" I really hate people doubting me like I'm a big liar.

"I don't know, but it ain't a flying saucer," he maintained again. "Well, let's agree upon what it isn't then. But first let's just look at the matching geometrical shape of it and a saucer. It does look just like a round saucer that you put a cup on, now doesn't it? Let's also look at its color. It's silver, shiny, and spinning, right?" I fired all these questions at him before he could respond.

He really started looking hard and made it a point to challenge them all, but couldn't. He did agree that it was round, shiny, and moving. He started to say it was small until a commercial jet flew under it. I got his response at this point to use later on as a scientific witness who was challenging my claim. It was beautiful. Because after challenging everything else—shape, color, movement, etc.—he was forced to examine the last thing that would rule it out, its size.

I screamed as the airplane came toward it and said, "You see, there's your proof. It's huge." It was twice the size and he used the comparison of it being a fifty cent piece to the plane being a dime. I was blown away! I never thought I would get this lucky to have a comparison like that! He wasn't that impressed and even said so on the interview. But I was and he said that, too. I asked him to clarify that he had in fact been shown a UFO by me over the billboard and that it definitely wasn't a star, planet, weather balloon, plane, satellite, etc. He did!

"Finally," I asked one more time, "what did it look like?". He said it was round, shiny silver, and spun as it moved.

"Well, wouldn't you say that it matches a flying saucer?" I asked, not able to help myself emphasize again the matching evidence.

He said he didn't know because, personally, he had never seen one. I couldn't argue with that. I was so tired of arguing. Hell, I just wanted the world to be perfect, anyway. What's so wrong with that? God does, too, I thought to myself, but doesn't make it so. I knew better than to touch that—all hell would break loose. It already had.

This is hell, not being able to discuss it, without all the hell. Why are religious people so afraid of this evidence? I guess because the same questions really torture them, too. Well, that about rounded out the last of 2006, other than the few sightings I had in Nashville afterwards. It is Christmas Eve now and the Tennessee Titans play today for a chance at a playoff spot. We are all very excited and I still have a song to finish before next week. So, I need to get back on the storyline that left off with "CONTACT"!

They have landed! I wrote the ending in my last book. I am not a bible thumper, but I did write that the final battle would be in Megido, Israel. I only did this for reasons of following a fictitious story-line. I do, however, see that the religious community of Jews, Muslims, and Christians revere Israel. The evidence strongly points to them not believing the aliens. The Jehovah's Witnesses are now teaching their flock, like many other Christian sects, that they are demonic. The bible has a killing god who murders innocent children, wants to be worshipped, and plenty of lies. I don't see them changing their "minds." I also don't see an immediate transition from chaos to world-wide cooperation. I think that any if not all of these religious followers will go to Israel. The majority of this population is already there. The ending must entail a slow process of trying to clean-up the earth and re-introduce a whole new way of life into our society, which is now based on money. I have followed the evidence for the past fourteen years, since I started down the road of religious examination. And in doing so I have come to one conclusion. The story I heard all my life about the angels being thrown out of Heaven now is very simple to understand. It is a story of lusting for power, to be greater than god. This made me ask the ultimate question; "Who is God?" which is and should be the first lesson in Religion 101. It is, if you aren't already conditioned/"brainwashed" to think God is a given and it doesn't matter what "HE" is. The second should be, "When did it start?" and the third is obvious: "Why would they stay away?" I immediately challenged the magic God because he wasn't here and there wasn't any magic! This was logical, but not for the faithful. In asking these questions I repeatedly found that most of my family and all religious scholars are just that, conditioned to not know or challenge it. Therefore, I set out on my own and ultimately began to study with someone who was also supposedly "looking." However, he ultimately couldn't bring himself to prove his magic, spirit, omnipresent god, either! Both the new witness in this story and the old in the first are believers in religion's universal spirit god story. They both still "BELIEVE" this lack of evidence. I can't change them, and my evidence or their lack of it can't, either. They couldn't see the irony of challenging someone to have "PHYSICAL" evidence when they didn't either. Their bible doesn't heal people. I challenged them to do it repeatedly and never saw them or anyone else do it. This led me to a startling conclusion, which came from this simple angel story I learned, like them as a child. Its simplicity stuck out like a sore thumb, that "Heaven mirrored the earth." Wow! I could see our lust for outward beauty and power was ruining our perfect existence as well. Could these angels be gods/aliens who all looked the same and were only capable of power over one another from scientific means like human creations? I was certainly more than convinced of this possibility, when the ancient evidence showed statues of god as an alien. His story clearly shows that he knew his "origins" from the universe as well. Adam/Atum is the atom! Yeshua said "we are gods" and was killed for saying he was god. "God" is everything in it, and it came from nothing. John Lennon and Carl Sagan said the same thing. The god story is one of evolution, by which these angels/gods became gods themselves and lusted for outward beauty and the powerful advantage over one another that it would give them. They were able to do this through the creation of man on the eighth day, out of clay, according to the Bible. The sixth day is their evolution from nature/God, who they are. I found that 666 is just the three stages of time, and a metaphor, showing they always make man. The universal atom symbol has six points. Adams are made up of atoms. He is the biblical quote, "What *isn't*, was, and will be cast into the lake of fire." *Isn't* is the key word. We didn't evolve . . . we're scientifically created. The gods/aliens "evolved"/ always existed, just like nature and the atom, "What Is."

All the other creation stories are the same, just like god being from the sky! The Easter Island god is "Make-make," and his creation of man and woman is exactly the same as the Bible's eight-day creation, down to anesthetizing Adam to make Eve. The ancient statues of gods/aliens all look the same and are outwardly ugly. This would make them equal and powerless over one another.

This was all making perfect sense. Outward beauty rules here, and it must be hell. The evidence sure says so. If we mirror them then it must there as well. According to all ancient texts, they also saw themselves evolve and realized that nature created them and the only way to achieve this unique power was through the scientific power of creation itself. They created man for his service and for his ***power through unique beauty of the flesh***. They conquered human creation, space, and "death." They know there isn't an ending to anything, only its image. Our problem and their addiction is just that, an image that is destined to doom, a scientific creation for power!

Nature creates uniformity within one's own kind. They evolved this way, one species who conquered space. We celebrate and applaud diversity and unique greatness. But it doesn't take a rocket scientist to see our problem, nor this contradiction. The idea of creating bodies for the "soul" purpose of outward immortal beauty is the goal of humanity. If we want to kid ourselves we can, but the religious Armageddon will be all about this one issue. It isn't possible to be intelligent, beautiful, and not know this. Hell, it isn't possible if you're dumb and ugly either. Wanting to be pretty is a terminal disease resulting directly from our mental sexual desire for power. The mother goddess statue makes this so obvious that it is pathetic. The stories of these beings looking "DOWN" on the daughters of man and seeing their outward beauty is painfully clear. They are ugly and wanted to be pretty. This story is the flood story, which is rooted in the universal mother-goddess worship.

These ancient statues have heads of aliens and pretty bodies! Aliens are "outwardly" ugly! The evolution of primitive man served only one purpose to them, and that was the vehicle to scientifically upgrade it. Modern man is a product of this scientific creation; primitive man is nature's creation. Mankind is "GOD'S MYSTERY." The evidence says that primitive man's God is an Alien! The trafficking and ongoing scientific creation of humans is why this mystery exists. It can't be stopped. We aren't a "good" thing. Nature is the "good" thing. They don't want to hurt us' they just want to be us! And all for the purpose of sexual power. Most of us, if not all, lust for outward beauty, to have it, be worshipped by it, and last but not least, yes, BE IT! We are sexual "BE"INGS! Actually, I think we all do! I do!! Desire for sex tortures me. It tortures my children who don't want mommy and daddy to be sexual. But the Buddhist monks are the ones who show that they have truly overcome this disease! They are celibate, bald, all look the same, and they don't want to save us. Just like the aliens. Wow!

I know I've gotten repetitive, and I'm sorry. But I want to make one last theory about the universe to go along with this ancient "GOD"/ALIEN evidence. On Michio Kaku's homepage, he is accepting people's theory of everything. Mine is solely based on today's knowledge of the atom. The very definition of it is says it can't be created nor destroyed. I have put this on the last page of evidence. Therefore, it has no beginning, only the "THREE" different forms of it. The universe consist of infinite "non-thinking" energy, that is constantly giving birth to matter and repeating it again through its inevitable death. This invisible creator of life is religion's god and irrefutably not a person. Yet, in religion, it is what makes the person. They are one and the same. This is why you have the confusion of god being an individual and everything else, too. It also applies to the multiverse theory, which states that one consists of an infinite "many." And they are infinitely giving birth to "NEW" ones, which is really the recycling of old ones! The structure of the universe is flat, due to the spinning composition of it and the atoms that make it. Even the smallest parts of the atom are held within a flat circular motion due to this centralized giver of life, the nucleus! The membrane theory is supported by many ancient carvings/sculpture of grids with stars and planets. Many even show modern airplanes! This theory does not stand in stark contrast to Michio's umbilical chord theory! As a "matter" of fact, they could be one and the same. The fields of membrane could indeed be spreading out in a round fashion, held together by the gravitational field of its nucleus. It would still be flat. This single field of matter in an infinite universe allows for constant multiplication and the ability to escape the contraction of it. The loophole to conquer the inevitable death of our species would require space travel. They both agree on this "matter," as I do!

That's why it is so scientifically important to see the "UP" evidence of ancient religion. Their art might shed some light on the structure of the universe. We must escape the stronghold of matter, by going "UP"! The membrane theory is different from Michio's, in that it doesn't relegate them to be adjoined as bubbles. Michio's does! There is ancient evidence to support this theory. He maintains that the resulting death of a universe will create babies through an umbilical cord. The umbilical cord could be the black hole, which is blowing out matter on the other side. It produces light/"white" matter and is called a white hole. Is it possible to use these to accelerate matter outside the realm of gravitational pull. The yin and yang represent just exactly this premise and that possibility! Like I said before, I had used this symbol to prove the angel/alien story and what they looked like. I now am using it to support Michio's theory. It makes sense to travel through the black hole to find a much younger, "WARMER" universe! It is giving new birth to old matter. I know we can't do this now, but I think it could be possible in the future. Maybe, just maybe, it's the beam me "up" Scotty story! *The Mayan ball game suggests so.* Maybe the aliens are doing it, now! They live "UP" in the sky.

Well, either way, there's no doubt anymore where heaven is. HEAVEN IS SPACE . . . UP! People, for god's sake. We found ancient statues of aliens and flying saucer art. We filmed flying saucers and still can. They are not hurting us. Please give our evidence a chance? "SEEING IS BELIEVING"! IT IS THE PROOF WE ALL WANT.

"FINALLY", you can "SEE" it for yourself in "The Jeff and Mike Show, Real-Life Flying Saucer Hunters!" Send $4.95 (S&H) with proof of book purchase for a free DVD, *Why The Blank Don't They Care*, to: Mike Brumfield, 1066 Golden Herren Rd., Sparta, TN 38583.

Please look for my next book **The Discovery**. It is not part of this storyline. I will write it as a fiction, based on my dream about the mystery of our species. I've already got the plot "in my head." The inspiration behind it comes from an unknown advanced scientific extraterrestrial intelligent being addicted to outward beauty, and my lifelong experience with déjà vu. You might even say it could be my own "guardian angel's" perspective. I'll leave that up to you.

Either way, "again" we all know, that everybody loves a good mystery. Especially me, so please enjoy it. Solving it is my dream and living it becomes mankind's worst nightmare! Little will I know, until the end, that these could be one and the same! Ultimately, this will depend on the way you "look" at it. But remember this: "SEEING IS BELIEVING"! Even if you don't believe it. Follow along as the horror unfolds, if you dare! Don't be afraid; after all, it's only a dream, or is it?

**To see the evidence in *"Heaven is Space . . . UP,"*
please buy yourself a copy.**

ALIENS
Gold
Tenth
Planet ...
PRIMITIVE MAN'S SEED
ALIEN SEED
"Amazing scientific evidence links the Roswell alien with the seed of primitive man!"
MISSING LINK?
Read the SHOCKING new sequel to the best-selling novel,
The Two Witnesses and The Religion Cover-Up!
BY MICHAEL

Second Book

WHAT A CLIMAX TO THE MOST EXCITING TRILOGY EVER!
THE FUTURE
ALIEN CONTACT!
ALL SPACE IS HEAVEN
IT WILL SOLVE RELIGIONS MYSTERY!
THE GODS/ANGELS ARE THE ALIENS AND FLESH & BLOOD
FLYING SAUCER
CAVE DRAWING FRANCE CIRCA 15,000 BC
READ AND FIND OUT
WHAT THEY LOOK LIKE
WHY THEY DON'T SHOW &
WHEN THEY POSSIBLY WILL!
LOOK EVERYBODY!!
"JOHNNY CASH"
LOOKING "UP" AT AN ALLEGED FLYING SAUCER
"REAL PHOTO" AROUND 1980
MORE PICTURES INSIDE
NO WONDER PRIMITIVE MAN SAID HEAVEN IS UP!
WHY WOULD SPIRITS HAVE DIRECTION?
HOW CAN SPIRITS HAVE SEX WITH MAN?
DO SPIRITS REALLY EXIST?
FIND OUT HOW HEAVEN BECAME A SPIRIT REALM!!
AREN'T WE SEEING THEM NOW?
READ THIS RIVETING ENDING TO THE PREVIOUS TWO BOOKS
FIRST "THE TWO WITNESSES AND THE RELIGION COVER-UP"
SEQUEL "ALIENS GOLD TENTH PLANET"
SEE BACK COVER FOR WORLDS LARGEST ANCIENT SCULPTURE OF FLYING SAUCER
WARNING,
THE FUTURE IS BRIGHT,
WEAR CHEAP SUNGLASSES!
AND ALIEN GOD! SEE THESE AND MUCH MUCH MORE ANCIENT
BY MICHAEL
EVIDENCE INSIDE THIS SHOCKING FINAL STORY!!!
NEW BOOK!

Third Book

I found it overwhelming that history itself was based in gold mining and universal religious stories of people living "UP" in the sky. This proves they are real flesh and blood people like us. We use gold to live "UP" in the sky too!

Fourth Book

The Video/Picture Evidence

Conclusion: My ability to film flying saucers matches the ancient art and universal religious stories of people living in the sky. The evidence shows them to be equal in looks like the Easter Island picture on page 285 reflects. This evidence clearly shows them to be like all other life on this planet—EQUAL IN LOOKS! I can only conclude them to be nature's creation. The evidence says we are their creation for the "SOUL" purpose of working for them and worshipping their power. Could we be the 1/3 of the angels/aliens experiencing power through the outward uniqueness of our looks? We now clone. My final thought is the "Beginning of Everything." The atom says there is no beginning and so does Religion's God! Will we let the evidence rule? Why would anyone be afraid of "THE EVIDENCE?" (Oh yeah, I almost forgot myself . . . us beauty addicts!)

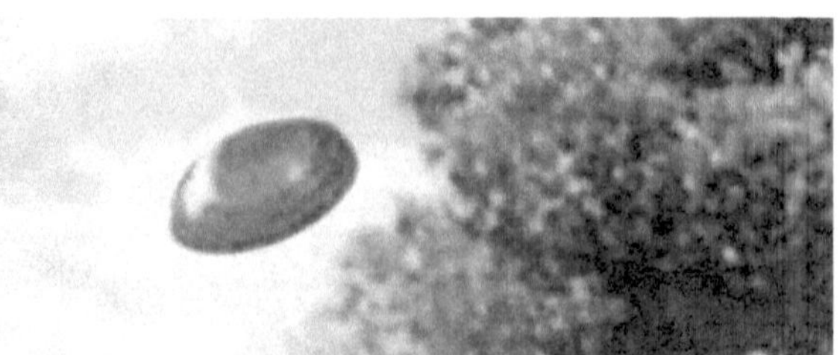

Paul Villa photo of flying saucer circa 1960.

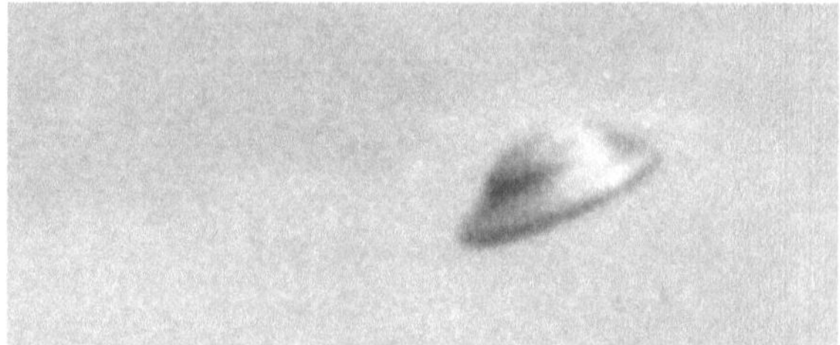

Picture on front cover of third and fourth book. How can these match when they are taken twenty years apart. Again, these "MATCH" ancient cave drawing on front cover. World's largest saucer on head of Easter Island, and aborigine saucer and alien's gold halo above (back cover) protecting it in space.

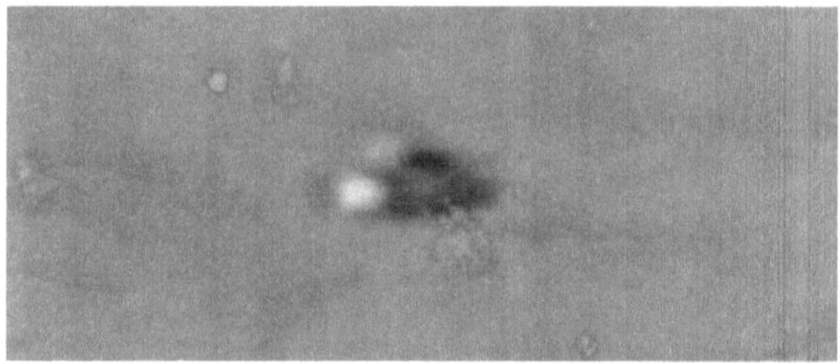

Video taken in 2003 by Jeff Willes of Phoenix, Arizona. To buy video, type his name in computer or call 623/847-9132.

Video taken in 2006 by Mike Brumfield in Phoenix, Arizona.

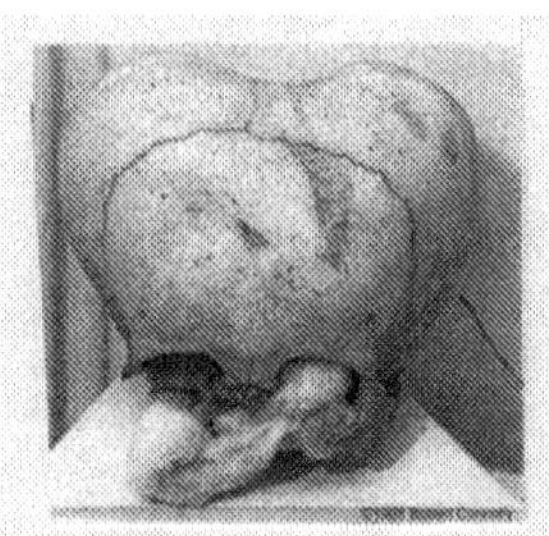

Oldest rock art on record catalogued by the Leakeys, ca. 50,000 years old, from Africa. Clearly shows little alien highlighted in box. It also shows another taller species restraining one of their own. The two heads above it were found in modern-day Israel, and are Sumerian; approximately 10,000 years old. The skull (from Peru) also supports ancient rock art of aliens in Africa. There are universal religious stories of two creations of man. Does this give us proof that they first tried to manipulate their own species to serve their needs?

Oldest Sumerian/Ubaid "God" statues on record in Museum of Antiquity, Cairo, Egypt. Clearly shows male and female gender and alien-looking beings. Picture, lower left, even shows mother nursing baby. Zechariah Sitchin claims these are android robots. They are, for God's sake, real "PARENTS!" If these are the most ancient statues that don't look like us, could they be primitive man's universal god/angel? Look at "Mother Goddess" statues on the following pages. They clearly are the god/angel that mixed with the "pretty daughter" of man.

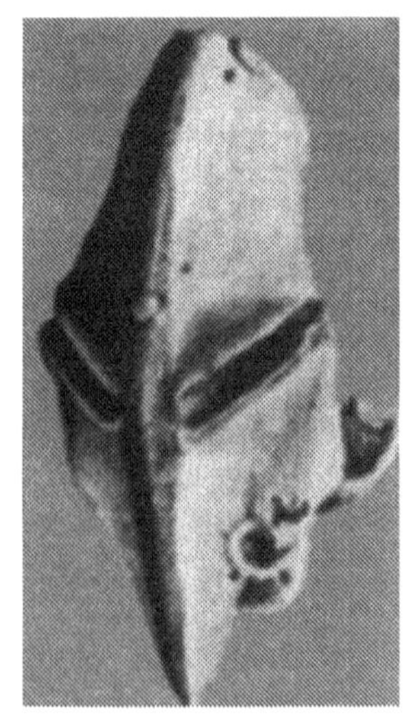

Ancient Sumerian King and Queen and Priest. Notice Priest has bald head—indicative of Alien God. Also notice big eyes.

The Sumerians carved statues of the gods from stone. From the statues we can see what they thought the gods looked like. Many gods looked like short people with round bellies. They had thin lips and big noses. They wore skirts made of sheep's wool. In fact, many statues of the gods looked like the statues the Sumerians made of themselves!

What Did the Sumerians Believe About the Meaning of Their Lives?

The gods of Sumer looked like men—and they acted like men. The gods liked good food and nice clothing. They got married and had children. Sometimes they were kind. Sometimes they were cruel. Either way, the Sumerians believed they had no control over what the gods did. Rather, the Sumerians believed that they were slaves of the gods. This story tells why.

THE SUMERIAN STORY OF THE CREATION OF MAN

The gods had always worked for a living. But when the goddesses were created, the gods had to work even harder to keep them happy. Then the gods had great trouble getting enough bread to eat

This is the oldest known historical record of Mankind's "God" story. It clearly shows they were real flesh and blood people. It also shows they created Mankind to work for them. This is an excerpt from an educational text called *Ancient Civilizations*.

Mother goddess statue from Catayal (modern-day Turkey), ca. 8000 B.C. It clearly shows an alien head representing God and a beautiful woman. This story is also universal in religion and reflects Gods/angels mixing with "pretty" daughters of man.º

This is the "head/person" that should be under the gold halo. Funny how the book cover shows the shroud which looks like space beneath it. Because it exemplifies what the cover-up in religion is all about. What heaven's occupants look like? And where are they? The evidence says clearly that they are aliens UP IN SPACE! If you don't follow evidence or can't imagine a new discovery of an ancient relic that could solve our mystery, then please watch "The Planet of the Apes." The apes ignore scientific evidence over their religious stories of God creating them, just like my story today! Why the blank don't they care! Check out my video. Are we all addicted to outward beauty? Hell, yeah!!! Can't, couldn't do anything. I've always said instant creation/magic wasn't possible, but if it is, I guarantee it to be scientific. And then, it couldn't make this universe perfect. Babies are being raped. Finally, people . . . please answer for yourself why anybody would let this happen if they could stop it. I promise you, there's only one logical answer . . . they can't.

To see the rest of the ancient statues/artworks of aliens and flying saucers, please buy a copy of my fifth book, *Heaven Is Space . . . UP!* There's lots more!

THE BASIC ELEMENTS OF MATTER

What is **matter**? ★ Why it didn't and doesn't come from something!

Matter is anything that takes up space and has mass (or weight, which is the influence of gravity on mass). It is distinguished from energy, which causes objects to move or change, but which has no volume or mass of its own. Matter and energy interact, and under certain circumstances behave similarly, but for the most part remain separate phenomena. They are, however, inter-convertible according to Einstein's equation $E = mc^2$, where E is the amount of energy that is equivalent to an amount of mass m, and c is a constant, the speed of light in a vacuum.

In 1804, the English scientist John Dalton formulated the atomic theory, which set out some fundamental characteristics of matter, and which is still used today. According to this theory, matter is composed of extremely small particles called atoms, which can be neither created nor destroyed. Atoms can, however, attach themselves (bond) to each other in various arrangements to form molecules. A material composed entirely of atoms of one type is an element, and different elements are made of different atoms. A material composed entirely of molecules of one type is a compound, and different compounds are made of different molecules. Pure elements and pure compounds are often referred to collectively as pure substances, as opposed to a mixture in which atoms or molecules of more than one type are jumbled together in no particular arrangement.   341

Atoms are invisible to the naked eye, can't be created, and make up ALL matter, just like religions spirit/God. With this evidence, why do we still question an atom's creation? Why don't religious people question God's beginning? Why do we not question "Nothingness?" Do we really "KNOW" what it is? Why can't we just accept a possible infinite existence with nature? After all, we are atoms.

Big Bang Theory disputed

"Space and time go on forever and the so-called Big Bang said to have started the universe is actually part of a repeating cycle, according to a new paper that challenges conventional wisdom in physics. Infinite space and time would contradict the generally accepted notion of a universe expanding abruptly out of nothing 14 billion years ago, said Neil Turok, a professor of mathematical physics at the University of Cambridge in England.

Turok wrote the paper in the journal *Science* with Paul Steinhardt of Princeton University. An ongoing expansion and contraction is more likely than a Big Bang as supported by Cambridge physicist Stephen Hawking and other cosmologists building on the work of the late Albert Einstein," Turok said in a telephone interview.

In the words of Michio Kaku, "Let this investigation begin." Could all the ancient sacred stone circles like Stonehenge represent saucers? They do match! They also match a type 3 civilization like religion describes. Check out Michio's website to see what a type 3 is. Heaven is a type 3 civilization!

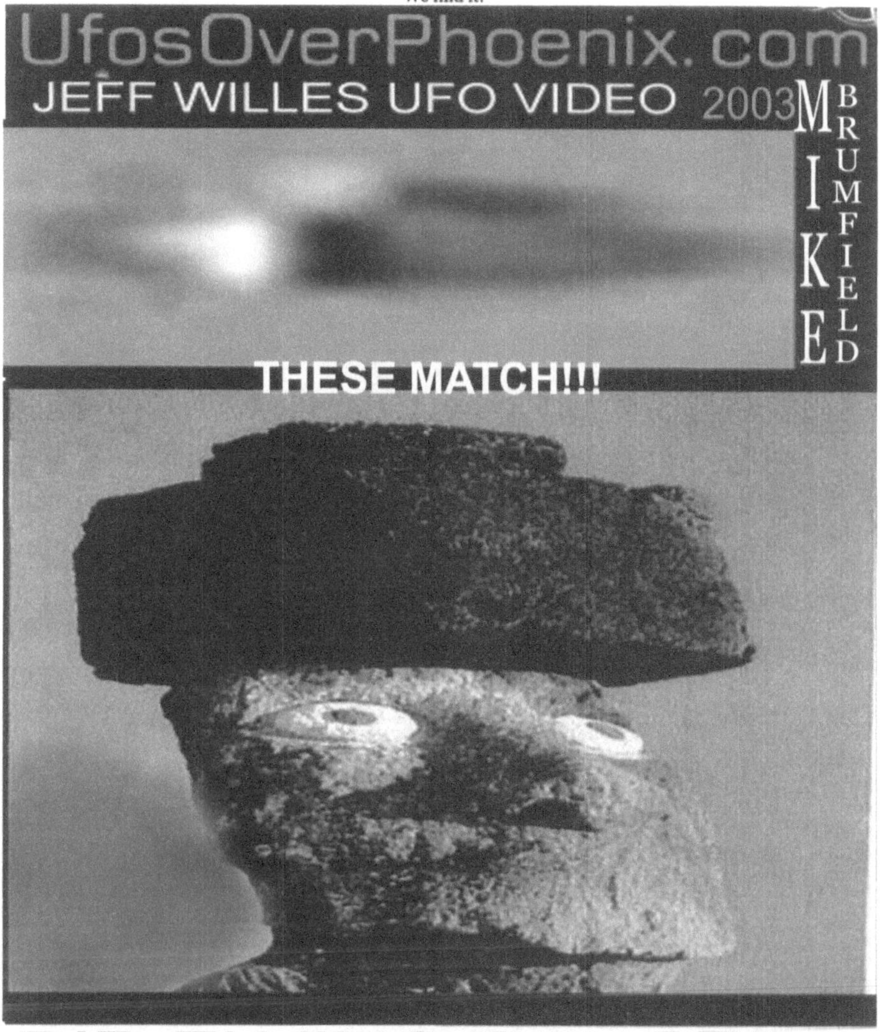

ARE WE *REALLY* READY?

What if we find it "Heaven" and they want us to give away all our money and follow them?

(I am not a bible-thumper; just pointing out that simple message of all religion is anti-materialism. This was Atlantis and all other pre-flood stories perfect culture's "DOWN-fall." Word up people, equality!)

JESUS SAID UNTO HIM, IF THOU WILT BE PERFECT, GO AND SELL THAT THOU HAST, AND GIVE TO THE POOR, AND THOU SHALT HAVE TREASURE IN HEAVEN: AND COME AND FOLLOW ME.

—MATTHEW 19:21

This scripture says we must give away our money to be perfect!
I can't tolerate religious people not recognizing the evil of money or anyone else!
This is a no-brainer. If you think it's not, try being poor!

READY OR NOT, WE ARE FILMING FLYING SAUCERS.

GET READY FOR THE "ANSWERS."

THEY ARE IN MY NEW BOOK,

COMING SOON,

THE

EVIDENCE

"Flying Saucers Created Religion"

(IT IS MY DISCOVERY!)

FINALLY, IF HEAVEN MIRRORS EARTH . . . THEN HUMAN CREATION FOR THE PURPOSE OF POWER THROUGH BEAUTY IS WHAT OUR MYSTERY IS ALL ABOUT.

First of all, for those of you thinking that we "could be" an experiment. Well, at least that's better than "are" an experiment. Because religion's destiny rules out us being an experiment, they know our ending. I find that the addiction to human creation by aliens explains our short recorded history, reincarnation, religion's story of people living in the sky, and most of all, the gold thing. It solves our mystery better than traditional magic religion, because the evidence matches! Secondly, for those who think we're being tested, this makes their omnipotent God cruel and a contradiction. He's omnipotent, remember? Again, He has no doubt and knows our future decisions. Third, for those who "say" there are good and bad angels/aliens/ or life watching us in the universe, why wouldn't the good guys help us openly or just show they exist in the sky? On the other hand, why wouldn't these "powerful" evil spirits rule us openly or just kill us? Finally, bad guys don't wait to rule/kill. There's only one logical answer . . . Maybe evil spirits don't exist, or worse, maybe we're them, and "spirit" is a scientific function to live through our scientifically created body to experience outward beauty.

PEOPLE, POWER CORRUPTS!

We are beauty addicts. Maybe we could be *them*.
If they conquered space, isn't it possible they could make new species?

FACTS: FIRST–   Plastic surgery is the fastest growing medical field.

SECOND–"UP" being heaven in religion is the most important evidence in solving our past!

THIRD–   The universe is made of an invisible "creator" that can't be created; it's called the atom, adam. Man was created with it and is it, now please *get it*. It's called scientific creation.

"I am the eggman . . . Imagine"
—John Lennon

THE EVIDENCE
"Flying Saucers Created Religion"

"Where the future was our past, the present is painfully obvious, and what will be is unstoppable."

MOST IMPORTANT FACT OF ALL: *When we land on a planet, they will say we came from "UP."*

Word **"UP,"** *you all . . .* **EQUALITY**

TRAGEDY: *Religious people teach their children to worship God's power and don't "SEE" or "MIND" it.*

NO BRAINER QUESTION: *If power corrupts, could this be their god's "DOWN"fall?*

WARNING: *This book is dangerous to all wealthy and beautiful "powerful" people from George Bush to Oprah Winfrey (oh yeah, me too!)*

"Final Thoughts"

Finding Heaven can only be done "scientifically." Sadly, religious people don't "know" where it is. **But even worse, they already know they are going, and "WE" aren't!** They also "know" they've got a front row seat at the foot of their killing god. Question that, and the majority will kill you. Scary, huh? People, surely we must think life exists elsewhere and is more advanced than us! If so, wouldn't we be looking "UP" for their spacecraft?

LAST QUESTION: *The evidence says, HEAVEN IS IRREFUTABLY UP! Survey question: Do you "BELIEVE it?"*